D1473720

SUNSET COAST

Susan DeVore Williams

CROSSWAY BOOKS • WHEATON, ILLINOIS
A DIVISION OF GOOD NEWS PUBLISHERS

Sunset Coast

Copyright © 1995 by Susan DeVore Williams

Published by Crossway Books
        a division of Good News Publishers
        1300 Crescent Street
        Wheaton, Illinois 60187

Cover design: Cindy Kiple

First printing, 1995

Printed in the United States of America

Library of Congress Cataloging-in-Publication Data
Williams, Susan Devore.
    Sunset coast / Susan DeVore Williams
        p.   cm.
    I. Title.
PS3573.I455614S8 1995   813'.54—dc20   95-15716
ISBN 0-89107-854-1

03		02		01		00		99		98		97		96		95
15	14	13	12	11	10	9	8	7	6	5	4	3	2	1

With love and immense gratitude to
my friends and family—

and most especially to "St. James,"
whose faith continues to
move mountains

Author's Note

The events and characters in this book are entirely fictitious, and the settings that are real are used fictitiously. There is no St. Stephen's-by-the-Bay in northern California (so far as I know), but there *is* a place that resembles it in many ways. It has been my heart's home for many years.

I want to make it clear that although Amos Whitcomb does not exist, his personality owes much to several old friends of mine who are, if anything, even more wise and delightful than the man I made up. For the privilege of knowing such men, I give thanks.

Award-winning liturgical artist Marjorie Hennessy, whose work is mentioned here more than once, is a real person and a dear friend. My thanks to her for letting me use her name in this story.

1

Remember how the autumn air smelled of burning leaves when you were a kid? Maybe not. Maybe you're not over forty like me, or maybe you grew up in the city, where leaves had to be bagged or neatly piled at curbside for pickup by one of those wretched mechanical claws, and where, if you dared to set a match to them, the Fire Department would roar up and slap you with a hefty fine. Or—worst of all possible fates—your environmentalist neighbors would accuse you of criminally polluting their air space.

I could be wrong, but I suspect that America was a lot better off when a fine night's entertainment consisted of standing around with Dad and a handful of friends watching a bonfire burn down in the chilly October twilight. As far as we were concerned, it was a bonus that our sweaters and jackets gave us a whiff of smoky incense each time we put them on for weeks afterward.

It was exquisitely romantic, that autumn scent, so sweet and full of promise that even now, when I'm of an age to know that memories aren't always reliable and promises are often broken, I mourn the loss of it—and, come to think of it, the loss of a way of life that made it possible for such subtle pleasures to leave indelible impressions on youthful psyches.

These days, for better or worse, most kids can't look forward to the scent of burning leaves in the fall. Instead, they get the acrid, eye-watering petrochemical perfume of fake fireplace logs. I suppose there are actually a lot of children growing up nowadays who will one day look back on this aroma with a certain amount of sentimental longing. Which seems symbolic of many things to me, most especially of the fact that the phrase "scientific progress" is more often than not an oxymoron.

At any rate, I mention autumn and burning leaves because when I think of Matthew Clement ("Mac") McDonald, the first boy who ever loved me, the picture that comes immediately to mind is of the two of us walking together like the young couples on greeting cards, hand in hand through the crisp, burning-leaf-scented air of New England. Derry Mills, Vermont, to be exact. September 1961.

Mac and I were seniors at Middlewood Academy when we met that fall. He had transferred from another, more exclusive and pricey boarding school after his father had resigned as chairman of the family business (Clement-Stowe Corporation, the giant defense contractors) to pursue a career in politics—or "public service," as Mac liked to call it. (It made his father sound nobler than a mere politician, right?)

Not that I had reason to doubt Congressman McDonald's nobility. According to Mac, his father had resolved to repay the nation for all that the McDonald clan had received from its bounty since they'd arrived in America a few years after the *Mayflower* landed.

Surprisingly enough, Congressman McDonald actually did repay the nation with interest, if you ask me. According to a profile in *Time* that fall, he had given away 97 percent of his vast fortune to charity by the time he was elected to the House, He'd even sold the palatial family digs in Palm Beach, Long Island, London, and Zurich along with a *pied-a-terre* in Monaco, dividing the proceeds among several relief organizations. By the time he was elected, the McDonald family had taken up residence in their sole remaining home: a fifteen-room colonial in the Virginia countryside near Washington, D.C. Mac's mother, a good sport if there ever was one, had dubbed the house *Sans-a-Maid*. The much-publicized divestiture of the McDonald family turned them into virtual pariahs in A-List social circles.

Thus, although Mac arrived at Middlewood as scion of one of the oldest and most powerful families in the East, the "ruling class" at school never treated him as one of their own. And in keeping with the relatively austere lifestyle his family had adopted, Mac did without the accouterments of wealth many Middlewood students took for granted: the European sports cars, the charge accounts, the Leica cameras, the Christmas holiday outings to Gstaad or St. Moritz. He didn't seem to resent the privation. In fact, he seemed eager—maybe even proud—to sacrifice for the sake of high principle.

I had arrived at Middlewood that year on the dole, having transferred on full scholarship from public school in Woolwich, my hometown, about ninety miles away. Miriam Toohey, an English teacher at Woolwich High, was an alumna of Middlewood. During my junior year she came to our house and announced to my parents that I was prime Middlewood material, and she wanted to recommend me for an Alumni Scholarship at her alma mater. It was, I learned years later, an honor bestowed upon no other Woolwich student during all the years Mrs. Toohey taught there.

I could never have attended a school like Middlewood *without* a full scholarship, you understand. My father, Ellsworth Alexander, town veterinarian and friend to humans and animals alike, could not have afforded it. We weren't poor by any means;

but as Dad always said, we didn't exactly live high on the hog either. Deep in his heart I think my father believed he should pay his patients for the pleasure of treating them; this made it tough for him to collect when their owners failed to pay for his services. As a result, luxuries like private schools were never an option in our family. That is, until Mrs. Toohey called on us that day.

As the youngest of three girls (the one Mom often introduced by saying, "And this is Sally; if you don't see the family resemblance, it's because she was left on our doorstep by a roving band of Gypsies"), I quickly saw this as my big break. It was a chance to be first and best at something, to do something that might make my parents proud, and above all to move out from under the shadow of two older sisters who had been the toast of the town all their lives.

Betty, six years older than I, had all the first-child qualities everyone admires: charm, intelligence, poise, a strong sense of responsibility, and a down-to-earth approach to life. She was not beautiful, but she had a certain elfin quality that caused everyone to call her "cute." In those days, *cute* was something girl children sought to be. She had been class president and a cheerleader in her junior and senior years. The yearbook had named her "Most Likely to Succeed."

Abby, the middle child, was a born flirt. Boys made fools of themselves over her, gave her their letter sweaters and class rings, and sacrificed themselves on the field of honor just to be able to walk her home from school. Like most born flirts, she took this for granted. Everyone—including Abby—knew she would always have a man around to pay her way. As a result she never gave a thought to a career or to anything much more serious than how to get a perfect tan by June 15th of each year. Which was no small feat in Vermont, I'll grant you.

Abby was crowned Miss Woolwich by the Chamber of Commerce when she was seventeen. Personally, I always felt she won at the moment when Hugh Seidel, the pageant director, asked her what she hoped to accomplish in the next five years of her life, and she answered, "World peace." Since Hugh taught classes in Esperanto and was the organizer of the disarmament rallies in Montpelier every year, it seemed safe to assume that her adroit response had clinched the title. She's never forgiven me for attributing it to that. And anyway, her response (she says to this day) was utterly sincere.

Compared to my social butterfly sisters, I was only a caterpillar. The whole family was delighted by Miriam Toohey's offer because they hoped Middlewood might help to "bring me out"— out of my cocoon, out of my private world, or at least out of my room, where I'd retreated for most of my sophomore and junior years to read the Great Books and ruminate about the meaning of life.

My parents meant well, of course. When it became obvious that I would never become the third Alexander daughter to be pursued by the most eligible young men in Woolwich, Mom naturally worried about my prospects for marrying well (a prime goal of most mothers of that era). While Middlewood was not known as a "finishing school," she couldn't help hoping that its well-bred, Eastern-establishment aura would rub off enough to make me a magnet for the right kind of suitor.

All I hoped for was to find a place where I could be myself— whoever and whatever that turned out to be. The biggest problem I'd faced at home was that my parents and sisters were natural-born extroverts who suspected, as extroverts tend to do, that anyone less gregarious than themselves must be marginally retarded. Actually, I had an IQ nearly thirty points higher than either of my sisters, a fact I didn't discover until I was tested for Middlewood. When I found out, I asked the counselor not to tell my parents. The prospect of having to change my role as "The

Slow One" in the family hierarchy just didn't seem worth it. It was simpler to stick with the status quo.

Anyway, it turned out that Miriam Toohey was right: Middlewood Academy and I were made for each other. I fit right in—a fact that pretty much bowled me over, since I had never seemed to fit in much of anywhere before that. My passions for reading, writing, jazz, and impressionist art had branded me something of an oddball among my peers at home. But Middlewood classmates accepted these passions as normal, even praiseworthy. Which is to say, most of them had passions, too, like Morty Quimby's fascination with his mammoth collection of authentic antique toy soldiers or Elizabeth Pritchard's obsession with calligraphy projects (she claimed to have copied in exquisitely illuminated lettering every poem e. e. cummings ever wrote). In the company of kids like these, I was run-of-the-mill.

Of course, most of them had grown up in cities where it was possible to pursue interests other than eating, sleeping, skiing, and engaging in lewd or lascivious conduct, which as far as I could tell were the only available extracurricular activities for kids growing up in Woolwich. After years of feeling like a stranded alien, I finally belonged somewhere. Maybe the other Woodies gave me a break because I was the new girl. Whatever the reason, at Middlewood I felt the way a two-headed man might feel after moving to a colony of blind people: relieved to be "normal" for the first time in my life.

Mac McDonald introduced himself to me on paper during the second week of French class. I had no idea where the note came from; it simply fell onto my desk as I concentrated on drawing an unflattering caricature of Mademoiselle DeVille, our teacher, who purported to be from Paris. The outside of the folded note had my name printed in block letters: SALLY WIG-GLESWORTH ALEXANDER. How, I wondered, had someone found out my middle name? I was faintly embarrassed but figured that's what I got for putting my full name on the class roster. Inside, the note read simply, "Will you go with me to the mixer on Saturday night? I'm three seats behind you, one row to the right. If you don't like what you see now, remember that I'll be better looking by the time I'm forty-five or so."

I resisted turning around as I passed back a note that said, "Maybe you should ask me again—in about twenty-eight years."

His response was a classic assumptive close: "Shall I call for you at 7?" Feeling reckless, I scribbled "*Oui*" at the bottom of his note and sent it back. His reply: "I like your French accent. Very alluring." He knew how to turn a girl's head. I was sure nobody had ever applied a word like *alluring* to Abby. The boys she dated wouldn't be caught dead using words like that.

Mac turned out to be tall and blondish with that windblown, slightly disheveled, tanned-and-freckled look usually associated with Ivy League boys who wore loafers with no socks and spent their summers on tennis courts or racing around on sailboats. He didn't sail (his father had sold the family's forty-foot sailboat, too), nor did he play much tennis, but he looked the part. He also had the palest blue eyes I'd ever seen.

But he wasn't really my type. My type had dark hair and important muscles and glimmering eyes that always seemed faintly amused in a worldly sort of way. The Tony Curtis type, if you go back that far.

Mac won me over on our first date, however, by speaking seven words that are still etched in my memory while thousands—well, maybe hundreds—of other endearments have faded away. He said them with a perfectly straight face as he walked me back to the dorm after the mixer. "You're everything I admire in a girl," he said.

It sounded natural and unrehearsed; he'd probably heard it in a Cary Grant movie or read it in a novel, but at the time I was sure it was original with him. He looked right into my eyes as he spoke; his voice seemed deeper than usual and full of conviction. His words told me that after nearly seventeen years of waiting to be discovered by someone—*anyone*—who could appreciate the qualities in me that the world had hitherto completely over- looked, my life was turning around.

Mac had something else going for him that helped cement our relationship. When we sat down together at the mixer, I noticed right away that his thighs were bigger than mine. Not that my thighs were huge, you understand, but I was 5'9", well- rounded (as they said back then), and terribly self-conscious about my size. It was significant that I felt less like Jane Russell and more like Sandra Dee when I was with Mac. It takes a woman my size and age to appreciate that, I suppose.

At any rate, Mac's solid legs and above-average intelligence, added to his obvious devotion to me and my alluring charms, qualified him to be my steady date—at least until Tony Curtis came along. Actually, he was the only boy who'd ever shown much interest in me. That, of course, was a bit of information I hid from him as carefully as I might have hidden a copy of the True Map to the Treasure of Sierra Madre. Mac was convinced, against all odds and all reason, that the world's most fascinating female had miraculously chosen him to be her escort out of the hordes of eligible boys who probably wanted that privilege even more fiercely than they wanted a red and white Corvette. And I saw no reason to let him know otherwise.

We became pretty much inseparable that fall. Mac was a true gentleman, which began to worry me after a time. He kissed me good night but never tried the off-limits kinds of things the other girls complained about with obvious glee after *their* dates. Not that there was much opportunity for that sort of thing, with chaperones lurking behind every tree and statue on campus. But his apparent lack of interest in serious necking eventually led me to wonder if he found me physically attractive. When I finally got up the courage to ask him about this, Mac responded by laughing almost hysterically for several minutes and then kissing me more passionately than I'd ever imagined he could. After that he apologized profusely and promised it would never happen again. From this I understood that our relationship would have to flourish along other lines.

I was somewhat relieved, actually. Mac had a certain boyish charm, but his most appealing qualities were (at least to me) mental, not physical. Thus, the kind of relationship Mac wanted suited me just fine. He offered me things nobody else ever had. For example, he actually *listened* to me—not casually, but with an intensity that often amazed me. He remembered the things I said and pondered them at length. Days (or even weeks) after a discussion about General MacArthur's being fired by President Truman, for example, he might suddenly say, as if we'd addressed the subject only moments before, "You know, I disagree with you. Truman should have let MacArthur finish the job in Korea. In twenty or thirty years we'll regret pulling back to the 38th Parallel." It was exciting to know that my ideas and opinions were important to Mac. It was probably more exciting, in fact, than any amount of necking might have been.

Mac was also immensely intrigued by my philosophical and spiritual ruminations. Both he and I thought about such matters a lot, as some teenagers will, and we pored over the trendy books of the time—everything from Ayn Rand to Carl Jung to—okay, I might as well admit it—Kahlil Gibran, whose quasi-religious writings I decided to study after they were quoted in place of the Scriptures at one of our campus chapel services. A careful reading of *The Prophet* opened my eyes to the fact that a lot of otherwise rational people were vulnerable to any pundit whose words lent themselves to embroidery on a pillow.

Mac and I talked endlessly about things like this, convinced that we might be the only people on Planet Earth capable of drawing ultimate conclusions about the problems that had confounded the human race since Day One.

Mac, the only person of faith I'd ever known, tolerated my proclivities toward religious skepticism with a grace I look back upon with awe. He listened, argued, challenged, and provoked, often countering my sweeping dismissals of Christian orthodoxy by quoting his own favorite writer, C. S. Lewis. I learned to deeply resent Lewis, mostly because his irrefutable arguments left me with so little excuse for doubt. When Mac cited Lewis to bolster his viewpoint, my usual response left me feeling somewhat less brilliant and sophisticated than I liked to believe I was: "Oh, big deal. What does *he* know anyway?"

At any rate, Mac hung on every word I said, it seemed, and meditated on our conversations just as Moses probably meditated upon his experiences on Mount Sinai. Every woman should be worshiped once in her life. It was my only experience with it, and I have to admit, it was extremely edifying.

Mac knew I wanted to become a writer as much as he wanted to become the editor of a big-city newspaper. He saw himself as a defender of justice and probity. (For that matter, so did I.) He pushed me to write so he could practice his editing and critiquing skills on my work. He cackled at my humor pieces, thoughtfully studied my serious prose, and once actually wept over my poetry. Sometimes I resented his criticisms, but he was generally sensitive and managed to avoid crushing my embryonic creative spirit. He was positive I'd be a best-selling author by the time I was twenty-five, positive we would together win all the best awards and prizes, positive our futures were tied together by an unbreakable cord. I didn't share his vision of a joint destiny, but I have to admit that it was probably because of him that I began to believe I could one day be a real writer.

One last thing about Mac made him very hard to resist: he accepted me without reservation. When I complained about gaining weight, Mac said—you guessed it—it only gave him more of me to love; when I berated myself for biting my fingernails at exam time, he told me I looked good with short nails. He claimed to love my straight, mousy brown hair, but when I lightened it several shades one Saturday and met him on the dorm steps completely transformed with a new upswept hairstyle, suntan makeup, and bright pink lipstick, he looked me over, raised his eyebrows, and said approvingly, "Wow."

I wondered, sometimes, what it would take to make him hate me. Maybe, I thought—just maybe—he'd be a little put off if I poisoned his entire family, including pets. Then again, he'd probably forgive me, attributing it to temporary insanity.

He did, of course, have a few important flaws. For one, he was a conservative Republican. We frequently fought about politics; I tried to convert him even though I felt he was genetically incapable of holding liberal views. (His father, after all, was a leader of the Republican party in our state.) Mac didn't parrot all his father's views, by any means, and I'll admit that he wasn't obnoxious about his opinions. Nevertheless, he *was* a Republican. That was a strike against him in my mind.

And that leads me to a more formidable flaw: Mac was—well, I guess I saw him as sort of *beige*, inside and out. Mister Vanilla. He lacked pizzazz. I mean, heads never turned when he entered a room. Nobody thought, "Wowie zowie" when they met him. Certainly I didn't. He was—*ordinary*, I guess, in a lot of ways that mattered to me at that age. These days women talk about a lack of "chemistry," and I suppose that's what it amounted to. He wasn't The Man of My Dreams.

There was also his spelling problem. Come on, you're saying, give me a break. Look, I'm trying to tell the truth, no matter what that may do to your opinion of me. The fact is, Mac was the worst speller I ever knew. I, on the other hand, was the best. His poor spelling undermined my respect for him, however subtly.

When he wrote his romantic little notes to me, he always spelled "gorgeous" without the e and "cuddle" with a "ttle," as in cuttle-fish. It was hard to take seriously a boy who wrote that I was "gorgous" and "cuttly." Sometimes it exasperated me so much that I gave his notes back to him, corrected in red pencil. This may seem petty and cruel to some, and perhaps it was. Okay, of course it was. But at the time I felt justified because I believed nobody could amount to anything unless he was a good speller.

Even so, I dated Mac exclusively that whole year. Several times I flirted with Jerry Herzog, our basketball star, and Pete Parsons, the quarterback, who was the fantasy of every girl in my class. I suppose I hoped they'd ask me out just so I could say they had, but I probably would have turned them down because I wouldn't have wanted to hurt Mac. I cared enough about him not to want to hurt him, but not enough to overlook his conservatism, blandness, and lousy spelling. I don't know what you'd call that kind of relationship. One-and-a-half-sided, I guess.

When June of 1962 rolled around, Mac and I made plans to visit each other three times during the summer. He would be heading for Stanford University in the fall—some 3,000 miles away—while I'd decided on nearby Rigby College, the school that had offered me the biggest scholarship. Mac and I wouldn't be able to get together until Christmas; so we'd have to make the most of the summer.

Before the end of the school year at Middlewood, Mac had started telling people, without consulting me, that we were "engaged to get engaged." When he said this in front of me one day, I took him aside and told him he shouldn't announce something like that without asking me first. He replied cryptically that he would ask when he was "prepared to ask properly." That meant, I assumed, when he had earned enough money to buy me a ring. He was proud of earning his own money for important things and never would have used money his father gave him to buy me an engagement ring. Considering the relatively non-committal way I felt about Mac at the time, you'd think I might have hinted to him that a ring would be premature. I didn't. And I can't offer any excuse for that.

Not surprisingly, the summer separation—even the first month of it—didn't make my heart grow fonder toward Mac. Three weeks before Mac's planned first visit for Fourth of July week, I met Peter Brigham, the new boy next door. Actually Peter was the grandson of Addie and T. J. Brigham, who lived in the rambling Victorian-era house just north of ours. He had arrived in June with plans to spend the summer.

Peter had black, gleaming, curly hair and black, gleaming eyes and the tanned physique of a bodybuilder. He was a senior physics major—near the top of his class—at Princeton. He was twenty-one, and he winked at me within the first few moments after he met me, which added substantially to his attractiveness as far as I was concerned. He had pizzazz aplenty. A far cry from Matthew C. McDonald.

Peter invited me out to a movie while I was planting strawberries in a small garden between our houses. I accepted, never for a moment thinking about Mac. I only felt guilty when, after Peter drove me home in his red and white 1958 Corvette—one of only 9,168 that had been built that year—he kissed me more passionately and expertly than Mac had ever dared, and I responded with a fervent enthusiasm that surprised even me. Yes, The Man of My Dreams had arrived.

By the time Mac arrived for his first visit on July third, I'd tasted hard liquor and engaged in serious physical contact with Peter on at least six occasions. I was heady with the newfound knowledge that Mac McDonald was not the only pumpkin in the patch. Peter was dazzling, no question about it, and everyone (including my sisters) envied me when they saw that I was becoming his steady date. Nobody had ever envied me—not that I knew of, anyway—as the object of Mac's affections.

When I was with Peter, I felt lucky to be in his company, lucky to be the girl he squired around town, lucky just to be alive in the same world with him. Peter was going places, was going to do exciting things, and I wanted nothing so much as I wanted to be at his side when he did them. Whatever it might require of me, I was willing to do it just to make that happen.

Mac did not take it well when I tried to tell him it was over between us. I'd avoided writing to him, telling myself it would be easier to break the news in person when he came to visit for the Independence Day weekend. I was wrong.

"I don't understand," he said, his eyes large and round like a doe in hunting season as he sat across from me in our living room. "What do you mean, 'things have changed'? *I* haven't changed. Have *you* changed?" He glanced at the small, blue, zippered satchel he'd carried in with him when he'd arrived at our house a few minutes before. A ring was in there, I suspected, and I didn't want to see it. I was determined to keep talking so we didn't have time to get to the ring.

"We shouldn't tie each other down at this point in our lives," I said. "You need freedom as much as I do. It will be better for both of us if we spend some time apart." It was the classic line every heartless two-timer seems to use instinctively.

"If you want more freedom, I can understand that," he said, glancing again toward his satchel. He paused, then shook his head. "If you're saying you want to date other guys, I guess I can understand that, too. But we can keep on seeing each other, can't we?"

I was getting nervous. He didn't get it. He wasn't being good old reasonable Mac. "No," I said resolutely, "I think it's better that we don't. At least for a while."

He didn't respond for a few moments. Then he looked at me

sharply. "Sally, what's going on?" he said. There was a bewildered expression on his face that made me look away.

I sighed heavily. "It's hard to put into words, Matthew." I had only called him Matthew on about three occasions. At that moment it somehow seemed more appropriate, more dignified. "It isn't you, it's *me* . . . I need to find myself . . . I need to be alone for a while." I don't know where the words came from. Maybe lines like these are part of human DNA. They might be located on the same strand of genetic material that contains such phrases as "the check is in the mail" and "no, of course that dress doesn't make you look fat."

"I can't believe this," Mac said, looking dangerously close to tears. "Maybe you need some time to think things through. I could go home and come back next month. We could write to each other, talk on the phone."

Panic set in as I realized Mac didn't understand that it was totally, irrevocably over and that he had to be on the road in one hour flat or he'd come face to face with Peter, who was picking me up to play mixed doubles.

"No, Mac," I said as solemnly as I could. "No. I don't want to hurt you by dragging this out. You deserve more than that. Please just go. This is hard for me, too, you know." I tried to look sad.

He stood there staring at me with that awful directness, that see-into-your-soul gaze that had always unnerved me a little. Then he pulled himself out of his slouched stance and reached out to take my hand. "If this is what you really need, I'll go," he said.

"It's what I really need," I said, pulling my hand away. He picked up his satchel, went to the door, and then silently reached into his shirt pocket and pulled out a small folded piece of paper. He turned and handed it to me. I closed my fingers around it and said nothing.

I watched him drive off in the dilapidated Nash he'd bought

with his own money the summer before and then stuffed the folded paper into my pocket. I didn't open it until late that night, when I was sitting alone on the window seat in my bedroom after Peter brought me home. On the paper was a poem copied carefully in Mac's best handwriting:

> ... *Others because you did not keep*
>> *That deep-sworn vow have been friends of mine;*
> *Yet always when I look death in the face,*
>> *When I clamber to the heights of sleep,*
> *Or when I grow excited with wine,*
>> *Suddenly I meet your face.*

At the bottom of the sheet he had written, "So Yeats knew you? I'm jealous." Except he'd spelled it "jelous." I shook my head. Amazing, I thought. How could I have wasted a year of my life on a hokey guy who didn't even know how to spell?

It wasn't until years later that I learned in a trivia game that Yeats, too, had been a terrible speller. Life is so circular.

2

Some two years later I married Peter Brigham, in the social event of the season, at his parents' estate on Long Island. After the wedding I quit college and took a job as an editorial assistant at Princeton while Peter finished his Ph.D. Shortly after that he was recruited by M.I.T.'s physics department, and we settled into life in the suburbs of Boston. I signed on as an assistant editor for a regional magazine with offices a couple of miles from the M.I.T. campus. A couple of months after I started at the magazine, I was invited to contribute an article about my favorite country inns and hotels. This led to a monthly feature that gave me the perfect excuse to traipse around Massachusetts on an expense account in search of the Ultimate Inn Experience.

Meanwhile, Peter's parents had bought us our first house as a "late wedding present." It was a smallish, two-story clapboard on a heavily wooded lot, and it was quickly furnished in Peter's family's preferred style, which I privately dubbed Liberal Chic. I don't know why all the liberals I knew furnished their homes with this sort of stuff. There were about fifteen utilitarian teakwood bookcases throughout the house, most of which were filled with African death masks, sexually explicit fetishes, clumsily made pottery with muddy-looking glazes, and books about obscure tribes of Indians, the practice of yoga, Bohemian life in Paris in the 1920s, and impending nuclear holocaust. (These items probably represented a profound collective theme, but I was never able to discover what it was.) One of the biggest book-cases housed professional-grade stereo components carefully chosen to provide perfect fidelity for the playback of solo lute music, which happened to be Peter's favorite.

The house itself boasted beautifully polished blond hard-wood floors (totally devoid of rugs, even in the ceramic-tile-floored bathrooms) and flying-saucer shaped light fixtures that made everyone look anemic and hungry. The living room and bedrooms featured a collection of natural-wood-and-sling fur-niture I suspected was designed by a committee of Scandinavian socialists who believed that if a single worker of the world was suffering, we had an obligation to suffer with them. Redemption through furniture, so to speak. I always felt we'd have been cozier in hammocks. I myself yearned for extravagantly clubby, com-modious sofas and easy chairs covered in bright chintzes or jewel-toned velvets. I couldn't admit this, of course. It was, after all, pretty ungrateful of me to wish for something other than the house my husband's parents had so generously provided.

Peter's colleagues and friends all told me what a great house we had, and I accepted their compliments graciously. Their homes were, for the most part, half-baked copies of ours. I fan-tasized for several years about arson, especially when the Brighams shipped us new additions to our modern expressionist art collection. But I finally reconciled myself to the Brigham style by telling myself that anything that annoyed me so much surely must be good for me. It was during this period that I began a slow, silent, steady transmogrification to Republicanism. Laugh if you like; there are worse reasons to become a Republican.

My job offered good hours and decent pay plus plenty of free time to think about the kind of writing I really wanted to do—mystery and adventure novels. I also toyed with some non-fiction pieces that were accepted in the big women's magazines. One editor, who noticed that I had a unique ability to change writing styles according to subject, suggested that I might make a good living as a ghostwriter.

I did. In the process I began to make a name for myself in publishing circles. I quit my full-time job at the regional magazine before the end of our first year of marriage and soon doubled my income as a freelancer. I was full of hope, full of dreams about how great life would be when I finally became a best-selling novelist. That kept me going.

And I was happy for a time. At least I think I was. You know how you can look back and wonder, "Was I really happy, or did I kid myself?" I'm not sure of the answer to that question, even today. At the time I believed that as long as Peter was happy, I must be too.

From the beginning of his tenure at M.I.T., we had an understanding about our work: I didn't bother him at the university when he was on a research project, and he didn't bother me on weekends when I was trying to write my "creative" stuff. He read some of my writing but showed no genuine enthusiasm for it. Once, at a faculty dinner, I heard him laugh deprecatingly as he told several people that I was "trying to break into writing." He never mentioned that at that moment I was earning more than he was and that my ghostwritten work was appearing in some of the biggest magazines in the country every month. I didn't mention it either. After all, no matter how I would have explained it, it would have sounded petty. And it would have annoyed Peter—which was something I was learning to avoid at all costs.

Peter didn't resent my work so much as he just didn't understand it. He never read for pleasure. To him, reading was a necessary evil—something you did to keep current in your field, or to gather esoteric information so you could impress colleagues at faculty meetings. Occasionally when I asked him why he was reading this or that book, he'd respond, "So I can say I've read it." At least he was honest.

In fact, that was why he traveled, why he did an incredible variety of things—so he could say he'd done it. The experiences themselves meant nothing to him. He rushed to get them over with so he could call someone to brag—tastefully, of course— that he'd done these things.

Once, in Paris, Peter tried to convince me to taxi across town in a pouring rain to see a small museum neither of us had the slightest interest in exploring. When I joked, "Let's not and say we did," Peter looked at me as if I'd suddenly solved a problem he'd been puzzling over for years. "That's a great idea," he said. By the time we got home he'd concocted an elaborate story about how we'd been the last people in the museum that day and had been treated to a tour of a "secret collection" by the curator; we'd seen paintings that only a handful of European connoisseurs had been allowed to view. Listening to his colorful narrative, I suspected that Peter himself believed it had happened exactly that way.

After that, when the opportunity presented itself, Peter would send me off to a concert or lecture he didn't want to attend, grill me about it later, and then tell people at our next dinner party that he'd been there, giving my impressions as his own. He never seemed embarrassed to do this in front of me, and I never exposed him. I wondered from time to time whether our relationship depended on my silent assent to his fibs. It probably did.

Anyway, Peter simply couldn't understand why anyone would want to write except to convey facts; so he had an attitude of mild condescension toward what I wanted to do with my life. It was understandable, really. The truth is, I felt sort of the same way about his physics research. I was proud of him for becoming something of a pioneer in his field at a very young age. But why, I wondered, would anyone want to spend the precious hours of his life firing atoms from one end of a linear accelerator to the other?

But we cared for each other. We didn't have to talk about it— it was just there. At least it was there in my mind. We had basic differences that manifested themselves in frustrating little ways, of course. But isn't that true in every marriage? For example, I had this thing about jazz, if you'll recall. Ever since I was about twelve I'd loved it. Not just modern jazz, as in the Dave Brubeck Quartet and Ahmad Jamal and his contemporaries, who were already becoming cult figures when I was a teenager, but other kinds of jazz as well. I was in love with the twenties and thirties and forties, too—Benny Goodman, Woody Herman and the Woodchoppers, and every early and modern jazz band in existence. Big bands, little bands, ragtime bands, hot pianos, swinging singers, cool cats—I loved 'em all. Peter despised my music, preferring ethnic recordings that apparently reminded him of his travels to Tibet, West Africa, and the Middle East. About three months into our marriage he actually said to me, in his sternest and most imperious voice, "I *forbid* you to play that jazz of yours in our home. If I hear it again, I will personally smash every record in your collection."

So I took to listening to my music furtively, secretly, feeling as guilty about it as if I were filching money from the household accounts to support a drug habit. That bugged the daylights out of me. But everyone has these little things to put up with, I told myself. Everyone makes tradeoffs. In spite of our differences, we lived our lives on a pretty even keel and I had nothing to gripe about. And as long as I didn't play my music in his presence Peter seemed content.

Things did change, or at least I first noticed it, when our baby was born four years after we were married. Peter had wanted to put off a family for at least ten years, maybe more. I was on the cutting edge of the birth control movement because The Pill was pretty new at the time. I felt safe. But even with the high doses of estrogen they put in those early pills, failures occasionally happened. I was one of them.

Peter didn't fly into a rage when I told him I was pregnant. He just shook his head as if I'd driven the Volvo through the back wall of the garage, cursed at me, and said very quietly, "Sally, how could you?" That was all.

The next day he called me from his office. "I talked with my father," he said, "and he knows a discreet doctor. He can take care of everything." I thought for a moment he was saying he had found an obstetrician to take care of me through the pregnancy. Then I realized what he meant.

"You want me to get an abortion?" I said.

"Well, what else can we do?" he asked, remaining very cool. "This is not the time for us to have a baby."

I felt stabbed through the heart but said, almost instantly, "Oh, well, I suppose that's true."

"Okay, then," he said. "I'll make the arrangements."

After he hung up, I thought, *He's probably right. A baby wouldn't want to grow up where it's not wanted. Surely it would rather not be born than to live where it's not wanted. An abortion would be a favor to this baby.*

That night Peter came home with a doctor's name and address on a slip of paper. "Thursday morning," he said and walked off to his study. It was Tuesday. The slip of paper said I was supposed to call the doctor directly to get instructions about how to prepare for "the procedure." That was a word I liked: "procedure." It took all the emotion out of it. It was science, not humanity.

Long after Peter went to sleep, I lay watching the shadows on the ceiling. At about 3 A.M. I turned on the light and shook him awake. He hated being awakened, but I did it anyway.

"I'm not going to have the procedure," I said.

He stared at me. "What?"

"I'm not going to do it. The abortion."

"Isn't it a little late to change your mind?"

"No. It isn't too late until it's done. And I'm not going to do it."

"Come on, Sally, you're being hysterical." I wasn't hysterical. I was calm and in control. Why was he saying this?

"I just thought you should know. I'm not going to do it."

He frowned. "We'll talk about it tomorrow when you're thinking more clearly. There really isn't any choice, Sally."

"What do you mean?"

"I mean, there isn't any choice."

"Of course there is," I said. "I just made it."

With a great sigh Peter shook his head and yanked at the covers, pulling them over his shoulders as he turned away from me. He went promptly to sleep.

I lay awake until dawn, a pillow clutched to my stomach.

By the time Peter got up the next morning I *was* hysterical. He seemed shocked and aggrieved that I would arbitrarily make a decision that could inconvenience him for the rest of his life. He reasoned with me, pointing out that "this mass of cells" I called a baby was half his, and he wanted his half aborted. He cajoled, pleaded, ranted, denounced me, threatened to have me psychoanalyzed (as if that were the worst thing he could do to me), and finally stormed off to work leaving me to wallow in my puddle of hysteria. I called the doctor Peter had set up and told him, without explanation, that I'd changed my mind. He was matter-of-fact, as if I'd simply decided not to have a face-lift after all.

Within a few weeks Peter developed an attitude of sarcastic resignation toward "baby Matthew," as he began to call the child-to-be. I hadn't suggested the name, but I was secretly pleased with it because it conjured up memories of Mac and simpler, easier days.

In fact, I'd left the choice of names entirely in Peter's hands, hoping that would soften him toward fatherhood. Given the task of naming the baby, Peter consulted with his parents and decided on Matthew if it was a boy and Martha for a girl. It turned out his mother's grandfather's name was Matthew and her mother was Martha. I suggested a few alternatives, but Peter and the Brighams had decided, and that was that.

Then in the sixth month he announced to me that he was positive it was a boy, that boys ran in his family, and after all, a boy was the only kind of baby he could possibly have anything in common with. After that he dropped all references to "baby Martha." Soon his mother announced that she had decided to surprise us with an early baby gift: she had hired a decorator to create a boy's nursery in the spare bedroom. Occasionally, during the last part of the pregnancy, I felt that Peter and his parents had murdered baby Martha in cold blood. It was just hormones, of course.

The baby had the good sense to be born a boy. He was an easy child to love, but he's told me since that he never felt loved by his father. I understand what he means, although at the time it seemed that Peter was making heroic efforts to act the part of a good parent. He didn't enjoy holding or playing with Matt, but he did talk to him. When Matt began talking several months ahead of schedule, Peter viewed it as a personal triumph. "Genes will tell," he said. I knew he meant his genes, not mine, but I went along with him because I figured a little paternal pride couldn't hurt. During Matt's toddler years, Peter actually took the boy to work with him several times to show him off. Matt apparently performed well.

For his sixth birthday Matt received a microscope from his

father, and it was the only gift I ever saw the two of them enjoy together. Matt was a curious kid, always looking beneath the surface of things. Over several months they spent many hours outdoors looking for things to examine under the lens, tramping back into the house carrying plastic baggies full of rotting leaves, pieces of colored glass, flower petals, rust scrapings from the lawn furniture, fur from the neighbor's dogs and cats, large and small insects, and swamp water. I was thrilled.

But for the most part the two of them coexisted in our house in a way that suggested that Matt might be a foster child sent to us on a trial basis. He could always be sent back if he didn't work out, Peter seemed to be thinking. He talked to me about looking into boarding schools, particularly one in Switzerland that he felt would "turn the boy into a man." I resisted Peter for the second time in our life together, insisting that we were better equipped to raise our son than the citizens of a nation whose entire history had culminated in the invention of yodeling and that now existed for the sole purpose of providing secret bank accounts for tax dodgers. He acquiesced with great reluctance.

I continued to freelance after Matt arrived, churning out nonfiction articles and books on subjects that were "acceptable" in our world: self-actualization and self-discovery, the New Left, trends in health care, psychoanalysis, environmental topics. Once I started doing books under my own name, Peter sometimes brought out copies to show to our guests, hinting broadly that he had "inspired" my work. Guests usually went their ways assuming that Peter did most of the creative work while I took the credit. I never bothered to disabuse them of this. I was not willing to give Peter the opportunity to call me paranoid or petty.

I was, however, enjoying motherhood in a way I had not anticipated. I was actually pretty good at it, in spite of everything. Peter more or less observed and kibitzed where the nitty-gritty of parenting was concerned. He didn't do diapers, didn't do cleanups, didn't do baths, and didn't do feedings except when we had guests, who were treated to an elaborate "Mealtime with Peter and Matthew Show." He joked that babies were too "sticky and gummy" for him, saying he'd prefer to do the fathering things for which he was best suited. Those included such activities as chats about nuclear physics, word games, talks about music theory, and demonstrations of mathematical principles, which Matt seemed to enjoy as much as he enjoyed anything with his father. Matt was precocious and funny, the sort of child who can be either a pleasure or a holy terror. To me he was almost entirely a pleasure.

I adapted and accommodated to the changes in my life as best I could. After all, I told myself, I had nothing to complain about. I was lucky to be the wife of a dazzling young physicist, lucky to be the mother of his child, the envy of other faculty wives and even of Peter's female students. Occasionally one of them would sidle up to me in a shop or grocery store and gush, "I just *love* your husband, Mrs. Brigham. You're so *fortunate* to be married to a man like that." Peter and I didn't argue very often, but when we did I usually backed down as I remembered how many women would give anything to be in my place.

We spent summer hiatuses at the Brigham compound on Long Island, traded in our twin Volvos every other year, dressed well, and ate out at chic restaurants. Under most circumstances Peter was charming and articulate, a man to be proud of. When he drank too much he thought himself immensely droll and debonair, and of course he was wrong; but he didn't drink heavily except on holidays and birthdays, which didn't seem excessive when I compared him to the other men in our circle.

Our day-to-day life together revolved around dinner parties at our house or someone else's, mostly with Peter's colleagues and friends. We also belonged to a country club; Peter didn't play golf, but was a fierce competitor at tennis. He played almost every day. He was such a cutthroat that I stopped playing with him after a couple of years. Winning didn't satisfy him; real fun came only through totally humiliating his opponent. I wasn't a good enough sport to enjoy this, so we each found other partners. We'd have dinner together as a postlude to a game—Peter and his partner and me. My partners never seemed to be free to join us.

Peter didn't really dislike my friends; he simply couldn't help treating them with a certain *noblesse oblige* attitude. They were not our kind of people, he'd say, meaning they didn't come from the right kind of (liberal) money or go to the best schools or think the right thoughts or sprinkle their conversations with the trendy psychobabble that was so fashionable in university circles. Of course neither did I, which only kindled the fires of insecurity that burned twenty-four hours a day in the furnace of my soul.

Didn't any of this bother me, you ask? Sure, and from time to time—especially after Matt came along—I felt vaguely depressed about the direction in which our lives were drifting. But the truth is, I had so totally immersed myself in Peter that I was unable to figure out what was wrong. I believed—probably correctly—that everything depended on my ability to play my assigned supporting role in Peter's little show. I continued to do what I'd done from the time I was born: I acted the part of the person I was expected to be. I was, by this time, a professional chameleon, keeping my true colors well hidden lest he (or his family or friends) toss me aside like a piece of *déclassé* jewelry.

Only my closest friends knew the real me, or what little there was of me at that stage in my life; and my relationships with them were only possible because they almost never saw me when Peter was around. Once, about six years into our marriage, I threw a party that included all of our friends—both his and mine. That was a great mistake. One of my friends commented later that I'd become "a different person" around Peter and his entourage, and she didn't like Sally the Sycophant very much. That troubled me, but I didn't know what I could do about it. My friendship with that woman gradually died, and I told myself it was for the best. She didn't understand how difficult my position was.

During the worst moments of my marriage to Peter, on the few occasions when awareness of my capitulation to him became obvious even to me, and when I caught glimpses of my own culpability, I managed to avoid total despondency by attributing much of it to hormones. Mine, of course, not his. When I couldn't do that anymore, I learned to give myself pep talks. I was being neurotic, I told myself. I had a great life, a life everyone envied. Peter was a brilliant, attractive, successful man. I had a great little boy and work I enjoyed. How could I *not* be happy? I had everything. *We* had everything.

These little talks did not work very well, but they did keep me in a frame of mind where I could continue our marriage.

When I began to notice somewhere around our tenth anniversary that Peter's work schedule had increased well beyond his usual fifty-five-hour week, I asked him about it. He shrugged and said, "We're shorthanded because of the budget cuts. I have to do the work of two people these days. It's temporary." When I reminded him that we hadn't had a full evening or weekend alone together in months, he responded without looking at me. "I'm glad you're giving me space, Sally. I couldn't handle a nagging wife on top of all the other pressures I have to deal with."

I had learned never to put pressure on Peter, because pressure gave him migraine headaches. And I'd learned to avoid saying or doing *anything* that might give him cause to label me a nagging wife. Fortunately, I was good at being alone. That was, as Peter reminded me many times during the early years of our marriage, a requisite for survival as a faculty wife. At least he gave me some credit for the way I handled it.

Then one day several months after I'd complained about his work schedule, I took Matt with me to a three-day writer's conference in Stockbridge, Massachusetts. He was always eager to accompany me on my business jaunts, and this one was a special, relaxed treat. Peter had encouraged us to take an extra day to comb the countryside, wander in antique shops, and take lots of photos. He'd planned to use the extra time alone to put the finishing touches on an important research project.

Matt and I had a memorable time. We stayed at the Red Lion Inn, and he got to eat like a grown-up in a big chair in the main dining room. Finally, both of us decided we'd had enough of rural Massachusetts. We drove home seven hours early.

I carried my suitcase into the master bedroom to find our bed unmade and the room reeking of Frappe Rosé, which I had always called the most fetid fragrance ever to assault the human nostril. The wastebasket from the kitchen, which sat by the bed with the melting remnants of about ten trays of ice in it, held an empty French champagne bottle. A crystal finger bowl containing half a can of caviar and a demitasse spoon sat on my nightstand alongside two initialed, hollow-stemmed champagne glasses that had been a wedding gift from one of Peter's cousins. Classy.

I drove Matt to my friend Tessa's, the friend of mine Peter disliked most. I didn't explain except to say that Peter and I had to talk. Taking note of my grim expression, she didn't pursue it.

Then I came back to the house and sat in the bedroom until Peter walked in about an hour later. Seeing me, he glanced around the room, taking in the bed, the champagne glasses, the caviar, and finally my puffy eyes and red nose. For just a moment I thought I saw panic well up in him, but almost instantly he recovered.

"I suppose you've drawn all the wrong conclusions," he said coolly, "and this is going to be a real scene."

"Tell me what conclusions I should draw," I said, gesturing toward the empty glasses and the fishy-smelling caviar, which I'd decided to leave there to stink up the room as much as possible. It was better than Frappe Rosé.

He stood in the doorway staring at the floor for perhaps twenty seconds, then sighed and shook his head. "I can't live a lie any longer," he said. *Good grief,* I thought, *what kind of stuff has he been reading to pick up this kind of dialogue?*

"So now you know. So I've been seeing someone," he went on, pacing back and forth in front of me. "So sue me." Why did he suddenly sound like Henny Youngman doing a *shtick* at some resort in the Catskills? And why was I shivering uncontrollably? You know how they say, "my blood ran cold"? Well, that may sound stupid, but if you've ever been in a situation like this, you'll know it's an apt description of what happens at such a moment.

"I never wanted to hurt you," he continued, "but I guess you had to find out sooner or later. I've never brought anyone here before. *Never.*" He looked at me as if I should say, "Thank you." I didn't.

"It's just—something I *need,*" he continued, gesturing grandly. He was Tony Curtis again, grinning and soft-soaping and conning his way out of a little jam. "I like women! I can't help it. And being married doesn't change that. It's my nature."

I can't explain how silly he sounded to me all at once. I don't know if it was his stance, or the words themselves, or the vision that came to me of Tony Curtis in *Some Like It Hot,* all gussied up in a frumpy wig, a print dress, and a pair of high heels. I had a peculiar urge to laugh, but I stifled it.

Peter went on to tell me, in language that made me feel he'd rehearsed it many times, that he'd *tried* to resist the advances of other women, had made up his mind many times, in fact, but that he guessed he just wasn't built to be a "one-woman man." Then he actually said, "It isn't you, Sally. It's *me*. I need to find myself. I think you do, too. It's a *good* thing that this has happened . . . You'll see. Really good. In the end we'll both be happier."

I stood up then, dry-eyed but still shaky, and said, "Peter, it won't play in Peoria."

He looked at me quizzically. I shrugged and then asked him kindly to pack up and move out. He didn't argue; so I presumed he'd already made some sort of contingency plan, just in case. As he carried the last of his suitcases out the door to the Volvo he smiled an ingratiating Hollywood agent kind of smile and said, "I know I can count on you to be civilized about this. I expect to pay child support, of course, but let's not turn this into one of those tacky, bitter divorces where people end up hating each other. You make almost as much as I do, so let's skip the alimony, okay?"

I was too astonished to speak for several moments. Then I found my voice and said, "I made exactly $14,740 *more* than you did last year. Maybe you'd like to sue *me* for alimony."

"Come on, we can be friends, can't we?" he said, ignoring my sarcasm. Then, head cocked, he smiled the commendatory sort of smile he usually bestowed on Matt when he was being particularly clever. "You're going to make some man very happy someday," he said, and held out his hand. "You're quite a girl."

That was when I did the one thing that seemed appropriate at the time. I kicked him in the shins. Very hard. Hard enough to make him howl with pain and scramble out of the house shouting threats over his shoulder as he hobbled his way to the car. I'm not proud of it, but I still sometimes feel it was the only sane response I could have made.

By the time the divorce was final, the house had been sold and Matt and I were packing up for a move to Minneapolis, a city

I had learned to appreciate after several business trips there. I'd found a part-time job as an editor with a small publishing house about twenty minutes from the high-rise condo Matt had helped me pick out on Lake Calhoun. I'd also gotten an advance to write a guidebook to the most romantic country inns and restaurants of the Midwest. It surprised the daylights out of me that the most important elements in our future seemed to be falling into place without a tremendous amount of struggle. I'd always heard that "major life crises" like divorce, job changes, financial reverses, and cross-country moves devastated one's ability to cope. Given all the crises I was dealing with at the time, I half-expected to wake up one morning unable to face the task of brushing my teeth. It never happened. Once the habit of living with (and accommodating to) Peter was broken, Matt and I managed remarkably well. We waded through a few episodes of depression together, which turned out to be good for both of us.

Peter wanted nothing from our life together—not Matt, of course, not the furniture, not the silver or the china, not even family photos. This puzzled me somewhat until I learned that one of his current girlfriends—the one who liked Frappe Rosé—was a psychologist who had recently sold an article titled "How to Get Over a Bad Relationship" to a women's magazine. The first thing she advised was to get rid of all objects that might remind you of the person you want to erase. So Peter took only his clothes, his own jewelry, and our entire portfolio in stocks, which presumably would not remind him of me. He gave our original art back to his parents and offered me the ugly furniture and the limited-edition prints he claimed were worth "far more than the stocks." I said fine and sold almost everything at an auction, netting about $5,000. Peter's mother came to bid on the prints, finally buying three pieces nobody else wanted. She'd never forgiven me for joking at dinner one night that those prints were original blots from the first Rorschach Test. She gave the auctioneer a check for them and left without speaking a word to me.

The $5,000, added to my half of the money from the sale of the house, was all I really wanted. Peter volunteered, within three days of his departure from our house, to pay $400 a month in child support until Matt was eighteen. In addition, he had his lawyer put $25,000 into a trust fund that Matt would come into on his twenty-first birthday. In those days that was a healthy sum. What surprised me was that it took that much to appease his conscience.

B.O. Plenty, the labrador retriever we'd gotten the summer before the winter of our discontent, made up his own mind where he wanted to live. A couple of weeks before the divorce was final, while Matt and I were packing for the move to Minneapolis, Peter came to retrieve the last of his clothes and, it turned out, to take the dog. Matt and I were shocked. We'd assumed B.O. would stay with us because Peter hadn't mentioned him at all in the months after he'd moved out, much less in the property settlement.

But Peter had other ideas. "After all, Sally," he said, "you have Matt, so I should have the dog." Well sure, I thought, it's an even trade. Why didn't I think of that?

When I pointed out that he'd never seemed to like B.O. in the first place, he stared at me as if I'd lost my mind. "How would *you* know what I liked or didn't like?" he said, his voice dripping with sarcasm. *Oh good, we are finally going to get into it,* I thought, *and all because of B.O. Plenty. I never understood you or listened to you, never appreciated you, never plumbed the depths of your sensitive psyche. Only a twenty-eight-year-old who bathes in Frappe Rosé can understand your love for this dog.*

Finally, with all the hearty ebullience I'd grown to detest, Peter looked at the dog and said to me, "I'll tell you what—we'll let B.O. decide! He can tell us who he'd rather live with." Without waiting for a reply from me, Peter clapped his hands on his thighs and grinned at the dog in his most playful and ingratiating manner. "Hey, boy, wanna come live with me? Wanna play Frisbee?"

Now, "Frisbee" was a word that normally sent B.O. into frenzies of leaping, bounding ecstasy. Peter had occasionally played Frisbee with him in our backyard. Matt and I did it almost every day during good weather. So the utterance of the word "Frisbee" was a cinch to push all the right buttons with B.O.

This time, however, B.O. merely looked puzzled as the word was spoken. Then, inexplicably, he curled his upper lip and bared his sizable canines while glaring menacingly at Peter. As Peter reached out his hand, B.O. growled. A small tendril of drool oozed from his mouth. Peter's face fell. He glanced at me as if to catch me giving him secret signals of some sort. I was merely astonished. Peter stepped toward B.O., but the dog backed away, still growling, and finally scuttled sideways to stand behind my legs. I suppressed a smile. *I can put this dog in commercials*, I thought. *We'll be rich.*

It was one of the sweetest moments of my life.

3

It took Peter no time at all to get over me, presumably, since he had help from his how-to expert. He didn't want visitation rights with Matthew, he said through his lawyer, feeling it was "better for the boy" that he make a clean break, and anyway he had total confidence that I could rear him "without the interference of a backseat driver."

What it really boiled down to, I decided, was that Peter was already getting on with his new life while Matt and I were still trying to figure out what had happened to our old one. As far as Peter was concerned, we were already relegated to being just two more annoying little delays in life that he had finally been able to dispense with, like the ten minutes you're forced to listen to Barry Manilow or Tom Jones when you call your local electric company. Being a father or a husband was such a demanding occupation that he was relieved to be freed from it so he could pursue the things that really mattered in life.

Usually I was able to persuade him to talk to Matt on his birthday and Christmas; but that was the extent of his willingness to participate in his son's life. When I tried to convince him to let Matt visit him during summer vacations, he was always just leaving for Africa or India on business. What sort of physics business could he be doing, I wondered, in countries where electric power was available only on alternate Saturday nights and people spent their whole lives waiting for their next meal?

I finally gave up on the father-son relationship the day I phoned Peter to tell him Matt had just racked up the highest scores in his school on a series of achievement tests. He said that was great, but he couldn't talk to Matt because he was still in pain from surgery.

"What surgery?" I asked, wondering if he'd had some sort of accident. It was that right ear, he said, the one that was always just a tad bigger than the other one, causing it to stick out slightly. It had bothered him all his life, so he'd finally found a great plastic surgeon and had it fixed. He was going to feel much better about himself now.

Maybe Peter was right after all. If I had never noticed that asymmetrical ear, maybe I hadn't really known him at all.

Matt grieved less than I thought he would over the loss of his father. I took him to a child psychologist friend of mine for about ten sessions, thinking he must be carrying a load of pain inside. She finally took me to lunch one day and said, "Look, Sally, I think Matt is a normal, very bright, basically well-adjusted boy who isn't mourning the loss of his father very much because he never really had one to begin with. He knows how much you love him, and that seems to be enough."

I mulled that over and decided she could be right. And except for a couple of heart-wrenching episodes of depression that lasted about two weeks apiece, Matt did fine, just as she predicted.

It took me a while, but eventually I recovered too. It was a shock to discover how little I missed Peter. I had expected he'd be on my mind constantly, out of habit if nothing else. But after the shock wore off, days sometimes passed when he never crossed my mind. Then I'd catch a glimpse of a man wearing a custom-tailored shirt like the ones Peter used to buy or hear someone with his self-conscious, staccato laugh, and there would be a brief pang of indefinable sadness—quickly followed by a wave of relief that this man was *not* Peter, and best of all he was not my husband.

It helped that I liked our new life in Minneapolis an awful lot. I liked the fact that I was responsible only to myself and, naturally, to Matt and B.O, and I could play my jazz collection whenever it suited me. I also liked not having to worry about a man—or men. I liked not having to *accommodate* constantly. I finally got over the lonely, black-hole-in-the-chest anxiety that haunts you for months after a divorce, although it occasionally returned on rainy Sundays when my cohorts were out of town and Matt was sleeping over with other kids. But for the most part I was more and more contented as time passed.

Then one Saturday morning about two years after the divorce I looked around our two-bedroom condo that looked out on Lake Calhoun from the eighteenth floor, the home I'd decorated with eclectic abandon, just the way I'd always wished I could, and realized that my life now resembled all the teenage fantasies I'd had about how good my life would be when I made it as a novelist. I wasn't, of course, a novelist yet, but I was a respected author and editor. I had my son, enough income to provide for our needs, several close friends, and a lifestyle that satisfied me in almost every way I could imagine. I was Mary Tyler Moore, the strong, self-assured career woman taking her brisk morning walks around Lake of the Isles—which was only a few blocks away, by the way—living the single woman's dream. Little Sally Alexander was happy at last—happy, without needing a husband there to make it so. I suppose I had become something of a liberated woman, but I wouldn't have said so at the time because I hadn't set out to arrange my life that way. It wasn't a crusade. It just happened.

I had no interest in ever marrying again. Some women will say this because it sounds so admirable, so modern, so independently Steinem-esque. But I didn't think in those terms. I only knew I was building a decent midwestern life for myself and Matt, and I was—to use Hubert Humphrey's favorite phrase—pleased as punch. The only thing I didn't like about life in Minneapolis, actually, was the fact that Hubert Humphrey and Fritz Mondale, the ultimate Democrats, were always in the news. But as I said before, there are always tradeoffs in life, and as tradeoffs went, I figured this one was bearable.

My friends went through phases where they tried to match me up with eligible men. I discouraged this, telling them I'd grown addicted to the relaxed feeling that I could be myself on every occasion. I had no intention of accommodating once again to someone else's vision of the role I should play. With Peter, I'd come to think so little of myself that when other people liked me I'd always assumed it was either a mistake or pure luck. I would never go back.

In the period after the divorce I also studiously rediscovered my own True Self, as the self-help pop psychology books said we all should. I spent time thinking about what I really believed in, what I wanted to accomplish by the time I died. I discarded a lot of debris in the process.

For one thing, I gave away all of my faculty-wife clothes and started buying only the things I loved, discovering in the process that I was a colorful, multifaceted, paisley kind of woman. I started speaking my mind again—or maybe for the first time in my life. It was disconcerting to realize, as I looked inward, that I had a number of strongly held convictions I'd never had the courage to publicly embrace or defend before. I suppose it went to my head. For a few months I became something of a loudmouth about these convictions, prompting my friend Biba to tell me I made her sweat when we were with other people because she knew I'd get into a shouting match with somebody before it was over. I decided to tone myself down after she hissed at me (for telling an artist friend of hers that I thought collage took less talent than fingerpainting, and it turned out to be his favorite technique) that I had turned into a "strident, rude, opinionated broad"—the sort of woman I'd always detested. It was a watershed experience, and after several weeks of self-examination, I emerged a new woman.

After that I really blossomed. I started laughing without worrying about how it looked, as I always had after Peter had explained that my gums showed and it wasn't pretty. I made lists of the things I thought might give me joy and started doing them. Matt made a similar list for himself, and together we figured out how to go about making ourselves and each other happy. I took piano lessons, joined a Dixieland and ragtime club (I was the youngest member by fifteen years), ate greasy hamburgers with raw onions, and in general began doing a lot of the things I had always felt I had no right to do because Peter—or my family before him—expected me to do other, more *correct* things. I was learning to play a role of my own making, and it felt very, very good.

And okay, as long as this is true confessions time, I'll admit it: I also stopped shaving my legs every morning. This, I found, was a truly liberating experience. It became symbolic of the transformation that was taking place inside me. The stubble on my legs, which had up till then been a reproach, became a song. Occasionally I let them go for a week at a time. The way I saw it, these cumulative small acts of courage eventually turn one into a fearless and bold human being.

For a while I told myself that I'd never have been free or happy if Peter had stayed with me, never would have found my True Self because Peter would have kept me browbeaten and servile and afraid. Then one day in Dayton's luggage department

I watched a middle-aged couple looking at suitcases. She was drawn to an elegant tapestry softsided carry-on while he lugged two gigantic steel-gray Samsonites to the counter. The wife glanced at her husband, surreptitiously opening and then guiltily rezipping the tapestry piece like a kid sneaking a peek at a hidden Christmas present.

"What are you doing?" her husband called irritably from the counter, where he was handing the clerk his charge card.

She saw me watching and immediately gave me an apologetic smile. "Nothing," she said to him, and quickly walked over to stand at his side. "Those tapestry suitcases are lovely," she said, glancing back at them—and at me, standing beside them. "But I suppose they're impractical."

He looked over at them and muttered dismissively, "Only an idiot would buy one of those." His wife nodded, I guess in agreement.

At first I wanted to scream at the man, "Listen, moron! Don't you get it? Your wife wants tapestry, and you have no right to force the Samsonite down her throat! Knock it off!" Then, in an instant, my wrath was aimed at the woman instead. "Hey, nebbish!" I wanted to yell. "When are you going to speak up? Tell him you want the tapestry! Don't let him bulldoze you!"

As I fought off the surprisingly powerful emotions their little tête-à-tête had stirred up in me, I had a flash of personal illumination. It was a moment when a major piece of the truth about my relationship with Peter finally dawned on me: For the first time I understood that although Peter may have been a domineering moron—and in fact, he had been exactly that, by almost any standards you might use—I also had been a nebbish—too timid to stand up for myself. He had bulldozed me, yes; but I had offered little resistance. Worse, I had abused me almost as much as Peter had. I had made the choices that had sculpted my life up to then, I realized, and I would go on making them. It was time to get down to brass tacks, decide who and where I wanted to be in twenty years, and start taking the steps that would lead me there.

So, just for the joy of it, and as a gift to myself to celebrate the new me, instead of doing another book in my Country Inns of America series, I decided to write a romantic mystery novel featuring a female detective named Bridget Caulfield, a widowed former housewife with a thirst for adventure. She was the perfect mouthpiece for my quirky ideas. Bridget was fortyish, smart, independent, and tough. And unlike most of the female detectives who were being introduced to the reading public, she didn't curse or sleep around. She had a friend—Bert O'Hara, a police detective she'd known for years—with whom she shared Sunday brunches and walks on the beach. But theirs was a new kind of romance. Chaste. Innocent. I wanted to write something I wouldn't be ashamed to let my mother or son read.

My agent said this sort of book would never sell without O.S.S.—"Obligatory Sex Scenes," as William F. Buckley likes to call them. Actually, the manuscript was picked up within two months. My agent told me not get my hopes up, however, since the publisher was a little worried about the lack of sex, too, and was planning a fairly small initial printing just to see how it would go. I decided to look on it as a grand experiment so I could remain detached about the outcome. I didn't even tell most of my friends I'd written the book.

After a slow start, the adventures of Bridget and Bert gathered steam and became the surprise hit of the season. Reviewers called them the grown-up Nancy Drew and Ned, comparing their relationship with those of all the screen greats—from William Powell and Myrna Loy to Hepburn and Tracy. The book didn't make the *New York Times* Best Seller List, but still it was a success in terms of sales. The advance on the second Bridget and Bert mystery was exactly ten times what I got for the first. My agent actually apologized. You'd have to know my agent to recognize what a significant moment that was.

Through all of this I dated occasionally but without much enthusiasm, because (like Bridget Caulfield) I resented the fact that most men who asked me out seemed to believe they were entitled to sex because they'd spent a few hours or a few dollars on me. I was not willing to give up one more centimeter of myself for the sake of anyone or anything, especially anything as fleeting as a sexual encounter. It wasn't that I lacked desire; it was just that the idea of casual intimacy was repulsive to me. I didn't share my toothbrush or my comb; why would I share my body with someone who wasn't a permanent part of my life? It made no sense to me, even in those inevitable moments when the moon was full and the man I was with seemed overwhelmingly tantalizing.

Thus, I felt a little foolish dating at all. Too many men assumed, for some reason, that I'd eagerly succumb to the Primal Urge after a gourmet dinner and a fancy chocolate dessert, while I knew in advance that this wasn't going to happen. I tired of the looks men gave me when I tried to explain, as delicately as I could, that a physical relationship wasn't in the cards. You understand, these were the days before AIDS, when we were being harangued by psychologists, politicians, and liberal theologians to cast off the shackles of sexual repression and—well, in the words of the favorite counterculture bumper sticker of the day, *If it feels good, do it.* This catchy concept covered a lot of ground, offering a blanket excuse for engaging in every kind of self-indulgent and destructive behavior from nail-biting to dope-smoking to blowing up nuclear power plants.

At any rate, I rehearsed several tactful, sensitive, reasoned explanations for my celibacy to use with the men I dated, sometimes even warning them in advance so they wouldn't spend twenty-five or fifty bucks under false pretenses. A few of them seemed nice enough that I really hoped they might agree to my terms. In fact, out of the fifteen or twenty relatively normal, intelligent fellows I refused to sleep with over the years, five responded by asking me to marry them. (I suppose if it had been a strategy for getting marriage proposals, it could have been viewed as a resounding statistical success.) The rest of the bozos I dated aligned themselves with noted philosopher Joe Namath, who once asked, "If you aren't going all the way, why go at all?" They walked away without a backward glance. There were no regrets on my part either. And it seemed more and more a waste of time to date anyone when I had nothing to gain and everything to lose. After about five years I discovered I wasn't going out at all, and I didn't miss it. The lamp of romance in my soul, which had dimmed to a faint glow while I was married to Peter, had finally flickered out.

Okay, I'll admit that I did think about Mac McDonald once in a while during the years that followed my divorce. Usually it was when the quarterly *Middlewood Academy Alumni News* carried a brief story about his exploits as a newspaperman. I couldn't help smiling a bit wistfully when I saw the photo they ran of an older but still slightly disheveled Mac sitting behind one of those proverbial battered manual typewriters in the office of a small newspaper he'd just bought somewhere in the wilds of northern California. On the desk was a little plaque that was only partly visible, but I knew from the few words I could read that it was one of his favorite maxims: "Never explain; your friends don't need it, and your enemies won't believe you anyway."

And I was duly impressed when I saw that he'd received a major award for an investigative report on water pollution by an industry that employed several thousand people in his area. He'd been threatened and sued but finally had won in the courts; the industry involved was forced to clean up its act. Chalk up one for justice and noble values. It looked like Mac had become the man he'd set out to be all those long years before, at least where his career was concerned.

And I briefly wondered about what might have been when I saw announcements of Mac's marriage (at thirty), followed by the birth of a child, Christopher (after Mac's great-grandfather, I was sure) a year or so later.

Then, some half-dozen years after that, a small notice appeared in the magazine stating that Sarah Deerfield McDonald, thirty-four, and her son, Christopher, five, had died in an automobile accident on New Year's Eve 1981. Memorials could be sent to the Chapel Fund of the Academy. They ran a photo of the stylishly slender, quite beautiful Sarah holding little Christopher, a golden-haired replica of his father. That brought a lump to my throat. And yes, it crossed my mind that Mac and I were both single again, but I wasn't interested in pursuing that line of thinking at all. Honest.

I did wonder, however, if anyone had bothered to call him to offer sympathy. I didn't, though I sent a $500 check to the Chapel Fund in a gesture that puzzled me because it seemed gratuitous, and I tried not to do gratuitous things anymore. A condolence card was called for, certainly, and I actually bought one. I sat down at my desk one night and spent a strange few hours sipping countless mugs of Good Earth Original Blend herb tea while I scribbled about fifteen different versions of notes that didn't come close to saying anything that might comfort a man who'd lost his wife and only child. Finally I gave up and spent the rest of the evening on the floor in front of the fire, tossing in the entire collection of crumpled notes one at a time, asking myself what on earth that had been about.

I remember a funny moment that took place at around 11 o'clock that night; it's stayed with me ever since. Just as I was pouring the dregs from the teapot into my mug, I glanced down at the *Alumni News*, which still lay on the floor by the fireplace—

the one with Sarah and Christopher McDonald's picture in it. I thought, "I wonder if Mac and Sarah were faithful to each other?" That wasn't so strange, of course, considering my own experience. But then I remembered Mac's and my year together at Middlewood and realized, with a flash of insight, that Mac was the only person I'd ever known who was incapable of cheating. And I'd known a lot of people, many of whom I'd thought exceedingly virtuous.

That scrupulous integrity had been a disconcerting facet of his character, I remembered—not one I'd valued much at the time, primarily because I hadn't yet experienced betrayal first-hand. I remembered the time he'd talked me into refusing to look at a copy of an upcoming history exam that had been obtained by Charlie Hanrahan, our class treasurer, and shared with every-one who'd pay him a dollar. Mac and I had gotten the only B's on that exam, and he'd refused even to discuss it with our classmates. "Honor doesn't have to be defended," he'd told me with great seriousness. I'd responded that he sounded like Senator Everett Dirksen, arguing that it was also important to get the scholarships we wanted, to get A's like everyone else, and to avoid becoming the butt of jokes among our friends. He'd listened thoughtfully and replied in his staunch, high-minded way, "Being approved by people who cheat isn't a priority for me." It was infuriating.

Now, the night all of this happened—my attempt at the con-dolence note and the mellow reminiscences about Mac's singu-lar value system—was the night before my son's thirteenth birthday. He'd been in his room most of the night working on an English paper, and I'd kept out of his way. At about 11 o'clock Matt wandered out with a notebook and pencil in his hands and sat down in the chair by the fire. He glanced at the *Alumni News* lying open on the floor and then at me. I must have looked strange to him, because he gave me a thoughtful, questioning frown. I smiled but didn't say anything. He watched me for a few seconds and then went back to his notebook, chewing on the eraser of his pencil.

As I sat there next to him one of those moments happened where time collapses into itself like one of those tricky plastic travel cups, a moment when the past looms up on you as if it happened only a few hours ago. I was lying in bed next to Peter again, the night after he'd arranged for the abortion, trying to make up my mind whether having a baby was really worth what it might cost me in terms of Peter's esteem and acceptance.

I stared at Matt until he felt it and looked up at me from his notebook. "What's going on, Mom?" he said, and I started to cry. Then I hugged him to me and said, "I was just thinking how glad I am that you were born." He hugged me back and grinned, probably attributing it to an attack of galloping nostalgia brought on by my alumni magazine. And who knows, maybe he was right.

After a few minutes he got up and walked back toward his bedroom. At the door he stopped and turned around to look at me. "Can we go to the Calhoun Beach Club tomorrow for dinner? Can I order lobster?" he said.

The kid was already a master of timing. He knew the exact moment to go in for the kill.

"Tomorrow," I said, "the world is yours."

○

———

4

It was six years later, the summer of 1987, when Mac's face appeared again in the *Alumni News* in a group photo of Middlewood's newly elected Alumni Board of Advisors back in Derry Mills. I was shocked to see how dramatically he'd changed. He was still fair-haired, though a little darker, still tall and square-shouldered with a slightly unkempt look, but the thick hair had moved back on his forehead about two inches and he'd added a good fifteen pounds. He wasn't fat, but now his legs and upper torso seemed to fit together instead of being slightly mismatched, as I'd always thought they were. The dimple in his left cheek wasn't so prominent anymore, but his crooked smile was still crooked.

It struck me suddenly that he was middle-aged. Not middle-aged like George Hamilton, all manicured and razor-cut with chunky, white teeth gleaming from a chiseled, tanned face. No, Mac was middle-aged like a real forty-three-year-old person who didn't sit under a sunlamp and who exercised only when being chased by armed muggers. Sort of like me, you could say, except that I walked several miles a day, so I hadn't gained fifteen pounds. I'd only gained five. Well, possibly eight or ten. It's hard to remember that far back.

As I studied the photo I saw something else, something different. It was the sag of the shoulders, the slight downward slant of the eyes, the faint change of angle in his mouth that I'd never noticed in the other photos that had appeared in the *News*. I wondered about it. I knew that his newspapers—three of them now, in different smaller northern California communities—were prospering. I'd seen stories about them (and Mac) in the Minneapolis paper a couple of times. I had every reason to assume that his life was going well in most areas.

In fact, one of Mac's former reporters, Dave Higgins, had recently won a Pulitzer prize for his syndicated columns about small-town life that appeared in the *Star-Tribune*, among about a hundred other papers. He was, I gathered, California's answer to Garrison Keillor or Dave Barry. In his columns he occasionally talked about his former boss and (still) close neighbor Mac McDonald, who joined him for spirited political and philosophical debates on Mac's porch as the sun set over the Pacific Ocean. If you could believe Dave Higgins, these two bachelors were as happy as sea otters in a kelp bed with armloads of abalone. Not that you could trust much of anything a syndicated columnist might say.

Anyway, the photo could have been from a bad angle, but it set me to wondering a little more about Mac as if he were somehow an old friend I ought to be keeping tabs on instead of a boy I'd known twenty-five years ago who probably didn't even remember me. I thought about dropping him a line, just to say hello and to congratulate him on being named to the Alumni Board. And of course to brag modestly about my literary success just in case he wasn't aware of it.

But it was a busy time for me. I had a new book out, the seventh in my Bridget Caulfield series, and I was doing the publicity circuit. That meant long periods on the road, endless days sitting on folding chairs in shopping malls to autograph books,

longer nights in hotel rooms that all seemed to have been decorated by the same person, and countless mornings when I awakened to wonder where I was. Chicago? Atlanta? Miami? Los
Angeles?

But I loved every minute of it. It was like getting the world's
best massage every day of my life. I never tired of listening to
fans telling me they loved my work. Some writers found it weari-
some, no doubt, but you'd never hear that from me.

When I was on the road I used most of my free time going
to museums and writing to Matt, who was by this time pursuing
a degree at the University of Missouri journalism school.

For about a year, between the ninth and tenth grades, Matt
actually hoped to go to medical school. Then he learned that
medical students were required to do things to helpless research
animals that made the perpetrators' condemnation to eternal tor-
ment in the cauldrons of hell seem like scant justice. So he
switched to journalism, his second choice. I was overjoyed.

Anyway, I was about to say that I had little inclination to
write or even call my best friends back in Minneapolis, much less
enter into correspondence with a man I'd never cared about
deeply to begin with. So I forgot about Mac again.

Forgot him, that is, until a couple of weeks before
Thanksgiving 1991. I had landed in San Francisco at the tail-end
of a second ten-day promotional tour for my book. It was the big
pre-Christmas push, and I was pooped. The main thing that was
keeping me going was the prospect of heading back to
Minneapolis and my planned Christmas holiday reunion with
Matt and his new girlfriend from Missouri.

I was set to appear on two local talk shows, back to back, followed by readings and book signings at three B. Daltons. That
night I would appear on a call-in radio broadcast for half an
hour, after which I'd be treated to dinner at my hotel by the book
reviewer for a local newspaper.

By 10 P.M. I had grinned my way through fifteen hours of adulation and was bidding the book reviewer good-bye in the lobby of my hotel. I was frustrated. Here I was, Ms. Successful, staying in a VIP suite at the best hotel on Union Square, the world was at my feet, and I wanted nothing more than to go to bed. Alone and quietly. Well, I was middle-aged, after all. If you're not there yet, you soon will be. Then you'll remember how you used to be amused by people who said this kind of thing.

I started to walk toward the elevators and heard the music wafting down from the small open piano bar several steps up and to the left of the main lobby. Never too tired to listen to a good piano, I pulled off my shoes and made my way up to the vacant table I spotted near a giant palm. I sank into the upholstered chair and closed my eyes.

When the waiter came, I asked him for a club soda on ice with a twist—to his credit, he didn't smirk—and sat back to enjoy "Come in from the Rain" and an evocative rendition of "Ebb Tide." I hadn't heard "Ebb Tide" since the senior prom at Middlewood Academy, I was sure. It was a wonderful song. The good songs were *passé*, I mused. Also the good singers and the good musicians. I was primed to be an old fogey. I sat there remembering Sylvia Syms, June Christy, Keely Smith, Helen O'Connell, Oscar Peterson, Joe Bushkin, Duke Ellington, even the Dorseys and Benny Goodman. Not to mention Art Tatum and Jimmy Rowles. I missed them. I was in that kind of mood. I had a nostalgic longing to go somewhere private and listen to their records nonstop for a week.

After about forty-five minutes of this, feeling dreamy and relaxed, I walked down to the elevators on bare feet that felt like overstuffed Polish sausages. I didn't care. I was going home tomorrow.

Once in my room I fell on the bed fully clothed and drifted

off. Some time later I awakened with a start at the sound of tapping on my door.

"Who is it?" I said stupidly, as if I expected to hear "Candygram!" or "Jehovah's Witness!" from the other side. But no, there was a brief pause and then, "It's Mac McDonald, Sally." Well, sure, we say in unison. Who else?

What I did then was amazing: I scrambled to my feet, pulled frantically at my wrinkled navy and white plaid wool skirt in an attempt to smooth it, then ran to the wall mirror—mortified to see, in a blinding moment of truth, that I looked exactly my age, not thirty-five as I'd been telling myself I did—and then ran back to stand several feet in front of the door, completely paralyzed, watching the door handle as if it might attack me at any moment. After a few seconds I glanced down and noticed that my off-white cashmere turtleneck sweater had little wooly pills all over it. I plucked at them. Finally, after some moments of this, I spoke irritably to the handle: "Who?" I waited for the handle to answer.

Mac saved me. After a couple more interminably long moments his voice came through the door again: "Sally, do you remember me? From Vermont. We knew each other in high school. Matthew McDonald?"

I was hyperventilating. *God, please, I'll never ask another thing if You'll help me out here. No matter what happens, I will look back on this moment and say, "It's okay, I already had my one big favor."*

There was no sound from the other side of the door. Had he gone? Panic seized me. I lunged for the door and yanked it open.

"Hi," Mac said.

Words weren't forming in my mind. I was still half asleep, I told myself. Nobody, absolutely nobody could hold me responsible for the way I was behaving. After about three seconds I took a deep breath.

"Well, hi," I said. You had to be there to know how brilliant that was under the circumstances.

Mac just stood there looking at me with a smile on his middle-aged face.

"I was asleep," I said. "I'm not thinking very clearly. Sorry." I smiled apologetically and looked down at my sweater. Mac seemed not to notice the pills. *How about this,* I said to myself, *I've managed to move back to square one in about fifteen seconds flat. I'm standing here thinking about the pills on my sweater, actually wondering whether they will make me unattractive to this man. It's 1962 again.* Like somebody said, you're only young once, but you can be immature all your life.

"I know it's late," Mac said, "but I saw you downstairs in the lobby. I wasn't sure it was you in the dark. I mean, it's been— what?—twenty-five years, I guess. But when you walked to the elevators I knew." He smiled that one-dimpled smile and shook his head. He was dressed in a gray tweed sportcoat, charcoal pants, and a light blue buttondown oxford cloth shirt. No tie, open at the neck. "It's taken me forty minutes to get up the nerve to come up here," he said.

I smiled back at him and said, "Twenty-six."

"What?"

"It's been twenty-six years, I think." Did I actually say that? Yes. I turned pink. *Come on,* I told myself sternly, *act your age. At least act thirty-five.*

Recovering quickly, I smiled a dazzling, public-relations smile at him and said, "I'm glad you recognized me. Do you have time to come in?" I gestured toward the yellow overstuffed chairs facing each other in front of the fireplace behind me. I was proud of myself. I was on my way to being cool and collected, the seasoned doyenne of the literary world who couldn't be ruffled by anything.

"I'm sorry I woke you—I won't stay," he said. "I just wanted to say hello."

"No," I said. "If you just wanted to say hello, it wouldn't have taken forty minutes for you to decide to do it."

He grinned and raised his eyebrows in that owlish way I remembered. "*Touché*," he said. He came into the room, hands stuffed in his pants pockets, and headed for one of the chairs.

"Do you have any ice?" he asked.

"No, but I can have some sent up. What would you like to drink?"

"Just water," Mac said, still smiling. Neither of us had stopped smiling from the minute the door had opened. "I don't really need the ice." I sat gracefully in the chair next to the phone, crossed my legs the way the TV consultant said to, high on the thigh, and dialed room service. Mac watched me as I spoke to the operator and hung up.

"I was afraid you wouldn't remember me," he said after a brief silence. "I felt like I was seventeen again, standing out there."

"Some parts of us never grow up, I guess," I said. Feeling profound, I waited. "So—" I said after several seconds. I was getting a feeling of *deja vu*. What was it? Then it came to me: I was trying out for a class play and had forgotten my lines.

Mac looked at me, his smile a full-blown grin by now. "So, here we are," he said, "two quick-witted individuals, both of us earning our keeps with words, neither of us having any idea what to say at a time like this."

I put my hands over my eyes. "Speak for yourself," I said. "I for one feel perfectly articulate at the moment." I took my hands away and managed to smile back at him.

Mac to the rescue again. "Speaking of words, I suppose you're here promoting a book. You know, I buy them for my friends and brag that I used to go out with you. I don't think they believe me."

"You've made my day," I said.

"You don't need me to make your day. You're a good writer. The best." He waved his hand slightly. "But you know that. I'm sure everyone tells you that."

I was speechless with pleasure. If I opened my mouth I'd gush, so I kept it shut.

"Tell me what else you're doing," Mac said. "I've read that you live in Boston, and you're married to—is it a radiologist?"

"Close. He was a physicist. I've been in Minneapolis now, hmmm, I'd guess about fifteen years." Fifteen years, three months, and fourteen days, to be exact, but who was counting?

"Oh?" His look was a question mark. I realized he didn't know whether my husband had died or we'd been divorced, so he didn't know how to respond.

"His name was—is—Peter Brigham," I said as blandly as possible. "He had problems with monogamy. He took his problems elsewhere." I shrugged, not knowing what else to say.

Mac looked at me, then down at his hands. Suddenly he was serious. "I'm sorry, Sal. You deserved the best." He paused. "Any kids?"

"One," I said. At least we were finally on a topic I could handle. "A boy. He's the perfect son, and I'm not the only one who thinks so. He's finishing his Bachelor's in journalism at the University of Missouri."

Mac raised his eyebrows again. "No kidding? That's great. What's his name?"

"Matthew," I said. The eyebrows shot up even higher, so I hastened to add, "My husband named him—after his mother's grandfather's somebody-or-other."

Mac smiled but didn't respond. I got up and went to the bed, where my purse lay open where I'd dropped it earlier. I took out my standard issue Mothers' Photo Book and pulled out the best snapshot of Matthew, handing it to Mac.

"He looks like you," he said. "I'll bet he's very bright."

What could I say? "He is. And he gives me great one-liners for my books." I gazed fondly at his picture as I put it back in my purse.

"You haven't remarried? I mean, it's hard to imagine you alone for long. There must have been a lot of men who wanted to take you out of circulation..."

Take me out of circulation? Wow, I thought. There were still people who weren't embarrassed to say things like that.

"Well," I said, slightly flustered, "I wasn't entirely alone. I have a lot of good friends who are like family to both Matt and me. And there was B.O. Plenty, our guardian angel. He disguised himself as a dog." I smiled, remembering B.O. "He died two years ago. He was faithful." I sighed. "As rare and wonderful a quality in a dog as in a man."

Mac eyed me with an expression I couldn't read.

"And yes, there were men who wanted to take me out of circulation," I continued, "but it wouldn't have added anything to our lives if I'd married them. So I passed." Well, it wasn't so far from the truth. I had to say *something*, didn't I? Otherwise he might have thought nobody wanted me.

Mac leaned farther toward me. "I don't know what to say," he said. "I'm sorry about your divorce, but you seem to have turned your life into exactly what you wanted it to be in spite of it. It must have been difficult for you. Especially doing everything alone."

"Piece of cake," I said lightly, reminding myself that this was not an in-depth conversation; it was merely *hello, how nice to see you again, goodbye.* "I've learned how to be happy on my own. My friends don't seem to understand it, but it's true. A woman's magazine recently called me 'the ultimate feminist,' but I'm a long way from that. I didn't set out to arrange things this way. It hasn't worked out for me to be married, that's all. It's just how my life turned out—nothing to be proud of or sorry about. I'm not a courageous heroine." I paused. "Anyway, I like men. Half of my closest friends are men. I mean, my closest friends are half men." I rolled my eyes. What a time for a brain cramp.

He nodded, seeming not to notice my pained expression. "I think I understand how you feel. I've learned to be happy alone, too, although I didn't choose it. People have finally given up trying to pair me off with somebody who can make my life complete. I suppose they realize I'm too old to change now." He grinned again, boyishly. Well, we'd gotten that much out of the way anyway.

I waited for a moment and then said, "I'm sorry about your wife and son, Mac. I read about it in the *Alumni News*. I can't imagine how awful it must have been." Immediately I wished I hadn't opened my mouth, but the words hung in the air between us and couldn't be retrieved. How was it possible, I wondered, that I could have said anything so banal and so hackneyed about what was probably the most traumatic event of Mac's life? He stood, walked to the mantel, and glanced up at the painting that hung above it, not really seeing it. His hands were stuffed into his pants pockets again.

"Yeah," he said after a few moments. He studied the painting, a generic hotel suite floral that picked up the colors of the room. "Chris would be fifteen now. I expected time to make it easier, but it doesn't." *Oh, dear*, I thought, *I didn't mean to stir this up.*

"Sarah and I were in the midst of a divorce, too. That's when it happened," he continued. "We hadn't been together for almost a year. Chris was living with me, but she had picked him up for the after-Christmas holidays." The recollection brought that shadow of sadness to his face, the one I'd seen in the *Alumni News* photo. I fervently wished I could change the subject but knew there was no way.

"I was at the stage where I thought I no longer cared what happened to Sarah," he went on. "But she was my son's mother, and I realized after she died that you don't stop caring because somebody says it's over." He turned, walking back toward the chair. "At least I don't."

I do, I thought. When Peter had said it was over between us, I'd stopped caring about him almost overnight. For a moment I felt ashamed of myself. I made a mental note that I needed to think about that sometime later.

"Mac," I said, "It's just dreadful. I'm sorry."

"I'm okay," he said. "I'm living the life I want to live, doing things that matter to me. Great losses tend to help you rearrange your priorities. That's not news to you, of course."

"I've seen bits and pieces about you in the *Alumni News*," I said. "It sounds like you've become the crusading journalist you always wanted to be. I've gotten a kick out of the stuff about you in Dave Higgins's column, too."

"I'm proud of Dave. He was the smartest kid I ever met when he walked into my office the first time. He started out hoping to be a hotshot reporter, and he's already a legend in his own time. Deservedly so, of course." Mac sat back and relaxed, stretching. He crossed one ankle over the other, smiling at me.

My face was getting tired of smiling, but I kept it up. "You love your work as much as I love mine," I said. "Are you a workaholic?" It was always good to get a man talking about his work. It eliminated awkward silences.

Mac looked at me. "I don't think so," he said. "I have a lot of fun with it, but it isn't what I set out to do. I wanted to be a journalist, or at least an editor, and I've ended up as a business owner. I've got three small newspapers and don't really edit any of them. I'm smart enough, at least, to leave that to people who are better at it than I am. So I'm an entrepreneur, a policy-setter, even a consultant maybe, but hardly a 'crusading journalist.' What I really do is enable other people to be crusading journalists. And I have some fun with that, I'll grant you."

I was surprised. "Are you saying you'd prefer to act as a managing editor instead of as owner-publisher?"

"In some ways I would, sure. But I like the clout, frankly. Owning the papers gives me a powerful voice in the community. If I had to answer to somebody else at this point in my life, I'd probably have a hard time with it. I can be pretty stubborn."

"I never thought of you as stubborn. I always thought of you as accommodating and agreeable." I knew several other nice euphemisms for wimpy, too.

"I've developed a number of character traits over the years that would probably surprise you."

"What, besides stubbornness?"

His eyes narrowed. "Hmm. This is one of those job interview questions, isn't it? You're asked what your faults are, and you have to come up with something cagey, like 'I'm so obsessive about my work that I think of nothing twenty-four hours a day but how to make more money for the company.'"

"Right. Quick, two faults."

He smiled again. "Okay, but on short notice I can't be cagey. How about this: I no longer laugh at jokes I don't think are funny. In reality, that does have its positive aspects, since it's reduced the number of speaking engagements and party invitations in my mailbox. Oh, and I'm overly picky, Dave tells me, especially where women are concerned. I tend to prefer the company of seventy-five-year-old widows to that of over-the-hill cheerleaders. And that's just for starters."

"Wow, I'm thanking my lucky stars I was never a cheerleader."

"I wouldn't have admitted it at the time, but I didn't like cheerleaders even when I was seventeen. If you'd been one, it might have caused me to miss out on you."

"You missed out on me anyway."

"Only for twenty-six of the last twenty-seven years."

"You're a pretty weird guy, Matthew."

He leaned forward and brushed something off the knee of his left pants leg. "You and Dave have a great deal in common," he said. "Your opinion of me, for example."

"Come on. His opinion of you makes my newspaper sticky. It oozes from between every line in his columns about you. In fact, tell him he'd better lighten up or people will start talking."

He laughed. "He doesn't lay it on that thick, does he?"

"So tell me," I said, "are you taking steps to broaden yourself as a journalist, or are you going to stay in your lucrative and cloutful rut?"

His face went serious. He seemed to be thinking it over. "I've been spreading my wings a little to make things more interesting; so the rut isn't as deep as it would seem. I'm even doing some writing—the occasional feature, investigative stuff, whatever appeals to me. But I haven't organized my thinking about what I want to do with the rest of my life. Maybe I'll be a late bloomer."

"Better late than never. But aren't you being overly modest? Most people would call you an early bloomer, and it wouldn't be flattery. You've been a success for years, by almost any standard you'd care to use."

He smiled again. "That's another of my peculiar qualities. I don't measure the success of my life according to traditional standards."

"Do you measure other people the same way?"

"I try not to measure anyone else's life, but when I do, it's not by traditional standards either."

I was enjoying Mac the iconoclast. Where had this side of him come from? I wondered briefly how he'd measure the success of my life, and it surprised me that I cared.

I eyed him over steepled fingers. "Marching to this different drum of yours is part of what keeps you in thrall to seventy-five-year-old widows, I presume."

"You're extremely perceptive."

"Am I to conclude from your non-traditional stance that you are no longer a Republican?"

He grinned broadly. "I haven't gone over the edge completely."

"That's a relief. You had me worried."

"You've grown more politically tolerant with age," he said, lifting his eyebrows.

"I've grown more Republican with age. Marriage to a Democrat transformed my thinking. Once, not long before Peter left, I even had a dream in which Gerald Ford and I carried on a memorable romance—after Betty foolishly left him for their pool man." I'd actually had that dream. Nobody believed me, but it was true. And—no joke—it was the most sensuous dream I'd ever had. I never saw the man on TV after that without blushing.

I smiled at Mac, realizing that there'd been a time when he'd reminded me a little of Gerald Ford. Hey, I thought, maybe Mac, too, had a few surprises hidden behind that mild-mannered exterior. Sure. And maybe Jane Fonda ate three Dove Bars before bed every night.

"A dream like that could be transforming all by itself," said Mac. "Even to a lifelong Democrat."

"I never thought of it that way. That could have been what clinched it, all right." I paused. "So to speak."

Room service rescued me by picking that moment to rattle up to the door with ice, several bottles of Perrier, and a plate of neatly sliced and seeded fresh limes. Mac tipped the waiter, closing the door after him and pouring glasses for both of us without asking if I wanted any.

"My wife was a registered Republican," he said, "but we never agreed about politics. So one of us was not really a Republican, I guess."

"I have a feeling I know which one."

He seemed to be thinking about it. "It would appear," he said finally, raising his glass in a toasting gesture, "that you and I both managed to marry people who didn't appreciate us. But we've triumphed over that and built lives of productivity and purpose anyway." The crooked little smile was still there. "Even if one of us hasn't bloomed yet."

I clinked my glass on his. "I'm proud of us," I said. "And who knows, maybe our real blooming seasons lie ahead of us."

He gave me a smile that was both wise and quizzical. "As you say, better late than never."

I stared at him, studying the differences between the Mac who was sitting with me and the one I'd dumped twenty-six years before. His straight posture, his restrained gestures, even his warm, smooth voice—all were eerily unchanged. But at the same time this Mac was far more assured than the old one, which I suppose was natural. I mean, you gain assurance with age and success. He also had gained, somewhere along the way, a kind of deep-in-the-soul dignity that shouldn't have surprised me but did. *In another fifteen or twenty years*, I speculated, *he could be the next Walter Cronkite*. The thought made me smile. "Good night and good luck," I could hear him saying, eyebrow lifted. He even had the voice for it.

He was studying me. "You are about ten times prettier than the pictures on your book jackets," he said. *No*, I thought, *twice as pretty maybe, but not ten times*. Still, those pictures *were* pretty awful. Then I thought, *Well, it wasn't necessarily a lie on his part, just hyperbole*. I forgave him.

"Thank you," I said modestly.

Then, quaffing another slug of Perrier, he asked, "How long will you be here in San Francisco?"

"I'm going home tomorrow night. It's the end of my tour."

He nodded but said nothing. I waited and for a little while found that I was content just to sit there with him and drink lime-

flavored Perrier and be quiet. It was a pretty strange scene: two
gunslingers in a saloon, each wondering if the other was going
to draw. Mac made no attempt to carry on the conversation. He
looked at me with an easy, eye-crinkling half-smile and we just
sat there like that, neither of us disturbing the silence, for several minutes.

Finally I broke it. "What brings you to San Francisco? Don't
you live some distance up the coast?"

He nodded. "Newspaper business. I also have orders from my
doctor to take a week's vacation. He claims I'm going to be an
early victim of heart attack unless I learn to take better care of
myself."

"As Noel Coward said, work is a lot more fun than fun," I said.
"How can it hurt you if you're having a good time?"

"He doesn't buy that argument. What do doctors know?" He
paused. "Will you have time to eat lunch tomorrow? I'd like to see
you again."

I reached for my purse on the table and pulled out my Day-
At-A-Glance. "No, it doesn't look like I can manage it," I said. I
read off the list of scheduled activities that took me up to departure time. Whew, that was close.

"It's a shame, after all these years," I said lamely. "There's so
much to catch up on." I tore a piece of blank paper out of the
calendar and handed it to him. "Give me your address and we'll
keep in touch," I said. "Next time you're in Minneapolis or I'm
in California we can get together."

Mac stared at me for a few moments and then wrote on the
paper. "Give me yours," he said. I wrote it on a card he pulled
from his shirt pocket and handed it back to him.

We stood and Mac smiled again, holding out his hand. I
shook it. "I'll send you a Christmas card if you promise you won't
correct my spelling," he said.

"I promise," I said, walking with him to the door.

"Bye," he said. "Take care of yourself."

"You, too," I said. "Thanks for taking the trouble to find me."

He started down the hall toward the elevators. When he got to them he turned, walked back, and came up to me with his hand raised slightly as if he'd forgotten to tell me something. Then he put his arms around me and hugged me. I was taken completely by surprise. Honest. In fact, it was sort of shocking, probably because it had been so long since anyone had hugged me in any way other than the comfortable, A-frame way old pals hug and pat each other on the back. This was a *hug*, the kind where bodies actually come into contact with each other and communicate things other than *bonhomie*. I found myself wrapping my arms around Mac and holding him only a little less enthusiastically than he was holding me, my head on his shoulder and his chin on mine. There wasn't any patting.

After approximately fourteen and a quarter seconds, we stood apart and Mac took my right hand, turning the palm up and looking into it. Then he surprised the daylights out of me by carefully turning my hand over and kissing it very gently. I started to speak—I don't know what I wanted to say—and then stopped.

"It wasn't just a coincidence that I saw you downstairs," Mac said.

"How do you mean?" I asked. Ah yes, of course. It was *fate*.

"I saw an ad for your book-signings at B. Dalton's in *The Chronicle* yesterday and decided it would be interesting to try to track you down. I did have some business here, and my doctor did tell me I needed to get away, but I actually came to see you. I missed you at B. Dalton, then came over here and lurked in the lobby for about four hours. When I saw you leave the piano bar I followed you up to your floor. Then I chickened out and went back downstairs. The part about taking another forty minutes to get up my nerve was true."

"Oh," I said. Still the same old Mac. Couldn't cheat, even a little. At least not for long.

"I'm glad I found you," he said.

"So am I," I said. Still the same old Sally, too, I thought. At least in one way.

"I'll find you again. Okay?"

I gave him a look that probably wasn't what he was hoping for.

"Yes," I said. "That would be nice." He was still holding my hand. After a few moments I pulled it free and touched his cheek with it and then backed into the room and closed the door.

5

It took me all of two weeks to put Mac totally out of my mind again, I can tell you that. Even in the pre-holiday rush, his face kept popping up in my mind, and of course the scene that kept coming back to me was the one at the door where he kissed my hand. Men just don't know what that sort of thing can do to a woman. If they did, naturally they'd be doing it all the time and it would no longer work, so it's better this way.

It was, at any rate, business as usual in Minneapolis. The new Bridget Caulfield mystery was selling well by Thanksgiving. My agent called on my birthday, December 7th, Pearl Harbor Day, to wish me well and to announce that I had just made #9 on the *New York Times* Best Seller List. My friend Biba Mariani was unexpectedly called out of town on business (she's a P.R. consultant) and wouldn't be there to gloat with me over one of our ceremonial birthday brunches. I didn't want to substitute one of my other friends for Biba since it would have broken a nine-year tradition; so I spent the morning opening cards from friends and fans, sipping freshly ground dark-roast Colombian coffee, solving cryptogram puzzles I'd collected from the newspaper, and idly wondering how I might celebrate the day.

Matt, good son that he was, called me around noon and made

jokes only a twenty-three-year-old could make about people my age. He told me he loved me and and would see me in less than two weeks. Words to warm the cockles of a mother's heart. He couldn't wait for me to meet Valerie, his girlfriend, who dreamed of becoming a mystery writer. *Yah, sure, yewbetchuh,* I said to myself Scandinavianly. Then I said to him that *of course* I'd be delighted to read one or two of her manuscripts and make any suggestions I could think of. I know, I know, my child had me wrapped around his finger. But what's a mother for?

After his call I decided I'd get dressed, go for a walk, and have lunch at whatever deli captured my fancy along the way. Today I undoubtedly deserved to top off my meal with a jumbo hot fudge sundae at Swede's Cafe. The walk would earn it for me, right? You know how these inner dialogues go: a twenty-minute walk will cancel out a 1,200-calorie hot fudge sundae.

I took my time dressing, opting for my old favorite, a red pullover sweater, white turtleneck, gray pants, and a pair of new red suede ankle-high boots. I felt terrific. Not to mention colorful.

I grabbed a scarf and my navy pea coat and threw open the door, running like Mary Tyler Moore down the hall, into the elevator, and out into the 20-degree sunshine of a perfect day in Minneapolis. (Twenty sunny degrees was about as perfect as things could get in Minneapolis in December.)

Yes, I was forty-seven, and I was ready for anything. Well, almost anything. I have to admit that I was not totally ready for what I encountered at that point. There, emerging from a cab on the corner of Lake Street at Dean Parkway, was Mac McDonald.

He eased out of the cab and grinned at me. "Hi," he said. "Happy birthday."

I was speechless.

"Are you on your way somewhere?" he asked.

"Yes," I said. "I mean, no. I was just going for a walk, to find a place for lunch." I felt embarrassed, as if I shouldn't admit that I was alone and looking for something to do on my birthday. "What brings you here?" I asked casually.

He glanced down at the sidewalk and then back at me. "You," he said. He always had a way with words.

"You came all the way from California just to wish me a happy birthday? I don't believe you."

"I tried to call, but you have that machine turned on all the time. Then last night I realized it was your birthday today, so I decided to take a chance and hop a plane. Besides, my doctor told me to leave town for a few days. I figured if you weren't here, at the very least I'd get to see the Twin Cities."

"Your doctor gives you a lot of orders."

"I don't know why I'm making excuses. I just wanted to see you. Do you mind?"

"I'm flattered. I don't know what to say."

"Let's get some lunch, then," Mac said, stuffing his hands into the pockets of his tan Eddie Bauer raincoat. Beneath it was a cobalt blue pullover sweater and gray cords. He held out an elbow for me to put my arm through. *Oh, well,* I thought, *if I wasn't meant to see him again I'd have left fifteen minutes earlier.* He'd flown here from California; the least I could do was have lunch with the man.

I took his arm and began to steer us straight to Swede's, down near Hennepin and Lake, where we got a table right away. All I could think of was hot fudge, but I felt compelled to do the refined thing by ordering some lunch first. I studied the menu. What the heck, I wasn't interested in veal cutlets. I told Mac I was going straight for a jumbo hot fudge sundae with extra hot fudge. He decided on a cheeseburger with grilled onions and a side of fries.

He rubbed his hands together as we faced each other across the table. His cheeks were rosy, as I presumed mine were.

"Your nose is running," he said, grinning.

"How kind of you to point it out," I said, reaching for a napkin.

"Are you cold?"

"Not now," I said. "I'm fine." I blew my nose noisily.

He looked around for a waiter, signaling when he saw one. The waiter ignored him, concentrating on the more important job of placing butterballs in little bowls. Harp music was playing from speakers over Mac's head. The song was "'Til There Was You." I remembered the first time I'd heard that song, when an elfin-faced woman named Mimi Heinz had sung it to her husband on the old Jack Paar *Tonight Show*, causing Jack to weep. An extraordinarily beautiful moment in television history.

I studied Mac's face as he tried to get the waiter's attention. There was something about him in that light that reminded me of someone else. As he looked at me and smiled that quirky half-smile of his I made a connection. Tom Brokaw. The evening news.

"Do people tell you that you look like Tom Brokaw?" I asked.

"No," he said. "You think I do?"

"Just a little. Around the eyes and mouth when you smile a certain way."

"Somebody told me last year I look like William Hurt, but I wasn't sure that was a compliment. Is Tom Brokaw a compliment?"

"Millions of fans can't be wrong," I said noncommittally. William Hurt, I thought. Yes, that's it. Much closer than Tom Brokaw. Mister Soft-Serve All-American Nice Guy.

Mac smiled his William Hurt smile. "Do you have plans for tonight?" he asked, getting right down to business. No shilly-shallying for him, no sirree.

"You're not supposed to ask a lady if she has plans," I smirked. "You assume she has. You assume she's booked solid for months at a time. Especially on her thirty-sixth birthday."

"Sorry." He grinned blandly. "I did try to call you. I apologize for putting you on the spot like this. I don't blame you for being annoyed. I feel like a jerk."

"I'm not annoyed," I said. "I'm just—oh, I don't know. I'm just—annoyed." I shook my head. "And yes, as a matter of fact, I've been invited to dinner. With the governor." He looked impressed. My wit was lost on him.

"However," I said, "since you've come all the way from California, I know the governor will understand if I take a rain check."

"The governor must be a Republican," he said, straight-faced. Maybe my wit wasn't lost on him.

"To the core," I said.

"Can I leave it to you to choose your favorite restaurant?" he asked.

"Sure. I'll make a reservation."

There was a pause. He leaned forward, elbows on the table, chin resting on his hands. "Well, what do you know about that," he said.

"What?"

"We're going on a date."

"Oh, my goodness," I said. "I wish you wouldn't put it that way." Now I was going to have to shave my legs.

He smiled his half-smile and sat back in his chair, a happy man.

6

Mac and I chatted spontaneously and, I thought, chummily through lunch. We caught up on each other's lives the way you always seem to do when you're with somebody you haven't seen in years—by relating little vignettes that sum up whole segments of your life, so you don't get bogged down in too many details that can't possibly be covered in a short time.

We parted at 3:30 in the lobby of my building, where the doorman called a cab for Mac. We agreed that he would pick me up again around 7. He headed off to the Walker Art Center to look for a couple of special gifts for friends back in California and then, presumably, to his hotel down on the Nicollet Mall.

This was turning into a fairly nice birthday, I told myself as I walked back into my apartment. A nice, friendly, happy birthday. I pulled off my clothes and put on my yellow terry-cloth robe, shuffling through the stack of mail I hadn't finished opening that morning and snapping on the burner to heat some water for coffee. I was having a good time. It was fun to be wined and dined by an old friend. Why not?

It crossed my mind, of course, that Mac's agenda here was different from mine. I felt a bit guilty but brushed it aside. The man's forty-six, I reminded myself, and he can take care of himself. None of this was my doing. He was the one who'd flown out here unannounced; he was the one who wanted a friendly dinner out. We'd have a nice evening and that would be that.

Now, I have to say in my own defense that I was not normally quite this dense and self-deceptive; it was merely a self-indulgent lapse that occurred during the three hours while I was alone between lunch and dinner with my high school sweetheart. By 6:30 the true picture was beginning to dawn on me. I had spotted the little worm in my shiny red apple. Mister Nice had not flown halfway across the nation purely to wish me a happy birthday. He had come to court me; that's what he had come to do. And I, of course, was going to have to put a stop to that. Fast. Birthday or no birthday.

He arrived promptly at 7 dressed in an expensively tailored, navy gabardine suit with a power tie—navy silk with red pin dots. He looked like an anchorman. Yes, William Hurt in *Broadcast News*, but slightly older and better padded. The hairline, the eyes, the overall evenness of his coloring, the posture, the winsome smile—the resemblance was rather striking.

"You look terrific," I said. What the heck, it wasn't such an exaggeration.

I was wearing the only "little black dress" I owned, which showed a little shoulder and cleavage but was modestly hemmed below the knee. I also wore my mother's pearls.

"You look better," he said, beaming at me.

"Better than what?"

"Better than anybody."

I have to tell you, I blushed like a schoolgirl.

He turned and began to walk around my apartment, first through the living room and kitchen, then standing in the doors of the bedrooms to peer in discreetly, finally landing in the large dining alcove I'd converted to a den. There I kept my computer, files, and about a thousand books in floor-to-ceiling white book-cases that covered three walls. After inspecting the computer he went to the sliding glass door that looked out from my balcony toward Lake Calhoun. It was dark, and the city lights were twinkling. The only sound was the low hum of traffic on Lake Street that snaked past the building and out toward St. Louis Park and the western suburbs. I pointed out landmarks, some of the other lakes, St. Paul, the Mississippi River. You couldn't really see the river or St. Paul from there, but you could see where it would be. The lake was calm, and the moon had already started to rise.

"I can see why you live here," he said. "This is something." He cocked his head at me. "Does the height bother you?"

"Not anymore," I smiled. "It did for about a week." He remembered my fear of heights. The man had a better memory than the Amazing Kreskin.

"Do you own or rent?"

"I bought it a couple of years after I moved to Minneapolis. Before that I lived in an apartment in the building next door. When my financial planner said I needed to invest in real estate, this seemed preferable to becoming a slum lord."

"Good choice," he said.

I offered something to drink. To my surprise, he chose hot cider over my secret blend of dark-roast Colombian with Mocha-Java coffee. I added a stick of cinnamon to our mugs. Then he asked me to tell him about each painting on my walls, which took a while because there were a lot of them. I was a collector, and the real decor of my apartment was the art. Hardly a square foot of wall space remained vacant.

I walked around the apartment with him, explaining where each piece had come from and why I liked it. He was particularly interested in a small painting I treasured, the work of my friend Marjorie Hennessy, who lived just a couple of miles away. It was one of her earlier works, *Flight into Egypt*. She specialized in liturgical art and had become something of a celebrity in the last few years. This one had won prizes at a couple of major shows. Mac studied it for some time and then wrote her name on a card and put it in his pocket. I hoped she'd end up selling him something.

His comments on the rest of my collection were informed, articulate, insightful. I was impressed and a little surprised. The man was urbane, even sophisticated. It caught me off guard, as if William Hurt had suddenly started talking like Vincent Price, but without the sissy accent.

At last we finished the grand tour, and Mac sat in the chintz-covered chair by the fireplace. I'd lighted a Duraflame log earlier. It flickered artificially on the grate.

"This is a comfortable place," he said, rubbing his palms on the arms of the big chair. "It's like you—stylish and classical, but still warm and easy."

My word, I thought. Is that how I seemed? I'd never thought of myself in those terms. It sounded like something a judge might say about a glass of cabernet at a wine tasting.

I took our empty mugs to the kitchen for a refill. As I started back into the living room I found Mac leaning against the kitchen door frame watching me. He didn't smile, didn't say anything, just stood there. I stopped, the mugs held out from my body.

He pushed himself away from the doorway and came toward me, taking the mugs and setting them on the counter to my right. *Oh, boy*, I thought, *here we go*.

In the midst of the embrace, I gave in and let myself enjoy it. Why should I be so noble? It was my birthday, after all.

"You feel extremely good," he said, moving to wrap his arms more snugly around me.

"Why, thank you," I said into his shoulder. "As a matter of fact, so do you." He wasn't trying to kiss me. He just wanted to hold me, I guess. It was nice.

We stood there for some time, I don't know exactly how long, until Mac pulled away from me slightly and said, "Let's go stand outside on the balcony."

"Okay," I said. It was by now about about 22·degrees, of course, but it still sounded like a splendid idea. I grabbed an afghan as we passed the sofa on the way to the balcony door.

Outside, we leaned against the railing. I was swathed in the afghan, trying not to shiver. The wind chill up on the eighteenth floor was reducing the temperature, so I tried to think warm. "Sometimes," I said, "in the warm months I sit out here at night and watch the headlights coming down Lake Street, the planes flying over, the boats at anchor out on the lake, the lights blinking from the skyscrapers downtown. It's quite a sight. Matt used to come out here with me, and we'd pick out all the constellations we could find on a star map."

Mac draped one arm around my shoulder, casually, the way boys used to do in a theater on a first date.

"When you were a kid," he said, "did you ever lie in the grass on a clear night and watch for shooting stars?"

I smiled at the memory. "Sure. I'd imagine I was soaring through space, out past the edge of the universe, out where there were no more stars, no more anything. And then I'd blow my mind by trying to picture what I'd see when I looked past that. And past that." I stared upward, recapturing the old feelings. "What do you think is out there, outside the edge of the universe, where there isn't even *nothingness* anymore?"

"God," Mac said.

I looked up at him. His face was serious; he wasn't being clever. I was surprised. It was an answer Malcolm Muggeridge or C. S. Lewis might have given, or even Charlton Heston, but I didn't personally know any men who would respond that way to such a question.

Without saying anything more, Mac moved to stand behind

me, wrapping both his arms around me. I could feel his warm breath in my hair. We stood there like that for about five more minutes, freezing our fannies off.

At 7:45 we left for dinner. I'd made reservations at an Italian restaurant near downtown, a place reputedly frequented by majordomos of La Cosa Nostra, if you could believe Minneapolis had a Mafia branch operation. I figured it was just P.R. designed to lure the local Scandihoovians. We were only admitted after being inspected through a face-sized peephole on the big, black front door of the place. The little door opened; a menacing face appeared, looked us up and down, and then the door snapped shut. It took another minute or two for them to open up. It was a nice, sinister effect.

Inside we found a sizable eating establishment that looked like a B-movie version of a *trattoria* in Sicily. Dusty-looking plastic grapes hung from arbors that ran up the walls in unexpected places. Everyone sat on wrought-iron ice cream chairs at big, round tables that were covered with red and white checked cotton tablecloths. Empty Chianti bottles hung from the ceiling, and more bottles squatted on the tables, each with a dripping candle burning in it. Hidden speakers played an Italian song, and the singer sounded just like Eddie Fisher. Maybe it *was* Eddie Fisher. I wondered what he was doing nowadays.

The tables around us were filled with hearty-looking women and their slightly less hearty husbands, all of them in a mood to sing and dance, which they did several times. There were children around who seemed to belong jointly to everyone in the restaurant. They cruised from table to table, begging desserts and soda crackers.

We had the seven-course Fiesta Dinner, which I'd had the only other time I'd dined there, several years before. As we ordered we were informed gravely that it took two hours and forty-five minutes to finish the complete dinner. Our waiter,

Mario, a jocular fellow who seemed to speak very little English, treated us like family, plying us with gelato between courses to cleanse our palates.

Mac ate all of his first-course antipasto salad and all of the incredibly savory lentil-and-okra spicy soup that came next. I hung back, knowing the best was yet to come. By the time the fourth course arrived—braccioli and manicotti—Mac was full. We both refused the seventh course when Mario arrived with a gigantic rolling cart of obscenely enticing dainties. It was hard to say no because dessert looked better than anything we'd eaten, and that was saying something.

At the end of the meal Mario and another waiter carried in a white cake with just-lit sparklers spewing tiny hot coals from it and invited the patrons to serenade me with a rousing Italian rendition of "Happy Birthday to You." I wondered how Mac had arranged it, then realized he must have done it when he'd gone to the men's room earlier in the evening. They probably kept birthday cakes on hand in the freezer for such occasions.

Mac waited until the commotion and applause died down before he handed me a small box with a card. I was feeling contented, warm, even a little giddy. I felt lucky not to be in a coma. My blood sugar was probably in the minus zone.

I opened the card first. It was not a birthday card. It was a tasteful, heavy white card with an embossed border and a poem professionally calligraphed on it:

> *. . . Others because you did not keep*
> *   That deep-sworn vow have been friends of mine;*
> * Yet always when I look death in the face,*
> *   When I clamber to the heights of sleep,*
> * Or when I grow excited with wine,*
> *   Suddenly I meet your face.*

Mac didn't move, didn't say a word. He just waited. So did I. I was dumbstruck.

Finally I picked up the box and opened it. A smaller box was inside. A ring box. *Oh, no*, I thought. *No, no. N-O.*

Courage, I told myself. I went ahead and opened the box carefully, as if one of those joke snakes might spring out at me. Inside was a simple gold ring with several small rubies in a cluster on top. It was sweet and old-fashioned, almost like a child's ring. I looked up at Mac.

"It's twenty-nine years old," he said. "I was going to give it to you that summer we broke up. I don't know why I kept it. Pure sentiment, I guess. When I decided to fly out here, it occurred to me that you might like it, just as a keepsake." I noticed an inscription inside the ring and held it up to the light to make it out. It said: "Love forever, Mac."

He got me. What can I say? Things were not going at all as I had envisioned earlier when I'd made up my mind to put a stop to things.

"Mac, thank you. I'll always cherish it," I said. Trite but true. I was touched. I put my hand on his, squeezing it.

Mac was thrilled. "Good. I was worried it wouldn't be appropriate." *No, you weren't, you old fox. You knew.*

"It's perfect," I said. I put it on my right hand. Naturally, it fit. I was glowing like a stoked-up, pot-bellied stove. And speaking of bellies, mine had reached capacity. There was not much that could top having a full, happy belly and a new (or old) ruby ring on one's forty-seventh birthday.

We each nibbled at the cake—just because it was there—glancing at each other self-consciously between bites. Then Mac ordered espresso. Over in a dark corner near the entrance, a reptilian senior citizen Mario described as "the boss" was holding court with assorted children of various ages. A steady stream of customers greeted him at his table and then retreated from his presence, bowing and scraping as if they were afraid to show him their backs. He rested his hand on an ebony cane that appeared to have a carved silver top. Occasionally he tapped it loudly on the floor to signify approval of something someone said to him or to get the attention of one of the children. We stared at him while we sipped the coffee. I wondered if he were an actor from the Guthrie Theatre, hired to impress the patrons.

"Do we kiss the godfather's hand as we leave?" Mac said.

"Risky," I said. "The wrong kind of kiss, or the wrong hand, and we could end up treading water in cement galoshes."

He laughed an easy, slightly sleepy laugh and sat back in his chair. "How did you find out about this place?" he asked.

"A reporter friend of mine from the *Star-Tribune*. He claimed, but I don't believe, that a Mafioso was actually shot down in here some years ago. I was here once before. I'd been hoping for an excuse to come back." I pointed toward the door at the back of the room that led to a smaller dining room. There was a plastic bead curtain covering the opening. "That's where it supposedly happened. The shooting, that is."

Mac looked in that direction. "Seriously?"

"Seriously."

"Far out," he said.

What else?

We went from the restaurant directly to Mac's hotel. There was a little bar there that featured a pianist I'd heard before, at a big wingding out at a mansion on Lake Minnetonka. His style had reminded me of Dorothy Donegan, which surprised me because he was much too young to remember her. If you remember her, you'll know how I could be lured to a hotel bar to listen to this guy in spite of the fact that he was playing in the kind of place I didn't frequent. In fact, the only other time I'd been in a hotel bar in my whole life was that night in San Francisco when Mac and I had met again. I didn't see it as a trend.

The music was terrific. I was enjoying myself immensely, in spite of the fact that I was getting minor guilt pangs each time I found myself flirting with Mac. I suppose you could call my behavior dense and self-deceptive again, but at the time I was focusing almost entirely upon the moment. Once in a while, on birthdays, it would seem we should be entitled to that.

Mac requested some songs like "I've Got You Under My Skin" and "Day In, Day Out." His renditions suggested to me that the pianist knew very well who Dorothy Donegan was. And the fact that Mac requested them suggested that he knew as well. When "Moonlight in Vermont" started up, I was sure about it.

"Don't tell me you're a Dorothy Donegan fan," I said. Well, of course I had to say it. Entire relationships have been built on a whole lot less.

"I only have one of her early LPs," he said. "I'd like to find more." He paused. "You wouldn't believe my record collection. It's embarrassing."

"How do you mean?"

"I was a disc jockey on the campus station at Stanford. I got turned on to old records. Since then I've picked up better than six hundred of them. I have cases full of old 78s."

My, my, my, I said to myself. Imagine that. Had I perhaps been a tiny bit premature in making up my mind about Mac? After all, there was nothing that said this relationship had to come to a *complete* halt. Was it really so far-fetched to imagine that we could become—and remain—good friends? The sort of friends, for example, who might exchange tapes of their jazz collections? Friends did that kind of thing for each other all the time; it was something I had done for at least one friend in the past, on a limited basis. Mac, I was sure, would be delighted to do it for me.

These were my thoughts. I don't deny them.

We launched into a lengthy discussion about the relative merits of Dixieland, ragtime, modern, and progressive jazz. By the time we finished talking about all our old favorites it was pretty late. We'd covered everyone from Duke Ellington to Jellyroll Morton, and I was amazed to discover that Mac knew a lot more about jazz than I did. Clearly, I decided, friendship was not out of the question. One of those long-distance friendships that existed almost entirely by mail would be perfect. I was a great letter-writer.

After the pianist finished a set of Count Basie standards, I knew the evening couldn't be topped, so I suggested it was probably time to head home. Also, I was barely able to keep my eyes open. It could not have been my age, so I expect it was the excess food.

My apartment was dark when we got back. Mac flipped on the light inside the door. He put the key in my palm and looked at me—first at my hair, then at my shoulders, then down to my feet, finally coming back to my face. I felt like Nancy Debutante saying good night to her new beau. Mac's eyes were, if anything, both paler and bluer than I'd remembered.

He looked at me the way I'd been told I should look at a TV talk show host for maximum "eye sparkle": his eyes darted quickly back and forth between mine. I'd never believed it could work, but sure enough, it made his sparkle.

I was feeling warm. I wished I could open the balcony door and stand outside again for about twenty minutes. I didn't want to invite Mac inside. Even the idea reeked of disaster. I was about as susceptible as I'd ever been or was likely to be.

"Thank you," I said, standing resolutely in the doorway, "for a memorable birthday."

"Thank you for being born," he said. It was a great parting shot.

But he wasn't finished. "I've got three more days on my plane ticket. I'd like to spend them with you," he said. "Is that possible?" His smile was beguiling.

"What did you have in mind?" I wasn't saying yes, mind you. I was just asking.

"We could start with a late breakfast tomorrow morning. Then we could see what develops."

"Tomorrow morning?"

"Unless you're meeting the governor to make up for tonight."

"No, that's next Saturday."

"So what do you think?"

I thought. "Ten o'clock would be good. Why don't we eat here?" A workable scheme had come to me. Here in the privacy of my condo we could talk. I could explain to him how we were going to be friends instead of paramours without being interrupted by waiters or overheard by nosy brunchers. I could, at some appropriate moment, show him my original Benny Goodman and Muggsy Spanier records and talk to him about taping his collection for me. I loved it when a plan came together.

"Nifty," he said.

Just to keep me off balance, I'm sure, Mac didn't touch me. He turned and walked down to the elevator and got on. I watched him. He held up his hand to me as he stepped into the car and punched the Down button. He leaned against the side of the elevator and crossed one leg over the other as the doors started to close. He was Fred Astaire bidding Ginger a jaunty farewell.

"Night," I said, and he waved. I thought, *A friendly birthday hug would have been all right*. I wouldn't have turned it down.

7

I think it was Mark Twain who remarked that life would be much happier if only we could be born at age eighty and gradually approach eighteen. That seemed like a better idea than ever as I waited for the buzzer to announce Mac's arrival the following morning.

I had spent a good three hours trying to get to sleep the night before, mostly because of alarming and persistent longings stirred up, no doubt, by his crafty, hands-off farewell tactics. I reminded myself that I was no longer an adolescent victim of my hormones, that the plan of the day called for breakfast, pure and simple, and that what I was experiencing was a mild form of temporary insanity. Like everything else in life, it would pass. Moreover, I was too old for it. Didn't need it, didn't want it. Not even if I were approaching eighteen instead of eighty. Period.

It wasn't that I didn't like or enjoy Mac, of course. He was far more interesting at forty-seven than I'd imagined he could become when we were seventeen. Even so, I was not prepared to let him shake up my life—not even as a harmless little diversion. I'd sworn off such shenanigans long before this, and that resolution had served me well. Why should I change now?

Eventually, at around 4 A.M., I'd managed to fall asleep. At 9 in the morning the alarm had rung me out of bed in a stolid and determined mood.

Mac arrived at my place at 10:04, grabbing me around the middle the moment I opened the door, picking me clear off my feet. Thankfully, he did not groan or reach for his back after he did so. He let me slide slowly to the floor and, before I could object, kissed me on the mouth. He smelled like Old Spice. Did they still make Old Spice? I guessed they must, if that was what he was wearing. I had always liked Old Spice. The newfangled men's colognes, even the expensive ones with names that hinted of European nobility, all smelled to me like something John Travolta might wear to a masquerade ball on the French Riviera, if you know what I mean.

Mac's kiss wasn't casual. It started out tender, almost hesitant, then grew intense. After about fifteen seconds I pushed half-heartedly against Mac's navy blue sweatered chest. He drew back a little and looked at me.

"Ahem," I said, raising an eyebrow.

He loosened his hold on me, running the fingers of his right hand very slowly and gently down the side of my face as he looked right into my eyes. It was an extraordinarily sensuous gesture for a Republican.

Just as he started to turn from me, he glanced down at my right hand, where I was still wearing the ring I'd forgotten to take off the night before. He looked up at me and smiled, and I felt as self-conscious as a fifteen-year-old on her first date. I wanted to look away from him, hide my embarrassment, but for some reason I couldn't. We just stood there and looked at each other for several long seconds. Maybe it was the fact that my sensual responses were so out of practice, I don't know. But it sure was something.

Collecting myself as much as possible under the circumstances, I pulled Mac to the kitchen, where I served a three-cheese-and-onion omelette with garlic and fresh spinach and herbs, just so the cholesterol molecules already in our bloodstreams from the night before would have plenty of company. I also rationalized that I was going to need fuel for what lay ahead.

We ate at the kitchen table, both of us famished, and afterward I ground coffee for cappuccino and started it brewing while Mac watched with such fascination that I felt he must not have seen it done before. They probably didn't know about cappuccino or even Italian roast coffee in the isolated backwoods of northcoast California, I mused. What with the marijuana and everything they grew out there, everyday drugs like caffeine probably seemed pretty mundane.

Mac carried the breakfast dishes to the sink, then rinsed them and put them in the dishwasher while I steamed the milk. When the cappuccino was finally ready, we took our cups into the living room. Mac set about building a real log fire in the fireplace—as real, that is, as the perfectly cut and bundled eighteen-inch sterilized oak logs I could buy at Lund's Supermarket. Outside, the sky was overcast, threatening. The lake looked steel-gray and coldly angry. Snow was on the way. The fire looked cozy and inviting. And so, I might add, did Mac.

We sat facing each other, Mac in the blue easy chair and I in the matching chair on the other side of the fireplace, the afghan covering my lap. It was a fluffy red and blue plaid afghan that nicely coordinated with Mac's navy pullover and my red sweater-vest, white shirt, and navy wool slacks. We could have been hung on a flagpole on the Fourth of July. Our navy blue stockinged toes wiggled and stretched four inches apart on the ottoman.

We talked quietly for a time about the Ordway Music Theatre in St. Paul, home of the St. Paul Chamber Orchestra, which (along with Orchestra Hall in Minneapolis) had become one of the premier concert halls in the nation. Mac had also heard about the Minnesota Zoo, the Guthrie Theater, and, of course, the World Theater, made famous by Minnesota Public Radio and Garrison Keillor. We covered most everything worth talking about in the Twin Cities and then lapsed into silence, watching the fire and the lake outside the window. The Benny Goodman Quartet was swinging softly on the stereo. I was planning how I'd segue casually into the topic of exchanging tapes and then into a warm and friendly farewell scene as I showed him the door.

"Have you thought about what you'd like to do?" Mac said before I could put my plan into operation.

"About what?" I knew, of course, but I was stalling.

"The next three days. I'd like to do things you'd enjoy as much as I would."

I took a deep breath. Well, it had to come. Couldn't avoid it forever.

"Mac, I've been thinking. The next three days may not be such a good idea."

"What do you mean?"

"I mean I don't think it's realistic. There's no future for us, not in the way you're thinking." I hadn't planned to let the words come out that way. They just did.

"I wasn't asking you to spend the rest of your life with me," he said impassively. "I was asking you to spend three days. Or part of them, anyway." He was cool, I had to give him that. It annoyed me. Why couldn't he be more of an oaf?

"Come on," I said. "You didn't fly across the country just to have a little birthday dinner and go sightseeing with me. You came to see if we could pick up where we left off in San Francisco. And in Vermont."

"You have a point," he said, now smiling a little. "But I didn't come here thinking in terms of the infinite future. I just said yes to an impulse. You've been on my mind a lot since San Francisco."

"You've been on my mind, too. But that's no reason we should involve ourselves in something that could cause both of us a lot of problems."

He raised his eyebrows, then sat back and frowned. "Go on," he said.

"There's nothing to go on about," I said. "What we have here is an impossible situation, and we'd both be crazy to pursue it."

"What are you afraid of?" he said.

Cheap shot, I thought. "I'm not afraid. And that's a cheap shot."

He waited. I hated that. Men who could wait like that were too sure of themselves, maybe even arrogant. I added this to my mental list of Mac's irritating qualities.

"Okay," I said, unable to bear the silence any longer, "maybe I *am* a little afraid. I've finally reached the point where I like my life exactly the way it is, and it's taken a long time to get here. I don't want to change things. I don't know about you, but I'm not looking for a casual affair . . . Or any kind of affair. I don't need it, and I don't want it." I sounded fierce and brave. Little Miss Marker.

"That wasn't what I had in mind," he said. I glanced up at him. Heavens to Betsy, he looked like he meant it. That threw me for a moment, but I plunged ahead.

"Mac, neither one of us needs a relationship that will require us to rearrange our lives—or the people and things that mean a great deal to us," I said. "We're not blank slates, you know. We're heavily written upon." What can I say? Even writers can lapse into this kind of dialogue.

Mac's face didn't change expression. "Sally, how do you feel about me?"

Out of the blue like that, I wasn't prepared for the question.

You try to prepare for any contingency, but some idiot always throws in something like this from left field.

I gave it a few moments' thought. Finally I said, "I don't know. I guess I feel a lot of things that make me uncomfortable because they don't fit in with the way I'd like to relate to you. I mean, nothing would make me happier than if we could just be friends, see each other from time to time . . ."

"'*See* each other from time to time?'" he echoed. "We could meet for lunch every year or two, trade clever quips, tell each other about our work, talk about our record collections, and then send snapshots to each other in our Christmas cards? What a terrific idea."

Low blow. Very defensive and very immature.

"Why not?" I said maturely. "We're not kids. Of course we can be friends." My back was up. And, of course, there *was* still the matter of his jazz collection.

"This is not a Neil Simon play, Sal. Come off it." *My goodness*, I thought, *what is this?*

I sat back, and he stood. He put his hands on his hips, then put one in his pants pocket and ran the other through his hair— definitely William Hurt gestures. I watched him, fascinated. He had just told me off, he was acting like a jerk, and suddenly, inexplicably, I found him completely charming. I couldn't believe it. Women. You never know, do you?

I gave this a few moments' thought and decided that charming was not enough. I'd made up my mind, and I was not going to let him rattle me with this unexpected behavior.

"Mac," I said in a conciliatory tone, "it would be different if you and I were leading empty, lonely lives. But we're not. We don't need a romantic involvement—especially one that could hurt both of us more than we can imagine right now. Friendship is one thing. I mean, you can always add to your store of friends. Life expands infinitely to include friends. But my life just can't expand at this point to include you in any other role." We looked at each other. I thought I was getting my first migraine headache.

"That's it?" he asked. "That's the best you can do?"

"Yes." I refused to dignify his comments by rising to his bait.

I stood, went to the glass doors, and opened the slider about two inches. The cold wind felt good slicing at my face and body. I moved from side to side to catch it.

After a few moments Mac sat down on the ottoman, elbows on his knees. "Let me get this straight," he said briskly. "You're saying you're happy, and I'm happy, so why risk messing that up with anything as pointless and complicating as love? Right?"

"I object to the subtle editorial comment inherent in that statement, but it covers things pretty well."

"You're ignoring the alternative. We might actually add something to each other's lives instead of subtracting. Is that such a remote possibility?"

"Yes."

"Why?"

"Because as I said, one or the other of us would have to leave behind a lot of things that are important. *Vital.*"

"Like what?"

"Well, do you want to move to Minneapolis?"

He stared at me for about five seconds. "I hadn't thought about it. But if it came down to that, we could figure something out. I might even learn to like the snow."

"Do you see what I'm saying? Already you're looking at the possibility of giving up your home, your work, your friends. How could you trade all that for me? I'd never let you do it, even if you wanted to."

"Don't worry," he said, smiling faintly. "I wouldn't give up my throne and scepter."

"That's the real problem, I think. I'd end up being the one

who'd give up everything. And it would make me hate you eventually. I'm no Duke of Windsor, either."

He looked a little puzzled. "This isn't an all-or-nothing situation, you know. There are a lot of ways to work out a relationship besides having one person give up everything for the other."

Now I was the one who was startled. "That's how relationships always work out," I said. "People talk about other ways and promise each other that *this* time it'll be different, but it never is." I stared at him for several seconds. It was odd, I thought, how it had come out. I'd never before managed to distill the problems I'd had with love relationships into one nice, neat, succinct statement. But that was it, all right. In a nutshell. I felt embarrassed and exposed.

Mac was watching me, his eyes thoughtful and slightly surprised. He'd caught it. Shoot.

"Thank you," he said.

"For what?"

"For making an honest statement about your feelings. I have a glimmer of understanding now. Just a glimmer, but at least it's something."

"I'm glad it makes you happy," I said, still embarrassed.

"I didn't say that." He was looking right into my eyes.

"What *are* you saying?"

"I don't know. Maybe I'm saying we're both creative people, so we can think of some way to work this out if it's important to both of us."

"Mac, I can't start a relationship with you on the vague premise that we'll find a way to work it out. That's the stuff of teenage song lyrics, not life. I've stopped doing things like that. I look at long-term consequences and try to make plans that will take me where I want to go. It works out a lot better."

"I took the Management by Objectives course, too. But like the man said, life is what happens while we're making other plans. We can't plan everything, Sal. And we don't have to know how the story's going to turn out while we're still reading the first chapter, do we?"

"We're not reading this story, Mac. We're writing it. And if we have any sense, we'll decide right now how it's going to turn out. If we wait until we get farther into it, we both could face some nasty surprises."

He was watching me, his eyes very serious. "Or some nice ones. Life has endless possibilities."

"Life also has possibilities that end. This is one of them." I didn't know where the line came from, but it was right on target.

"I see," Mac said. It had stopped him.

"I'm sorry," I said. "Please try to understand."

"That's asking too much."

I was getting a brain cramp. Why was I doing this? This man was not, after all, The Man of My Dreams. He had, I admit, become substantially more appealing to me in the last twenty-four hours, but I didn't need this. I owed him no explanations. I could just ask him to leave, and that would be that. I'd feel guilty for having hurt his feelings twice in a lifetime, but I could live with that. Definitely. I could even live without his jazz collection. Or at least I could try.

I turned to look at him. His eyes were steady and pale. I sighed. "Mac, what can I say?"

He looked down at his hands, then back up at me. "I'll tell you what. Tell me you don't care about me and I'll disappear forever."

I stared at him. That was the lowest blow of all.

"Well?" he said, still watching me.

"I can't say that. My feelings for you are a little unsettling right now. But that doesn't mean I have to do anything about them. Neither one of us does, Mac. Sometimes there are feelings that reek of disaster, and when we're faced with that we can walk away from the feelings and save ourselves. I guess that's what I'm doing."

His eyes searched mine. Neither of us spoke for a long time. Finally Mac stood and picked up both of our coffee cups and carried them to the kitchen. I continued to stand in the partially opened door. He came up behind me and put his arms around me, shoulder high. I could feel his breath on the side of my head. He kissed my hair.

We stood there like that, looking out on the lake for several minutes. His arms were wrapped very tightly around me, and my arms finally went up and wrapped around his. Then I felt him brush aside the feathered hair on the nape of my neck and kiss it very softly. He let go of me and walked back in the direction of the fireplace. I didn't turn.

A few moments later I heard the door open, heard the click of the lock, and knew he was gone. I pulled the door shut, went slowly to the chair he'd sat in all morning, sank into it, and rubbed my hands on the heavily padded arms, noticing once again the little ruby ring on my finger. Then I cried for the first time in a long time.

8

After I finished crying, I decided the only thing to do was to run over to Summit Avenue and talk to Saul Resnick. Saul was a psychiatrist from St. Paul I'd met at a booksellers' convention about a year before. A good friend of mine, an editor named Mary from Doubleday, had introduced us over lunch. She'd rejected a manuscript he'd sent her but had liked his convoluted suspense plot enough to suggest that he meet with me to see whether we might try to put something together as a team. She'd heard me talk about doing a medical thriller often enough, and she knew my writing well enough to imagine that Saul and I could hit it off.

We had. And I had seen the same potential in his plot that Mary had seen. Since then he and I had spent our spare evenings at my place working on the computer and going through the usual give-and-take that collaboration requires. He thought I was the finest wordsmith since Ellery Queen, which of course proved that he was both perceptive and worthy of my help.

Just for the record, Saul made a pass at me at the beginning of our relationship. Actually two or three passes. Even if I'd been interested in that sort of thing I wouldn't have been interested, if you know what I mean. He was Richard Dreyfuss in his bearded phase, except that Saul's hair was silver-gray and frizzy. Not my type at all, even when I *had* a type. Anyway, my refusal to receive his passes hadn't fazed him. Apparently he didn't consider it a rejection of himself; in his mind I'd simply made a choice, and that choice was nothing he should take personally. He was disappointed but perfectly amiable about it. I admired him for that.

Now he was engaged to Angela Gunther, a beautiful blonde internist twelve years his (and my) junior. When I first met her I immediately suspected, in a moment of cattiness, that Saul only wanted to marry her because when people met her they'd wonder if they'd misjudged old Saul in thinking him unattractive. "Well," folks would say, eyebrows arched, "if he looks good to *her*..."

Eventually I understood that Saul was as attractive in his way as she was in hers, and I began to see that they were a perfect match. They had virtually nothing in common—except medicine, which is a dubious sort of bond, to say the least; yet they clearly belonged together. They were living proof that some things in life cannot be reduced to a scientific formula.

Angela was one of the smartest and wisest and warmest people I'd ever known. She was such a fantastic person, and so flat-out gorgeous, in fact, that it took several months for me to stop being cold and indifferent toward her for being so perfect. Finally I broke down and decided we could be friends. After that, the three of us had become like family.

Saul and Angela and my other best friend, Biba Mariani, had been the only people I'd told about Mac after our encounter in San Francisco before Thanksgiving. Biba had held her cards close to her chest, not offering anything positive or negative in the way of comment or advice, remaining neutral but supportive. She was half Swedish, after all, a neutralist by genetic predisposition despite her Italian father's chromosomal contributions.

Angela's comments about Mac, on the other hand, had been typical of her straight-to-the-heart-of-things attitude: "Don't be a ninny. Go back out to California and track him down," she'd said. "You're too conservative. A little fling would do you good." You never had to wonder what Angela was thinking.

Saul had waved her comments aside. "Angela," he'd told her indulgently, "you are a know-it-all. This is a grown woman who knows what she wants. Let her have it. Then, when she comes crying on our doorstep that she's lonely, you can say, 'I told you so; it's exactly what you deserve.'"

You could say my friends represented every possible viewpoint regarding my personal life, and that was the way I liked it. Balance in everything, that was my motto.

So as I was saying, about an hour after Mac's departure from my place on December 8th, I went over to Saul's, counting on him to affirm the wisdom of what I'd just done. If Biba had been in town I might have gone there instead, and if I had—well, things might have turned out differently. Then again, who knows? The hinges upon which life turns are often so small.

In spite of the fact that he was a shrink, I had faith in Saul's essential levelheadedness and keen discernment. So he was an excellent alternative to Biba. When I got to his place, Angela was there cooking a late brunch. She didn't live with him and usually didn't cook; so it was a nice surprise to find them together at that hour. She knew the minute I walked in the door that something was rotten in Denmark.

I told them the whole story then, sitting on a stool in the kitchen while Angela worked at the stove. I cried again when I got to the part where Mac had walked out the door. Angela came over to me, wiping her hands on her apron, and put her arms around me.

"Sally, you've made a big mistake," she said, patting my back. "Why don't you call him down at his hotel? He probably hasn't checked out yet. Meet him somewhere and talk it out."

Saul had been studying me. "Now wait a minute," he said, hands up in a gesture crossing guards employ to keep school-children on curbs. "Just one minute. Let's not rush off and do something rash. Let's think this through." The voice of reason, crying in the wilderness.

Angela gave him an irritated glance. *Men,* her look said. *Why do we bother?*

"I'm trying to look at this as a dispassionate observer," he said. "As a counselor, not just as a friend." That was a relief. Heaven knows I wouldn't have wanted him to look at anything as a friend.

"What occurs to me," he continued, "is that Sally may have made the wisest and most astute decision possible. Look, we all have times in our lives when we feel vulnerable—for whatever reason. Sometimes it happens because we realize we're getting middle-aged, losing our youth, whatever. Sometimes we're in a rocky period, either in a marriage or in a divorce, or the kids are driving us crazy and we wish we could run off to a desert island. Or we hate our work. There are people who feel vulnerable when they achieve great success and discover that it isn't as ecstatic an experience as they always thought it would be."

Angela was looking at him, not tapping her foot on the floor, but wanting to.

Saul read the signal. "Okay," he said, "I'm getting to the point. Whatever it is that causes us to feel vulnerable, one of our com-monest responses is to start going back over our lives to look for the things that gave us comfort and satisfaction in the past. Men sit around during these phases hauling out high-school year-books, looking longingly at the pictures of the sweethearts they left behind. 'She was the best thing that ever happened to me,' they moan to themselves. 'I never should have let her get away.' Or whatever."

Angela was listening. "The yearbook syndrome is not entirely a male malady, doctor," she said.

"I realize that, thank you, Ms. Freidan," Saul said, nodding in her direction. "All I'm saying is that it's not uncommon for people in this frame of mind to want to escape into the past. They look back and idealize the images they have of the people long ago who meant a great deal to them. And these idealized images usually have nothing to do with the real people as they exist today. I've had patients spend months searching for high school or college sweethearts during one of these obsessive phases, only to come to me amazed that they now had absolutely nothing in common and no longer felt the slightest attraction to this person—the person they'd remembered as the most attractive, the most passionate, the most understanding creature in the world. Most of us never actually look for or find these fantasy people, of course, and it's almost always better that way."

"So what?" Angela said.

"So the best course of action when we find ourselves faced with one of these windows of vulnerability is to simply acknowledge that these feelings exist, that they're common and normal, and that—as Sally has so wisely observed—we don't have to act on them. They'll fade and die. And we'll be better off for *not* having acted on them. Most people who act on them end up regretting it."

Angela sniffed. "But Mac and Sally *do* have an attraction that still exists. It isn't all in the past. Furthermore, Sally wasn't obsessively looking for Mac to compensate for vulnerability. So your theory doesn't hold water. Back to the drawing board."

It was sweet. They were arguing over me.

"Angela," I said, trying to head them off at the pass, "Saul has a point. I mean, look at what's going on here. Yesterday was my birthday. I may be entering that middle-aged window of vulnerability he's talking about. Yes, I have everything I want, I have my son and my work, and I've been contented and happy. But Matt is out of the nest now, getting ready to go out into the world on his own. I'm shifting gears. I'm wondering, ever so subtly, what I'm going to do now that I'm grown-up and don't have to be Mommy anymore. Maybe I'm having a mid-life crisis. And maybe Mac is, too. He could be at the same vulnerable point in his life. After all, he's questioning the direction of his work, and possibly a lot more. Maybe he *is* a victim of the yearbook syndrome."

Saul was nodding, crunching on a celery stick he'd been using to stir a giant glass of vegetable cocktail.

I went on, "The fact is, Mac is the last person in the world I should get involved with. Truly. If I'm vulnerable, I should do exactly what I told Mac I was going to do, which is the same thing Saul suggests—simply acknowledge the feelings and then let them fade and die."

I could be so logical and insightful sometimes.

Saul was thrilled with my breakthrough. "There, you see? You were right all along!"

Angela looked at him, still thinking. "You're both talking logic and reason. I'm talking feelings. Gut-level feelings."

Saul shook his head. "Those will get you in a peck of trouble."

"Like the peck of trouble you and I have gotten into, for example?" Angela said. "You and I are, as we all know, a couple with every logical reason to be together."

"Are we in trouble? Why didn't you tell me?" Saul said.

She glared.

"You and I are different, my dear," he said. "You, most especially."

Angela wasn't going to let it drop without getting the last word. "Saul, you're eliminating the love factor. Love isn't something you can turn on or off according to how logical or convenient it is."

I sat there listening and thought, *Hey, when did this discussion turn out to be about love?*

"Oh, but it *is* something you can turn on and off," Saul said. "Love isn't a feeling that sweeps over us out of the netherworld, making zombies of us overnight. We *choose* to love or not to love. It's not just glands. Feelings are too fickle to be trusted with a job as important as loving somebody. Sally certainly can choose not to love this man, regardless of the feelings she may be experiencing as a result of her own vulnerability. It is entirely within her power." He was wiggling his fingers, touchy-feely style, looking pleased with his discourse and pleased with himself.

Angela wasn't impressed. "That may be true, Saul, but I still say people sometimes just *need* other people."

Saul didn't bat an eye. He did, however, arch an eyebrow. I groaned, knowing what was coming.

"People who need people," he said, "are the luckiest people in the world."

I SENT A CHRISTMAS CARD to Mac a week later, telling myself it was a gracious, adult thing to do. It contained a breezy holiday message, a paragraph about what I'd been doing, and a snapshot of Matt. I only briefly mentioned that I envied him his record collection. Mac sent a card back. His didn't have a snapshot, and it didn't refer to the record collection. It was signed simply, "Love, Mac." I guessed it was his way of saying, "It's okay, I forgive you." I felt vaguely sad about the situation, but I knew it was for the best. I had finally learned how to make sensible choices, and I was pleased about having done so well with this one.

By the start of the third week of December I was well into the first draft of the new Bridget Caulfield book, humming along on my Macintosh computer at a brisk ten-page-a-day rate. I was working overtime to give myself a Christmas break when Matt and his girlfriend would arrive home from school on the 23rd for their planned ten-day visit.

Saul was at my place on the night of December 22nd, hunched over the computer with a look of deep concentration on his face. We were doing a marathon work session on our collaborative book because we wouldn't be able to get back to our manuscript until after New Year's, when the kids went back to school.

Saul looked like a mad scientist, his hair zooming outward as if—my dad would have said—he'd stuck his finger in a light socket. He was dressed in his Medical Thriller Writer costume, a green surgical scrubsuit he'd gotten from a colleague who'd stolen it from Fairview Southdale Hospital.

"This section isn't right," he said over his shoulder at me. I was reading a printout. The pages were stretched out several feet in front of me on the floor.

"Which section?"

"The one where Tom is talking to Denise in group therapy. Remember?"

"Um-hmm."

"We're going to have to make her promiscuous. It would be more realistic."

"Can't she just be neurotic? You have a fixation."

"Neurosis is hackneyed. Readers love sex stuff. Authentic details."

"Sex isn't hackneyed?" I glared at him.

"You're a Calvinist," he said.

"Calvin was a swinger compared to me."

"Sexually repressed," he said. "You should look into that with the help of a competent therapist. Like me." He looked at me and wiggled his eyebrows up and down like Groucho Marx.

"You should be ashamed of yourself. Poor Angela."

"Angela is neither poor nor repressed," he said. "Let's say Denise is promiscuous because she's on drugs. She started hooking to support her habit." He rubbed his hands together and started punching at the keyboard.

"Saul, let's stick with it as is and rewrite it later if it doesn't gel."

"No, I think I'm onto something here. Let me do it, and you can see what you think."

I sighed. "Okay." I would erase it all later in one quick blip of the computer.

"You're too good to me," he said.

SEVERAL HOURS LATER, around 2 in the morning, Saul left with his copy of our night's work in his battered brown leather Gucci briefcase. I started cleaning up our mess, then heard Saul back again, pounding on the door.

"The car won't start," he said. Now his hair was really zooming. The wind and blowing snow had turned it into a silver corona around his head.

"Want to call Triple-A?"

"No, I think I should leave it until tomorrow. It's snowing pretty hard, and I've been having carburetor problems. I'm afraid I might get stranded again on the way home. I'll get Mercedes R Us to pick it up in the A.M. if you can give me a lift."

"Mercedes R Us?"

"On my honor," he said.

"Sure," I said, pulling on my heavy red wool coat.

I WAS MAKING THE TURN onto Lake Street when I noticed how slippery the streets were. It was so close to 32 degrees that ice was forming in a thin glaze on the untraveled parts of the road. I slowed down and drove the length of Lake Street at about twenty-five miles an hour.

What I remember next is a little hazy. I was just entering the first intersection across the Lake Street Bridge over the Mississippi River when I saw a truck moving toward us from the right. It was a battered blue Chevy pickup with something large in its bed. It ran the red light, and it was moving fast, I know that much. Saul saw it first. He sucked in his breath and started to point to his right, and then I saw the headlights heading right into Saul's side of the car. He dove out of his seat toward me, looking like he was trying to protect me from an assassin's bullet. I remember thinking, *Oh my, I hope I'm wearing my new underwear.* I don't know, maybe Saul thought the same thing.

The next thing I recall is that panicky feeling I always got when I woke up in a strange hotel room in the middle of the night on one of my book tours. No matter how many years I'd done it, the feeling was always the same. Where was I? Where was the door? If I got out of bed, would the floor be there, or would I step into eternity?

I wanted to move, get up, but I hurt everywhere. The pain clubbed at me. My body was heavy, impossibly heavy. Something was tightly pulled around my head, around my whole body. I couldn't move a muscle. I decided that was okay. I didn't want to move a muscle.

I strained to see some familiar object in the partially lit room, but my eyes felt swollen shut. All I could sense were vague moving lights. Soft, brisk-sounding voices were talking somewhere near me, but they seemed strangely far away. Did they want something from me? I couldn't make out the words. Then I went to sleep again. They tell me I was unconscious for most of ten days.

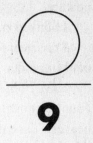

9

Angela was there the next time I opened my eyes, wearing her white doctor coat with the stethoscope slung around her neck and the little beige plastic badge on the breast pocket that said "Internal Medicine" under her name. *Come on*, I thought, *you don't have to impress me.* I tried to speak, but words wouldn't come out.

"Welcome back," she said. "Don't try to talk." She was patting my shoulder. It hurt. "Just stay quiet. Okay?"

Okay, I thought. *Just stop touching me.*

"Sally, do you know where you are?" She looked at me expectantly. There was another man with her, also in a doctor coat. Didn't know him. Didn't want to. "Can you blink once for yes, twice for no?" the other doc asked.

I blinked twice.

Angela smirked. "Well, at least we know good old Sally is in there."

The other doctor didn't get it. "Please blink once for yes," he said. He was no fun. I blinked once.

"Is that yes, you know where you are? Or yes, you can blink? Or yes, you can obey orders?" Angela said, suppressing a snort. The other doc looked confused. She smiled at him apologetically.

"I'm sorry. We'll start again." Then, to me: "Do you know where you are?"

I blinked twice.

"You're ensconced in the bridal suite at glorious University of Minnesota Hospitals," she said. "You've been here for ten days. I've been keeping an eye on your doctors so they didn't cut your heart out for an organ transplant. These guys are such eager beavers." The man next to her didn't smile. She was quiet for a minute.

"You've been unconscious. Do you remember anything? Do you remember the accident?" She waited for a reaction. When there was none, she said, "You're going to live. Actually, the eager beavers have done a heroic job."

Angela put her hand on my shoulder again. I wished she'd stop that. "Saul was banged up, but he's going to be okay," she said. "It's amazing, considering the fact that the car was hit on his side. But he stayed in the car and you didn't. The emergency people always say that's the secret. In this case it sure made the difference. His right hand and arm got mashed pretty bad, but I think he'll be able to use it with some more surgery. Anyway, it's lucky he's left-handed. He also has some pretty severe trauma to his whole right side, but he's in much better shape than you are. I know he's okay because he's cursing himself for not being a surgeon so he could retire like a king on disability insurance. He was released in my care yesterday. He's driving me crazy. Everything they say about doctors being the worst patients is true. Actually, everything they say about doctors in general is true. It's very depressing."

The doctor next to her glanced in her direction as she said this. Then he looked at me, turned, and glided out, like an undertaker respectfully leaving the widow with the dearly departed.

Angela seemed not to notice his leave-taking. She looked at me, organizing her thoughts. "Let's see . . . I called Matt late on the night of the accident. He came right out. Valerie didn't come with him, but she flew out the day after Christmas. They've been here ever since. We've been talking to him about getting back to school. He knows that's what you'd want. Starts again on the 4th—that's Monday. Now that you're conscious and blinking, I think they'll feel better about leaving." She paused. "Matt is really a super kid, Sal," she said. "I want one like him. Oh, and you'll like Valerie. Your son has good taste."

I wondered idly if Matt and Valerie were sleeping together in his bed at our apartment. You never stop being a mother, do you? Even on your deathbed.

Angela stood back one step and started picking nervously at her thumbnail.

"Sally, I've got to tell you something else."

I waited. Nothing could faze me now, I decided.

Angela cleared her throat. She wasn't looking at me. "The thing is, I called Mac."

No, I thought. *You didn't.*

"I know you'll be upset with me, and I don't blame you. I— well, it just seemed like the right thing to do at the time. I take full responsibility." She sounded like a Navy officer explaining how she'd accidentally fired six nuclear missiles at an unarmed Caribbean cruise ship.

"I called him the morning after the accident," she continued in her briefing-officer voice, "when we didn't know if you were going to live. He wasn't that hard to find."

I sighed. Sighing hurt, too, I noticed.

"Sal, I thought that if you weren't going to make it, he would want a chance to do something. Send flowers. Buy balloons. I don't know. I couldn't deny him that. Saul told me to mind my own business, but you know me."

I did. But for reasons I could not muddle through right then,

I was not all that displeased that she'd called Mac. If I'd died, I would have wanted him to know.

Angela was quiet for a few moments. Then she cleared her throat again, and I realized I'd never seen her nervous before. It was sort of endearing.

"Well, anyway," she said, "Mac flew out here the same day I called him, on the 23rd. He's still here. Right outside, I mean. I think he's taking a nap." *Just like in the movies*, I thought. Then, surprisingly, another thought flickered through my bandaged head. Did I look as bad as I imagine I must look? And why did I care? Because, I decided, when you're on your deathbed you're supposed to look wan but ethereally lovely, so your friends can be sympathetic but admiring. This is the picture of you they'll carry with them forever, after all.

Angela walked around the bed, standing where I could see her straight on. "I hadn't realized that Mac's wife and son were killed in an accident during the Christmas holiday season some years ago. That's probably part of the reason this hit him so hard. Anyway, he wanted to be here, and I didn't try to stop him."

She was still picking at that thumb. "He's a good man, Sally," she said. She shook her head. "He loves you." She stared at me, a funny little smile on her face. "What's more, I don't think there's much you can do about it. He is *persistent*." There was about a ten-second silence while she tried to read my thoughts. When she couldn't, she waved a little wiggly wave, said, "I'll see you soon," and walked out of the room. I fell asleep again.

MAC WAS SITTING NEXT TO THE BED in a straight chair the next time I opened my eyes. It was not dark in the room, just gloomy, like one of those moody fifties black-and-white movies that starred Marlon Brando or James Dean. A liberal, depressing kind of movie. He glanced up at me, saw my eyes watching him, and smiled. I couldn't follow suit.

"Hi," he said. Then, without warning, there were tears in his eyes. He didn't try to cover them or wipe them away. It was strangely touching—not the tears so much as the fact that he didn't try to hide them.

I couldn't move my lips. I wanted to, just to try them out, but I didn't have the will or the energy. Also I decided they'd probably break if I moved them.

"It's almost 7 o'clock," he said. His voice sounded rough, tired. "It's January 3rd. Happy 1992." He took in a deep breath, let it out, and shifted in his chair. He turned the book in his hand upside-down and placed it carefully on one of those tables that can be cranked up, down, every which way. I noticed that I didn't care what book it was. That wasn't like me.

"Can I do anything for you?" Mac asked.

I tried to move my head from side to side. It wouldn't move in either direction.

"Don't try to move," he said. "Just blink once for yes, twice for no." I felt helpless and anxious. Why did everyone want me to blink?

I had to speak. Just to prove to myself that I could. I pried open my lips by sheer force of will and whispered, without opening my teeth, "No." It was a lot more dramatic than anything I'd seen on the silver screen.

Mac was quiet for a minute. He was wearing a pale yellow crew-neck sweater with a light blue button-down shirt under it and navy chinos. A plain gold watch was on his wrist. I couldn't see his feet, but I knew he'd be wearing brown penny loafers. Polished. His hair was slightly disheveled, as always. He looked very, very tired and about ten years older than the last time I'd seen him.

"Matt's down getting some dinner with Valerie. They'll be

back soon. Your sisters have been calling. Betty wanted to come out, but her kids are on Christmas vacation, so I told her to wait. And she has a cold, so she shouldn't be here anyway, passing it on to you."

I fought tears. I hadn't been close to my sisters for years, not close like we'd been in our twenties. Betty was the closest, mostly because she'd gone through a divorce just three years after I had, and there was the bond from sharing similar tragedies. When our parents had died several years before—Dad in a head-on collision with a tractor-trailer rig during perfect weather, Mom of a heart attack right in the middle of a garage sale only two years later—the three of us had drawn together for a short time to share the grief. Then we'd drifted apart again. My work probably had something to do with that. My schedule. My whole life, I guess. All of our lives. I wanted to talk with Betty. Just for an hour or two. And Abby, of course. For about thirty or forty seconds.

Mac pulled a Kleenex out of a hospital-sized box and dabbed at my eyes. I looked at him gratefully.

"About fifty plants and flower arrangements have come since you've been here. Your publishers have been sending something every few days; they're very solicitous. And there's a bunch of cards, telegrams, letters. A lot of friends have wanted to see you, but there's been a 'no visitors' order. Angela convinced your doctors that Matt and Valerie and I wouldn't do you any harm." He paused, rubbing his face and eyes with his fingers.

"They wouldn't allow the plants and flowers in the room. I guess they carry bacteria or something. I took pictures of them and kept the cards for you." He looked over at a table by the window where a neat stack of cards and envelopes lay. "I can read those to you when you're ready."

I thought, *If this man were not here right now, I would die. I would just close my eyes and not wake up again.* Considering my condition, it was not such a surprising thought. I might have thought the same thing about Geraldo Rivera.

"Anyway," Mac continued, his voice straining to be cheerful, "Matt and I took the flowers and plants to the nursing home down the street. Except for three or four exotic types that we took to your apartment." He smiled again. "I'm watering your plants.

"Angela and Saul convinced me to stay at your place," he went on. "Actually, Angela went to my hotel room and moved everything while I was here at the hospital. She called and said not to go back there, just to go to your place." He looked slightly embarrassed.

"She's a very straightforward woman." He grinned. "Anyway, I hope you don't mind my being at your place. Saul said you'd want me to act as chaperone for Matt and Valerie, anyway. I've been sleeping on the sofa bed, and Val's in your room. It's worked fine. I have the distinct impression they'd much rather be alone there, but they've put up with it well."

"Good," I managed to whisper between clenched teeth. Mac looked extraordinarily pleased with me.

There was a five-second pause. He sat down again, then looked at me as if he'd just realized he'd been rattling on, stream-of-consciousness style, about a lot of stuff that probably sounded disconnected to me. It did, but somehow it also made sense. I clung to his every word.

"Do you want to know about your injuries?" he asked.

"Yes," I squeaked. How could saying such a little word take so much effort?

He took a deep breath. "You had head injuries, as you've probably gathered. Your car was hit on the passenger side by a pickup truck doing about thirty miles an hour through a red light. Do you remember?"

I was suddenly too tired to speak again. I blinked once. That was almost as hard as speaking. Mac understood me and moved on. "The impact of the crash threw you out of the car, and that's when the head injuries occurred. Your doctors can tell you the technicalities about what happened to your head. I don't fully understand the details. But the good news is that they're now saying that in time you can fully recover from the brain trauma. In the beginning, before you were transferred here, the doctors were talking like you'd have major disabilities—if you lived at all. Now they're saying you probably *won't* have permanent disabilities, but they're taking a wait-and-see attitude. You've been having seizures off and on.

"Let's see . . . what else? Your left arm is broken in two places. You had a neck injury, but *it* wasn't broken, at least. You're in cervical traction for a while, anyway. You have two fractured femurs, but your legs are okay below the knees. The legs are in traction now, too, as you realize, but in another three weeks you'll have a body cast from the waist down, and a month or so after that you'll probably be able to graduate to crutches. There were internal problems, grouped under what I think they called 'interabdominal injuries.' About the only injury you *didn't* have was a ruptured spleen, but you could have lived without it even if it had been."

I was ready for him to quit. I wondered, idly, what the spleen's job was that it was so expendable. I wondered if it was what made me crave hot fudge sundaes. It would be just my luck to have that be the only organ that escaped undamaged.

Mac went on, "In case you're wondering, your face is pretty badly beaten up right now, but it will probably heal without permanent scars. It'll just take time."

I stared at him. He was saying I looked pretty ugly at the moment.

"Other than that, Mrs. Lincoln," he said, a small smile at the corners of his mouth, "how was the theater?"

What started out to be a small laugh erupted into wheezes and coughs, followed by searing pain. I had never felt that kind of pain. I thought of the old punch line, "It only hurts when I laugh," but that made it worse. Mac looked distressed and pressed the button that summoned a nurse. By the time she arrived I'd calmed down. She touched me in several places just to be sure I hurt and said I needed sleep.

Mac waited until the nurse rustled out of the room, then sat on the straight chair again. Why, I asked myself, did so many nurses rustle when they walked? Did nurses' shops sell special rustling nurse dresses and pantyhose? As I lay there I really wanted to know. Now, of course, it seems somewhat less important, but I'm still curious.

"I'm sorry," Mac said, looking guilty. "I didn't mean to make you laugh. I'll try hard not to be funny." I didn't blink. He waited.

"I'm going to stay awhile," he said finally. "In Minneapolis, that is. I've got everything set up. I can be here a couple of months. I'm going to get you home and see that you're back on your feet before I leave." A feeling of despair swept over me. The chapter summary that flashed across my mind read: "Heroine, now a helpless invalid, meekly accepts benevolence of former suitor." My life was flushing down the toilet.

"I'm not doing this because I feel sorry for you," he said. "It's just what I want to do. You'd do the same for me if our positions were reversed. Very simple, basic stuff. Okay?"

I considered it. *No*, I thought, *I wouldn't do the same if our positions were reversed. I'd send you cheerful get-well cards and that would be that.* Then, ashamed, I thought, *Well, I suppose anything is possible.* I blinked at him once. I couldn't think in complex terms. Simple and basic was fine.

"Okay," he said. "Your job is just to heal. Relax and let it happen."

He stared at me hard for a minute.

"Okay," I whispered.

"She speaks!" Matt said from the doorway. "All *right!*"

My son and his girlfriend ran to the side of my bed with looks of unrestrained glee on their young faces. *A sight for sore eyes*, I thought, and then I thought, *So that's what that old cliché means.*

Matt took my hand—which actually had no bandages on it—as if it were a priceless Rodin sculpture, carefully pressing it with gentle reassurance. This was nice, though painful. It made up for the nights I'd sat up worrying about him. It even made up for the occasions when he'd told me to get off his back.

"You look like the Mummy's Curse," he said.

"Hi," I whispered, glancing up at the dark-haired girl who stood by his side. She looked like a young Elizabeth Dole, which was surprising to me. I wouldn't have thought she was his type.

"Mom," he said, remembering her, "this is Valerie Holden. Val, this is my Mummy." He giggled. When were kids supposed to stop giggling, anyway?

Valerie didn't giggle. She touched my hand briefly and said, "Hello, Mrs. Brigham. I feel like I already know you. I'm glad you're better. We've been so worried." At least she knew what to say at a time like this. That was something. The fact that she called me Mrs. Brigham instead of Ms. Alexander could be chalked up to youth and inexperience.

Matt was as happy as a clam. I squeezed one of his fingers a little. The three of them stayed with me for a couple of hours. Then around 9:30 Nursie rustled in and said it was long past my bedtime and she really *must* insist. Matt had talked more or less nonstop for two hours, much of the time about Valerie and their school experiences, and it had been better than either the proverbial or literal shot in the arm for me. I was exhausted, but there was no denying the salutary effects of Matt's presence. Now Mac was telling me that the two kids were heading back to school on the 7:45 flight the next morning. Matt hung his head as Mac explained it. Clearly he felt guilty about leaving me.

"I want you to go," I whispered to him. "Don't feel guilty."

Mac smiled at me. "Oh, let him feel guilty," he said, glancing at Matt and Valerie. "That way he'll call every day or two and write once a week."

"I will," Matt said earnestly. "I promise. You know I will."

"Yes," I said.

"We'll see you soon, Mrs. Brigham," Valerie said, touching my hand. "We can see the sights together, all of us. And celebrate your recovery."

Sure. In about five years. But she was a nice girl. By George, my son did have good taste. This had to be one of those rewards of motherhood the women's magazines mentioned vaguely all the time.

Matt looked exhausted. "I love you, Mom," he said. "We'll see you soon." He kissed my cheek. For some reason I couldn't feel it.

"I love you, too," I whispered. It was a beautiful scene. Just beautiful. A bit overdone perhaps, but an editor wasn't going to touch this one, so it was all right with me.

Matt self-consciously brushed at his face. Valerie had walked to the door. Mac had joined her. Matt got up and stood there with them. They looked like three contestants on *Wheel of Fortune*, waiting for the final spin.

"Night, Sal," Mac said. "I'll see you tomorrow after I've dropped these two off at the airport. Around 9, I expect. Sleep tight."

"How else?" I croaked with the last ounce of energy in me.

After they left I immediately fell asleep and dreamed of Lon Chaney. He was lost in the Great Pyramid. A creature that seemed to be wrapped from head to toe in Ace bandages was trailing him from room to room.

10

It was a mild January in Minneapolis, little snow, more sunshine than usual. Betty came to spend a day with me on either the 7th or the 8th, hastening to get home in time for her sixteen-year-old's birthday. She cheered me immensely. Abby called the same day Betty was there; so it was like Old Home Week for a little while. There was still hope for the American family, I decided. At least for *our* family.

After that I had other visitors, one at a time. Biba had been in and out of town a couple of times since the accident, but after the 5th of January she was there at the hospital almost every day. She flirted with Mac much of the time. I figured it was a good distraction for both of them. Biba was one of those women who looked like she was born to be a mother: wide pelvis, ample breasts, strong legs and arms. She was vivacious and quick-witted and seemed to enjoy playing the perennial bachelorette despite the fact that her single status might mean she'd never bear the twenty or so babies her anatomy would have allowed. At forty, her biological clock was running out, and she didn't seem terribly concerned about it.

Her visits were always a high point in my day. And Mac's, I have no doubt, especially after she developed a habit of patting him on the fanny in a friendly sort of way as she said good-bye to me. I think it was purely instinctive on her part; I just waited for it to happen each day so I could smile inwardly about it—sort of the way audiences wait for Oliver Hardy to tell Stan Laurel, "Well, here's *another* fine mess you've gotten me into!" It may be stupid, but it's always good for a laugh, even when you've seen it a thousand times.

Angela and Saul continued to be the daily rah-rah team. They'd come in, usually individually, telling jokes or gossiping about hospital infighting and giving me the old "win one for the Gipper" routine. Angela talked about her patients, and I suspected that she was getting her stories from the same medical joke service Saul subscribed to. One day she told me a female patient had come to her complaining that a gynecologist had diagnosed her problem as "fireballs in my Eucharist," which upon further investigation turned out to be "fibroids in her uterus." The patient wondered if she needed an "hystericalectomy." For some reason I believed this story.

Most days the entertainment was distracting and pleasant, but there were also days it depressed me or made me irritable and sullen. I knew it was me, not them, and I knew my brain was not firing on all cylinders; so I didn't overtax myself worrying about my attitude. Anyway, they were very understanding; when I snapped at one of them, I never got snapped at in return.

Mac, to his credit, did not mother me. Or father me. He didn't chide me for being churlish with the doctors, didn't recite positive little homilies when I got depressed and cried, didn't lecture me about how I should be thankful that I wasn't more badly injured. He was as noteworthy for what he didn't do as for what he did do.

Doctors multiplied in my room. Neurologists came in packs, like wolves, circling my bed and finally announcing that my brain was relatively intact and the headaches would eventually subside. They promised pain relievers and more tests.

Despite all this attention, I was getting better faster than anyone expected. Angela, who ought to know, assured me I'd had the best care available in the U.S. I didn't doubt it, but it did make me think seriously about what was going on in the world of modern medicine. One smarmy whitecoat, a super-specialist with a big name at the University, spent the first ten minutes of his visit listing his medical credentials and academic triumphs, as if it were vital to my cure that I know these things before he laid hands on me. Then, after much probing and a half dozen undecipherable and ominous-sounding murmurs, he confided in hushed tones that he was always shocked to see what the human body could endure and still survive. I suppose he thought that bit of news would aid my recovery. Who knows, maybe it did.

Something was aiding it, that's for sure. One doctor commented that my rapid recovery was, even in the face of all the medical miracles they'd pulled off, basically an "unexplained phenomenon." I figured it was my one chance to be placed in the same category as spontaneous combustion and UFOs.

And just a day or two after that, there was a quirky little thing that happened while Mac was performing his ritual of reading aloud to me the morning's letters and cards. When he finished the last card he said, "Oh, I almost forgot to tell you—I got a call this morning from Annie Bosworth and Amos Whitcomb. Annie's the lady who runs the prayer group at my church back home. And Amos is one of my best friends. They both said to be sure to give you their love."

Surprised, I said, "You belong to a church?" To myself, I said, *Uh-oh. What do we have here?*

"Oh, sure," he said. "They're great people. You'd enjoy them. They're my family, I suppose." That was a relief. It wasn't so much religious fervor as a need to *belong.* Religious fanatics troubled me. Especially when I was bedridden and defenseless.

"What kind of church is this?" I didn't really want to know, but I was a nice person. I showed interest in others.

"Episcopalian."

I pictured the Episcopal churches I'd been to in my life. I hadn't realized they actually allowed or encouraged people to pray without a script. In fact, I had thought Episcopalians read out of the *Book of Common Prayer* so as not to offend the Almighty with ordinary, spontaneous, unofficial prayers or acts of worship. One wouldn't want to embarrass God by catching Him unprepared, would one?

"Well, say hello to Annie and Amos for me," I said. "It was nice of them to send their love when they don't know me from Adam."

"I called them the day after your accident, before I came out here, and I've kept them posted. They know you pretty well by now. Annie's group has been praying for you."

"Isn't that like doing surgery without the consent of the victim?"

He smiled his inscrutable smile. "I didn't think you'd mind having God look after you. If it bothers you, I could ask Him to take back what He's done so far."

"No, that's all right. Unless He was the one who caused the accident to begin with."

His eyebrows went up like Groucho's. "Does God drive a blue Chevy pickup?"

"Nah. A Jeep Cherokee. I suppose it couldn't have been Him."

Mac was eying me, trying to read my real feelings, which were buried about eight feet under this mountain of clever dialogue.

"Is Amos Whitcomb in this prayer group, too?" I asked. I

couldn't picture anyone who was one of Mac's best friends involved in anything like that.

"Well, sure. He's the parish priest."

I sighed. "Tell Annie Bosworth and Amos Whitcomb I appreciate their petitions on my behalf," I said. It couldn't hurt. You learn to hedge your bets when you find yourself strapped to a hospital bed. "Tell God, too, if you like."

"Tell Him yourself," Mac said.

ON THE MORNING of the 23rd of January, Saul and Angela came in the room with Mac and packed up all my hospital possessions in sacks and cardboard boxes. About three hours later, after various doctors had checked and probed me one last time, I was put into a wheelchair and ushered outdoors. Two of my nurses came to say good-bye, bringing with them copies of Bridget Caulfield mysteries for me to autograph. By this time I could actually sign my name if papers were held up for me.

I was hoisted into another wheelchair Mac had rented, lifted into the back of a huge van Saul had borrowed from someone, and chauffeured home like a potentate.

The three musketeers got me into my place and comfortably settled in bed with about sixteen pillows behind me. I felt like Bette Davis playing the Queen. The TV remote control was strategically placed by my right arm, the CD-stereo remote control beside it. A stack of magazines and books lay to my left. Angela looked for places to arrange several of the goofy hospital gifts that had been sent to me by friends and fans. My favorite was a toy gun that shot out a little flag when you pulled the trigger. The flag said, "Go ahead. Make my day." There was also a plastic music box that played "Look for the Silver Lining," a mobile featuring dangling molded plexiglass replicas of body organs, and a brightly painted wooden parrot with metal magnet feet that could be attached to the edge of the hospital table. Tell me, if people didn't get sick or injured, how would the manufacturers of these products make a living?

Angela unpacked the rest of the hospital stuff and put it in the drawers of my bureau, probably observing that I didn't neatly fold or iron my pantyhose. Mother had always told me I should have neat drawers because you never knew who would get into them some day. I had, of course, snickered over her choice of words and ignored the advice. Now I thought, *Laugh at your mother and it'll always comes back to haunt you.*

The apartment was immaculate. Did Mac really live here? I thought only homosexuals and the terminally henpecked of the male species kept their living spaces immaculate. It made me wonder for a minute. Then I thought, *Nah, he just cleaned up so I wouldn't have a stroke when I came in.*

He was busy, wandering in and out of the bedroom to ask if I needed anything or wanted a pain pill. No, no, no, I kept saying.

Saul finally came in and sat on the edge of the bed. "So, kiddo, you made it." He was using a cane, but otherwise—except for his right arm and hand, which were wrapped and in a sling— he seemed fine. Maybe Annie Bosworth and Amos Whitcomb were praying for him, too. I hoped so, because I didn't want to be the sole focus of their religious enthusiasm.

"Yes indeed," I said. "You, too."

Angela called over her shoulder from the bathroom, "Hey, did you hear they arrested the guy in the pickup?" Saul looked at me.

I was shocked. "Do you mean they didn't know who it was before?" I was disconcerted that in all this time I hadn't thought to ask about the other driver.

"Yeah," Saul answered. "The pickup was totaled, but the driver took off. Turned out the pickup was stolen. There was a witness who described the driver, but the I.D. was so vague that I didn't really think they'd get him. I didn't get a look at him at all, with the snow falling and everything."

"But they got him?"

"Yesterday. The witness identified him positively. He was wanted on a couple of felony warrants. He'll probably be out on the street before you're out of this bed, however. He wasn't badly injured in the accident. Just a few bruises. He was probably drunk or on drugs."

I thought about all that. For some reason, it didn't bother me as much as it should have. I was tired, which undoubtedly blunted my feelings. In a couple of months I'd probably want him executed.

Angela walked back into the room and came over to check my pulse. "You want to know what I think?" she said to Saul. "I think we should get out of here and let the patient sleep."

I smiled at her. Sister Angela. My patron saint.

She dragged Saul to his feet and pulled him out of the room, wiggling her fingers at me, imitating him. I heard them talking with Mac in the living room. After a while I heard Mac say something that sounded like, "I wish she would too, but I don't think it's likely." A few moments later the front door closed.

Mac didn't come into the room right away. I drifted off. When I awakened, the room was dark. A shaft of soft light fell onto the floor from the living room. Piano music was playing faintly. It sounded like one of my old Joe Bushkin records. It made me nostalgic.

I lay there motionless and listened, my mind a blank. It was nice.

After about half an hour I saw Mac standing in the doorway looking in.

"I'm awake," I said.

He walked inside. "Want the light on?" he asked.

"Okay."

He switched on the lamp by the bed and sat on the edge of the chair next to it. "How are you?" he said.

"Dandy," I said. "It's good to be home. Thank you."

"My pleasure."

"I want to hire a nurse," I said. "Will you help me?"

"What for?"

"A nurse could stay here until I can manage on my own."

He raised his eyebrows. "Am I failing to measure up in some way? You have only to speak, Effendi."

"Mac, you've been in Minneapolis for a month. It's time you got back to your work. I feel guilty. Guiltier than I've ever felt in my life."

"Well, now," he said, "there's something."

"What?"

"You feel guilty."

"Very guilty."

"Obligated? As if you can never repay me?"

"Yes."

"Hmmm," he said, still smiling. "A pregnant situation if I've ever seen one."

I admired the phrase for a moment, wondering why he didn't do more writing. "Mac, be serious. It's absurd for you to have taken a month out of your life to be my caretaker. I can't let you do anything more."

"Sure, you can."

"No."

"We'll talk about it tomorrow. Or next week." He stood.

"Mac."

"Yes?"

"What do I have to do to get you out of here?"

He thought for a minute. "Hire a hit man," he said. "Maybe the old guy at the Italian restaurant would know somebody." Sure, it was corny. But in my condition, it also seemed cute.

THE DAYS PASSED QUIETLY. I had hoped that Biba might be able to come over each morning to help me with what the hospital nurses tactfully called my "personal hygiene matters," but she was traveling so much that there was no way she could offer continuity. She could do weekly shampoos and manicures, that kind of thing, but not daily care. So Mac did it—in a completely platonic way, believe me. He insisted that it made him feel good to be able to take care of my needs, that he would be hurt if I didn't let him.

Saul told me two days after I got home that I should stop fretting about it, that Mac was benefiting because it was resolving some of his grief and subconscious guilt over the loss of Christopher and Sarah. The way he explained it, I was sort of a substitute for them, psychologically speaking. Mac had had no opportunity to do this kind of thing for them, and now I was offering him a second chance. It was a favor, Saul said, so don't feel guilty. Just accept and enjoy it. Sure.

Mac would come in after I awakened each morning to help me with the bedpan. It embarrassed me, but he was nurse-like and matter-of-fact, and soon I was resigned to it. He helped me change gowns, which embarrassed me even more for some reason, made the bed, fed me pills, took my pulse and blood pressure. He helped me brush my teeth and hair. He even washed my hair and blew it dry a couple of times when Biba was out of town and I was desperate.

After all his morning ministrations he'd serve me breakfast in bed, then clean up the dishes and get me into the wheelchair. The casts would be coming off the lower half of my body and my arm soon, and I couldn't wait. I wanted desperately to be able to move again like an actual person. Several times each week Mac drove me to the hospital for therapy and checkups, and I was seeing progress. I began to believe I would one day be my old self again.

Biba usually managed to get there at least twice a week in spite of her schedule. She gave me occasional sponge baths, something I never imagined I could let anyone do. The hospital had taken away the last shreds of modesty. Angela looked in most days and did things an internist should do. So I felt well attended.

Mac and I talked a lot, of course, since we were together virtually all the time except for his occasional outings to run errands or buy groceries and supplies. Strangely enough, we didn't talk much about feelings or personal things. Mostly we confined ourselves to politics, literature, his work, my progress, philosophical and social issues, and speculation about the weather, which was unseasonably warm and spring-like this year. Mac was very busy for two or three hours every day calling or writing people in California and Washington about issues in which he seemed heavily invested. We talked about these issues, which ranged from international relief efforts and even several individual families in northern California who had lost homes or families to fires and other natural disasters, to the reelection campaign of a Republican congressman whose wife and children had been kidnapped—and finally released—by terrorists. Surprisingly, we found quite a bit to laugh about, too. I was a good little trouper. So was he, as a matter of fact.

A few times I caught Mac watching me with one of those looks you could have poured on a waffle (as Ring Lardner would have described it); but by and large we managed to keep things on a friendly, warm, companionable basis. It was pretty relaxed, considering. I suppose we were both aware that if we let things get too personal, that could make our living arrangement sticky to impossible. So we instinctively kept it loose. When you're over forty, this sort of thing comes easier.

Even so, two things struck me as touching about what was going on between us. I thought about these things a fair amount as I began to mend and stopped being totally preoccupied with my own discomfort. The first was that I was on the receiving end of the most selfless beneficence I'd ever experienced. I had, in fact, never known that one human being could actually treat another human being with the kindness and devotion Mac showed toward me. Sometimes I was suspicious of it, thinking his behavior had to have strings attached, and I felt it was only a matter of time before the emotional blackmail would begin and he he'd start wanting me to reciprocate in ways I'd find difficult or distasteful.

But that never happened. If anything, he seemed to bend over backwards to be certain there was no possibility of that. Several times I caught him covering up things he'd done for me, and I understood eventually that he did this because he didn't want me to feel grateful for what he'd done or uncomfortable that I couldn't do these things for myself. When I called these to his attention he seemed genuinely irked that I'd found him out. I knew there were probably dozens, even hundreds, of these things that I never knew he did, and it moved me to realize that he wanted it that way. The thing I marveled at many times was that with all he was doing for me, he never took on the faint air of saintliness and nobility to which he might have been entitled.

The other thing that touched me was related to the first one. It was that—as Angela had so astutely observed when I'd awakened after ten days of unconsciousness—Mac really did love me. With incredible persistence. That sort of love had never actually impressed me before, maybe because I'd never understood it or believed I needed it. But it did impress me, increasingly, as I experienced it over the weeks that Mac and I were together almost constantly. It finally dawned on me that, improbable as it seemed, Mac loved me irrespective of my feelings or even of my actions toward him. In fact, it seemed (though I only barely grasped this) that this love didn't even depend on *his* feelings about *me*. It existed almost as an independent state. This was awesome to me; and although it was largely beyond my comprehension, it became the focus of many hours of thoughtful contemplation on my part. One day when Saul stopped in for a visit while Mac was out buying groceries I mentioned this to him, asking what he thought about it all.

"I think," Saul said, "that Mac has a profound understanding of what love is all about, and I think that's about as rare a quality as you're likely to find in a human being. We could all do with a big dose of it." He gave me one of his wise, insightful looks and let it go at that.

I had to agree. Yes, Mac was really something. I had never known anyone like him, that's for sure. I wondered about the experiences that might have built such a man, wondered how it was that loss and grief and pain did different things to each person. Sometimes they turned decent citizens into ax murderers. In Mac's case, they seemed only to have made a good man better.

Once I was able to be up and around in the wheelchair most of the day, Mac invited me to watch while he worked on my computer daily. We discussed his editorials, which appeared about once a week in each of his papers, and the various administrative and investigative kinds of things he was doing by modem and phone. A small-town paper was very different from a city paper, I learned. The issues and standards were different. People were more fervent, more intensely personal in their opinions and demands—or at least it seemed that way, because they weren't anonymous in the way people can be in a city. The focus of the news was almost entirely local, or at least regional. The paper was part of the community, reflecting what was happening on a day-to-day basis among individuals who knew each other, loved and hated each other, fought and reconciled, married and divorced, and occasionally even committed violent acts upon each other. Everyone paid close attention to what was in the paper and read it from front to back. Nothing was missed, not even the public notices.

His work was clearly a passion with Mac, in spite of the small doubts he'd expressed about where it had led him. I could see the passion in the way his color heightened while he read and wrote, the way he talked with his managing editors and even some of the staff writers, thought about this or that story, demanding that it be thoroughly explored and honestly reported. One day as I watched him in the throes of this passion my mind flashed to that scene in the movie *Patton* where George C. Scott as the general stood looking out on a battlefield littered with corpses and the charred remnants of tanks while trumpets played eerily out of some other century. I could still see his face as he gazed at the carnage and whispered with a fervency that few other men could capture, "How I love it!"

I remembered the scene not only because I saw the same passion in Mac's face, but also because I'd felt that same passion in my own work, felt it as the mystical process of creation began in my brain, as synapses fired and thoughts organized, felt it as the people and events I created began to live and breathe almost independent of me, eventually leaping off printed pages straight into the minds and hearts of readers in Savannah or Des Moines or Santa Fe, completing the circuit. When this occurred I always thought—after I thought how I loved it—that I was born for this, and that nothing else in my whole life, other than Matt, had any real significance compared to it.

It was a thrilling thing to me, that passion. I was glad that Mac felt it, too, for the work he was doing. I wondered if anybody who'd never felt that passion could say he'd really lived.

MAC WAS HARD AT WORK one morning after breakfast about two weeks after I came home, when he said, "Have you ever considered doing a syndicated column?"

"Not lately," I said.

"Does the idea appeal to you at all?"

"I don't think so. Why?"

"I just think you'd be good at it. You're a keen observer of the human condition."

"Not as keen as you," I said.

He looked at me quickly. "I'm not the writer. You are." Modesty became him. He had such a sincere, boyish look when he was being modest.

"You're a very good writer," I said.

He pecked at the keyboard for a few moments. "Do you think so?" he said. He was not fishing for compliments. He never fished for compliments without announcing it. "I'm asking for a kind word," he'd say, "so tell me something nice."

I sighed. "Yes, Mac, I think you're an *exceptionally* good writer."

"Seriously?"

"Yes."

"Well," he said. He pecked some more.

"Maybe *you* should write a syndicated column," I said.

Peck, peck, peck.

Then he stopped and pushed his chair back. "Maybe I should," he said. He flashed a half-smile at me, nodding slightly.

He was quiet for a while, working steadily. I watched him, wondering what it was that prompted him to bring up the subject of a syndicated column. Then I wondered what prompted him to do a lot of things. For instance, what was it that caused Mac, a conservative Republican, to lead a crusade against oil drilling off the coast of northern California? Or to organize a rally in Sacramento to promote the funding of twenty-five new drug treatment programs in California? I wondered about the conversation I'd overheard between Mac and someone in his office in California, in which Mac suddenly snapped into the telephone, "I don't care what it costs, Jack. That's my problem, not yours. I told you the day you started how it was going to be. We do what's right, even if it's not profitable. You want to work in a strictly capitalist enterprise, find another job." That kind of heresy would have given Ronald Reagan an anxiety attack.

A few minutes later Mac sat back in his chair and looked at me. "Want some coffee?"

"No, thanks."

"You look pensive," he said. "What are you thinking about?"

"I'm wondering what makes you tick," I said.

He grinned crookedly, pushing his chair farther from the desk and leaning back so he could lift his stockinged feet onto the edge of the desk. I wished I could do that.

"There's no mystery about me," he said. "I'm an open book."

"Hardly," I said. "Charlie Chan couldn't figure you out. Not that he'd want to."

"I'm that mysterious?"

"In many ways. Mysterious and annoying."

"How do you mean?"

"You're far more complex than you seem on the surface, and you keep me off-balance by doing or saying what I least expect. Just when I imagine I can predict what you'll say or do next, you blind-side me with something off-the-wall. It's disconcerting. I'm a pretty astute student of human nature, and I like to think I can ferret out most people's motives and hidden agendas. But you have me pretty well flummoxed."

"Great word, flummoxed."

"I like it."

He was silent for a few moments.

"I'd have to say that according to your definition, you're something of a mystery to me, too," he said. "That mystery is an extraordinarily appealing quality, I might add." He widened and then narrowed his eyes, the way William F. Buckley often did, in a way that hinted of secret delight over the words he'd just spoken.

"Life is a mystery," I said.

"You could cross-stitch that and frame it, it would probably sell."

"Don't laugh. That's how I'll probably have to earn my living from now on."

I was reduced to this sort of banter, I thought, by a drunk redneck in a blue pickup. Execution was starting to sound too good for him.

"Seriously," Mac said, "what can I do to enlighten you about my hidden agendas and unfathomable motivations? I hate to annoy you."

"I was thinking while I was watching you work, how much I know *about* you, but how little I really *know* you, even with all the time we've spent together. You're an enigma, you know? That's what's annoying. I suppose I just enjoy being able to make assumptions about the people I know. It gives friendships a pleasant, comfortable kind of predictability. I know it can be boring to be able to predict *everything*, but I enjoy the fact that the people I know well can be depended on to behave the way I expect they will most of the time. You aren't like that."

He studied me. "Being able to predict behavior gives a sense of control, I suppose."

I smirked. His look was inscrutable. I didn't read disapproval in his face, however, so his comment didn't feel like criticism. I gave it some thought.

Finally I said, trying to avoid sounding defensive, "I hadn't looked at it that way, but you're probably right. The surprises in my life haven't been good ones. I like to avoid them. Self-preservation, I suppose." I was going to have to discuss this with Saul and Angela, I thought. At length. In the abstract, of course.

"Is that why you've tried so hard to avoid getting involved

with me?" He leaned toward me and smiled. "Is that the bottom line?"

I took a deep breath, then turned to look out the window. "I'm not sure what you mean," I said.

"I don't follow your script, and that threatens your sense of control. I don't fit the role you want to assign to me. I'm a free agent." He paused.

"That's nice and pat. And it paints such a pretty picture of me."

"I want you to let me into your life, Sally, but you've refused to do that. I'm just trying to understand why."

"I didn't invite you to get involved in my life, you know."

"Ah. It has to be you who invites."

"Yes." I said it quickly, without thinking, then realized it was true.

"Tell me, Sally, just how do I get on your invitation list?"

"You don't."

"Why?"

"We've had this conversation before, Mac. You know why."

"I know the reasons you gave me in December, which didn't make sense then and still don't. I think we're getting closer to the truth right now. Don't stop. Keep talking."

"I'm tired of talking." I sighed.

"Too bad, because we're just getting started."

I thought how ironic it was that thirty years ago, it had been Mac's predictability and controllability that made me want to walk away from him. Now I had to admit that it was just the opposite. I wondered briefly whether I might have invited him into my life now if he were still the boy I'd known in high school.

Mac was staring at me. "Self-preservation. Interesting concept. Are you saying you can't preserve yourself unless you can predict how I'll behave? Come on, now. You don't believe that."

"That isn't what I meant."

"I'll tell you what. Where you're concerned, I don't *know* very much, but I think we're really talking about the fact that you're scared to death, Sal."

I started to reply, then closed my eyes. Why did I suddenly feel like crying? I took several deep breaths. I hated this conversation. I wanted to end it, but something was drawing me along, and I couldn't seem to resist it. A death wish, that's what it was.

"Tell me," Mac said. I could feel him watching me.

"Oh, rats." I sighed heavily, feeling a large tear trickle slowly down one cheek. Mac said nothing, just waited. There he went again, doing the unpredictable. I somehow expected him to rush to comfort me. Not that I wanted him to.

Finally I stopped the flow of tears and sniffled miserably. Still Mac didn't move or speak.

"I hate you," I said finally. Mac didn't answer.

"You're the only person in the world who could make me feel this confused and rotten." I was whining. I could hear it, but I couldn't stop it.

"Ah," Mac said. "Progress."

"Quit being clever and droll."

"It won't be easy," he said, "for one endowed with wit and a steel-trap mind."

"Try anyway."

"Well, just for the record," Mac said, pulling his feet down from the desk, "I'd like to say that I find mysterious, unpredictable personalities appealing."

"Oh? Sounds like you're talking about yourself."

"Give me an example."

I thought for a few seconds. "I guess I assume, or at least expect, for one thing that since you proclaim yourself to be a devout Republican, you'll look at the world in a fairly traditional, *laissez-faire*, Republican sort of way. But then you surprise me with your attitudes toward the world community, the environment, political corruption, the poor and the homeless, racial equality, even women. Republicans aren't purported to care very much about those things, but you obviously do."

"So do you. And you're a Republican."

I gave him a wry little smile. "I care in a different way than you do."

"How's that?"

"My caring is about 80 percent mental or emotional. I feel bad and talk about these problems, or vote for someone who says he'll take care of them. You *do* things. You make things happen. Look at what you've done since you've been here—not just the things you've done for me, but the things you've done by phone and mail on the West Coast and in Washington, the people you've called to help solve problems in your area, the letters you've written, your editorials exhorting people to take action on any number of problems. When you're at home I know you're knee-deep in all that action, too. I tend to sit back and just cluck my tongue. Not always, but more often than I like to admit."

He was turning this over in his mind. "I don't do as much as you give me credit for. But I do what I can, yes. I don't believe in a passive existence. Emotionally, and especially spiritually, I believe in action."

I thought about it. "That doesn't compute. To me, spirituality is passive by definition. Spirituality is God doing things *for* us or *to* us, to make us better—or at least to keep us from doing evil. Even prayer is passive. You ask God to do something and then sit back and wait for Him to take care of things."

He looked at me, squinty-eyed. "Nah," he said.

"*Nah?* What do you mean, *nah?*"

"That's not what I mean when I talk about spirituality. You're talking about religion. I'm thinking about spirituality in Christian terms. The two are worlds apart."

I was starting to wonder why I'd brought this up. I could have just sat there and watched him work, like the helpless lump I was. But I was still a sucker for a good talk about matters philosophical.

"Okay, I'll bite. What's your definition of Christian spirituality versus 'religion'?"

"Well, the whole point of most religion is to make people good by giving them rules to follow. If they follow the rules, they end up being defined as 'good'—that is, 'good' in terms of that religion. And they get rewarded for that."

He reached down and pulled up his socks, then leaned toward me, elbows on knees. "Christianity is a radical departure from that. It's a radical departure from all the other religious systems the world has ever known, in fact. It says the point is not merely to become a good person or to follow rules. The point is to know God, to be His friend, to invite Him to be intimately involved in everything we do and everything we are."

"But Christianity involves obeying the rules, too. The Ten Commandments, the Sermon on the Mount. Isn't that the point?"

"The point of the the Commandments is that nobody can keep them. We're not capable of being truly good on our own. Unless we have God's own life and Spirit in us, we're not capable of fully obeying the law of God."

"You really believe a person can know God?"

"Yes."

"And you think you do? Know Him, I mean?"

"It's a lifelong process, like any relationship. I know Him, yes. But my knowledge is imperfect. It leaves plenty of room for growth."

"It sounds too simple," I said.

"It *is* simple," he said. "But it's true, nevertheless."

"How can you be so sure?"

"A man I trusted convinced me to take a blind leap of faith—to respond to what God has revealed of Himself; and to my astonishment, God was there to catch me. After that, my life began to change. Certainty came gradually, as I got to know Him better."

I pondered this. "In what ways did your life change?"

"My focus shifted—away from my own desires, toward God and His purposes. I knew I wasn't responsible for the shift. I hadn't even been aware it was possible. After that, I suppose you could say I learned to relax and enjoy. I was able to stop feeling like everything on Planet Earth revolved around me. It was a shock to find out that it didn't."

"Sure doesn't sound like any conventional religion I've ever studied."

"Well, I've never been a particularly conventional thinker."

I looked up at him. He wasn't? Since when? "I've always thought of you as pretty conventional," I said. "*Very* conventional, in fact."

"I know," he said, a little smile appearing. "You've always been wrong about that."

That made me laugh. "What else have I been wrong about?" I asked.

His eyes crinkled up in a bigger smile. "You think you can get rid of me."

"Oh, that," I said.

11

I was determined to hire a nurse as the third week of February wore on. Mac seemed entirely unconcerned. It began to worry me that he might somehow stay on indefinitely unless I took matters firmly in hand.

Our arrangement was not uncomfortable, as I've said, and that was part of the problem. It was easy simply to let it continue. But as I grew stronger and less dependent, I began to see that our relationship inevitably would have to move either toward something permanent or toward oblivion. I could not imagine us as "good friends" forever, mostly because I knew Mac would not accept that. And the stronger I got, the more I resisted the idea of a long-term commitment to anyone—even Mac, of whom I'd admittedly grown very fond.

I wanted my old life back, that was what I wanted. I didn't want to think about rearranging things to accommodate whatever "creative" ideas Mac might come up with so we could be together. In spite of everything that had happened between us, and the admiration and affection I felt for him, I grew more and more resolute about rebuilding my old life pretty much as it had been before Mac had come into it again. I suppose it was a natural longing to cling to the familiar, the tried and true, which were a lot more appealing to me at that point than the unknown qualities of a possible future with Mac. Such a future, at least in my mind, also carried with it the possibility of more change than I ever wanted to experience again. I wanted back my world of predictability and contentment.

I know that all this may seem selfish and ungrateful. And it was, of course. But Mac knew as well as I did that I could not choose to be with him out of gratitude. He didn't want that, obviously, and that was part of the reason he'd gone to extremes to keep me from feeling indebted. So in a strange sense, I suppose my determination to bring things to a halt was an outgrowth of Mac's unselfishness in our relationship. The irony of that was not lost on me.

Since Mac managed to ignore my increasingly frequent suggestions that we look for a nurse, I finally started calling agencies to arrange some interviews on my own. He saw my notes and asked about it.

"I called a couple of home nursing services. I have two interviews tomorrow. You can help me," I told him.

"It's going to be crowded here with another person underfoot," he said.

"There won't be another person. This one will take your place."

He clutched his chest and made a wheezing noise. "How can you say that? You're kicking me out?"

"I'm not going to joke about this. It's time. Okay?"

"Let's talk about it tonight."

"Tonight never comes," I said.

"Didn't the Platters sing that?" he asked.

THAT NIGHT AFTER DINNER we sat, or rather he sat and I was cast down, in front of the fireplace. We were drinking low-cal cocoa out of bowl-sized blue cups, snug as two bugs in a rug, with Bix Beiderbeck on the stereo. Mac had brought a dozen or so of his records with him when he'd flown out the day after my accident. I don't know about you, but I called that foresight.

I had decided it would be the ultimate test of my true character if he forgot the records when he left to go back to California. Would I remind him? Or would I wait, hoping he'd never miss them? I'd probably remind him, mostly because if he eventually remembered them I'd feel like such a creep if I hadn't. There are certain people who believe that jazz music has a corrupting influence on the human race, and I was beginning to think they were right.

I was halfway into the best book I'd read in a long time, a suspense novel in which the good guys were beating the bad guys with brute strength and exceptionally witty dialog. I was feeling good. The casts were coming off my legs in two days, and the world would be mine. I was going to be a new woman.

"So, let's talk about the nurse," Mac said. That surprised me. I thought he'd try to avoid it again. Maybe he was beginning to see the inevitability of it.

"I figure that after the casts come off, I'll be able to get around enough to spend the nights alone," I said. "I'll be able to dress myself, get to the bathroom without falling. I'll only need a few things that will require help. And someone to take me to therapy, help with meals, shopping, those sorts of things. In a month I'll be able to handle everything. Maybe sooner. A visiting nurse would be ideal."

"I see."

"Mac, you should be relieved. This has been a long, long couple of months for you."

"What makes you say that?"

"Oh, I don't know. I suppose I'm telepathic."

"Ah. If I'd known that, I'd have guarded my thoughts."

"Well, anyway, it's time. Don't you agree?"

His look said, *No, I don't agree.* Maybe I *was* telepathic. His eyes flickered, reflecting the fire.

"You've lost two months of your life over me," I said. "I don't want you to lose any more. It's enough already."

"There hasn't been any loss on my part," he said. "Believe me." His face was serious.

"Sure," I said.

He watched me, trying to squeeze into my head via my eyeballs. I looked away.

"Okay," he said. "Let's hire a nurse."

He stood, brushed at his pants, tucked in his blue and red plaid shirt, put his hands deep in his pockets. "Okay," he said again.

"Thank you," I said, finding it hard to speak.

"You're welcome," he said.

THREE DAYS LATER Nurse Ratchet came. She was credentialed, efficient, and had the face of a barn owl. Among six candidates we interviewed she was the best, and I was resigned to having her with me ten hours of every day for a month. Her name was actually Mildred Clarkson, but we dubbed her Nurse Ratchet from the minute she left after her interview. Not exactly original, of course, but apt.

Mac was packing the last of several boxes containing the materials people in California and Washington had sent to him over the last couple of months to enable him to run his little empire from my place. On crutches, relieved of the weight of the casts, I was feeling frisky. I'd been ordered not to walk around without support for a couple of weeks, but I was still a new woman.

I crutched my way into my son's room, where Mac knelt on

the floor next to a pile of books and computer printouts. He didn't look up.

"Can I help?" I asked.

"I'm about done," he said. He stacked several books on a chair. "I'll leave these books for you. You might enjoy them. And the records."

My heart went pitty-pat. *Shucks*, I thought, *now I'll never know about my true character*. "Thanks," I said. "I'll take good care of them. And I'll think of you when I listen to them."

He didn't reply. He sealed up the carton on the floor, then lifted and carried it to the group that stood piled by the door. "There," he said.

"Will you need to take those to the Post Office?"

"UPS is going to pick them up this morning," he said.

"Oh." Silence.

"We have managed," I said, "to get ourselves into something of a predicament."

"Yes," he said, coming up to me and leaning against the wall, his arms crossed. I shifted from one leg to the other and moved the crutches under my arms. "'Life isn't a spectacle or a feast, it's a predicament.'" He paused, then added, "That's Santayana."

"Auntie Mame would disagree, of course," I said.

He was gazing at me with a small frown. "I don't want to leave. I was thinking a while ago that this is the hardest thing I've ever done."

"Me, too," I said.

"Oh?"

"Yes."

"Then why are we doing it?"

"Because."

He looked down at his feet, then up at me, sharply.

"That's a good reason if I've ever heard it," he said.

"It's inevitable," I said.

"You would have made a great Buddhist."

I pulled myself straighter and crutched over to the dark red leather chair by the desk, settling onto it as gracefully as an over-stuffed pelican.

Mac sighed, walked over, and pulled up a little straight cushioned chair so he could sit facing me. Our knees were almost touching.

"I wish you'd come out to California for a while," he said. "I have a small guest cottage where you could finish recuperating. You'd have space, privacy, no pressure from me. You could start working again, or just lie around and do nothing. Give it some thought, and in a few days I'll call."

"I don't think that's a good idea," I said.

He looked at me, frowning, then looked down at the floor again.

"Come on, now," I said. "What would happen if I went out there? It would compound the predicament."

"You are certifiably nuts," he said.

"Probably. But I think you know I'm right."

He leaned forward, put his hands on my shoulders, and looked straight into my eyes, deeper than I'd ever felt him look before. I couldn't look away. "What I know is this," he said, "I will love you forever. And there is nothing you can do to stop that. Nothing."

Sir Lancelot would have said that to Guinevere, Romeo to Juliet, Jimmy Stewart to June Allyson. It took my breath away.

"You love too much," I said after several seconds, my voice faltering. "You always have."

"No," he said. "Nobody can love too much." He paused, dropping his hands from my shoulders. "In fact, nobody can ever love *enough*."

He stood, leaned over, and kissed me on the top of my head for about four seconds, then straightened and walked out of the room. A few minutes later I heard him talking to Nurse Ratchet. Then the doorbell rang. The UPS man came in and carried out the boxes using a big metal hand truck. The front door opened again, then snapped closed quietly, and I knew Mac had gone. Again.

I sat back in the chair and took three deep breaths, letting them out slowly. I was going to get through this, I reminded myself. I would survive. So would he. And I would never let myself get into this kind of fix again.

Nurse Ratchet rustled into the room. "We have a very nourishing soup for lunch," she said. "Are we ready to dive in?"

I stared at her. "Are we ever," I said.

12

Saul and Angela dropped in the next night on their way home from a concert. Saul made popcorn, heavy on the butter, while Angela put together root beer floats for the three of us, serving them in my big cut crystal glasses. We—or at least they—sat comfortably in front of the fire. Saul's hair was combed back, making him look about ten years older than usual.

"To us," Angela said, lifting her glass. "Long may we live."

We all clinked glasses.

"Seems odd without Mac here," Angela said. "I miss him."

Saul looked at her pointedly and lifted an eyebrow.

"It's hard," I said. "But I'll feel better when I'm working again. I'm going to get back to the new Bridget book tomorrow. I was about halfway into it in December." I didn't like to say, "When the accident happened." I was still in a denial mode.

Saul rubbed his hands together. "Do you feel like getting back to our book, too? I mean, I don't want to rush it, but if you feel ready . . ."

"Sure," I said.

"Sure?"

"Sure."

"Okay," he said. "I'll bring the manuscript up before we leave tonight. I have it in the car. I've done a little work on it, but I'm stuck. I need my collaborator."

"Saul," Angela said, "maybe Sally should go at this slowly. See how it goes with the Bridget book, you know, and then decide about the other one." She glanced at me, sympathetic and concerned.

"I'm okay," I said. "It would feel good to work hard. I want to be a little pressed. That's the best cure for post-parting blues."

"Right," Saul said.

Angela looked at me, at Saul, and then back at me. "Could I ask a personal question?" she said. "I mean, the one we're all avoiding so carefully?"

"Which one is that?" I said innocently.

"About you and Mac."

"Surprise, surprise," I said.

"When are you going to see him again?"

"Never, " I said.

"You're kidding," she said, her green eyes very wide.

"You're kidding," Saul said, swallowing a large gulp of his root beer. The ice cream was melting, and it left foam on the hairs of his upper lip.

"I am not kidding."

They looked at each other.

"You don't understand," I said.

"True," Angela said. "So, tell us, what is this—you're giving him up for Lent? You can't seriously mean you aren't going to see each other again, ever."

I felt like Oliver North at the Iran-Contra Hearings. I stared morosely at my glass.

"Sally, forgive me," Saul said, "but I think you're off in Banana Nu-nu Land here."

I blinked. "Is that a psychiatric opinion?"

"Yes," he said.

"Well," I said, "what do you know about that."

"Why are you cutting off a relationship that could be one of the best things in your life?" he said.

"Or one of the worst," I said.

"Life is full of risks," he said.

"I choose my risks carefully."

"I guess you do." He stared at me psychoanalytically. He was sitting cross-legged on the floor, elbows on knees, fingers steepled in front of his face. He reached for a fistful of popcorn and tossed it in his mouth, chewing loudly.

Angela leaned forward. "Sally, do you love the man?"

That surprised me. Another one of those left-field questions I'd somehow failed to include in my planning.

"I don't know," I said.

She pursed her lips at me.

"I don't know!" I said, exasperation rising. "Is that a crime? What does it matter, anyway?"

"Matter? Obviously, you know that he loves you," Angela said.

"Of course I know that," I said. "The entire population of the free world knows that. But I don't know whether I love him, and it's actually beside the point. I'm not going to pursue the relationship; so my feelings don't matter."

Saul shook his head. "I can't believe you're being this neurotic."

I glared at him. "Saul, what is this? You of all people should not be pushing me like this."

"If I don't, who will?" he said, tossing more popcorn into his mouth.

"I will," Angela said, pointing a pink-polished fingernail at her own chest.

"You are both being obnoxious. Stop it," I said.

Angela glanced at Saul. Saul took another handful of popcorn. Crunch, crunch, crunch. His mouth had a greasy, disgusting shine all the way around it. There were bits of popcorn caught in his beard.

"It wouldn't have worked," I said. "Never in a million years."

"Oh? Tell us about it," Saul said.

"Stop playing shrink for a minute, will you?" I said.

"Only if you stop acting like a nut."

I stared at the fire, angry. I didn't have to defend my feelings, my choices, to these people. They were two of my best friends, yes, but friends should not demand explanations.

Well, maybe they should, I thought after a moment. If they don't, who will?

Angela pulled her knees up and wrapped her arms around them. "Sal, you know I love you. You're the most level-headed person I know. Your judgment is flawless. I really feel that way." She looked at the fire. "The thing is, I feel—and Saul feels, too, don't you, honey?—that you're not thinking straight about Mac. You're not seeing, ummm, the *possibilities* in your relationship."

She pulled in a deep breath, took a handful of popcorn, and played with it in her palm. "Look," she said, gesturing helplessly with her right hand, "we just see these two terrific people who would be even more terrific together, and it makes sense that they would ride off into the sunset hand in hand. Instead of that, the man rides off into the sunset, alone and sad. The woman sits in her apartment with Nurse Ratchet, planning her future as a lonely old crone. I hate stories that end like that. I just hate them."

"So do I," I said. "But I will never be an old crone."

"Well," she said, "you're the creative genius among us. I can't believe you're incapable of producing a more satisfying *denouement* than this." She pronounced it the French way. Angela could carry it off.

I sighed. "What do you suggest? That I break up housekeeping, explain to my son that I'm going to sell our home, move out to the Sunset Coast, and try to forget how much our life here means to us? Forget you and Saul? Forget all our other friends, my work? I *love* this city. I love the Twins. I love the Vikings. I love the lakes, the trees, the Swedes, the Zoo, the Golden Gophers, Minnehaha Falls, the Ordway, the wind and snow, I love *everything* and *everyone* in the Twin Cities!"

"Mac would move here," Angela said, kindly ignoring the tone of my outburst. "That's pretty rare all by itself. Anyway, these are just details." She made a dismissive gesture with her hand.

"*Details?* Angela, these details are the people, the places, the things that make me happy! These details are my life!" I slurped noisily at my drink. "And yes, Mac would probably move here if I asked him. Good grief, he would probably donate all his worldly goods to the Socialist Party if I asked him! I couldn't deal with another sacrifice on his part," I said.

"Aha!" Saul said. His eyebrows popped up, and his index finger pointed at the ceiling. I looked at it, and he pulled it down, crossing his arms. His hair was zooming again. Now he looked like Richard Dreyfuss in a fright wig.

I breathed deeply. "What I mean is, neither Mac nor I should make that kind of sacrifice. If either of us gave up everything else we love just so we could be together, we'd regret it in a hurry. We'd eventually hate each other." I thought for a moment. "Or more likely, I'd hate him, because out of guilt I'd end up being the one giving everything up and it wouldn't be fair to expect him to stand in the stead of everyone and everything else I love. And in the end he'd be hurt, too, because I would leave him. Without a doubt."

"And to think," Saul said, "that we were looking on this as a simple open-and-shut case. Clearly he escaped just in the nick of time."

I glared at him again. "Saul, give me a break. Can you try to see it the way I do? Mac and I were both happy, individually, before we saw each other again," I said. "We can be just as happy again, when this—this *vulnerability* fades a little. You're the one who pointed out that time takes care of these things. And besides, I'm no good at living with a man. Any man."

"There have been so many?" Saul said, eyes wide. "This is amazing news."

I ignored his barb. "Look, when Peter and I were married I realized that I have a terrible tendency to *accommodate*. It's my nature. Maybe it's the youngest child syndrome, I don't know. As soon as I got married I became two people. There was this creative, bright, slightly off-the-wall woman who existed when Peter was at work or away from home. I liked her. But then there was the other Sally—the Incredible Shrinking Woman, a mealymouthed, self-sacrificing creature with hardly an idea or desire of her own, who existed only for Peter. 'Yes, dear—no dear—whatever you'd like is fine, dear—I am so *lucky* just to be with you.' I knew it was going on, and I was powerless to do anything about it. He didn't do it to me, you understand—I did it to myself. It was pathological. I look back now and puke."

"Is that true?" Angela said, wonder in her voice. "Were you really like that?"

"Yes. Yes, yes, yes," I said emphatically. "So you see, musketeers, I am not playing the martyr. I am engaged in self-preservation. I want my happy life back. I want to hang on to the Sally we knew and loved before Mac wandered back onto the scene. I am engaged in an attempt to safeguard the person I am, or at least the person I was a few short months ago, whatever that may cost me. A noble cause, and a thankless one." I raised my empty glass, held it in the air, and on an impulse threw it in the fireplace. It shattered noisily. A small shard landed in my lap. It was a grand gesture, I thought. Well worth the $19.95 it had cost me.

Saul flinched, shook his head, then stared at me with one eyebrow up, making a diagnosis—manic depressive with schizoid tendencies, I figured. He began to pick pieces of crystal from his lap. "You are absolutely crackers," he said. At least I was close.

I shook my head. "No," I said. "Only repressed and neurotic."

"My father always said it's a dangerous and ominous thing when a woman thinks too much," he said, dropping several pieces of the crystal into Angela's empty glass.

She looked at him lovingly and patted his cheek. "Isn't he precious?" she said brightly. "Just like G. Gordon Liddy."

Saul kissed the air in her direction. "Have you considered the possibility, sweetie," he said to me in his most pedantic voice, "that as an insightful, mature human being who learns from past errors you are now in a position to avoid repeating the behaviors that have caused you to loathe yourself in previous relationships? Surely you realize by now that relationships don't have to be an all-or-nothing proposition."

I glared at him. "That has been pointed out to me before, thank you."

"Apparently you need to have it pointed out again," he said. "Has it occurred to you, as well, that it might actually be exhilarating and self-affirming to be with this man and not allow yourself to become a toady? Come to think of it, I have not seen you acting the toady during the last several months in Mac's company. Is it possible that this part of you no longer exists? I only ask you to consider it."

"It's not possible," I said, running my fingers through my hair. "You don't understand how incorrigible I am. I would revert to type overnight as soon as I allowed myself to love him. Love does that to me—at least the romantic kind of love does. The toady is still there, lurking down at the bottom of my soul, just waiting for the chance to come out and finish me off."

"Yuk," Saul said.

"Maybe you should kill the filthy little beast first," Angela said profoundly. "In hand-to-hand combat."

It sounded pretty profound to me, too.

After that the three of us stared at the fire for a while, silent. The logs cracked and hissed and finally burned down to a flickering pile of embers. Peggy Lee was now singing huskily in the background. Saul got up, dusted the salt and butter off his hands with a napkin, wiped his mouth and beard, and carried the popcorn bowl out to the kitchen.

I reached out and put my hand on top of Angela's. She gave it an affectionate squeeze. Saul returned and knelt down, placing his hand on top of both of ours.

"All for one, and one for all," he said.

It had to be the root beer.

13

Saturday, March 26th. The day before Palm Sunday, a week before the start of Passover—a gray, blustery 52-degree day in the Twin Cities. My favorite weather. The wind skidded across the little whitecaps on the lake. The snow was long gone, and the *Star-Tribune* was full of ads for bright spring clothes and sales on lawn equipment. My new Bridget Caulfield manuscript was in the mail to my editor. I was walking well now and had several days earlier burned my cane in the fireplace in a solemn and moving little ceremony. Nurse Ratchet was off doing her thing with some other pathetic invalid.

My good old life and my good old self were within my grasp. Saul and I had been working steadily at our book, for which we'd received a respectable advance. We'd finally decided to call it *The Lockworth Prescription*. Lockworth was one of the villains, a sinister psychiatrist with delusions of grandeur. I wasn't crazy about the title, but Saul and Angela had come up with it, and I had nothing better in mind. Somebody would change it before publication, anyway. They always did. Later that night Saul and I were scheduled to do another few hours together at the computer, while Angela went off to a medical meeting in Burnsville. Things were back to normal.

At 6:30, just as I was about to sit down in front of a plate of sautéed soft-shelled crab I'd been hoarding in my freezer for two weeks, the phone rang. A salesman, I grumbled. But since it could have been Saul, I picked it up.

"Yes?" I said irritably.

"Hi," Mac's voice said.

The effect on me was truly amazing. The hairs on my arms stood straight up, so help me. You might have expected this, but believe me, I did not.

"Hi," I said.

"How are you?"

"Fine," I said. "No, better than that. I threw away my crutches, burned the cane, and I haven't had a headache for two weeks. I'm into a walking program."

"Wow," he said. "That is incredible."

"Yes, it is. I had great rehabilitative care."

"Nurse Ratchet was that good?"

"No. You were."

There was a pause. "I've been thinking," he said.

"Yes?"

"I have this recently redecorated guest house. Well, maybe redecorated isn't the word. It has new carpeting in one room. And the fireplace was just swept. Think of it as a charming bed and breakfast in one of the most sought-after tourist destinations in America."

"Oh?"

"I called my travel agent, and she claims she can have a round-trip plane ticket in your hands in two hours flat. You could be here early tomorrow afternoon. Call it an Easter vacation."

I was holding my breath. I let it out.

"Oh, dear," I said.

Mac didn't respond. He was waiting. If he'd been born a girl and had entered a Miss America pageant, he could have introduced "waiting" as a competitive talent—and could have won on that basis alone.

I let him wait while I mulled things over. Finally I spoke. "Round trip, you say?"

"Yep," he said in a John Wayne voice.

"Sort of like winning a sweepstakes, huh?"

"Sort of," he said.

"Well, hmmm." I was trying to sort out the 379 random thoughts that were ricocheting at high speed off the concave interior surface of my skull. I can't offer much in the way of rational explanations about this, of course, but the idea of flying out to California for a few days was not one I immediately threw out the window. It could have been the suddenness of Mac's call, the effect it seemed to be having on me, or even the fact that it was just awfully good to hear his voice after such a long few weeks. Who knows? It even could have been the barometric pressure.

The doorbell rang before I could come up with a reply to Mac's suggestion. *Saved by the bell*, I thought. I asked Mac to wait while I let Saul in.

"Tell him hello, and I'd like to see him. And Angela, too," Mac said before I put the phone down.

I let Saul in. "Mac's on the phone," I said, and he raised his bushy eyebrows at me and gave me a surprised smile. "He says he'd like to see you and Angela."

Saul said, "Tell him we'll fly out soon. We'll call him."

I went back to the phone in the kitchen and let Saul seat himself in the living room.

"Here I am," I said. "Saul says he and Angela will come out to see you." I wondered if I should be writing these messages down.

"You were about to say yes," Mac said.

"Oh?"

"Weren't you?"

"What time does the plane leave?"

"Nine twenty-five."

"Where would I land? I mean, what city?"

"I'll pick you up in San Francisco. That's easiest."

"Do you believe the travel agent can really get the tickets here in two hours?"

"Yep." It was Gary Cooper, not John Wayne. I was still thinking.

"I guess I'll see you tomorrow, then," I said after about fifteen more seconds. I heard a noise behind me, turned, and saw Saul standing at the kitchen door with his arms folded across his chest and a grin spread across his face.

"That's great," Mac said. "I'll be at the gate."

"I'll see you there," I said.

We hung up. Saul kept leaning on the door frame, watching me.

"Well, well, well, well," he said.

"Shut up," I said. "You were eavesdropping. Where are your ethical standards?"

"You're looking at a man who eats table grapes while sending money to the Cesar Chavez Memorial Fund. What do you want from me?"

"About five minutes of silence."

I went to the stove, picked up the plate of cold soft-shelled crabs, and scraped them into the garbage can. Saul gasped.

"Were those soft-shelled crabs?"

"Yes, they were."

"You could be struck dead for that."

"Saul, why did I let Mac talk me into this?" I turned to look at him.

"Did he really do that? Doesn't sound like Mac to me."

I pondered it. "No," I said. "He only invited; *I* talked me into it. But what possessed me, Saul? I was getting back to normal. I promised myself I would avoid this sort of thing. Now I'm going to have to get over him again."

"Maybe not."

"Oh, yes, my friend, I will."

He looked at me owlishly. "Don't be so negative. Maybe this will be a watershed experience. Consider the possibility—just the possibility—that starting now, you can let yourself love somebody who loves you back, and you both can just keep on getting better at it until you die. Without having it turn into something you have to get over, like the flu."

"If you say, 'love means never having to say you're sorry,' I'll cut out your tongue."

Saul smiled. "Actually, love means having to say you're sorry just about every day of your life. Among other things."

"Thank you, Leo Buscaglia," I said.

He shrugged, came over to where I was standing, and put his arms around me. I leaned against his chest and sighed deeply.

"Why are you encouraging me to make a fool of myself with a Republican?" I said. "Haven't you taken some sort of oath that prevents you from doing this?"

"My oath requires only that I do everything in my power to prevent Republicans from mixing with Democrats. The theory is that since a Republican couple will have sex only once every leap year, eventually there will be none of you left. So far, it's working beautifully."

I looked at him. "Actually, you may have something there. As an evil plot, it could work."

"Well," he said, eyebrows up, "loose lips sink ships. Now that I've spilled the beans, you'll probably go right out to California and nip our dandy little plot in the bud, so to speak."

"I think you're still safe."

He shook his head and looked at me gravely. "I won't make any bets until you get back."

SAUL DIDN'T STAY LONG. He volunteered to take me to the airport the next morning since he had no patients scheduled until noon. At exactly 8:15 that night, as I was about to get ready for bed, the doorbell rang. A messenger had arrived from the travel agent. A computer-printed note in the envelope read: "Ms. Alexander, this ticket shows a return date one month from now, but Mac asked me to explain that it can be changed to any date you wish with twenty-four hours' notice. The Easter weekend is difficult because all flights are heavily booked, but I'll work with you." At the bottom it said, "Anne T. Bosworth," with a 707 area code phone number. Why did the name sound familiar?

Later that night as I lay in bed trying to sleep I remembered Annie Bosworth, the lady who had that prayer group at Mac's church. *The lady's into travel and prayer*, I thought. *A Renaissance woman.*

Just as I was getting ready for bed, Matt called from Missouri. He'd called the week before to ask whether I'd mind if he spent spring break with Valerie's family instead of coming home. I'd insisted that he do just that, making a brave front by telling him I was too busy with Saul's and my book to spend much time with them anyway. Mothers are good at these self-abnegating sorts of things.

But that night Matt was having second thoughts. "Mom," he said, "I've been thinking . . . I know Val will understand if I take a rain check. I want to spend the time with you."

I smiled. "You're a good son," I said. "I appreciate the sacrifice, honey, I really do. But I've made some plans of my own, so you're off the hook." It felt good. *I* was the one who was busy.

"Plans? What kind of plans?"

I hesitated. Did I really want to tell him I was going to spend a few days—maybe more—with Mac? Well, what else could I say?

"Mac called earlier and invited me to spend Easter vacation in his guest cottage." Then, without taking a breath, I said, "On a wholesome and friendly basis."

"Keen," he said instantly.

"Keen?" I said. "Who is this—Pat Boone?"

"You're the one who said, 'wholesome.' I'm really glad, Mom. I think this is great."

"You think *what* is great?"

"You and Mac."

"There is no 'me and Mac.' There is me, and there is Mac. Don't start inventing or extrapolating. Besides, sons are supposed to be disapproving and suspicious of the men in their mothers' lives."

"Okay. Face it, Mom, Mac is a scumbag."

"That's enough."

"Okey dokey. Just trying to oblige. Make up your mind, will you?"

"I'll talk to you soon, honey. When you learn to talk like my son would talk."

"I'll call you on Easter . . . At Mac's."

"Okay, I'll give you the number."

"That's all right. I have it."

"You do?"

"Sure. I got it when you were in the hospital."

"Bye, honey. I love you."

"Bye, Mom. Have fun."

I fell asleep wondering whether northern California was spring-like at that time of year, and whether my sweaters and wool pants would be too warm, and whether I needed to take my quilted down jacket. Then I thought what a mundane and pointless thing that was to worry about when I was flying to my doom.

14

The airport was crowded, but Saul got me to the gate on time the next morning. I had a bad case of nerves. He handed me a small bottle of pills. The label had my name and the word "Valium," with directions. I put the bottle back in his hands.

"I'll be okay," I insisted. "That's nice of you, but no thanks." He put the bottle in my purse.

"They won't stunt your growth," he said. "There are only six. They'll help you relax for the flight."

"You're a pill-pushing quack," I said.

"Who happens to be worried about you," he finished. "Indulge me."

"I'm fine."

"Then why are you having trouble breathing? I'm about to call for oxygen support," he said.

"Am I that bad?"

"Yes."

"Saul, if I come back tomorrow will you and Angela still be my friends?"

"No."

"I see. Well, I just wanted to know."

He put an arm around me. I closed my eyes.

"I feel like I'm about to go down in flames," I said. "It's suicide, you know. There is no possibility that anything good can come from this. It must be what they call a 'fatal attraction.' It doesn't matter that it's going to kill us both, we just have to go through with this, Mac and I. We have to do each other in." I was chewing the inside of my lip.

"That's my girl," Saul said. "Stay positive. You're a regular Norman Vincent Peale."

He pushed me toward the attendant who stood ready to take my ticket. "The little lady is pregnant," he said to the attendant in a Texas drawl, saying it "preg-nent." She looked at me sympathetically. "Y'all take good care of her now, hear?" Saul said, winking at her and slipping a twenty-dollar bill into her hand.

She smiled, her teeth straight and white and sparkling. "Yes, sir," she said. "We'll be sure she's comfy as can be. It'll be our pleasure." Her own drawl was almost identical to Saul's. I wondered who was putting on whom.

I walked the last mile onto the plane without looking back, trying to waddle pregnantly. I skipped the Valium but drank five bottles of Calistoga water in the three and a half hours between Minneapolis and San Francisco. By the time we were ready to land, my ankles were the size of stovepipes. I squeezed my feet into my shoes and splashed Visine on my bloodshot eyeballs as we touched down. It didn't help the redness much, but it did smudge my mascara a little. I dabbed at my eyes to turn the smudges into something more attractive.

Mac stood at the gate dressed in tan chinos, a pale blue crewneck, and a yellow button-down shirt with a navy blue L. L. Bean jacket, the kind with the plaid lining. We looked like Bobbsey Twins. I had worn tan cotton pants, a yellow cotton turtleneck, and a medium blue crewneck sweater. I'd draped a long plaid scarf around my neck. Nobody stared at us.

He greeted me with a warm hug, picked up my carry-on suitcase, and started walking almost immediately toward the terminal. "Good flight?" he asked. He seemed not to notice our outfits.

"Yes," I said. "Thank you, by the way. First-class was an edifying experience. They waited on me hand and foot." Speaking
of feet, mine seemed to be making a disconcerting squishing
sound with each step.

"Great," he said. "You look rested. You look better than I've
ever seen you, in fact. You're walking just fine. No pain?"

"No," I said self-consciously. "No pain. I still get headaches
occasionally, but I'm not much different from 90 percent of the
adult population in that respect."

"You're a little thinner," he said. "Nurse Ratchet didn't serve
potato pancakes for breakfast?"

"Nurse Ratchet served gruel."

"Don't worry, Mrs. Whelan will fatten you up."

"Who's Mrs. Whelan?"

"My housekeeper. Not a gourmet cook, but she makes memorable sauces. Fresh herbs." Aha. We were already getting into
the leafy green stuff, were we? Next would come the Alice B.
Toklas brownies.

We continued to walk in silence, my arm through his. He
hugged it close to his body.

When we got to the sidewalk outside the terminal, he put
down the suitcases we'd collected and asked me to wait while he
went for the car. It was cool and sunny, Minneapolis spring
weather; but the air felt moister and slightly salty.

When Mac's Republican silver Buick pulled up, I waited
while he arranged my carry-on and two suitcases in the trunk. I
climbed into the car, and he shut the door.

He walked around to the driver's side and opened the door,
peering in at me. He stopped, not moving for a few seconds.

"What?" I said.

"You're here," he said.

"Yes indeed. I surely am."

He grinned happily and sat, inserting the key in the ignition. He looked tan and about thirty-eight years old. *Good,* I thought, *now I'm also too old for him.*

THE DRIVE TOOK US NORTH TO THE CITY, through what Jack Kerouac had called the "great hulk" of downtown San Francisco, across the Golden Gate Bridge, and up 101 toward Mt. Tamalpais and the junction with Highway One that eventually would have carried us all the way up to Washington. We cruised past mile after mile of the most spectacular shoreline I'd ever seen, then cut inland across the Point Reyes National Seashore. At Point Reyes Station, home of the historic lighthouse, we turned east briefly and then headed up past Tomales Bay through Marshall. We spun along the countryside in high spirits, windows open, sun pouring down through the sunroof.

At first I chatted amiably, living the moment, senses energized. Then as the drive progressed, everything my eyes took in was so lush, so wildly uncultivated, and so exquisitely beautiful that I fell silent for a long time.

"How are you holding up?," Mac said after some time. "Tired?"

"This is the perfect drive," I said, trailing my arm out the window. "The perfect day. The perfect place to be." It was. I flowed with it.

We cut inland past Bolinas Bay, following the highway through the sleepy town of Valley Ford and on to Bodega Bay. There, Mac asked if I'd like to stretch my legs. I said sure, and we parked at a bay-front eatery attached to a row of souvenir shops.

The air was fresh, the way I'd remembered the sea air in New

England. The sky was clear and bright turquoise. Seagulls cried and swooped in the sun. Only a few cars were parked in the lot.

We used the restrooms and bought small plastic cups of fresh crabmeat from the deli counter in the eatery, then walked outside and looked in the window of one of the souvenir shops. I wolfed down the crabmeat, scraping at the bottom of my cup to get every morsel, and tossed cup and spoon into a trash barrel. Mac came up to me with his plastic spoon full of crabmeat. He held it out, offering it to me. I stood there looking at the spoon, the crabmeat, and Mac and was struck by the feeling that this was an almost mystically intimate gesture. His face went serious, and I leaned forward and took the crabmeat into my mouth, squinting my eyes like an ecstatic cat as I chewed. He watched, smiled, then offered more. I shook my head.

"Go ahead, enjoy," he said, still holding the spoon toward me.

I shook my head again, returning his smile. "No," I said, "the secret is to stop before you get sick of it. It works with everything."

He didn't comment but went over to toss his cup into the trash. Then he walked back, slowly, and as he came up to me he wrapped his arms around me—casually, I thought. I put my arms around his waist and rested my head on his shoulder, feeling the warmth radiating from him. When we pulled apart, Mac leaned down and kissed me on the lips. I kissed him back. A very satisfying kiss, indeed. A snapshot flashed into my mind: Saul leaning against my kitchen door in Minneapolis saying, "Well, well, well, well . . ."

The air seemed cooler as we cruised northward toward Jenner.

Finally we hit an intersection, turned right, drove inland and upward for several miles on a winding, heavily wooded road, took a left, then another right onto a gravel road and across a ridge through gigantic trees with bark that seemed to be peeling off in long strips. Mac pulled to a stop. We had arrived a million miles from nowhere.

I climbed out of the car and looked around. The area was surrounded by trees and dense shrubbery. A medium-sized, white-painted house that looked like a magazine photo titled "California Country Ranch" stood about twenty yards down to my right. It looked old but well-kept. It was one-story, with two chimneys and a big porch that appeared to run all the way around it. There were flowers everywhere. They didn't seem planted or cultivated, as in a garden. They were just there, in profusion. I couldn't identify most of them. Some were huge, some smaller, some miniature, and their colors were intense and varied. The green leaves were much darker green than those in the Midwest and East. In the distance, through what appeared to be fog rolling either in or out, was the ocean.

"Wow," I said.

"Yeah," Mac said, coming to stand beside me with suitcases in each hand. "Sometimes I still get overwhelmed by it."

"No wonder," I said.

Some fifty yards from the house, a weather-beaten barn hunched among the trees. A fence next to it corralled several horses—a black one, a plain gray, a gray-and-white variegated one, and a red-brown, glossy one. I didn't know horses, didn't even know what kind these were, but they sure were handsome.

Mac carried the bags off toward the left side of the house, down a long path of worn stones that had tiny flowers growing between them. The luxuriance of the jungled landscape was awe-inspiring. About thirty yards down the path, through a bower of vines clinging to a trellis, we came to a small barn-red cottage with a black lacquered door and black shutters. The windows and door were outlined with white paint, giving the house a New England look.

On the door mat, looking as if she'd been arranged there by

a designer from *Architectural Digest*, was an extremely fat black cat. She was sleeping peacefully. She lifted her head at our approach, appraised us, and then squeezed her eyes almost shut. As we came closer she roused herself, arched her back in a shuddering Halloween-cat stretch, and slowly sauntered a few steps to the left to allow us to pass, yawning as she sat down to watch.

"This is Alistair Cooke," Mac said.

Why did I always think cats were female?

"There has to be a story behind his name," I said.

"Dave Higgins gave him to me. He said cats live up to their names. Trouble was, after Dave named him hoping to turn him into a dignified character, I started calling him Cookie for short. He developed a taste for sweets and has since become the Jabba the Hut of the cat world." Mac pushed open the door and waited for me to enter the cottage. "I advise you not to watch him eat. It's not a pretty sight. In fact, now that he's been put on one meal a day he's practically obscene. I know he's secretly snacking on mice." That cat smiled at us, proud of himself.

Inside, the cottage was open and bright. The beamed ceiling was whitewashed like the barn-board walls. Old oil paintings hung over the fireplace and in the dining area. I examined them briefly and decided they were very good, worth a bit of study later. The small kitchen was open to the living space, with an eating counter and wicker stools facing the stove to the rear. A picture window in the living area framed a view through the trees to the ocean.

The decor surprised me. Was it really Mac's taste? I'd pictured him as Early American. Another of my false assumptions. A large sofa at a right angle to the fireplace was covered in a red and green paisley print with a white background. An old Hamadan rug in dark reds and golds and greens lay in front of it under a country-antique wood trunk with tarnished brass hardware. A bean pot with fresh flowers sat on the trunk, as did a stack of books.

The floor was well-worn dark oak, not polished, just natural. Next to the whitewashed stone fireplace was a handsome brass pot, about two feet high, also unpolished, with kindling in it. Firewood was stacked in a wicker hamper next to it. An easy chair slipcovered in the same paisley print as the sofa was arranged on the other side of the fireplace, with an ottoman at its feet and a square table next to it. A white basket full of fruit was on the table, alongside a reading lamp that seemed to have been made from a colorful old cloisonné vase.

"This is wonderful," I said. "Did you do all this yourself?"

"Mrs. Whelan and Annie Bosworth picked out most of the newer furniture. They know my preferences pretty well. They worked with what I've collected over the years. I was going to rent it out but changed my mind. I mostly use it as a guest house for friends of friends who need a place to get away."

"You should charge them. You could probably get $150 a night for it. It's everyone's fantasy of a house by the sea."

"I enjoy making a gift of it," he said. The suitcases went in the bedroom, which was large and painted pale yellow, with an open-beamed whitewashed ceiling and fireplace. It was newly carpeted with Berber carpeting—thickly napped, oatmeal-colored, and probably very expensive. A queen-sized bed with a down comforter and about ten pillows sat plumply by a big window. On one side of the bed was a smallish antique *tansu* topped by a big Chinese-style brass lamp and bowl of flowers; on the other was an inlaid game table that looked mid-eighteenth century. An easy chair covered in flowered chintz was next to the fireplace. Unstudied, casual elegance. It reeked of good breeding. There was also a tall, fairly massive bleached wood cabinet-bookcase sort of affair on one wall that had doors. Two of the doors were opened, revealing a pullout desk with a Macintosh computer and printer on it.

"Okay, what's this?" I asked.

"I liked yours so much, I traded my IBM for it when I came home. I thought you might be inspired, so I brought it out here."

I walked over to the computer and examined it. It was the same model as mine. A box of blank disks stood in front of it. Several word processing programs were stacked on the side of the desk. This was a man, I thought, who left no stone unturned.

"I brought along the manuscript for Saul's and my book, just for bedtime tinkering," I said. "Maybe I'll feel like doing some real work on it. We're nearly to the last chapter."

"I'll need to use the computer while you're here," Mac said. He was opening the closet door and turning on the light. "I'll just come out here instead of taking it back in the house." I nodded. "I'm doing a column, by the way," he said.

I turned, startled. "You are?"

"I've sold it to nine smallish papers so far, all of them dailies. I get ten bucks per column."

"That isn't bad," I said. It sure wasn't. "Does it appear daily?"

"Twice a week," he said.

"Reflections on the human condition?"

"Sort of. A little humor, a little of this, and a little of that. I'm feeling my way along. So far people seem to like it. When I get it a bit more refined, I'll try to syndicate it."

"What do you call it?"

"I don't. I just use my name."

"Well, it's catchy," I said. "And better than 'Big Mac' or 'Mac-a-roni.'"

He smirked. "Or 'Mac the Knife.' I'm afraid to let you see any of them."

"Why?"

"You're a writer. You know why."

I thought for a minute. "Yes," I said. I'd never minded sending my manuscripts out to a new editor, to somebody who didn't know me. Showing them to an editor I knew, or to a good friend, was like opening a vein. You know how it is—impersonal criticism is just *life*; personal criticism is torture.

"You don't have to show me if you don't want," I said. "I do understand."

"No, I will," he said, waving his hand at me. "But not now." He walked to the bedroom door and put his arms up, bracing himself in the frame, rocking slightly. "I'm very glad you're here," he said.

"Well," I said, "so am I."

He let his arms drop, then held out a hand to me. "Come on, let's go over to the house and I'll introduce you to Mrs. Whelan."

SHE WAS PLUMP AND SIXTYISH, gray-haired, rosy-cheeked, and very hearty. She grabbed me as we were introduced, hugging me to her ample bosom. She was as good a hugger as I'd encountered. I laughed and glanced at Mac. He winked. "Welcome, welcome," she said jovially, patting me thoroughly and then letting go of me. I imagined that Willard Scott greeted people like that.

"Thank you," I said. "It's good to be here."

She regarded me carefully. "It's about time!" she said.

"For what?" I asked.

"Never mind. Just take the tour of the house, and I'll bring you two some cider and cookies. It'll be a couple of hours before dinner."

We left the kitchen, a flowery room that had a red tile floor, glossy dark green walls, and white window trim, with wood cabinets painted white and big brass knobs on the doors. The parlor, a big room with an open-beamed ceiling and a sixteen-foot-tall Monterey rock fireplace, featured a wall of window that looked toward the ocean. Through it I could see the porch that circled the house. Bleached wicker chairs with faded red India-print pillows on the seats sat facing outward on the porch, a weather-beaten wood table between them. I recognized this as the setting for the sunset chats Dave Higgins had talked about in his columns.

The furnishings here in the parlor were similar to those in the cottage, only more stereotypically masculine. The sofa was dark blue cotton duck, the rug a large, old red Bokhara that was still thick and beautiful. Two easy chairs slipcovered in a dark red and gold stripe faced the sofa next to the fireplace. Everything was nicely worn but not tattered. A lovely old oil painting of two dogs leaned against the wall on the single-beam mantel. Bookcases were recessed into the wall on each side of the fireplace, and they were crammed with books and memorabilia.

"Nice room," I said, walking to the window. "You'll have to tell me about each of your paintings, you know."

"Okay. But not now. Want to see the rest of the house?"

"Of course."

He led me to the small dining room that held a good-sized antique table and six chairs, a Welsh cupboard with assorted old pottery displayed haphazardly on its shelves, and a sideboard that matched nothing but fit perfectly in the room. Over the sideboard was a large mirror framed in mahogany.

Through a hallway we approached two bedrooms—the smaller one with a mahogany double-sized sleigh bed and a beautiful old dresser and mirror, also mahogany, on a large antique Kirman rug. The master bedroom was a very large chamber, at least 18 by 22, dominated by a stone fireplace Mac said was part of the original ranch, dating to the 1880s. The ceiling was beamed but whitewashed, the walls off-white and covered with more paintings that revealed Mac's eclectic taste. In front of the fireplace was a comfortable-looking sofa flanked by a pair of round antique tables and unmatched cloisonné lamps. One was lit, giving the room a cozy look. By the bed, on the floor, were two stacks of books and about twenty magazines in a pile. I turned and glanced at Mac, who seemed to be appraising the room and my reaction to it.

"You have great taste," I said. "This is a marvelous house."

He grinned at me. "It's home."

I looked back at the room again. "It sure is," I said.

We went back through the hall to the parlor. "Want to sit on the porch?" Mac asked.

"Sure," I said. We went out by way of the French doors next to the picture window and sat in the wicker chairs.

Mrs. Whelan came out then with the cider and cookies. Little sugar cookies with pressed designs, home-made and rich.

She stood by while we each ate a cookie. "Delicious," I said. She beamed and left us.

We sat and stared out at the trees, at the sunlight on the shrubs and flowers, at the ocean that looked like a vision of Xanadu.

"How can you work here?" I asked. "Aren't you constantly distracted by all this?"

"I was, the first few months I lived here. Then I started taking it for granted, I suppose. I'm still drawn to it, but it no longer pulls me away from anything important."

I thought about it. I guessed that after a time a person could take almost anything for granted. Even this.

15

Dinner was fresh salmon with dill sauce, spinach soufflé, sourdough bread, and tiny little boiled potatoes dunked in garlic butter and sprinkled with fresh parsley. We sat at the old round walnut table in the dining room, lights dimmed, fresh flowers between us, two pink candles lit. Mrs. Whelan had outdone herself. By now it was dark outside, the kind of inky dark you only see in the country or in the middle of the ocean. Mrs. Whelan came out of the kitchen and stood by the table with her hands on her hips, looking at the table and at us.

"I'll just be getting along now," she said. "I've got a meeting tonight, so if you want dessert it's in the fridge. Chocolate mousse, nothing fancy. Leave it if you don't want it, I won't mind." She started out of the room. "I'll see you tomorrow, kiddies," she said.

"The dinner is beautiful, Mrs. Whelan," I called after her.

"Nothing fancy, not like you're used to, but it's all fresh," she said. The back door slammed.

"She's amazing," I said.

Mac nodded. "That she is."

We ate for a while in silence, savoring the exquisite flavor of the salmon, the herbs, the garlic, everything. The Benny

Goodman Quartet was playing "Dinah" on the stereo in the parlor. Next came Earl Hines with "My Melancholy Baby" and Jimmy McPartland with "China Boy."

"Does Mrs. Whelan live here?" I asked, curious. I wondered if there might be other quarters hidden in the trees somewhere.

"No. She lives about six miles up the road. She's been a widow for some years. Has worked for me for five. She comes around when she gets ready, usually 10 or 11, and stays until after dinner. She's a good friend."

"I can tell."

We lapsed into companionable silence, eating until our plates were empty. We decided to put off dessert. Mac went into the kitchen to make coffee while I cleared the table.

Back in the living room, he built a fire and we sank into the easy chairs. I looked for the stereo speakers and found them built into the bookcases. Andre Previn's album *Music of Young Hollywood Composers* was playing, and it struck me that these composers were no longer young. The room smelled of good food and burning wood.

We talked about my finished Bridget Caulfield manuscript. Mac talked about his newspapers, about local politics and his latest activist projects. Then he told me about his horses and about the dead whale that had washed up on the beach several days before and was lying there, rotting in the sun, while officials tried to decide what to do with it. We went to the window and looked through the telescope at the stars, then walked out on the porch and sat on the railing, listening to the crickets and night sounds. Inside, a swinging rendition of "I've Found a New Baby" was playing.

"Is that the Chicago Rhythm Kings?" I asked, unable to believe my ears.

He nodded. "George Wettling's group."

"Charlie Teagarden on trumpet?"

"Mm-hm," he said. "Let's see if I can remember—Danny Polo on clarinet, Joe Marsala on tenor sax, Floyd O'Brien on trombone, Jess Stac piano, Artie Shapiro bass, and—hmmm—Bland, somebody Bland on guitar. Do you remember? Jake, no, *Jack* Bland."

I smiled. Mac seemed to take it for granted that I, the jazz aficionado, would remember all those great musicians. Actually, I figured, he and I might be the only two people within 500 miles who recalled that there ever *was* a George Wettling's Chicago Rhythm Kings band. I wondered whether he had their recording of "There'll Be Some Changes Made," the one with the vocal by Red MacKenzie. After a few minutes I asked him.

He didn't answer but walked into the house. In a couple of minutes I heard the scratchy recording start up. When he came back outside I beamed up at him. "You are a man of exceptional taste in music," I said.

We went on listening to more of his eclectic collection—Lena Horne's "Stormy Weather," Bing Crosby and Connie Boswell's "Between 18th and 19th on Chestnut Street," and Paul Specht and his orchestra's "Bye Bye Baby." We finished up with Woody Herman and His Woodchoppers—Joe Philips on sax, Sonny Berman on trumpet, Bill Harris on trombone, the great Jimmy Rowles on piano, Charlie Jagelka on guitar, Joe Mondragon and Don Lamond on bass and drums. And the incomparable Red Norvo on vibraphone. What a group!

By 11:30 I was yawning. I told Mac it was my bedtime. He nodded and got up, and we walked together to the cottage, hand in hand. At the front door he stopped and gently pulled me toward him, then reached out and touched my face, the same sort of gesture I remembered from the morning after my birthday in Minneapolis. He was wearing Old Spice again, too.

He kissed me then, very tenderly, and we held each other. A

lush orchestral arrangement of "My Funny Valentine" was floating down the hill from the house. Pure magic.

Finally, after several minutes, while we were still embracing, Mac spoke softly into my hair. "There's something I have to say, Sally." *Oh, no you don't,* I thought. Then I thought, *Saul was only kidding. He and Angela would still be my friends if I went back to Minneapolis tomorrow.*

There was a long silence.

"I have never wanted anything in my life," Mac said at last, "as much as I want to make love to you right now."

I breathed into his shoulder. What man had I ever known, in forty-four long years, who was capable of uttering such uncool, absolutely amazing words? Only Mac. I was nonplussed.

"Let me correct that," he added. "There's one thing I want more." I pulled away from him slightly so I could see his eyes in the dim glow of the lamp we'd left burning inside the cottage that afternoon. I didn't say a word.

"More than I want to *make* love to you, I want to *love* you," he said.

I blinked. It was the only response that occurred to me.

Mac was watching me intently. "I don't know what you expected when you came here," he said, "but I want to be very clear about everything that happens between us so there won't be any misunderstandings."

I blinked again. Holding up my end of this conversation was turning out to be easy, at least.

Mac's face was about five inches from mine. He drew in a deep breath and let it out slowly. "Right. Clear as swamp water," he muttered. "Hmm . . . What am I trying to say? I want to tell you what I'm *feeling* as well as the things I'm *thinking* right now. Does that make sense?"

"Oh," I said. He was peering at me, waiting for more. Instead of speaking, I raised my eyebrows questioningly.

He plunged ahead. "I *feel* extremely—ah—*passionate* toward you at the moment. But I *think* it would be a bad idea to cloud the issues we have to deal with right now by getting, well, too *intensely* passionate. So I'm *talking* about how I feel instead of *doing* anything about it. That way you won't have to play guessing games, and neither will I."

Good grief, I said to myself. *Where is this headed? Is he trying to be chivalrous or what? Does he think I came out here expecting to jump into his bed? The nerve of him.*

"I don't know how to respond," I said finally. "I'm not even sure I fully understand what you're trying to tell me." I was starting to wonder exactly what I *did* expect when I came out here.

"Okay," he said, staring down at his feet, thinking. "To put it as plainly as I know how, it's crossed my mind that you might wonder—if not now, maybe later—why I don't make, umm, well—physical *advances* toward you. Sexual advances. Because I'm not going to."

"Aha," I said. Things were getting clearer. Even in the darkness, I could see Mac was blushing. I wondered whether he could see me doing the same thing.

"I don't want to do anything that could leave us with regrets," he went on, "or with a need to ask forgiveness . . . From each other or from God."

"Aha again."

He stared at me. "Do you understand what I'm trying to say?"

I was thinking it over. "You'd have regrets if we made love and then didn't stay together forever?" It had been at least twenty years since I'd heard the words "made love" spoken aloud by adults. The more graphic terms for it were the only ones anybody seemed to use any more. That was too bad, I thought.

"Yes," he said. "I'd have huge regrets. Wouldn't you?" He was looking at me very seriously.

"Now that you mention it."

"Well," he said, "okay, then. Good. That much is cleared up, at least."

Yes, I decided, we were hopelessly square. So Saul was probably right about Republicans and leap years. Big deal.

Mac touched my cheek lightly. "What are you thinking?"

"I'm thinking," I said, "that you are the most singular, the most astonishing man on this planet. Without a doubt. I don't know what to do with you," I said.

"It's a start," he said, shrugging.

"Yes," I said. "I suppose it is that."

He hugged me to him again, and then we kissed one more time, a lingering and many-splendored kiss. I wondered how on earth he'd learned to be such a world-class kisser. In high school he hadn't done a thing to my pulse. For some reason I was jealous of whoever had helped him develop this skill. Probably Sarah, I decided. Then I thought, no, not the Sarah I'd seen in that photo in the *Alumni News*. It must have been somebody else.

When we let go of each other, Mac gave me a look that was full of longing. Then he smiled, took me by the shoulders, turned me around, and gave me a gentle push through the door. He turned and walked up the path toward the house. *How about that*, I thought. *He really meant it.*

For about an hour I lay on the bed in the dark watching the stars through the big window and listening to the crickets and night sounds. From the house, very faintly, I heard the last few notes of a Haydn string quartet. Then I drifted off.

16

The next day I slept until after 9, waking up refreshed and energetic. The room was cool, perhaps 55 degrees, so I turned on the space heater in the bedroom before I showered and dressed in navy and white checked wool pants and a red, bulky turtleneck sweater.

Mac was in the kitchen with Mrs. Whelan when I got to the house. He was outfitted like a cowboy in worn jeans, tooled leather pointy-toed boots that had seen better days, and a faded denim work shirt. He was making potato pancakes. Mrs. Whelan turned to look at me as I walked in.

"Morning," she said, smiling a secret little smile. "Sleep well?"

I nodded, straight-faced, as Mac glanced in my direction. "Like a top, thanks," I said. "You?"

Mrs. Whelan snorted. "I always sleep ... Like a dead person."

She was scrubbing a pot at the sink, working hard at it. Mac said, "I hope you're hungry."

"Starved," I said. He was at the stove, a big old cast-iron and porcelain affair. He was cooking the pancakes in a giant cast-iron skillet.

I got out the plates and some napkins. When Mac was finished, we took our pancakes and condiments out to the porch and ate them from our laps, feet braced against the porch railing.

"Yum," I said. "I will be fat and sassy after this."

"Let's go for a walk, then," he said.

"Good."

We walked along the roads around his property for about two hours, stopping to look at flowers, sitting in the shade of the big trees, looking at the ocean and the sky, holding hands. It was cool and sunny.

"There has to be a flaw in all this," I said as we stared at the scene from the top of a hill. "I'll bet the San Andreas Fault runs right under your house."

"Sorry," he said. "It runs out to sea near Point Reyes. In fact, Tomales Bay *is* the Fault. When San Francisco falls into the ocean, we'll be up here taking in the refugees."

"Ah," I smiled, "there's the rub. This whole area will be wall-to-wall interior decorators. Even the trees and rocks will have slipcovers."

"Look on the bright side," he said. "At least we'll get some good restaurants."

We went home about 1 o'clock, and I felt sleepy. Mac asked to use the computer in my bedroom to work on some columns. I napped on the bed, covered with a small quilt, while he worked.

Later Mac was bending over me touching my nose. I opened my eyes. Without thinking, I reached up and put my arms around his neck, pulling his mouth down so I could kiss it. It was extremely pleasant.

"You've slept for two hours. Need more?" he asked when we stopped.

I thought about it. "Nope."

"How about a drive?"

"Okay."

WE HEADED OUT ALONG THE SAME ROAD we'd followed getting home the day before, but turned north at the intersection with Highway One. Mac asked about Saul and Angela as we drove. He laughed as I recounted some of Saul's latest stories about his patients, which he swore were completely true.

One of them was about a twenty-year-old woman who was obsessed with a fear of death. Saul asked her why she was afraid of dying at such a young age, and she replied very earnestly, "I don't mind dying young, I just want to be as old as possible when I do it." Another story involved a woman whose sanity he was asked to evaluate for a murder trial. She had split her husband's skull with a carpenter's hammer. When Saul asked why she had used a hammer, she responded, cheerfully, "A fly landed on his head, and the hammer was there. I wasn't trying to hurt my husband—I was just trying to kill the fly. That's no crime, is it?" Saul claimed the woman was eventually let off with probation.

We drove for about an hour, cutting off to follow country roads, eventually pulling back onto Highway One north. He asked about Matt; so I told him about his studies, how brilliantly he was doing, what a fantastic kid he was. Just the facts, of course. He asked about Valerie and said he was glad they were still together. Then we spun along for a while without talking.

"Want to head home, or would you like to see St. Stephen's-by-the-Bay?" Mac asked after some miles.

"What's that?" I asked.

"The church I belong to. I promised Amos Whitcomb he'd get to meet you. He's a great fan of yours."

"Your priest friend?"

"Yes."

"By all means," I said. "I try never to miss an opportunity to reinforce the devotion of a fan."

A few miles north we cut off the highway again, headed inland and upward perhaps a quarter mile, then north again down a county road until we came to a turn marked by a large sign topped by a cross. The church name was in large, obviously hand-carved letters, and that was followed by a listing of the times of daily and Sunday services. An arrow pointed up the hill. We wended our way perhaps another eighth of a mile through dense trees and flowering shrubs, finally coasting into the court-yard of a small, red church. It reminded me of the old song that went, "Come to the church in the wildwood, come to the church in the vale." It was tucked into a hillside full of lush foliage.

As we parked, a priest bounded out of the side door of the church and across the gravel parking lot toward us as if he'd seen us coming. He was about sixty and silver-haired, a very tall man, slightly balding, wearing Earth Shoes and a long black cassock. His face was narrow and chiseled, with bright, very intelligent eyes and a long, aristocratic nose. This face was set upon very broad, muscular shoulders that made his cassock look like it was too small for him. It was the head of Edward Woodward, "The Equalizer," grafted onto the body of Victor from *Beauty and the Beast.*

"Halloo," he shouted at us, grabbing our hands and hugging us each in succession after he skidded to a stop. "So *this* is Bridget Caulfield! Welcome!"

"Father Whitcomb," I said with a smile. "It's a pleasure."

"When did you get here?" he asked.

"Yesterday." I looked around. "I haven't been to this part of California before," I said. "It's incredible. Other-worldly."

"Isn't it amazing?" Father Whitcomb said, swooping his arms outward to encompass our surroundings. "I am always astounded," he said, "to find that anyone could be depressed here. But they can. Just the same as anywhere."

"I suppose so," I said. "But I agree, it's hard to believe."

"Well, look at you—you're walking just fine! You know, we prayed for you around the clock after the accident. Are you 100 percent these days?" Father Whitcomb eyed me like a hawk spotting a mouse from the air.

"About 99 percent," I said. "Still a twinge in the head now and then. Nothing to complain about."

"Well, we must just keep praying," he said, grinning happily at Mac and me as if he were glad he didn't have to stop. "But isn't it a miracle that you're all in one piece? I remember when Mac called us and said they didn't expect you to live. This is a great day."

I looked at Mac. He put his arm casually around my shoulders. I moved away slightly.

Father Whitcomb glanced back and forth between us. "Well, come on inside," he said. "I'm just about to have some coffee. Freshly ground Jamaica Blue Mountain. My friends the Havermeiers from the City drove up and brought me three pounds of it today. Isn't that marvelous?" He was delighted, rubbing his hands together.

We went inside and chatted while he made the coffee, poured it into large brown mugs, and handed one to each of us. Then we followed him out the door again.

"You will want to come to a retreat," he said to me, walking along energetically. "We do nothing for two days but seek God. There's no conversation, no idle chatter. We just concentrate on knowing the Lord better. It's transforming. Right, Mac?"

Mac nodded. "Yes, it is," he said.

Did he mean it? I looked at him and decided he did. Two and a half days without talking? I could not imagine such an experience.

"The first one next month perhaps," Father Whitcomb said. "There's a women's retreat. I think all the retreats this month are fully booked."

"I'm afraid I'll be back in Minneapolis by then," I said.

He looked at me, stopping. He looked at Mac, eyebrows up. Mac shrugged.

"Ah, well," the priest said, smiling broadly, charging forward again. "We have plenty of time to change your mind."

"Oh," I said, laughing, "you and Mac have plans along those lines, do you?"

"No, no, no," he said. "I wouldn't bring Mac into it." He shook his head and wrapped one arm behind him, a beatific smile on his face.

I stared at him and laughed again. "I see," I said.

"Good," he said, giving me a sidelong glance and charging along a path that led straight up toward a stand of enormous eucalyptus. Mac and I were breathing hard from the exertion, but he was breathing normally.

He gave us the cook's tour of the grounds, stomping through overgrown paths and up steep inclines to show us every vantage point. I was winded. The church property apparently encompassed about fifty acres, most of it with ocean vistas.

"Mr. and Mrs. Leland Portsmith owned most of this area from about 1912 on. She sold off whole sections at a time, then sold individual pieces of land to people from the Bay area who wanted to build summer homes on it. Finally she was left with this acreage in addition to her own property, which is adjacent to this over the ridge. She was Episcopalian, and she wanted to be able to worship when she retired here in the late 1930s; so she donated this land to the Diocese and paid to build the church on the condition that they furnish a priest and pay for upkeep.

"I'm only the second priest to serve this parish," he went on. "The first one stayed almost twenty-six years. He died after delivering a sermon about the Resurrection. Just turned from the pulpit and dropped to the floor with a smile on his face." He grinned at us. "What a way to go," he said. There was envy in his voice.

"Has Mac told you about the retreat center we're building?" he asked me, glancing at Mac.

"No," I said, also glancing at Mac. He was standing with his hands in his pockets looking innocent. I guessed I was going to hear about the retreat center whether I wanted to or not.

Father Whitcomb pointed down the mountainside. I could see about six small white cottages sprinkled over the slope. "We'll have twenty more cottages within a year, each self-contained with a full bath and a living-sleeping room furnished with a good bed, a sofa and comfortable chair, and a desk. A fireplace for heat. Each cottage very private, with a small patio or deck. And the ocean view, of course." He smiled broadly, envisioning the cottages. "I'll show you the floor plans when you come again. Every detail will enhance meditation and reflection. The furnishings will be simple; most of the bedspreads and linens and even the slipcovers for the chairs and sofas are already being made by the seamstresses and artisans of the parish. A wonderful artist is doing a series of paintings, one for each cottage—based on the Psalms of David. We believe it's important that when people come here to be alone with God, they have comfortable surroundings, but with as few distractions as possible," he said. "So we are keeping everything quite plain."

"It's a tremendous undertaking," I said. "Especially for so small a parish." That was an understatement. It staggered the imagination. Even without the need to purchase land and using local labor, I guessed the twenty cottages would have to cost close to half a million dollars.

"I never in my wildest dreams could have envisioned that God could provide as He has for this project," Amos Whitcomb went on. "We've not had to ask for a penny from anyone. Of course, that's how this parish has operated ever since I got here. We never ask for money; we just let people give as they're moved by God's Spirit. As a result we have far more than we can use here, and we're able to help meet needs in the community and in other parishes. We give away more money to missions than we keep here for local use." He put his hands on his hips, looking across the hillside as he took in a deep breath. "Well," he said, "isn't it exciting? We begin construction next week. We've been planning for—what, nearly two years, Mac?"

Mac nodded.

"It sounds idyllic and restorative," I said. I meant it. I could imagine how it would look, how it would appeal to the weary sojourner looking for a couple of days' break from stress. It would even appeal to me.

"We'll follow the path down the other side of the hill," Father Whitcomb said, "and I'll show you the church."

The building itself, clearly the work of craftsmen, was a masterpiece of simplicity and understatement. Attached to the back end of the church by a long catwalk suspended over a small ravine was a little whitewashed stone cottage that was Amos Whitcomb's home. Flower-dotted vines nearly covered the side and back of the cottage.

He pointed at the deck that hung from the front over the ravine. "I sit here at night and know that I am the most fortunate man on earth," he said. "I've been here twenty-five years next month, and I feel like I've just arrived."

He took us into the sanctuary then. It was a larger church than it appeared to be from the outside. Maybe 250 people could squeeze into the pews if they all sat skinny. Father Whitcomb stood with us for a few moments, staring up at the tall, unadorned golden cross that dominated the main altar. Giant ceramic vases with bountiful bouquets of cabbage roses, irises, baby's breath, jonquils, and white field daisies stood on each side of the altar, clearly the gleanings of a local gardener. Father Whitcomb looked at me, his eyes asking if I felt as thrilled as he did. He didn't speak. He looked around the sanctuary, face alive and slightly flushed. I was reminded again of General Patton looking out over his battlefield. It was interesting, I thought, how passion could take so many different forms.

Mac looked at Father Whitcomb, then at me, smiled, and took my hand. Finally, as we started back to the car in high spirits, Father Whitcomb looked at his watch. His face went pale. "Oh, no," he said, panic in his voice. "I'm late for a counseling session *again*. Effie will be pulling her hair out. You must pray for me. I have absolutely no sense of time. There's no excuse for this." He held out his hand to me, then thought better of it and hugged me instead.

"Well, I hope we'll see you both on Sunday. I wait for Easter all year long. We'll have great music. It will be a fantastic celebration." He glanced over his shoulder. A sixtyish woman was standing on the doorstep at the side of the church looking like a mother about to yell, "Amos, you get in here right *now!*"

"Sally, we must get together," he said, ducking his head. "Mac, you arrange it with Effie and have her put it on my calendar. We have so much to talk about. I want to have a chance to get to know you before you try to escape." With that he hugged me again, as if unable to contain himself. I hugged him back, laughing. He hugged Mac, too. He was an even better hugger than Mrs. Whelan.

And off he went to meet the couple that now stood next to the older woman outside the side door to the church. I heard the man speak to him, watched him hug the man and then the woman, then both of them together. The woman appeared to be crying.

"Is Effie his wife?" I asked Mac. I wondered how the two of them could live in that tiny cottage.

"No. She's the church secretary and den mother. Amos was

married as a young man, for about seven years. His wife died of cancer shortly before he entered the priesthood."

"Oh, that's too bad. But that had to be thirty years ago or more. I'm surprised he's never remarried. He's an attractive man."

"He feels he is married."

I thought about it. "I guess he is," I said. Then after a moment I said, "I'd like to see him again." I meant it. He was intriguing, magnetic. I was beginning to understand why Mac would want to be close to him.

"Maybe he could come to our place for dinner one night this week. I'll check with Effie."

Our place? I smiled to myself. This man was as transparent as Saran Wrap. What *was* I going to do with him?

"That would be nice," I said. "Maybe Mrs. Whelan would let me cook."

"Sure," he said. "She'd think you were showing signs of settling into domesticity. It would make her day."

"Gulp," I said. "I may want to rethink this."

"How often do you get to make someone's day? And at so little cost?"

AS WE REACHED THE CAR I looked back toward the church. Amos Whitcomb had disappeared, along with Effie and his two counselees.

"Let's come to church on Easter," I said. I had the feeling it would be a spectacle, and I didn't want to miss it.

"Great," Mac said, giving me a look that said he hadn't expected this. At that moment I realized I'd just made a sort of commitment to stay another six days.

As he reached around me to open the car door, Mac glanced up into my face and crinkled his eyes slightly. Then the other arm came around me and he kissed me, right there in front of God and St. Stephen's-by-the-Bay.

I thought for a moment about Amos Whitcomb looking out a window and catching us. Then, in the same instant, I knew that if he did, he'd probably applaud.

17

Dinner that night was fresh bay scallops. Mrs. Whelan gave me her recipe:

2 pounds fresh bay scallops (enough for four people)
Flour for dredging
Sea salt and fresh ground pepper
5 shallots or 6-8 green onions, minced finely
3 cloves of garlic, minced
2 tablespoons of minced fresh tarragon
3-4 tablespoons of minced fresh parsley
1 cup of white cooking wine
Olive oil
Butter

Dry the scallops thoroughly, toss them in the flour mixed with a pinch of salt and a good sprinkling of pepper. Heat about two tablespoons of olive oil and two tablespoons of butter together in a big skillet. When the butter starts sizzling, shake off the scallops and cook them over high heat, stir-frying them quickly, for about a minute. They should be brown but not overcooked. Remove them to a warm dish.

Toss the shallots or onions and garlic into the pan, stirring them and scraping up all the leavings from the scallops. Then add the wine all at once. Bring to a boil, add the tarragon and parsley, and cook on high for a couple of minutes to reduce the liquid somewhat. Turn down the heat to medium, put the scallops back in the pan, and let them simmer in the sauce for about 30 to 60 seconds. Serve with rice, corn muffins, and a green salad with fresh, ripe tomatoes.

Mac and I lingered over the meal. The tiny corn muffins had been baked in a muffin tin that turned them into cunning little puffed animals—lions, bears, cats, birds. Sweet butter straight from a farm down the road made them better than dessert. After we'd finished, we were handed cups of strong decaffeinated French roast coffee to take out to the porch. Mrs. Whelan announced that there was no dessert except fruit. I was thankful.

As we sat on the porch with Mozart serenading us from the parlor, I heard a car pull up the gravel drive around the front of the house. Mac glanced over his shoulder, eased himself out of his chair, and went to see who it was. A few minutes later he came back onto the porch with a man following him.

"Sally, this is Dave Higgins," he said. "You've heard me talk about him." Alistair Cooke had followed them outside. He sat next to my chair watching the action with a look of bored skepticism.

I stood, surprised to see that Dave was shorter than I. "Hello," I said, shaking his hand. "I'm a fan of yours." I always thought celebrities were tall people.

"It's mutual," he said. He grinned at me for several seconds, then glanced at Mac. "Old man, you neglected to mention the fact that Sally and Jamie Lee Curtis could be sisters." So help me, that's what he said.

"You may gather," said Mac, putting his arm around my

shoulder in a proprietary gesture, "that Dave has an adolescent crush on Jamie Lee Curtis."

"Used to have. You are better," Dave said, still grinning at me. "Substantially better. For one thing, you are here—in the flesh, so to speak."

He had dark wavy hair, cut short, and eyes like Michael Dukakis, sort of squinty and slanting downward at the edges with heavy eyebrows over them like thick horizontal apostrophes. I could forgive him for that in light of his evaluation of me. Charity begets charity.

"The resemblance is phenomenal," he said, not letting go of my hand.

"Except for the fact that I outweigh her by a good thirty pounds, you're undoubtedly correct," I said. I wondered why nobody else had ever pointed out this resemblance. Maybe they were jealous.

"Fifteen pounds maximum," Dave said. "And she's too skinny, anyway. It's her only fault." *Well,* I thought, *Michael Dukakis isn't such a bad-looking guy when you get down to it. Sort of cute, actually.* I had known several cute Democrats. Now I knew one more.

Mac went to the end of the porch and brought back another chair. We sat. Dave could not take his eyes off me. I was getting fidgety.

"Well, I hope you two are having fun," Dave said, glancing sideways at Mac. "Seeing the sights and all."

"We are," Mac said.

"Right," I said.

"Glad to hear it," Dave said. Then, to me: "Have you ever thought of cutting your hair more shaggy? And wearing it all tousled?"

I grinned, realizing as I did so that my gums were showing. I smiled a smaller smile. "As a matter of fact, that's sort of the way I wore my hair in high school."

Mac laughed. "In high school you looked like Janet Leigh. Now you look like her daughter. That's what I call progress."

"I was devastating," I said. I wondered uncomfortably if both of them were putting me on.

"Do you have a picture from high school?" Dave inquired. He looked serious.

I looked at Mac. "He's serious?"

"You'd better get used to it. I think he's going to attach himself to you like a limpet. You'll never get rid of him."

Dave was gazing at me almost worshipfully. Mac shot him a glance that said, "Stop being a moron." He didn't stop.

"We drove over to St. Stephen's-by-the-Bay today," I offered, hoping to change the direction of the conversation. "Do you know Amos Whitcomb?"

"Very well," Dave said. "We play chess together every other Tuesday night. He always wins."

"Really?" I said, surprised.

"Amos is the only Christian I've ever known who hasn't tried to convert me," he said, "which probably means he'll be the one to do it." He looked over at Mac. "Even Mac tells me I'm a lousy agnostic. And since I'm not guilt-ridden enough to be a good Jew or Catholic, that leaves me in limbo."

I laughed. "A little guilt improves most people. Maybe you should work on that."

"No," he said. "If I felt any guiltier I'd have to give up lusting after women. And I can't give that up because it's the closest I come to having a virtue. You see what we're dealing with."

"Sounds like you're wallowing in filth and degradation to me," I said.

"True," Dave said. "But Amos Whitcomb plays chess with me, so I can't be hopeless."

We passed the next couple of hours in conversation about Dave's syndicated columns, which were now appearing in 112 newspapers. That day he had lampooned animal activists by focusing on the attempts of a group of marine mammal protectionists to cordon off an area of beach about a half-mile long to protect the carcass of the dead whale that still lay there waiting for somebody to decide what to do with it.

I defended the activists, Dave called me a bleeding-heart whale-lover, and the discussion degenerated from there. Finally I predicted that Dave's stand on the whale would cost him the Pulitzer prize. He countered that if Dave Barry could win it, anybody could, remarking that he and Dave Barry shared not only the same first name but also fell under the same astrological sign and owned identical cars. I was unsure what that proved, but thinking he might have been trying to impress me with obtuse Dukakis-style repartee, I generously let it pass without comment.

We ended the evening by listening to a few cuts of Teddy Wilson and his orchestra. I hadn't heard some of these, which featured Billie Holiday on the vocals and Benny Goodman on clarinet. "What a Little Moonlight Can Do" and "If You Were Mine" were followed by "Miss Brown to You." When Billie started on "I'm Just Foolin' Myself" I immediately felt like the felon on the lam who imagines that every police car in the state is after him.

Ah, Billie, I thought, *you and me both.*

TUESDAY MORNING MAC KNOCKED ON MY DOOR at 9:15, just as I was getting dressed. I opened to him, pulling on a crewneck multi-color hand knit sweater over my pale yellow cotton turtleneck and jeans as he followed me into the bedroom. He was dressed for business in a navy blazer and gray wool slacks. Just when I started to get down-home, he went formal. Wasn't that always the way?

"I have to drive over to Santa Rosa for a meeting this morning. Can you entertain yourself here, or would you like to come with me and do some shopping? I'll probably be gone until about 2."

I thought about it as I put on some lipstick. "Maybe I'll stay here and work on the computer for a while. I have some ideas I'd like to get down for Saul to work on until I get back. Do you think tomorrow we could next-day-air a disk to Chicago?"

"Sure. I'll be driving in to Sebastopol tomorrow anyway. You can come with me then, or I'll do it for you."

"Great," I said. Alistair Cooke had sneaked into the cottage when I opened the door for Mac, and now he was ensconced on the bed, head wedged between two pillows, blissfully asleep. I reached over and petted him. His ears twitched, but he didn't open his eyes.

Mac shook his head. "That cat knows a soft touch when he sees it."

I smiled at him. He was studying me. Probably thinking how much I looked like Jamie Lee Curtis. He walked over to me and said, "Good morning, by the way" and kissed me. It was not exactly a casual kiss. *Boy*, I thought, *there should be a kissing Olympics for somebody like this.* It was a much better talent than waiting. It had to be what he did best. Then again, maybe it wasn't.

After that, he waved good-bye and left.

I went over to the house a few minutes later, having reapplied my lipstick so as to avoid sniggering remarks by Mrs. Whelan, who seemed to believe something was going on between Mac and me, which of course it was not.

"Morning," she said heartily as I entered the kitchen. "I told him not to wake you. Has he left?"

"Yes. There's a meeting in Santa Rosa." Alistair Cooke had followed me from the cottage and was now sniffing under the cabinets next to the sink, looking for microscopic scraps of food.

Mrs. Whelan poured about half a cup of dry nuggets into a small bowl on the floor near the door. Cookie lunged for it, burying his face and crunching noisily the way you'd expect Garfield might.

"Guess you two had a meeting in your cottage, too," Mrs. Whelan snorted, chuckling as if she'd just made a witty remark.

"Can I fix my own breakfast? I don't want you to bother."

"No bother," she said sincerely. "I came over early so I could do it." She smiled to herself and went to the refrigerator, pulling out some eggs, bacon, heavy homemade whole-wheat-and-oat-meal bread, and butter.

I sat down at the big oak table in the kitchen and watched her doing her chefly duties. She was a model of efficiency, breaking eggs with one hand the way they teach you at Paris cooking schools, whipping them with a wire whisk for a few seconds until they were pale yellow, adding a few drops of water, and then scooping them into the waiting buttered omelette pan. She quickly stirred the eggs with a fork, shaking the pan to loosen the edges, and finally tossed in fresh herbs she'd already chopped on the sideboard. Last of all she added some green onions and shredded Sonoma jack garlic-and-herb cheese and slid the whole omelette onto a plate.

"You're a good enough cook to work at a four-star restaurant," I said. She looked at me as if to check whether I was serious.

"The only thing I know is how to be a wife and mother and cook," she said. "I was never trained for anything else. I'm happy to be able to cook for Mac and his friends. I'd be useless otherwise."

"Well, Mac certainly needs you. I don't know how he'd be able to get along without you."

She smiled at me. "He's a good man," she said.

"Yes, he is."

"He's more like a son than my own two sons," she said. "I

hardly see them anymore. They live in southern California—
L.A. They have their own lives. They're good boys, but they're
selfish." She set the table in front of me with a place mat, knife,
fork, spoon, and a cloth napkin. Then she put the omelette before
me, adding two pieces of toast to the plate before I had a chance
to take the first bite.

"Mmmm," I mmmm'd as I tasted the omelette. It was the best
omelette I'd ever eaten. Bar none. I told her so.

"It's the fresh eggs. Just laid at Mrs. Carpenter's before I came
here this morning. Still warm from the nest." I continued to eat
while she talked. "I like a woman who enjoys food," she said. "It
says something about her character. I never trust skinny women."
Well, say what you would about me, at least I was chubby enough
to pass muster with Mrs. Whelan. I decided then and there to
skip lunch. That's what Jamie Lee Curtis did, I was sure.

"By the way," she said as she sat down at the table to eat a
piece of toast with me, "Effie called to say Father Amos can come
to dinner tomorrow night. I told her 7 o'clock would be fine. I'll
fix beef if that's all right with you. Or are you one of those
women who feels sorry for cows?"

"No," I laughed. "Beef would be great. I feel sorry for cows,
but not sorry enough to stop eating beef." I thought about my
plan to cook the meal, then thought better of it. "I'd enjoy *helping* you with dinner if you can handle an amateur in your
kitchen," I said. "I could learn a lot from you, I think."

She raised her eyebrows skeptically. "I doubt it," she said.
"But you're welcome." She munched on her toast, dunking a corner of the remaining piece in her coffee. Then, without smiling,
she looked at me and said, "I like you."

Surprised, I didn't answer right away. Finally I said, "I like
you, too. I'm so glad you're part of Mac's life."

She glanced up at me from her toast. "I'd think you'd resent
it. I would if I were you."

"Why?"

"Well, you're the new woman in his life, and I'm here in the house doing things you'd probably just as soon do for him." She smiled guiltily. "If I were in your shoes, I'd want to kick me out." She seemed embarrassed to be speaking so frankly.

"Mrs. Whelan, I could never do your work as well as you, and I wouldn't try. Believe me, I'm thankful you're so happy doing all you do for Mac."

She smiled broadly at me.

"Besides," I said, "you're the one who's being generous. This is your domain. I'm just a temporary boarder, after all. It's good of you to be so hospitable."

She looked startled. "What do you mean, *temporary?*"

Now *I* was the one who was startled. "Well, I'm only visiting, after all."

"But you'll be back soon," she said.

"Maybe. This is a vacation for me. I don't take many vacations."

She looked silently into her coffee cup for some ten or fifteen seconds while I continued to eat. Then she looked up at me sharply. "If you break his heart," she said, "you'll have me to answer to."

I felt as if I were talking to Mac's mother and was about to get a royal chewing out.

"Mrs. Whelan, I don't plan to break his heart. He's a wonderful man . . . a dear friend. I care about him. But we have separate lives, in two different parts of the country—with different friends, different work. He has no illusions."

"Then why did you come out here? Mac isn't a man to invite a woman across the country for a little fling." She said it disdainfully but with dignity, the way Ethel Barrymore or Eleanor Roosevelt might have.

"This isn't *a little fling*," I said. Oh boy, this was getting sticky.

"What is it, then?" she said. It didn't occur to her that it was none of her business. Mac was her charge, and I'd better watch my step if I knew what was good for me.

"It's—well, it's friends enjoying each other's company without any preconceived expectations for the future." I liked the sound of that. Neat and modern and noncommittal.

"It's silly, if you ask me," she said, her mouth firmly turned down at the corners. She sipped some coffee, carefully returning the cup to its saucer. I wanted to say I *hadn't* asked her, but I wisely kept my big mouth shut.

"You won't find a better man than Mac," she said after some seconds. "Ever."

"I don't doubt that. But I'm not looking for a man," I said. "I was happy alone for many years before Mac and I met again. He's very special to me, but we're not lovers, Mrs. Whelan. We're friends." I was astonished that I'd said it. What had possessed me? I didn't owe her any explanations.

She looked at me, raising an eyebrow.

"If you were my daughter, I'd tell you to stop acting like a fool and start looking at what you're missing." She paused, taking another sip of coffee. "And I don't mean sex."

I suppressed a smile. "I understand," I said. "I might tell my own daughter the same thing if I had one. But I'd also try to understand that she could be happiest living the kind of life that doesn't include a husband. I'm not very good at being a wife, Mrs. Whelan," I said. "I'm good at living the way I've been living since I was divorced. I'm good at writing, at being a friend, at loving my son. And I'm good at living alone. Can you understand that? You're good at living the way you do, doing the things you're best at. I'm the same way."

She gave it thought. Then she said, "You shouldn't have come here if that's how it is. It can only lead to hurting Mac, and he's had enough of that in his life. He doesn't need more. I'm sorry, but that's how I feel."

"Don't apologize," I said. "I'm flattered that you care enough to say what you think. I admire it." I carried my plate to the sink and ran water on it.

"And, Mrs. Whelan," I said, turning to face her, "you may very well be right. Maybe I shouldn't have come. Maybe it was wrong of me. But believe me, I'll do everything I can to avoid hurting Mac. I promise."

She snorted. "Easy to say," she said. "The man is ga-ga over you. Anybody can see that. He doesn't look on you as just a good friend."

"I didn't mean to say that," I said. "I know Mac loves me. But I don't know what I can do about it at this moment."

She snorted again, a snort that said this is a *dumb* woman I'm dealing with. "Of course you do," she scoffed. "You can do what other people in this world do. You can love him back. And let your work and your friends and all the other particulars take care of themselves."

"Unfortunately," I said, "that's what I did in my first marriage. And it didn't work. It wouldn't make much sense for me to repeat that mistake, would it? Mac would be hurt more by that than he ever could be the way things are now." I paused, thinking.

"Hmmpfh," she said. It meant just what it sounded like it meant.

"You know," I said after a couple of minutes, "I can't explain why I said yes to coming here. I have no excuse, not even an explanation. Maybe when he called me I just lost my head. Maybe he called at a moment when I was tired of being wise and resolute. I'm very fond of Mac. I guess I just wanted to see him again, and he wanted to see me."

I felt helpless to evaluate the situation. Why in the world *had* I come? It wasn't smart, wasn't like me. I'd been foolin' myself, as

Billie would say. And fooling Mac. I'd been playing some sort of complex psychological game, a game I could not begin to fathom at that moment. I'd been pretending that anything was possible, but in reality nothing had changed. It would be a favor to both Mac and me if I paid close attention to that fact.

Mrs. Whelan pushed herself away from the table and stood, brushing at her apron. "Well," she said, "there's no sense beating a dead horse. You'll do what you want to do, and I can't stop you. But I don't like it."

"My promise still holds," I said. "I'll think about it, and I'll do everything in my power to avoid hurting Mac."

She turned away. "Well, I'll start dinner at about 5 tomorrow afternoon. If you come to the kitchen then, I'll put you to work. Tonight I'm just fixing chicken."

"At the moment I'm wondering if I shouldn't go back to Minneapolis tomorrow. I may not be here to help you."

She nodded.

"Thanks for being straight with me," I said. "I appreciate it."

She shook her head slightly and said nothing.

I felt awful.

WHILE MRS. WHELAN ATTACKED the kitchen floor with a scrub brush and a pail of soapy water, I took coffee into the parlor. I tried to persuade her to let me help, but she wouldn't hear of it. "Good for my back," she said. "Keeps me agile." She pronounced it "ay-jile."

I stood at the bookshelves to the right of the fireplace and browsed among the books and memorabilia Mac had arranged haphazardly. There was not an African death mask or fetish or clay pot to be seen. Not a single volume about Paris in the 1920s or the joys of Zen Buddhism. The books showed a wide range of interests, from horse breeding manuals to Lee Iacocca, from *The Medusa and the Snail* to *Fletch*. There were three copies of C. S. Lewis's *Mere Christianity* and a range of other titles with his name on them, from some children's books to *The Problem of Pain* to *The Great Divorce*. There were also three photo albums. I reached for one, then pulled back, feeling somehow intrusive and sneaky. Then I decided Mac wouldn't mind and took it out, walking over to the chair to leaf through it.

There were many shots of Mac's son Christopher, mostly alone or in Mac's arms. He was a good-looking child, all boy, his grin a carbon copy of Mac's. One picture was especially poignant, of Mac holding baby Chris close to his face with a stuffed animal between them. Chris's mouth was open wide with two teeth showing; Mac was laughing. I could almost hear the giggles and the joy. A couple of photos were of Chris with Sarah. Sarah seemed lovely but brittle. Not really cold, just fragile and guarded, as if she might not want to laugh for fear of causing a permanent wrinkle. I wondered whether this was wishful thinking on my part, then shook my head at the realization that I felt a little envious of Sarah.

The album followed the baby from birth through age five, then abruptly stopped, leaving about twenty blank pages. That left me feeling empty and broken-hearted. I put the album back on the shelf and took my coffee out to the porch. It was still chilly, and the fog had not burned off. I sat in one of the wicker chairs, put my feet on the railing, and wept for Mac.

After a few minutes I wiped my eyes and went inside. I thought about looking at the other albums but didn't. I'd ask Mac about them, and if he wanted me to see them, I'd look at them then. With him.

Alistair Cooke followed me back to the cottage and climbed up on the bed again while I took out the book manuscript and began to work at the computer. As my mind focused, the sadness began to subside a little. Then, about an hour into my work, I found myself staring at the screen with tears running down my face again.

I did the only thing I could think to do at that moment. "Oh, God," I said, and I guess it was sort of a prayer, "I don't know the right thing to do."

Then I thought, *I do know the right thing to do. I just don't want to do it.* And the sadness descended again.

18

I was still in the cottage when Mac's Buick pulled into the driveway at about 2 o'clock. I heard the car door slam, then the sound of his footsteps, then his knock on the door.

"Come on in," I called. I saved the work I'd done on the disk and started to make a backup copy.

Mac came in the room and sat in the easy chair. I smiled at him, hoping he wouldn't notice my puffy red eyes. I'd flooded them with Visine, but they still looked bloodshot.

"Get a lot done?" he asked.

"A fair morning's work," I said. "How about you? Was your meeting a success?"

"I think so," he said. "It was a building committee meeting for the retreat center at St. Stephen's. It's a good group. Everybody's pulling in the same direction. That helps."

"Are you in charge?"

"Sort of."

"I'll bet you're good at it," I said. "I mean, at leading them toward the goal, keeping them motivated." *The man could sell pork bellies to the Israeli parliament,* I thought. *Of course he's good at it.*

He was staring at me. "Have you been crying?" he said.

I managed a laugh. "It's just hormones. Women can admit that again, in case you haven't seen *Redbook* lately."

"Did something happen to bring it on?" He wasn't going to drop it.

"Not really, I just felt teary. The fog and everything, I suppose, added to pre-menopausal estrogen depletion syndrome."

He kept looking at me. I was getting annoyed.

"You wouldn't lie to me, would you?"

I laughed. "Oh, sure I would. At the drop of a hat."

He smiled. "I see."

"Have you had lunch?"

He shook his head. "Have you?"

"No, but I had a late breakfast with Mrs. Whelan. An incredible omelette. She's a national treasure."

"I know. Let's see what she's left in the refrigerator for lunch."

I stood and stretched. "Did she leave?"

"Her car is gone. Must have had something to attend to."

He held out his hand to me and took mine, holding it all the way to the house. It made me feel guilty, somehow.

We found homemade chicken vegetable soup in the refrigerator, with instructions to heat it in the microwave on 80 percent power for four minutes. My resolve about skipping lunch evaporated as I looked at the soup; so I made half a bowl for myself. No wonder I wasn't skinny and untrustworthy. The table was set in the dining room; so we took the soup and some of the homemade bread in there. I made low-cal instant cocoa for us. Nothing like a mug of non-nutritious hot chemicals on a foggy day, I've always said.

Mac talked about the building committee meeting for a bit, then asked what I was doing on the book. I started to explain the process of fleshing out characters.

"The way you describe it, the characters seem to have minds of their own," he said. "It's eerie."

"I suppose it is, a little," I said. "You create these people as stick figures to begin with. You know what they're up to, and you know how they're going to interact within the story you have to tell. But as you write, they become more and more real. You keep adding detail, and they finally start living and breathing. As you write you find yourself saying, 'What a surprise. I never imagined Mary would say that!'—the way you'd say it about a child who blurts out something unpredictable. She's like your child, sort of—the fruit of your mind instead of the fruit of your womb. Although you've created her, she's taken on her own personality. She can surprise you with ideas and thoughts of her own. You have the power to make her do anything you want, but you can also set her free to act on her own. Well, sort of. Naturally, that isn't actually possible." I was finding it hard to put this phenomenon into words.

I stopped and took a deep breath. Mac seemed fascinated.

"Amazing," he said.

"Yes," I said. "It is. It is the most incredible experience. And impossible to explain, really. Unless you've done it, you can't know how joyful, how almost *ecstatic* that experience can be." I was suddenly self-conscious. I knew my face was bright pink. "It's a type of passion," I said.

Mac was watching me, grinning, trying to imagine how any of this was possible—what I was saying as well as the way I looked. Then he sat back in his chair. "I've never heard a fiction writer talk about her work before—not in any detail. Journalism is so cut-and-dried compared to that. You just report the facts— or your opinions—with as much grace and style as you can manage."

"I did that, too, remember. And you know, it's not so cut-and-dried as you're modestly trying to make out," I said. "It's extremely difficult to do well. Fiction is easier, in my opinion.

That's one reason I tried it. Then I got hooked by the joy of it all ... And the freedom."

"I can see that," he said.

I thought for a minute while I sipped the soup. "I've never said this to a living soul before," I told him. "It sounds bizarre, I know. But there are moments—when everything is going right, when the creative juices are flowing and the characters and events in a story are just *unfolding* of their own accord, and profound truths are emerging from *somewhere*—not really from me, it seems, but out of the cosmos—well, in those moments I feel as if ... as if I've touched God, or God has touched me in such a profound way that it leaves me stunned and awed." I picked up another piece of bread. "Do you think that's crazy?"

He was studying me. His right hand held his soup spoon in midair, halfway to his mouth. "I think it's—hmm—" He searched for a word. "—fascinating," he said finally. "*Intriguing.*" He kept staring at me, his face serious, and then he put the spoon in his mouth.

"I don't normally think like that," I said apologetically. "I don't believe in magic."

He eyed me. "I do," he said.

A few moments later he said, "I'd enjoy hearing what Amos thinks about all of this. If he comes for dinner, do you mind telling him what you've just told me?"

"Oh," I said. "He's coming tomorrow night. I forgot to tell you. Mrs. Whelan says I can help her make beef. And I'd be interested in his thoughts about it. By all means bring it up." *If I'm still here*, I added to myself. The thought gave me a burning sensation in my chest.

We finished our soup, cleaned up the dishes, and went into the parlor. Mac built a fire. The fog still hadn't dissipated entirely, and the room was cool without the benefit of sunshine streaming through the windows. He put on a tape—Gould playing

Bach—and we sat back to listen. After a couple of movements I dozed off.

LATER THAT AFTERNOON Mac used the computer to work on his columns, finally sending them off to Never-Never Land by modem. I made some corrections to the material I'd printed that day and put it into one of the next-day-air envelopes I'd brought with me, already addressed to Saul. I could have sent them to my own modem in Minneapolis, but I'd never shown Saul how to use it. And I certainly hadn't planned to have a computer to use here.

We went down to the barn then, and I got to see the horses up close. They had eyes, as Dave Barry has described them, the size of cue balls. It was still chilly and humid, causing their breath to blast out of their nostrils like puffs of steam from the side of a locomotive as they pranced and played. Standing next to them gave me the the sort of thrill I always got from looking into the eyes of a tiger at the zoo with nothing but a narrow concrete moat and a flimsy three-foot chain-link fence between us. All that monumental strength, all that energy was capable of making mincemeat of me—but it didn't. These horses had teeth as big as piano keys, and yet they plucked sugar lumps from the palm of my hand like dainty dowager queens. Politicians could learn something from them, I thought, about the prudent and judicious use of power.

At 7 we had dinner, a chicken from Mrs. Carpenter. Raised without antibiotics or chemicals, Mrs. Whelan said, a happy, free-range chicken that enjoyed itself all the way to the chopping block. It took me a few minutes to get up the courage to bite into it. I had to admit it was exceptional. It tasted the way I remembered chicken tasting when I was a kid—roasted simply, without sauce or embellishment other than the hint of garlic Mrs. Whelan had apparently tossed inside before cooking. On the side were steamed new potatoes, crusty sourdough rolls, roasted yellow squash, and grilled fresh tomatoes sprinkled with Parmesan cheese and dill. A sumptuous repast.

Mac sent Mrs. Whelan home as soon as she'd served, insisting that we'd clean up when we were finished. She shot me a motherly warning glance that said she expected me to mind my p's and q's and bustled off, whistling the theme from *The High and the Mighty* softly to herself. I wondered if it was a deliberate comment. Or a warning.

After dinner we made quick work of the dishes, then put on jackets and went for a walk. The silence of the country was still surprising to me. Even with the constant noise from crickets and the rustling of small animals scurrying in the brush, it seemed like the quietest place on earth. There was no hum of traffic, no horns, no sirens, no neighbors having fights, no television turned up too loud, no rock music blaring from boom boxes hanging on the arms of sunglassed kids. There was only a hushed stillness that seemed to reach out from where we stood toward the horizon. There, the ocean lay waiting for the moon to pull it up like a blanket over the sleeping shoreline.

When we got back to the house, Mac built a fire and put on a tape of Barbara Cook singing some songs hardly anyone else could do justice to—especially Irving Berlin's "What'll I Do," which could turn most singers into comic caricatures. She soared through Janis Ian's "Stars" as we stared out the window in easy silence.

After half an hour or so I got up and made some decaf and brought it in. Mac was sitting on the sofa near one end and patting the cushion next to him so I'd join him there. I did. He put his feet up on the big trunk and rested his cup on the arm of the sofa. I crossed my feet next to his and leaned into him. His arm went around my shoulders. I felt him kiss the side of my head. I thought guiltily about my conversation with Mrs. Whelan that morning.

"Remember what you said earlier about your writing?" Mac said suddenly. "About how mystically it unfolds sometimes? How you set the characters free, and let them do their own thing?"

"Um-hm," I said. He still had that habit of thinking about my ideas for days at a time.

"Does this happen to all fiction writers or just to you?"

"I don't know. I've never asked anyone else about it. I suppose I'm afraid to."

"Why?"

I considered that. "Well, if it happens to all of us, that could mean it's not so magical, not so inspired. If it happens to writers of pornography the same as it happens to me, the magic would sort of go out of it, wouldn't it? And on the other hand, if it *only* happens to me, it could mean I'm loony tunes. So it seems better not to know."

Mac was grinning at me as I glanced up at him.

"I love your mind," he said. "I really love it." He gave my shoulder a squeeze. "And the rest of you, too, of course."

I opened my mouth to speak, then closed it. *We have to talk*, I told myself sternly. Waiting would only make things worse. But I couldn't get a word out. I sighed. I felt Mac looking down at me, wondering what the sigh was about.

I put my head back, nestled deeper into the crook of his arm, and closed my eyes, floating with Barbara Cook and the good feelings that were warming my toes. *Tomorrow*, I thought. *Tomorrow is soon enough.*

19

After breakfast on Wednesday Mac and I set off for Sebastopol dressed in yuppie country clothes—Mac with his plaid button-down shirt and tan chinos, and I in my navy cardigan, pink turtleneck, and gray pants. We looked like the centerfold couple in the Eddie Bauer fall catalog. It irked me that many of the liberals I knew were now dressing like this, and in my heart of hearts I was sure it was nothing more than a clever ruse. Disguised as William F. Buckley Republicans, ex-hippies and sixties subversives were now out-entrepreneuring the Hearsts and the Rockefellers. The difference between the new wealth and the old, it seemed to me, was that the old wealth was spread around to help the community to a far greater extent than the new. For all their lofty humanitarian rhetoric, these new capitalists seemed to me far more self-absorbed, self-indulgent, and self-deceptive than the predecessors they still vilified.

We caught Highway 116 south of Jenner, which took us along the Russian River through Duncans Mills and Guerneville and then south through Forestville on a winding, scenic road. In Sebastopol we found the UPS agency, and I gave them my padded envelope containing the disk for Saul. Then we strolled around for a while, looking into windows and enjoying the sunshine.

After about half an hour of wandering, we went into a shop that sold horsy things—saddles, boots, and all kinds of gear and equipment presumably useful for a horse or a rider. Mac talked to the guy behind the counter, a tall, thick-necked country boy in a western-style shirt and string tie who brought several items out of a back room for him—a couple of bottles of oily looking liquid, a can of leather conditioner, and a harness wrapped in a plastic bag bearing Mac's name written in Magic Marker. Mac paid him, and we left.

Out on the street, Mac turned to me.

"I have an idea," he said.

"What?"

"Let's go on a date."

"A date?"

"Tomorrow night. We'll drive up the coast to a restaurant I know. It's right on the beach. They have pretty good food, but the big attraction is live music and a little dance floor. We can flirt with each other and see what develops."

"I think you're flirting with me right now."

"You're very perceptive." He winked and wiggled his right eyebrow. "However," he said, "you ain't seen nothin' yet."

"This sounds like a reckless idea."

"Thank you," he said. He was waiting. "Well?"

I thought for a moment. How could I tell him no without getting into all the things we had to discuss later today—all the things Mrs. Whelan and I had talked about? And I didn't want to get into that standing there on the street in Sebastopol.

I looked at him. "I believe I'll be coy," I said. "I'll give you my answer later. You can just sit on pins and needles until then, Bucko." He laughed. The treachery of a woman's heart has no equal.

Back at the house, Mac spent time in the corral grooming the horses and mucking out the barn. I didn't watch. What horses did in the privacy of their barn was of no interest to me. The thing that did interest me, however, was the way Mac approached the entire process, dressed in extremely old non-designer jeans and a worn plaid work shirt, plus boots that obviously had been ankle-deep in horse manure on at least 850 occasions. He simply went to the barn without fanfare and got dirty and sweaty with the horses. After a couple of hours' work, he disappeared— apparently to shower and change—then reappeared, hair still damp, without mention of what he'd done.

What seemed remarkable about this was that I had never before been around a man who could bring himself to do anything *dirty*. My father had hired handymen to put the storm windows on our one-story house every fall, and Peter had wrinkled his nose at the very notion of what he called "manual labor"— which included things like changing light bulbs, hanging pictures, and spraying canned silicone lubricant on the automatic garage door opener chain once a year.

These thoughts caused me to reminisce about the time I had asked Peter to oil the squeaky hinge on the front screen door, an operation that took the better part of a morning. He first had to select an oil-the-door-hinge outfit, which turned out to be a pair of Calvin Klein jeans and a custom-fitted, neatly pressed Ralph Lauren plaid shirt. He came to the kitchen twice during the actual oiling ordeal to wash his hands and complain that the oil had gotten under his nails and the smell was making him gag. Then when he'd finished, he made me come out to the front door to see what a fine job he'd done. It was, in fact, the last household task I ever asked him to do.

At about 2 o'clock Mac saddled a couple of the horses, and we went for a long, lazy ride along the ridge. The sun was out, and the day was perfect—about 60 degrees. I loved the feel and even the scent of the horse beneath me, the rhythmic movement of shoulder muscles as he ambled along, the sound of his snorting and breathing. I smiled, imagining that Saul would call it Freudian. *No*, I thought, *he'd be wrong; it's a kind of primitive oneness with another living creature.* The horse and I were a single unit, each of us sensing the other's intentions without having to communicate formally. We had an understanding.

Believe it or not, I looked hard for an opening to bring up the dilemma of our relationship while Mac and I were riding, but I simply couldn't find it. Several times I asked myself if this was the moment, only to hear that peculiar little inner "not yet" that probably wasn't so much intuitive guidance as chickenheartedness. Finally, exasperated with myself, I made up my mind: after dinner, after Father Amos left, no matter what, Mac and I would talk.

When we got back to the house at around 3:30, I reminded Mrs. Whelan I'd be helping with dinner. She didn't comment or even look up from her work but simply nodded.

I joined Mac in the parlor, where he was pulling out some newer tapes of Diane Schuur with Count Basie's Orchestra. It was comforting. The future was not so bleak, after all, where music was concerned. Schuur probably had a good forty years of singing and playing ahead of her.

As we sat together in the afternoon sunlight I spotted the photo albums in the bookcase.

"I hope you don't mind, but I looked at one of your photo albums yesterday," I said. "The one with the pictures of Chris."

Mac was sitting with his head back on the cushion, eyes closed. He didn't move. "I don't mind," he said.

"He was a beautiful child," I said. "He looked so much like you."

He didn't reply.

"Actually, that's what I was crying about before you came back," I said.

His head turned in my direction, and his eyes opened to look at me with surprise. "You were crying about Chris?"

"I'm not sure. About Chris, yes, and about you. About Sarah. The whole thing. It broke my heart. I can't explain it."

He was looking off into space now, thinking.

"It's very sad."

"Yes," he said. "Sad but hopeful. Love can give meaning and significance to sadness."

I thought about that. I wasn't sure I understood exactly what he meant, but I didn't ask him to explain.

"Did you say you only saw one of the albums?" he asked.

"Just the one of Chris. After that I felt I should ask you. It seemed somehow—well, a violation of your privacy, I guess. It wasn't what I intended, but after I saw the one it bothered me."

He looked at me, then got up and went to the bookcase, pulling the other two albums off the shelf and handing them to me.

"Be my guest," he said. He went over and poked at the fire with a black wrought-iron tong that stood on the hearth. I opened the first album and saw that it contained photos of his parents and himself, from childhood on. Mac had been a regular Gerber baby, I noted, and he'd turned into one of those freckle-faced kids everyone pats on the head because he's so boyish and mischievous and cute. As a thirteen-year-old he'd looked gangly and shy, apparently getting his growth spurt early. A photo of him standing next to his father showed the two of them at the same height. The caption under the picture, apparently written by Mac's mother, said, "Our baby's 15th birthday, already over six feet tall!" I smiled. Mothers never thought about how such captions would read twenty or thirty years from the day they wrote them.

Tucked in the back of the book were obituary notices for the congressman and his wife, dated some years before. I recalled that the two of them had died in a plane crash while on a political junket to West Africa. I'd read about it several months after the fact in an old issue of *Time* in my dentist's office. I'd been traveling when it had occurred, and when I was traveling it was possible for World War III to start without my knowledge.

As I read through the obituary it struck me for the first time that Mac had lost the four most important people in his life in tragic accidents. No wonder my collision with the blue pickup had brought him racing to Minneapolis. It explained a lot about the two months he'd spent with me. Saul had been right—I had been Mac's chance to wrest something from the hands of a cruel fate. I wondered for a moment how Mac would have reacted if I'd died. I looked at the photos for some time but couldn't think of an appropriate comment.

Finally I opened the other, smaller scrapbook, which was crammed with hand-written notes that were slightly yellowed and frayed around the edges. It took me a moment to understand why they seemed familiar: they were all in my handwriting.

"Eeek," I said.

Mac, who was by this time back in his easy chair, turned his head toward me and grinned. "I thought you knew I kept those," he said.

"I did at the time. I never imagined you'd still have them."

I read a few of them, randomly. There were poems, mostly dramatic and pretty depressing poems by people like T. S. Eliot and Matthew Arnold, and comments about events we apparently were planning to attend together. Philosophical commentaries. Lofty statements about the meaning of life. Cutesy little maxims. At the bottom of one note I had written, "Will you still want me when I have wrinkles and weigh fifteen pounds more?" *Well,*

I thought, *at least I knew the answer to that one.* It made me smile. Mac caught it.

"What?"

"I'm reading where I asked if you'd want me when I got old and fat."

He stood up, then went back to his chair, grinning. "Still wondering?"

"Nope. Now I know."

"No, you don't," he said. "But it's something we can look forward to." I started to say something but stopped and shook my head.

Then I read more, amazed to be able to so easily climb back into the mind of the seventeen-year-old girl I'd been all those years ago. She was thoughtful, clever, but detached somehow. A character of some depth, yes, but one unwilling to trust anyone with her inner secrets, trying too hard to impress her suitor with borrowed quips and elegant philosophies and high principles. It was easy to be objective about her, observing her from this distance.

I felt Mac staring at me.

"What?" I said.

"I love you," he said.

"But will you love me when I'm wrinkled and fifteen pounds heavier?" I said without missing a beat. As soon as the words were out, I looked at him and put my finger up to my temple, like a gun. I pulled the trigger. "Sorry," I said. "Foot in mouth disease."

Mac's mouth turned up slightly. "Come out, Sally Alexander, wherever you are," he said. Our eyes were locked on each other. I couldn't even blink.

Finally I closed my eyes and sat back, sighing. "I don't know if I *can* come out," I said.

"It isn't a question of whether you can. It's a question of whether you will."

I opened my eyes and glanced over at him. "Stop being so profound. It gives me a brain cramp."

"That's not what's doing it," he said. "You're getting a cramp from holding on to the door so tightly."

"What door?"

"The one you've been hiding behind all these years."

"I'm here, aren't I? If I were hiding, would I be here?"

"I don't know. Maybe I'm wrong, huh?"

I stared at my lap for a minute. "I'm a mess, aren't I?"

He was smiling at me. "That's your word. Not mine."

"You'd think after more than a quarter century I would have advanced just a little."

"Don't be so hard on yourself. A lot of water has passed over the dam since then. Maybe you have more reason to hide now than you did then."

"Quit being charitable. I deserve a kick in the tail."

"You're doing that all by yourself. You don't need it from me."

"I need something," I said softly. "I wish I knew what."

Mac didn't respond but put his head back on the cushion and closed his eyes.

After about ten minutes I looked over at him. "Mac," I said.

He opened his eyes and turned to look at me.

"I don't want to hurt you," I said. "Please remember that, no matter what happens from now on."

"That sounds ominous." He was frowning slightly.

"I don't mean it to be. You are the most extraordinary man I've ever known. But I have to do what's right for me. Whatever that is."

"It sounds more and more ominous."

"I'm sorry. I'm not sure what I'm going to do. But if it ends up hurting you, please remember what I said."

He was silent for a couple of minutes. Then he said, "I'll remember."

20

I showered and changed into a navy corduroy skirt and a cobalt blue Angora turtleneck before joining Mrs. Whelan in the kitchen at 5. She gave me a huge apron and tied it around me before putting me to work.

"We're having beef tenderloin in my special Louisiana Sauce," she announced. She had everything organized in her mind. "I'm told this sauce is similar to one served in a famous restaurant called Masson's in New Orleans, so I decided to call it Louisiana Sauce.

"First, we're going to make a nice caramel custard for dessert. Then, while that's cooling, we'll make the rice. We'll put some celery and tomatoes in the rice, and that will be the vegetable. This won't be fancy, but it's one of Father Amos's favorites." She clearly enjoyed making him happy.

She told me to sit and watch while she made the custard. I was enthralled. The woman was all business, like a surgeon in an operating theater. She knew exactly what she was doing, and there were no wasted motions.

After the custard was finished, while the rice was cooking, she looked over at me.

"You can start the beef sauce by chopping up two carrots and two onions." She handed them to me. I nodded, pulling a knife out of the block on the counter. A minute later she came over to where I was chopping.

"Want these chopped very fine?" I asked.

"No, this is a chunky kind of sauce. Country-style." She put two large garlic cloves on the chopping block along with about seven or eight sprigs of parsley. "You can chop these, too," she said.

She clanged around looking for a pan. Soon she came to get the chopped vegetables and added them to a heavy 12-inch skillet that held what looked like about a cup of hot olive oil. Everything sizzled and bubbled. Nothing rouses the appetite like garlic and onions cooking in olive oil.

She sprinkled in about a half cup of flour and stirred it until it was blended well. Then she turned the heat down a little and let it cook about five minutes. After that she added two tablespoons of tomato paste and cooked the mixture another three or four minutes. I watched and salivated.

She then measured out a full cup of red cooking wine and added that to the skillet along with four cups of weak beef bouillon, turning up the heat as she poured. When it was blended, she waited for it to simmer and turned the heat down a speck, explaining that the alcohol and bouillon had to "cook away" until only about half the liquid remained.

While that was happening, she sent me in to set the table with bright paisley place mats and napkins and beautiful old baroque sterling flatware she said was "from the McDonald family back East."

Mac was sitting in the parlor reading the newspaper as I set goblets and water glasses on the dinner table according to Mrs. Whelan's instructions.

"You'd think Amos was Archbishop of Canterbury," he said.

"Mrs. Whelan does this every time he comes. He loves it, and she knows it."

"I think it's wonderful," I said. "She's in her glory."

Mac was staring at me.

"What?" I said, hands on my hips.

"You're beautiful," he said. I smiled a dazzling smile and pulled a stray strand of hair behind my ear where it belonged. *Jamie Lee Curtis, eat your heart out.*

I went back into the kitchen to find Mrs. Whelan pouring the sauce into the Cuisinart. She pureed it and left it in the machine while she went back to the stove.

"Now we cook a little more garlic," she told me. She quickly chopped up two more big cloves and tossed them into a little olive oil in the bottom of the skillet she'd used for the sauce— not really browning them, just softening them. She then poured this into the food processor. In what seemed to be an after-thought, she chopped up another small handful of parsley and threw that in, too. Then she zapped it for about one second and tasted it. A look of satisfaction spread across her face. She dipped another spoon in the sauce and held it out for me.

It was even better than it smelled, which was saying something.

"Now, then," she said, "when Father gets here, I'll just broil the tenderloins the way you all like them and pour on the sauce before I serve them. So you can go on in and enjoy the evening."

She dusted off her hands and wiped them on her apron.

"Bravo!" I said. "I feel as if I've just witnessed the creation of a masterpiece."

"Appreciate the help," she said and turned to the sink, all business. *So,* I thought, *we're going to be like this, are we?* Feeling guilty again, I went back to the parlor. You can never really escape from Mother, can you?

Father Amos arrived at precisely 7 o'clock. Tonight he was

in civvies—black chinos and a red plaid wool shirt, with a stiff clerical collar improbably peeking out at the neck. He hugged Mac and me and fell into one of the easy chairs next to the fireplace, lifting his Nike-clad feet onto the ottoman like a member of the family. Mac had a fire going.

"I smell Mrs. Whelan's Louisiana Beef," Father Amos said happily, rubbing his hands together. He took in a long, deep breath and relaxed into the plump cushions. "What a treat this is. It's been a long day," he said. "I was called out at 4:30 this morning. Ted Preston had a small stroke, Mac."

Mac expressed concern and promised to visit the man in the hospital. Mrs. Whelan entered the room bearing a tray of ice water with slices of lemon, which all of us took gratefully. She announced that dinner would be ready in half an hour and went back to the kitchen.

"So, Sally," said Father Amos, sipping his water, "have you been playing or working since you've been here?"

"A little of both," I said. "I brought along a manuscript I'm working on with a friend in Minneapolis. A medical suspense novel."

"It's a collaborative work?"

"Yes. It's the first time I've tried collaboration."

"I'm surprised. With your own books on the best-seller lists, what prompted you to do that?"

"His expertise. He's a doctor—a psychiatrist, as a matter of fact. The villain in the book is, too, and so is one of the key female characters. I've always wanted to do a medical suspense novel, but I didn't know enough about the field to do it authentically. Saul even came up with the basic plot, so it's a true collaboration. I'm not carrying him. Much of the time he carries me."

He was smiling at me. "It's refreshing to meet an artist who isn't territorial."

"You give me too much credit," I said. "I just want to have another best-seller on the charts. My psychiatrist friend offered that opportunity."

"I have a friend who's a psychiatrist. Fascinating man," Father Amos said, taking a long drink from his glass. "He's a priest now. I knew him first when he was still in medicine. You never think of psychiatrists as spiritual people, but most of them are, I think, whether they admit it or not."

"Now that you mention it, I suppose I'd have to say my coauthor is a 'spiritual' person, if you define that as someone who thinks in terms of things that can't be seen or touched, things that have to be taken on faith."

"That's not how I meant it, but it's an interesting definition," he said. "What I really meant was that my friend, like several other psychiatrists I've known, had a rather mystical belief system before he ever became a Christian. He believed that mysterious 'inner powers' guided him in times of crisis. He even prayed after a fashion, though he denied it was prayer at the time. He called it contemplation or meditation. But it was prayer, all right. He admits it now."

I smiled. The man sounded like Saul in a lot of ways.

"He was spiritual, too, in the sense that he knew, intuitively, how to get in touch with the spiritual dimension in his own personality. He used to say to me, back when he was in medicine, 'Father, you and I are on opposite sides of the fence,' and I'd say, 'No, we're on the same side, we're just on different ends.' Now he tells me, 'Father, we were always on the same side *and* the same end, weren't we?'" He smiled broadly, enjoying the notion.

I also smiled, thinking that priests are a lot like doctors in another way: they love calling themselves and each other "father" the way doctors love calling each other "doctor"—almost as a term of endearment. I remembered all the physicians I'd heard greeting each other in the hospital: *Doctor, how are you? Fine, doctor, how are you? Hello there, doctor. Good to see you, doctor.* Priests probably did the same at priestly gatherings. I wondered if nuns did, too. Come to think of it, lawyers liked to call each other "counselor," didn't they? Maybe I should start something for writers: *Hello there, author.* Nah, it didn't work.

"Have you done much writing?" I asked him, thinking that he ought to if he hadn't. He seemed to have the mind and heart for it.

"I write short pieces for a newsletter we send out once a month, but that's all I normally do. I don't consider myself a writer. I have some good ideas, but I never get the words down. I've often thought what a splendid thing it would be to be able to create characters out of thin air as you do," he said. "I can't imagine how you do it."

Mac sat forward, looking at me. "That reminds me. Tell Amos what you told me yesterday, Sal." He looked at Father Amos, then back at me.

"About creating characters, you mean?"

"Yes."

I explained what I'd told Mac the previous afternoon. Father Amos listened intently, nodding thoughtfully. When I got to the part about placing characters in scenes, fleshing them out, and then setting them free, and finally to the part about profound truths emerging from the cosmos and my feeling of having touched God, Father Amos's eyes widened perceptibly.

"Isn't that wonderful?" Father Amos said when I finished. "Isn't that absolutely *amazing?* What a gift! Of course, God *has* touched you in these moments. He has reached out to you, as He is always ready to do, and you have reached out to Him, and you have *connected.* Just as Michelangelo depicted it—your finger to God's finger. Zap! Creation!" His face broke into a huge grin.

Mac was staring at me with a mixture of awe and admiration,

as if I'd just won the California lottery and had donated it all to charity.

"Well," I said somewhat self-consciously, "it's certainly the best thing I've ever experienced. Nothing else even comes close. I have to admit that those periods of 'connectedness' are what keep me hooked on writing."

"I don't wonder," Father Amos said. "I'm green with envy." He drained his water glass and held it on the arm of the chair, shaking the ice so it made little clinking sounds. He picked the lemon out of it and put it in his mouth. My lips involuntarily puckered.

Mrs. Whelan came back into the room and announced that dinner was served. Father Amos almost leapt to his feet. He was infused with new energy by the prospect of Louisiana Beef.

We attacked the food after a brief prayer of thanks by Father Amos. It was, I thought, the first brief prayer I'd ever heard from a member of the clergy. Hunger was, of course, a powerful motivator.

Mrs. Whelan disappeared immediately after serving us, and Mac filled the crystal goblets on the table from a bottle that looked to me like it held champagne. The bottle was swathed in white linen, so I couldn't see the label.

Father Amos gasped with delight as he sniffed at it and then took a sip. "No! It can't be!" he exclaimed. "Mac, how on earth . . . ?"

"The Blaisdells had a case shipped to me during their trip to England last summer. Jeannie grew up in Surrey, you know. They stayed with some old friends who live a few miles from Thorncroft." Mac made a toasting gesture toward us with his own goblet. He was waiting for a comment from me. I took a sip, let the lightly sweet flavor linger on my tongue for a couple of moments, and swallowed.

"It's delicious," I said, "but what is it?"

Father Amos held up his goblet with a huge grin. "Thorncroft Vineyard's Sparkling Elderflower!" he told me. "An elixir unlike any other on earth! Ambrosia!"

I looked at Mac. "Sparkling Elderflower? Seriously?"

"Yep," he said, pulling the linen napkin off the bottle so we could see the label. Sure enough, it said, *Sparkling Elderflower.*

"It's made from essence of wild elderflower petals," Father Amos explained. "Plus a hint of fresh lemon. And pure spring water. Non-alcoholic and low-calorie. What more could anyone want?" He was sipping with his eyes closed, savoring the drink. "Ahhhh, yes, it's perfect! What a delightful surprise, Mac."

"I have several bottles set aside for you to take home," Mac told him.

"No, no," he protested. "Much better to drink it here, with Mrs. Whelan's food and your company. Such a rare treat has to be shared to be properly enjoyed."

I watched him talking and thought this was surely one of the most charming, urbane, intelligent men I'd ever met. How, I wondered, could such a man wind up living the way he lived? It was all so improbable.

We mmmm'd and aaah'd our way through each item on our plates: the beef, some dainty little steamed potatoes, and stir-fried summer squash. About halfway into the meal, I felt Mac looking at me. I was sitting next to him, between the two men. Father Amos was concentrating on his beef, savoring each mouthful. Unexpectedly, Mac reached out and put his hand on mine. It was a tender, loving, married sort of gesture, the kind of gesture Peter had never made toward me. It flustered me. Discreetly, I pulled my hand away. As I did, I noticed Father Amos looking at me. He glanced back and forth between Mac and me and went back to his plate.

"Tell me, Father," I said, shifting gears, "how did you come to St. Stephen's in the first place?"

He smiled. "You're asking for the story of my life." He glanced at Mac. There was a fondness between them that warmed my heart. "Mac's heard it too often. Some other time, perhaps."

Mac shook his head, laughing. "Come on, Amos," he said. "There's not going to be a better time. Don't play hard to get."

Amos Whitcomb laughed loudly and wiped his mouth. "The voice of my conscience! Always right to the bull's-eye," he said to Mac. Then, to me, "He doesn't let me get by with anything."

I nodded. "Well?"

"All right. But for all our sakes I'll try to be brief. Let's see, we can skip over my childhood and youth, which was fairly uneventful and relatively normal—whatever that is. My father was a surgeon, a brilliant man, but a man not given to much sentiment. Mother was a homemaker, a good woman, but she left most of the rearing of her children to the help—nannies and baby-sitters and cooks. And I have an older brother, the apple of my parents' eyes, who became a lawyer. I was headed in that direction myself—got my law degree and passed the bar by the time I was twenty-three. Thought I was pretty hot stuff in those days, in the way only the truly ignorant can think of themselves.

"At twenty-five I met my wife-to-be, Catherine. I'd been hired by one of the best law firms in Chicago. That's where I grew up, and that's where I chose to practice. I was going to make a lot of money, and it seemed to me it was time to settle down and have a family. That's the sort of man I was. I made all the important decisions of my life that way. I said, 'It's time to get married now,' and I set about to do it. It was my father's way, of course. I didn't know there *was* any other way.

"I don't know whether I thought I was in love with Catherine while we were dating, but she was a lovely, intelligent, charming girl, and I decided we were compatible," Father Amos went on. "I desperately wanted her, I can tell you that much. She wasn't about to give in to me before we were married. Of course, in those days that was unthinkable anyway. But I lay awake nights imagining what it would be like when she was my wife."

I felt Mac look over at me. I glanced at him, saw a small smile on his face, and quickly turned back to Father Amos.

"After we were married," he continued, "after the newness of the conquest had worn off, I realized that something was missing. There was no substance to our relationship, you see. At least not on my side of it. I knew a lot *about* her, but I didn't actually *know* her, if you follow me. I simply lacked the ability to love in any but the most trite and immature way. I admired her, even lusted after her, but I hadn't the slightest idea what genuine love was all about.

"I could act the part of a husband, of course. I could come home and converse at dinner, compliment her cooking, ask her about her day, even take pride in her and enjoy her as a person. We were socially active, had a large circle of friends. At least I called them friends. I didn't know *them*, either. But I had observed and read enough to know how a good husband or a friend was supposed to act, so that's how I acted. I did everything I thought I should do so nobody could criticize me for not doing enough. I did all this without knowing I was doing it with these motivations, of course. I felt I was a superb husband and a superb friend, as well as the best lawyer in the Midwest."

He took a sip of Sparkling Elderflower before continuing. "But all this was purely selfish on my part. I did the things I did in my marriage—and in all of my relationships—because these were the things I had to do to live a relatively friction-free, comfortable life. With Catherine, I did only those things I had to do to keep things pleasant between us. I wasn't interested in *her* happiness, only in my own. At the time I didn't understand that, naturally. And after all, I was only doing what I'd observed my own father doing in his marriage. It was all I knew."

I was listening to his story with a mixture of sadness and amazement. I was thinking of Peter again. Was this the sort of man he had been—unable to love, emotionally bankrupt, selfishly looking after nothing but his own comfort and convenience? It made me feel almost sorry for him. And for myself, in a strange way. I'd been the perfect victim in our relationship. I'd let him continue his charade without challenging his values or ethics—and without thinking about the way his behavior tied into my own.

"Looking back, I realize that it was the genuine love Catherine gave me that enabled me to see, finally, how empty I was," Father Amos said. He looked at both of us and shook his head sadly. "There is no emptiness like the emptiness of looking into your own soul and seeing a black hole, a vast vacuum waiting to be filled," he said.

He leaned on the table, hands folded. "That led me, not surprisingly, to a spiritual crisis. Many men in such a state look for another woman to take their minds off their problems. I never thought of that for some reason. As I contemplated my failure—my ineptness as a husband and in *all* my relationships—I somehow recognized that I would not find permanent solutions to my problems anywhere but in God.

"Certainly my wife was a catalyst in this process. I knew that she had faith in God, and I sensed that He was the source of the love she was able to pour out to me and to everyone else in her life. She never talked about this, I must tell you. Never preached to me. She just . . . *lived* it. I had never known anyone so courageous, so admirable, and I wanted to be like her, but it wasn't in me. That frustrated me in a way I can't explain.

"Anyway, I decided it would be good for me to become *religious*. But I wasn't the sort of man who would simply walk into any religion without investigating the available choices first. I studied various religions and came to the conclusion that the one most likely to make me into a person of substance—a person like Catherine—was Christianity. So I read the Bible and memorized the rules. I became a superb rule-follower.

"Now mind you, I was not totally off the track. I sensed that in Jesus Christ I would find life. I discovered Him through the Scriptures, which was a good step. But I was still going through the motions—these were just religious motions instead of regular, humdrum secular motions. This went on for a couple of years. My wife was unbelievably patient with me, bless her. She knew God; she had His life within her. She knew what He was able to do; so she waited and prayed without being a critic. It couldn't have been easy for her."

What had she looked like? I wondered. What had she thought of all this? I pictured her as a young Claudette Colbert, tiny and sweet and feisty. Somehow I could believe she was every bit as noble as Father Amos said.

"Then the worst thing imaginable happened," he went on. "Catherine developed uterine cancer. She was dead a year later. They were helpless in those days. Now they probably could save her." He toyed with his goblet, turning it slowly with his fingertips. "I sat at her funeral, and it finally struck me: I had been married to this woman for seven years, she had poured out her life to me, and I had never been able to love her. I had *believed* I loved her, of course, in the sense that I had admired her immensely. I suppose in a human sense I *had* loved her—the way the love songs and greeting cards describe it, anyhow—especially in the months before her death. But I knew that was not what she longed for. It was not the kind of love she deserved. And it was not the kind of love I longed to give her—the supernatural, God-filled kind of love she had given to me. I also had wanted desperately to believe that her death would not be the end of our relationship, but that seemed foolish and weak to me then.

"Her last words to me, a couple of days before she died, were the most amazing words I had ever heard. She whispered to me, 'Amos, God wants you to know Him. And I do, too—more than anything.' At the time I thought what a curious way it was of putting things. She hadn't said God wanted to know *me*—she'd said he wanted *me* to know *Him.* Mostly because they were her last words, I suppose, I couldn't get them out of my mind.

"All of this overwhelmed me at her funeral. It broke my heart. As I looked into her face before they closed the casket, I wept for the first time in my adult life."

I felt a lump in my throat the size of an egg. Mac was enthralled, leaning forward with both elbows on the table, his chin cradled in his palms.

"I went home and soon became convinced that God was calling me into the priesthood. I suppose I felt I might redeem myself from what I now saw as my total selfishness by serving God and my fellowman for the rest of my life. Within six months I had sold everything I owned and gone off to study at an Episcopal seminary. People thought I'd lost my mind. But I was doing the only thing I could think of to do. It was perfectly rational in a pathetic sort of way.

"But seminary only complicated matters. I finished first in my class, of course. But there still was no life in me. There were more rituals in my repertoire, and I had learned how to be gloriously religious, a great imitator of a disciple of Christ, but very little had changed within me. I went through a nine-month depression after I graduated from seminary. Absolute despair. There are no words for such despair.

"Finally I asked for, and was assigned to, a small parish in the slums of Chicago. I wanted to help people who were more desperately needy than I was. I believed that would be my cure. But there in the midst of all the pregnant children and devastated families, the druggies and the pimps, I was confronted once again with my own inner bankruptcy. I could do all the right things—

take food to the hungry, sit with the dying, visit the sick, march for better housing and social justice. But still—and by now I knew it—I was not ministering *life*, because in reality there was no life in me. The love of God was a total mystery to me.

"My impulses were drawing me in the right direction, you see, but I needed transformation, not education or a cause to champion. What I was doing was not a bad thing to do; it simply made no difference—either for my parishioners or for myself. I had followed every rule in the book, had done everything I knew how to do, and it wasn't working."

He sat back, wiping his mouth. "Isn't it amazing? How could I be so unbelievably dense for so many years?"

"You were unbelievably persistent," I said. "I'd think you might have given up by this time. I keep wondering where God was while you were struggling."

He pushed his chair away from the table a few inches and smiled. "Ah, well, that's the best part!" He looked at me for a moment, eyes wide. "God was busy setting the scene and fleshing out my character so He could reach down from the cosmos, touch His finger to mine, and bring me to life. He was there all the time, building a living, breathing person He could set free to really *know* Him."

Mac looked at me, grinning. "Gotcha," he said.

I smirked and shook my head. Father Amos and Catherine and Mac seemed to have a real thing about "knowing God." It was much more than a philosophy to them. It was a way of life. I picked up my Sparkling Elderflower and batted my eyes at Father Amos. "I guess my next line is, 'Tell me, Father, exactly how did that happen?'"

He grinned. "Right. It happened one night while I was still in Chicago. I finally came to the end of myself. I was lying in bed one night, utterly distraught, more despondent than I knew I could be. I began to weep from sheer anguish. 'God,' I said, 'either kill me or heal me! I can't go on another hour like this!' I just gave up. I was pondering suicide, but I didn't have the courage to carry it out.

"I lay there most of the night, not really thinking, just praying to die. I had no faith to believe I could be healed, so I presumed God would at least be kind enough to end my life. But He didn't.

"Instead, He did the the most amazing thing. As I lay there, new thoughts began to come into my mind—thoughts I'd never had before. I recognized almost immediately that they were not thoughts typical of me. I knew they were from God. My psychiatrist friend might have said, 'Aha! You had a psychotic break!' But these were not the thoughts of a lunatic, and I knew it. They were, in fact, the first truly rational thoughts I'd had in years. They were the breath of genuine life.

"The first thought that came to me was a question. It was very clear in my mind: *Amos, what do you think would happen if you gave up religion?*

He looked down at his plate. "What a question for a man like me!" He dabbed at his mouth with his napkin and refolded it. "After thinking it over I finally said, as much to myself as to God, 'I just wouldn't know *what* to do.' The thought actually scared me. I'd walked away from everything else in my life and had committed myself to the disciplined practice of the Christian religion. How could I think about giving it up?

"Then the next thought came to me—and this one, too, was very clear, quite a contrast to all the muddled thoughts I'd been wallowing in up to that point. This one was also a question: *Amos, what if instead of being so perfectly religious, you simply tried saying yes to Me, one moment at a time, for the rest of your life?*

"I was thunderstruck. Such an idea was totally foreign to me! I couldn't even comprehend it. It was absurdly, impossibly simple, the exact opposite of everything I had ever understood about religion and about life. Astonishing! At first I wanted to dismiss it. But I couldn't stop thinking about it."

Father Amos leaned forward in his chair. I took another sip of my drink. There was a long pause while he ate more of his meat and picked up some of the sauce in a teaspoon to pour it on his rice. We waited.

"Well," he said at last, "that was it. I had nothing to lose, you see, and everything to gain. And that is the ideal position from which to approach God. So, after lying there the rest of the night pondering these questions, I made the fateful decision: I would do it. I would stop worrying about playing the perfect Christian and the perfect priest and concentrate on saying yes to God Himself—one moment at a time. I would open myself to Him as I had never been able to open myself with anyone. I would get to know Him on a personal, human level instead of on an intellectual one. I knew somehow that the results could not be any worse than the results of my own attempts at religious life."

He sat back in his chair, resting his wrists on the edge of the table, looking back and forth between Mac and me. I found myself unable to take my eyes off him. For reasons I could not understand, my natural skepticism about the kinds of things he was saying had been suspended. His words had the ring of truth. It was a little scary, but moving as well.

He waited a few seconds, then went on. "Beginning that morning, I took off in a new direction. That's when the burden of my existence began to be slowly but surely lifted off my shoulders. I knew—deep within me, I *knew*, as I had never known anything before—that I was free for the first time in my life. I began to understand how limitless God's love was. He had loved me even when I'd failed or made terrible mistakes, had loved me in my selfishness and sin, even kept loving me when I said no to Him over and over again.

"He didn't condemn me as I had condemned myself. He just

loved me and waited for me to say yes. I had made it so hard, and it was so incredibly simple when it came down to it."

I was still staring at him. "I'm having a hard time imagining this." I pulled my eyes away from him and glanced at Mac. His look was inscrutable.

Father Amos drank down the last of his Sparkling Elderflower. "The moment I said that first yes to Him, God reached out His hand and touched me, infusing me with His own life for the first time. In that moment I ceased to be my own person and became His. This infusion of His life made me immortal, you see. I became a person with a future that stretches into eternity."

"I'm sorry," I said, "but I guess I don't understand the process. It sounds like something out of 'Invasion of the Body Snatchers.' Are you saying God came into your room in the middle of the night, took over the body of Amos Whitcomb, and replaced him with somebody else?"

Mac snorted. "Amos Whitcomb, pod-person," he said. "Word is out about you, Amos."

Father Amos burst out laughing. "I like it! I may steal it for a sermon. You won't mind?" He looked at me.

"Be my guest," I said. I didn't think it was that funny.

Father Amos's face went serious. "There was no replacement, I assure you. I was still Amos Whitcomb, more's the pity. But once God has our consent to go to work on us, noticeable changes begin to take place. His plan, as author of creation, is to help us become completely ourselves, and at the same time completely His. This is not instantaneous transformation, mind you, but a progressive, *collaborative* effort."

"Give me an example," I said.

"Well, in my own case, as the days passed I began to notice small, subtle changes. As I said yes to the Lord from moment to moment, as I learned to rely upon Him and invite Him to be involved in every area of my life, I found that I was finally able to begin to love others—in the way Catherine had been able to, without strings. I didn't have to control everything anymore. I was learning to *know* God, you see. I was connecting with Him deliberately, on a continuing basis, and He was revealing who He really was, letting me experience Him as a living, loving, forgiving friend. I was also learning, for the first time, that it was sometimes good for me to be weak, to be vulnerable, even to be dependent upon someone besides myself.

"Over time, I finally understood what it was that compelled Catherine to love as she had, what enabled her to resist becoming the critic she was entitled to be with me. It was God's own love. It filled her up and spilled into the lives of everyone who knew her. That was the transformation I'd been awaiting without knowing it.

"One incident sticks in my mind: two weeks after that night when I made my decision, I was approached at a convention by the bishop of this diocese about taking the pulpit here at St. Stephen's. It was pretty shocking. This was a parish I'd have felt insulted to be offered two weeks before. There were about thirty members, most of them elderly, and the church was in total disrepair. Old Mrs. Portsmith had died years before, leaving a bequest that paid for some of the expenses of maintenance; but the parish no longer had enough members to take care of the rest. By human standards it was a terrible assignment, though it was much better than I deserved. But God knew what He was doing. All I had to do was say yes." He paused, and I took a bite of squash. Cold.

"I reacted strangely to the bishop's request. Ordinarily I'd have become indignant and sunk into a three-month depression over such an idea. Instead, I went out for a walk and said, 'Lord, I'm going to say yes as an act of faith. If You don't want me at St. Stephen's, I ask You to give me no peace about it.' I knew the scriptural principle that God often reveals His will by giving or withdrawing His peace. We have to pay close attention to that, and this was one of the lessons God was teaching me at that point.

"I made a trip here to see the church and meet the congregation, and I found that I had great peace about it. They felt the same way. We went to the bishop and told him I was ready to make the move. He was amazed, I think. As we left his office I was more at peace than I could ever remember being. I knew I'd done the right thing. The joy I felt over that was inexpressible. And in all these years I haven't had a moment of regret over that decision."

Mac glanced at me. "And since then Amos has led this parish into a ministry that reaches around the globe," he said. "Thousands of lives have been transformed."

"Through the retreats you offer?" I said.

"Partly," Father Amos answered. "But we also have local outreach programs, and we support missions all over the world. The retreats simply make it possible for people to open themselves to the Spirit of God—often for the first time. Here they can encounter the real, living Christ and get to know Him. Sometimes it's easier for them to hear His voice here—that's all. He Himself does the real work. We just set the stage and await His creative touch. And of course no one is ever the same after being touched by God, as you can testify. Once one has tasted the Real Thing, even for a moment, he or she can never again settle for anything less."

He grinned at me, thrilled to the core. "That's the real secret of what God does, you know. His love makes everything else we've experienced dull by comparison. His love is irresistible, totally irresistible. If we can make it possible for people to know what that love is like, even for a moment, He's got them!"

Mac and Father Amos both smiled at the thought. So did I. I

didn't believe for a moment that he was making any of it up. This was not a man given to delusions or deceptions. Neither, of course, was Mac.

Mrs. Whelan came in to clear the table. We all expressed our appreciation for the meal, and I got up to help her carry out the dishes. But she shooed me out of the kitchen, saying, "Go sit with the men." I obeyed her. She was not in a mood to be disputed.

Mac and Father Amos had returned to the parlor, where Mac was adding a log to the fire. The flickering flames were the only light in the room.

"You're a born storyteller," I said, settling into the empty easy chair, avoiding Mac on the sofa. "You ought to write up your life story and publish it."

"Oh, no, I don't think so," Father Amos said. "It's the sort of thing you can only tell people when you're face to face."

"Father," I said after we were quiet for a while, "why do you think God waited so long to show you all of this? Why didn't He reveal it all before Catherine died, so you could share it with her?"

"Oh," he said, "it wasn't that God was holding out on me, if that's what you mean. He never barges in, you know. He waits to be invited, waits for us to say yes. I said no for a long time. For much too long. That was *my* problem, not God's. When He gives us free will, it is *truly* free. We have the power to say no, and He respects it. We often hurt each other terribly when we exercise that power, but God permits it because His love would have no meaning unless we were free to accept or reject Him. And don't feel bad about Catherine missing out. I'll share it all with her when the time comes. The last chapter hasn't been written yet."

The thought touched me. Nobody spoke, and the only sound was a log settling in the fire. After a few moments I said, "It's hard to imagine you saying no to God."

"Oh, but we all do it. It's the easiest thing in the world to say no. I was afraid of what might happen if I let down the barricades. Anything could happen, I told myself. I could become a raving lunatic, a holy roller, who knows what? We're terrified of things like that. We're also afraid of being hurt, being disappointed, looking foolish; or worst of all, we're afraid of simply not knowing what to do next. That was a very big fear of mine. It's much easier just to keep following familiar rules."

I smiled. I could understand that.

We were relaxed and thoughtful as Mrs. Whelan came in bearing a tray of caramel cream custard and mugs of decaf French roast. I had a strong desire to go to the cottage and sit in the dark so I could think quietly for a few hours.

Father Amos took his coffee and custard and smiled at Mac and me, looking back and forth between us as he seemed to be in the habit of doing. He sipped at his coffee and savored his custard. The fire flamed up, lighting our faces and casting dancing shadows on ceiling and walls.

"So tell me," he said innocently, "have you two set a date yet?"

You know that scene in the movie where a guy makes a shocking remark while another guy is casually drinking coffee, and in mid-gulp the second guy sprays a whole mouthful of coffee on himself? I did something like that, except the coffee didn't really spray. It just sort of dribbled out of my mouth, down my chin, and into the mug while I choked and sputtered. I grabbed for a napkin and blotted my face, humiliated.

Father Amos watched beatifically. "Oh, forgive me," he said, "Was my question premature?"

Mac was handing me another napkin, barely suppressing a laugh. "You did that for effect," he said to me. "And so did you," he said, pointing at Father Amos, who continued to look amused. I glared at both of them.

When I was nearly dry again I said, "I'd like to pretend the last several minutes never happened, please."

"What several minutes?" Mac asked. Then, still enjoying the moment, he stood and took my mug and the wet napkins to the kitchen. While he was there, from somewhere outside I heard a loud crash, followed by the sounds of horses whinnying. Then I heard Mac walk down the hall from the kitchen toward the outside door. He came back to the parlor and said, "Excuse me a minute, will you? I think we have a possum or a skunk in the barn. I'll be right back."

After a few moments Father Amos, still smiling a sly little smile, said to me, "One question."

"Yes?" I said.

"Why are you so unwilling to be loved?"

The question startled me. "What do you mean? By whom?"

"By Mac." He paused, then raised both eyebrows at me. "And perhaps also by God. What do you think?"

I gave it some thought. "I *am* willing to be loved by God. Why wouldn't I be? But Mac is another matter. You're asking a very hard question. If you pressed me, I'd have to say our situation is pretty much impossible." I hated having to be honest. It was like walking on tar paper. Sticky, sticky.

"Ah, *impossible!*" the priest said. "That's God's specialty! You're in a very good position, indeed."

I shook my head. "I'm in the worst position of my life. I'm afraid to hurt Mac by continuing our relationship, and I'm afraid to hurt him by ending it. Of course, I'm afraid of hurting myself, too. There's no way I can explain the complexities of it to you, but it's a mess. I know it can't go on, but—well, I'm stymied. I've gotten both of us into the mess by coming out here, and now I can't seem to find a way out that won't be painful. You might say I don't know what to do next." Surprise of surprises, tears welled up in my eyes. I looked at him and sighed heavily. "I am open to suggestions."

Father Amos gazed at me thoughtfully. Then he closed his

eyes. He didn't speak. Another one of those people who could wait. *Well*, I thought, *so can I.*

After perhaps two minutes, his eyes popped open.

"Are you willing to consider an experiment?" he said.

"What kind of experiment?"

He smiled. "An experiment to discover how creative God can be as an author. Let's say you give Him permission to write a chapter in your life story—perhaps one week's worth. Does that seem like a reasonable length of time?"

I laughed. "You're going fishing, Father. No fair!"

"Ah," he said, "I thought you were already hooked! Well, let's just say if you get hooked any deeper, it will not be I who have done it."

"Want to bet?"

"I'll bet you anything you care to bet. All I ask is that you wait one week before making a judgment about it." He looked at me eagerly. "Agreed?"

"Not so fast. Why should I want to get involved in your little experiment?"

He raised one eyebrow. "Just to see what will happen. And of course, to see whether God might be able to write a more satisfying resolution than you've been able to so far. What do you have to lose?"

I had to admit the man knew how to dangle the bait. "Just how would this experiment work?" I tried to sound casual.

He knew he was going to reel me in. It was no longer a matter of *if*, it was only a matter of *when*. He smiled broadly at me. "Simple. You go about your business as usual, except for this: you agree to say yes to God, starting immediately, for the next seven days. Now, this may seem obscure and difficult, maybe even scary to you at the moment, but God will make it clear as you move through the week. You're simply opening yourself up to His creative touch for a defined period of time—with an option to continue at the end of that time, if you wish. Call it a first step on a long journey. A radical and intriguing notion, yes?"

"You're suggesting that I've never done this before, that I've said no to God up to now. That ain't necessarily so."

He grinned again. "You tell me. Have you said yes—deliberately and consciously?"

I thought about it. "I suppose not—not in those terms."

"Then I ask you again: what do you have to lose?"

"Autonomy."

He laughed out loud. I hadn't been trying to be funny. "Sally, autonomy is purely illusory! It doesn't exist, you know, not as you're suggesting. The closest we can come to autonomy is to exercise the free will God has given us. We can choose among all available options. If we refuse to consider any of the options He offers, of course, we severely limit ourselves. But if we *will* consider His options, possible choices multiply exponentially." He paused, looking at me hard.

I studied him, and he studied me. We could have been two wrestlers circling each other, looking for an opening. The man could be right, of course. On all counts. If God was really God, He could open up a whole new range of options. Options I'd never considered before. Even I could see that it was possible.

"Suppose I agreed," I said. "Suppose I said yes, just to see what would happen. What do *you* think would happen?"

His eyes got bigger. "I don't have the slightest idea!" he said, apparently delighted with the thought. "Isn't that exciting? It will be a surprise to me, too!"

"I don't like surprises."

"You haven't experienced many of *God's* surprises, then. You'll like them. I guarantee it."

"All I'd be doing is saying yes? I can't imagine how that could change anything. Certainly I don't see how it could solve the problems with Mac."

"Good! It's better when you can't imagine it. Now, here is what I suggest." He sat forward and looked deep into my eyes. "You'll make this agreement with God: 'Lord God, I say yes to You right now. I authorize You to write a new chapter in my life. I open myself to Your creative touch. Enable me to recognize Your options when I see them, and to say yes to Your options—knowing that they're filled with love. Help me to trust You, and to stop being afraid of what You might do if I opened myself to You completely.'"

I realized suddenly that he had been praying with me. *Sneaky*, I thought, *very sneaky*. He was supposed to close his eyes and act pious so people would know. I smirked at him.

"Well," he said, "do you agree?"

I looked at him. Was I going to let him get away with this? Well, I thought, why not? Just to see what might happen. I had nothing to lose. And who knew what additional options might open? The situation couldn't actually get much more hopeless than it already was. The worst thing I could imagine was that I could end up selling all my possessions and living in the streets of Calcutta with Mother Theresa. I'd never been to Calcutta. There might even be a book in it.

I sighed. "Okay," I said.

"Yes?" he said, twinkling at me. "This is yes to God, you know, not to me. This is a moment of truth."

I felt like Joe Isuzu. Why did this man think I might lie to him or to God? Did I have that sort of face? Or did he know something? I cringed and bit the bullet.

"Yes," I said.

He beamed. I was in his net, on the way to the creel. *She can't get away now*, he was saying to himself. I smiled back at him and thought, *You old son-of-a-gun, you played me like a hungry trout*. But for some strange and inexplicable reason, I didn't mind very much. I felt sort of hopeful.

"This is going to be a week to remember," he said. "Remember, God does not always make things easy. Sometimes things get harder when you decide to choose His options. But He always makes life exciting."

Now you tell me, I thought.

"Well!" he said, standing and walking over to put an arm around my shoulders, "You've made a tremendous leap of faith! I can hardly wait to see what happens next!"

"To be honest," I said, "I feel like I've just invested a million dollars in a beachfront condo without even looking at the floor plans."

With a satisfied grin he began to move toward the hall. "Relax. Your investment is in good hands. Now, I must be going. Let's find Mac and see what's been going on with the horses."

As we headed out the door, Mac came toward us from the direction of the barn.

"The skunk wouldn't leave," he said apologetically, "and I didn't want to get sprayed, so it was a standoff. He left when he got bored, I think. What have I missed?" He walked to my side and took my hand. I started to pull it away, then stopped. Mac looked at me, squeezed my hand, and I squeezed back. I glanced up at Father Amos. The man missed nothing.

"I'll let Sally fill you in," Father Amos said. "The skunk's timing was perfect. Did you know that the Bible says the animals belong to God?"

Mac looked at me, and I looked back; then we both looked at Father Amos. I didn't open my mouth. All these looks were making my eyes tired.

Hugging me with gusto, Father Amos then grabbed Mac and patted his back heartily. "Thank you for another wonderful evening," he said. "I always leave here full of steam. Mrs. Whelan ran off, didn't she?"

He glanced at me. "You'll call me in a day or two to let me

know how the experiment is going, won't you? I'll keep you in my prayers. If you don't call me, I'll have to hunt you down."

"I'll call you," I said. Having seen him in action as a fisherman, I didn't want to become his prey on a hunt.

Beaming, he waved at both of us, charged out to his car, and pulled away.

Mac turned to me. "What in the world was that all about?"

I shrugged. "Saying yes, I guess." He gave me a quizzical look.

"Oh," he said, wondering whether to pursue it.

"I think I'd like to turn in," I said. "I'm tired."

"Good idea. Me, too," he said. I started off toward the path to the cottage. The gravel on the driveway crunched noisily under my feet. When I reached the path I stopped, turned, and looked back at Mac. He was watching me.

I stood there perplexed, then smiled to myself. *Okay, so here I am*, I thought. *Where are these new options I was supposed to start seeing?* I had planned to have that talk with Mac after Father Amos left, to tell him I was going back to Minneapolis. Now I'd embarked on this so-called experiment, and although it didn't actually preclude going home, it made me feel I should wait before making a new plane reservation. This wasn't as clear as I'd hoped.

I was staring at Mac as these thoughts went through my mind. He wasn't moving. He just stood there looking back, hands in his pockets, practicing his waiting skills. Come on, what was I supposed to do now? *Well*, I thought, *I could always walk back there and just talk for a while, and see what happened. Sure*, I said to myself, *that would be smart*. Then I thought, *This is not simple. What can I say yes to here that won't make matters worse?*

While I was standing there arguing with myself like that, Mac walked toward me, slowly; and when he got to me he wrapped his arms around me. I pulled in a deep breath. I put my arms around him without thinking about it and felt him relax. We stayed like that for several minutes, listening to each other breathe.

When Mac finally let go of me he said, "I'm still on pins and needles."

"About what?" I said.

"About our date. Tomorrow night."

"Oh." I'd forgotten about that. I had, I recalled, expected that I wouldn't have to deal with it, because I'd planned on being on a plane to Minneapolis by tomorrow. Now what? I pursed my lips. Mac waited.

I could still say no. I could still exercise my almighty free will and say the big N-O. I could still spare both of us the agony that probably would come unless I made that choice.

Ah, well, I thought, *a leap of faith every few years has to be good exercise for the soul.* There was always Calcutta. I looked at Mac. He would survive. So would I. I wasn't sure how, but we would both survive.

"Okay," I said. "My answer is yes."

"Whew," Mac replied.

21

The next morning, Thursday, the phone rang right in the middle of French toast with fresh boysenberry syrup. Mac and I were eating together at the kitchen table. He went to the parlor to take the call. A few minutes into the conversation I gathered that it was Saul. Mac called me to the phone just as I'd taken the last mouthful of French toast. Timing is everything in this world.

I hurriedly chewed and swallowed. "Hello, doctor," I said into the phone.

"I got your disk," he said, ignoring my sarcasm. "Haven't had a chance to look at it yet." It was good to hear his voice. It was home.

"Let me know what you think. I changed a lot in chapter 5."

"Okay."

"I miss you and Angela," I said.

"You're still there," he said. "You don't miss us that much, apparently."

"Well, you and Angela mean a lot to me. Our friendship depended on my staying, so I've stuck it out."

"Angela says to tell you she's never been a bridesmaid."

"Never a bridesmaid, always a bride."

"Cute. I always forget how cute you are."

"I'm not cute, I'm gorgeous, like Jamie Lee Curtis. I am *woman*."

"Says who?"

"Says a world-renowned expert on that subject, Pulitzer prize winner Dave Higgins."

"I stand corrected. And now that you mention it, he's right."

"Aw, shucks," I said.

"So what have you been doing?" Saul asked.

"I'm involved in an experiment, among other things."

"With whom? Mac?" I could imagine him wiggling his eyebrows.

"No. God."

"Well," Saul said. "Are there any other symptoms?"

"I woke up this morning feeling ravenous, and I've just eaten four large pieces of French toast with boysenberry syrup. And two sausage links. I may throw up."

"Perhaps it's not God. Perhaps you're just pregnant."

"No, it's definitely God."

"What is this experiment's purpose?"

"Just to see what will happen."

"This sounds more and more like medical school. Or government research. Are you working for the National Institutes of Health?"

"There is this priest, you see. Amos Whitcomb, a friend of Mac's. He's the one who got me into this." I knew I could count on Saul to tell me to stay away from priests.

"Amos Whitcomb? Oh, I know about him," he said. "He spoke at a symposium I went to last year in San Francisco. His subject was the impact of spiritual forces on physical health, the so-called mind/body connection, that sort of thing. Very heavy stuff. Actually very impressive stuff. So he's your mentor?"

"You could say that."

"You could do worse," Saul said. "*I* could be your mentor."

"Gasp."

"Well, as long as we know you're in good hands, we can stop worrying about you. What with Mac and Amos Whitcomb and Dave Higgins working on you all at once, we can expect things to start looking up pretty soon. I'll tell Angela. She'll go shopping for a bridesmaid dress."

"Tell Angela I'm turning her in to the IRS. She's going to be audited for the next fifty years."

There was a pause. "I love you, sweetie," he said. "So take care of yourself. And give Mac a hug for us."

"I will."

"And, sweetie—" he said.

"Hmm?" I said.

"Say yes."

I took a breath, then let it out slowly.

"'Bye," Saul said. And he hung up.

I went back to the kitchen, where Mac was telling Mrs. Whelan how much Father Amos had liked her meal the night before.

Mac looked up at me. "That was quick."

"Short and sweet. Is there more sausage?"

He ignored that. I really wanted another sausage. "What did he have to say?" Mac asked.

"All I can tell you is that Saul is a smart aleck who never should have been unleashed on the unsuspecting public disguised as a shrink."

"Oh, really? He said that much, did he?"

"He had *nothing* to say."

"Ah." He lifted his eyebrows and looked at Mrs. Whelan, who shrugged and turned toward the sink. I sat down and cut off a piece of the sausage on Mac's plate, running it through the syrup before popping it into my mouth. I'd eat myself to death, that would be the ticket. Sausage suicide. I would at least be off the hook.

Mac was looking at me with interest.

"What?" I said irritably.

"I was just thinking that you sort of remind me of W. C. Fields right now."

"Anyone who hates babies and psychiatrists can't be all bad," I said. I hung my tongue out. Then I realized it was probably purple from the boysenberry syrup, so I pulled it in.

"Have another sausage," Mac said. I took one from his plate.

MAC USED THE COMPUTER AND MODEM to send material to other modems most of that afternoon while I dozed in the sun for a while. I took a walk, alone, at 4 o'clock and thought about Amos Whitcomb's comment that he'd learned it was sometimes good to be weak and vulnerable and dependent, to rely upon someone besides himself. I wondered if I could learn that, whether it truly was a good thing to learn, or whether I had fought so long and hard to become strong and independent and self-sufficient that I could never seek a middle ground that included moments of dependency and weakness.

I also wondered whether a middle ground was really what I wanted. Why, I wondered, was I having so much trouble knowing what I wanted? I couldn't recall ever having this kind of problem before.

I stopped at the corral to visit the horses. They came to me, probably hoping I'd brought carrots or oats. As I patted them I thought, out of the blue, that I loved them. I softly ran my hand up and down each of their noses, wanting to communicate this somehow. It was strange that the more I rubbed and patted them, the more the love for them seemed to build.

As this was going on I looked into the eyes of the big gray

horse, Toby, and thought I felt him loving me back. *Dumb*, I thought. *This horse can't love me. He can only respond instinctively to kindness.* But then, as I stared into Toby's eyes, tears welled up in my own. Where had that come from?

Suddenly another thought ran through my head: *It doesn't matter if Toby can love me. I can love him.* And I stroked him again, lovingly. It was an extraordinary feeling. The horse continued to gaze into my eyes, and then, after some minutes, he reached up with his big mouth and—I could not believe it—with his huge, soft, whiskery lips gave my hand what looked and felt like a horse kiss. It made me laugh. Of course, he was just hoping I had a carrot, I told myself. After that I stood there rubbing him and grinning for some time—basking in it, not wanting it to end.

When I got back at about 5, Mac had left the cottage. A note was on the bed. It said, "We'll leave around 7. OK?"

At 6 I showered and changed into my favorite little dinner costume, a black Liz Claiborne wool and Angora sweater with soft shoulder pads that made me look thin and a straight black silk skirt. The sweater was covered with tiny gold beads, and it looked as smashing on me as anything could look. I sprayed myself with Guerlain's Liu, a softly romantic sort of perfume no longer available in America. I always felt rich wearing it, partly because I'd heard a few years after I'd started using it that it was the only perfume Ethel Kennedy ever wore. Probably it was propaganda started by Guerlain, but I bought three-year supplies of Liu on my infrequent trips to Paris anyway.

After embellishing myself with extra eye makeup and a pair of gold earrings, I admired the whole effect. Understated elegance. Mom would be proud.

My date arrived at my door promptly at 7, dressed to the nines in a navy blue suit and white shirt. A red tie with navy pin dots added enough color to keep him from looking stuffy. He was handsome, I decided. I was just going to admit it to myself: he was much better looking than William Hurt. Actually, I was noticing the resemblance less and less.

He whistled at me. "Wow," he said.

I glowed. "It's a special occasion."

He came close and sniffed. "Seductive."

I gave him a look.

"We have reservations," he said, pulling me out the door.

We headed up Highway One with George Shearing on the tape deck. "I'd forgotten all about Shearing," I said. "Where are new Shearings, I wonder? I suppose there isn't a big market for this kind of jazz."

"Probably not," Mac agreed. "But there are some talented young jazz pianists around. Diane Schuur, for one." We floated along while George played and sang "Send in the Clowns."

As we passed Sea Ranch it was already dark. The ocean on our left hypnotically ebbed toward shore. Near Gualala Mac pulled into the parking lot of a low-slung restaurant with a weather-beaten wood sign that read "The Sea Nymph—Fine Dining & Dancing." Beneath that, a hand-painted cardboard sign announced: "Amos Otero Quartet, thru Saturday."

Inside, the restaurant was dark and cozy. Fresh flowers stood on cloth-covered tables that were set with wine goblets and good-looking white ceramic candlesticks instead of those cheap, squat, mesh-covered globes everyone was using. The whole wall facing the ocean was glass. The moon was up, the view spectacular. The music had already started, and several couples were on the small dance floor to the side near the window, dancing cozily to the old Tony Bennett hit, "If I Ruled the World." Most of them were our age or older. There seemed to be no singer; the piano carried the melody. The quartet was young, all of them in their late twenties, I guessed, and they were good. My hopes for the future were improving by the hour.

We sat at a table by the window. It was just like everyone's fantasy restaurant on the California coast. Breakers hit the rocks below us and sprayed within a few feet of the window. *They should make a movie here*, I thought. As a set, this was better than anything Universal could invent. Anything could happen here—intrigue, murder, romance. It made me a little nervous.

We ordered a baked fresh shrimp appetizer. It had an oriental flavor; the waiter told us the shrimp had been marinated before cooking in soy sauce with safflower oil, garlic, and candied ginger.

As we finished the last of the shrimp, Mac nodded toward the dance floor. "Come on," he said. He walked around the table and led me by the hand. They were playing "What I Did for Love."

We danced the way we'd done it in high school, moving our feet just enough to keep time to the music so the chaperones wouldn't accuse us of making out. In high heels I was tall enough to put my chin on top of Mac's shoulder. I could smell his Old Spice. When the song ended we stood there with our arms around each other, not speaking, me with my head down, Mac watching me. It was nice and dark on the dance floor, and most of the other dancers were standing there, too, so we weren't conspicuous.

The piano player announced through a mike on the piano that they were going to do a set of Lionel Richie hits and that he was going to try to sing, and he hoped we'd bear with him. "Endless Love" started up, and we began to move again, very slowly, very close. The pianist began to sing the lyrics in an unschooled, George Shearing style, and I was charmed. After a few seconds Mac pulled my right hand inward and kissed it. Then he let my hand rest on his chest while he wrapped both arms around me, pulling away slightly to look down at me. I looked back and slid both hands up around his neck the way I'd done at the Senior Prom, and we danced like that, faces inches apart, until the pianist got to the heartbreakingly sweet phrase that went, "My first love, you're every breath that I take..." Mac's eyes smiled at me, and he came two inches closer, just barely touching my lips for perhaps four or five seconds. I shivered. It was, beyond doubt, the most romantic moment I had ever experienced.

When the song ended, we hugged each other without speaking and stayed on the floor along with most of the others. Just as the musicians looked ready to start a new song, Mac leaned toward me and said, "I have a request."

"You'd better get it in quickly. I think they're about ready to play."

"The request isn't for a song," he said.

"What?"

He smiled suddenly and looked down at the floor, scratching the back of his neck. "I'd like you to think about marrying me," he said.

I looked back and forth between Mac's eyes, checking for humor. This was not a jest.

"Before the main course?" I asked.

One corner of his mouth turned up slightly. "Before you go back to Minneapolis." As if on cue, the band started playing. The song was "Still."

"Well, that gives me a little more time." I leaned into him again and put my cheek close to his. Neither of us spoke.

When we finally went back to our table, the waiter brought plates of just-caught crab (he claimed) with mushrooms and tarragon. It was perfect. We lingered over the food, and I found myself watching and listening to Mac more closely than I usually did as he spoke and laughed and watched me back. Over dessert and cappuccino—they did know about it out here—we chatted about his newspapers. In the midst of this he told me, very offhandedly, that someone had called him to ask if he'd consider selling two of his papers. Mac had told him the papers weren't for sale for less than an excessively high price he'd quoted; so he assumed it would come to nothing. Most of these offers, he explained, were bargain-hunters looking for a free ride.

Then he said casually that if the right price *were* offered, he'd been thinking it might not be such a bad idea to get rid of all three of his papers, so he could concentrate on other things, like syndicating his column. What were my thoughts?

I couldn't believe he was serious. After all, newspapers were his passion, and could be even more of a passion if he rearranged his priorities enough to do more of the things he enjoyed most. "A man doesn't walk away from something he loves as much as you love newspapers," I said, "on the off chance that he can make it as a columnist."

"There are other passions in my life," Mac said. "Writing columns could easily become a passion if I didn't have to put most of my time into the newspapers." It surprised me. How could he so easily contemplate such a major career move?

He started talking about his columns then, in some depth, and I was surprised again by the light in his eyes as he spoke. Was he really a *writer?* I wondered. It was possible, of course. He was, without doubt, one of the smartest men I'd ever known in a lot of different ways that might make for brilliance in writing. His editorials had been exceptional for editorials, but editorial writing and feature writing—the only things of Mac's I'd seen— were different from what he was talking about. A columnist had to have a kind of fingerprint, a unique style that was his alone— a "voice" that readers connected with and waited to hear each day. Did Mac have it, or could he develop it?

I didn't want to squash his enthusiasm without knowing what kind of writer he was trying to become, so I didn't say much about these things. I just listened as he talked animatedly about the viewpoint he wanted to put forth in his columns. That viewpoint, curiously, was not necessarily a traditional Republican one.

It was not even political, although Mac said it might encompass politics sometimes. It focused on insights into relationships, observations about down-to-earth philosophical and spiritual issues couched in very plain, concrete terms to which most adults could relate. It occurred to me that his viewpoint might, indeed, be unique enough to catch on. If he was a good enough writer.

We'd been talking about all this, or rather I'd been mostly listening to him talk about it, for perhaps forty minutes when I found myself listening only halfway, fighting the urge to lean right across the table and kiss him in a shockingly bold manner. He must have seen how I was looking at him, because he suddenly stopped speaking in mid-sentence and smiled at me quizzically.

"Are you thinking what I think you're thinking?" he said.

I looked away, then back again. "Prurience is not illegal in California, is it?"

"Almost nothing is illegal in California. Least of all, prurience."

"That's what I thought," I said, "I suppose it made me lose my head a little."

"I've always loved hot-blooded women who are ruled by their appetites," he said.

"No, you haven't. You've always loved hard-hearted Hannahs who keep you in your place."

His smile crinkled his eyes. "I've always loved you," he said, reaching over to pick up my hand. He kissed it, watching me. I watched back, totally enchanted.

"Well," I said after a few moments, "this must be what they call *flaming desire.*"

Mac laughed, sitting back but not letting go of my hand. "Not yet," he said.

"Oh, my goodness," I said, "my palms are damp, my face is pink, and my heart is going pitty-pat. What's left?"

He raised his eyebrows. It was a pretty innocent gesture, but that didn't help.

I blushed, then blushed again because I was embarrassed to be blushing. Blushing sort of went around and around, I thought, like one of those perpetual prayer wheels they used in India.

"There's no waiting period in California, you know," he said.

"For flaming desire?"

"We could get a license and be married tomorrow. I'm sure Amos would be happy to accommodate us."

"You're serious."

He was. Thinking hard, I stirred my cappuccino. It didn't need stirring, since I hadn't added anything to it. Now what? Here I was again, not knowing what to do next. I thought about Minneapolis, about Matt, about my work, my friends, my condo, my agent, the Twins and Vikings, and even Dayton's and Eddie Bauer's and Orchestra Hall and the Swedish Institute. I was waiting for options to occur to me.

"Your silence is making me anxious," Mac said.

I glanced up at him. Now what? I couldn't say yes, obviously. But what else was there? My mind was a blank. None of this was as easy as Father Amos had made it out to be. Priests ought to be forced to wear warning labels, I thought: *Caution: This man may be hazardous to your health.*

"I'm not saying no . . ." I said after several seconds. Mac raised his eyebrows, smiling expectantly. "But I'm not saying yes, either." His smile didn't disappear. It was such an endearing smile, I thought.

"I'm going to look on this as progress," he said.

The music had started up again. They were playing Neil Sedaka hits this set, the leader announced. I loved Neil Sedaka, although I was ashamed to admit it to anyone. Mac came over and pulled me to my feet, saying, "Maybe another few turns around the dance floor will make you putty in my hands."

"Another few turns around the dance floor will start a meltdown in my reactor core," I told him. It was not much of an exaggeration.

We danced another twenty minutes. "Breaking Up Is Hard to Do" was the last straw as far as I was concerned. By the time it was over and we'd headed for the parking lot, I was thinking what a good thing it was that we hadn't drunk anything alcoholic and the musicians had run out of Neil Sedaka songs so quickly. I, for one, was about done in.

We drove south again slowly, windows down, savoring the sea air and the nighttime landscape. I wasn't worried about what the wind did to my hair. It would be better if I looked like Harpo Marx by the time we got home, anyway. I could use all the help I could get.

Mac said, "Sit next to me," and I did. I was becoming frighteningly compliant. He put his arm around me, and we cruised along like two sixteen-year-olds in dad's new Buick. I tried to focus on the moment, not think ahead. It was nice.

Back at the house, we got out of the car and stood there leaning against it, both of us quiet.

"It was a magical evening," I said finally. "Thanks. You are a terrific date."

Mac turned to face me. Without speaking he brought both hands up to cradle my face. He did that thing that made his eyes sparkle, and then he kissed me—a long, tender, adoring kiss. Then he stepped back and took my hand, starting off toward the path to the cottage.

I followed him. When we got to the door he opened it, reached inside, and turned on the light. I made no move.

"I think we'd better say good night," he said.

"Definitely." That was good, considering how indefinite I felt.

"Do I get extra credit for valor?"

"No. But you don't get demerits, either."

"Well, that's better than nothing," he said. He kissed me again, lightly, and looked deep into my eyes, trying to read my mind. Failing that, he left.

For about an hour I tossed around in my bed. It was one of those nights when I closed my eyes and was painfully aware of the way my eyeballs were darting around under the lids. I couldn't force them into a comfortable, relaxed position. Eventually I turned on the light and tried to read. It was almost 1.

I needed milk, I decided. Some soothing amino acids to counteract insomnia. I went to the window and looked up at the house, where the lights were on in the parlor, I thought, but not in the kitchen. I put on my red terry-cloth robe and my bunny slippers with the whiskers and floppy ears and padded up the path.

The sound of pouring milk attracted Alistair Cooke, who undulated around my ankles begging for a libation. Or maybe he was just attracted to the bunnies. I poured some milk into his food dish. He slurped at it. So much for the bunnies.

I switched off the kitchen light and peeked around the corner into the parlor. Mac was not there. He'd forgotten to turn off the lamp, I figured, so I went in to do it. Then I noticed that he was sitting out on the porch, his back to me, feet on the railing. I watched him for a moment, my hand on the lamp switch.

On an impulse I straightened and walked over to the French door. Mac couldn't see me because his eyes were closed. Had he dozed off? I wondered. I hesitated. I pushed the door open quietly, and Mac's head moved. He glanced over at me.

"Sorry," I said. "Were you dozing?"

"No."

"I couldn't sleep, so I came for some milk."

As I walked over to the empty wicker chair and sat, I noticed that his eyes seemed slightly moist. He didn't seem self-conscious about it, so I thought I might have been mistaken. Maybe he was just tired.

"I'd like to say something," I said. "About our conversation tonight."

"Which one?"

"The one where you asked me to marry you."

"Oh?" He was staring out at the stars.

"My response was unforgivable. I'm sorry. Sometimes I'm about as sensitive as your average brick wall."

He gave me a sidelong glance. "It's okay."

"Mac, I know how unfair I'm being." I sighed. "I need—I don't know what I need. I think I need more time. Another few days, at least." I sat forward, running my fingers through my hair. "Can you forgive me for the way I'm acting? You don't deserve it, that's for sure."

"There's nothing to forgive. I want you to take your time."

I looked over at him. "If you could wait forever, that would mean I'd never have to give you an answer." It was a bad joke. Or was it a joke?

"The default option in this program is no," he said. "So no answer would be an answer." He glanced at me again. He wasn't smiling.

"Yes or no, huh?" I wished people would stop talking about options. I was starting to feel like a high flyer on Wall Street.

"Are you avoiding answering because you're afraid, or just confused?" he asked.

I thought about it. "I don't know. Both, maybe."

"Don't be afraid," he said. "Be honest. That way, no matter what you decide, I can accept it."

I looked at him. I wasn't sure I was up to that. "I'll try," I said.

The stars were bright. I watched them for a few minutes, then I stood.

"I feel," I said, "as if I hold your heart in my hand."

He raised his eyes. "Don't worry," he said, "you're not holding it all by yourself."

I considered it. "Thanks. That helps," I said.

I went back to bed then and slept.

22

Dave Higgins, dressed like the Marlboro man in a worn buckskin jacket and cowboy boots, was in the kitchen when I arrived for breakfast the next morning. It was Good Friday. I'd often wondered why they called it "good." It was the day Christ died. Good for us, yes, but not so good for Him. Of course, if you wanted to get into the deeper aspects of things, I supposed you could make a case for calling it "good" from His standpoint, too. I wasn't feeling deep at that moment.

Mac saw me first, got up, and smiled a welcoming smile that brightened my mood. It was raining out—a misty, chilling rain that made me long to sit in front of a roaring fire with a mug of mulled cider and a stack of magazines.

Dave stood as he saw Mac look at me, spun around, and threw out his arms. I let him hug me. He wrapped his fingers around my waist, and I was positive he was estimating its size. I wondered if my waist was still 30 inches. I guessed Jamie Lee was about a 26.

"You look gorgeous with your hair all damp and wispy like that," he said.

"I use rainwater," I said. "Calvin Klein's private label rainwater. You just spray it on and everyone would swear you'd been in a downpour."

Mac wore his amused look, still standing with his hands in his pockets. In front of him was a plate of omelette and a cup of coffee. He was boyishly cute. For reasons I cannot explain, I had a strong impulse right then to go over and kiss him. I weighed it briefly, then walked over to face him, and he looked down at me, surprised, puzzled. Mrs. Whelan was bustling about the kitchen, and Dave had his eyes glued to me, his mouth slightly open like a dog waiting to be fed a rasher of bacon. I reached up without smiling and planted my lips on Mac's. He kissed me back without removing his hands from his pockets.

When I finished, I went around the table to sit across from him. Dave was standing there as if he'd been poleaxed, a goofy grin on his face. Mrs. Whelan had turned from the sink to watch, and she appeared transfixed. Mac had sat down again, and he looked perfectly normal, if somewhat bemused.

"Is it supposed to rain all day?" I asked.

Dave let out the long breath he'd been holding and sat down. "No, it'll stop around noon."

"Good," I said. "I'd like to drive over to St. Stephen's to see Father Amos for a few minutes if I can get an appointment. Could I use your car?"

Dave was still grinning a doggie grin. Only now he looked back and forth between Mac and me, waiting for an announcement. After all, why else would I be going to see Father Amos? I was afraid he was going to start panting. I imagined he was already fantasizing about the honeymoon.

"I'll drive you," Mac said. "I have to go over there for a couple of hours anyway. Whenever you're ready."

"Great. Thanks."

He gave me one of those smiles that could melt marble.

"Would you like an omelette?" Mrs. Whelan asked me.

"No thanks. I think just some of your toast, and maybe a piece of cheese." A worried look crossed her face. She was being Mother again. I loved her.

Dave stood, picking up a stack of papers and two computer disks that were on the table in front of him. "This is great stuff," he said to Mac.

"We'll see," Mac said.

"Hey, when a genius with a Pulitzer prize in his den tells you your stuff is great, it's sacrilege to doubt him," Dave said.

"Are those Mac's latest columns?" I asked.

"Yeah. Have you seen them?"

"Not yet. I'm waiting for permission from the author."

Dave shot Mac a look, then put the disks in his jacket pocket. "He's afraid you'll find out he's a hack writer with nothing to say. Not that I blame him. Once you learned the truth you'd probably trade him in for a real literary genius in five minutes flat. If one were available."

Mac said, "Don't you have something to do, Dave?"

"Yeah. Well, I guess I'd better mosey along," Dave said, looking at me and pulling one of the disks back out of his pocket. "I'm going to drop these off at Mac's office to be printed and mailed out."

"Be sure to run them through a spell-checker," I said.

"Oh, you know about Mac's problem, do you? I thought it was our little secret." He glanced at Mac.

"Don't worry," I said. "My lips are sealed. Do you think I want anyone to find out I associate with bad spellers?"

Mac was crunching on his toast. "Look at it this way: if it weren't for people like me, all those spell-check software companies would be out of business. There'd be hundreds more computer jockeys on the dole."

"At least they'd all vote Democrat," Dave said. "Oh—how about dinner tomorrow night?"

Mac questioned me with his eyes. I nodded. "That would be nice," I said.

"Where should we meet?" Mac asked.

"My place. A barbecue. I'll invite a few others who'd like to meet Sally. She can be the visiting celebrity. Sort of a 'welcome to our neighborhood' party." He nodded to me. "So you'll know we'd like you to stay."

I smiled. "Sounds like a plot to me."

Dave laughed. "Have we got plans for you!"

"I don't care what anybody says," I told him, "you're not a bad guy. I don't know about eating with you, though."

"Did you know," he said, raising an eyebrow and glancing at Mac, "that eating together is supposed to be as intimate an act as sex? I think I read that in *Psychology Today*. Maybe it was *Gourmet*, I can't remember."

"It was *Road and Track*," I said. "The issue with the Lamborghini on the cover."

He chuckled. Had I said something funny? "Six-thirty or 7 would be good. We'll eat before 8. Don't bring anything." He glanced at Mrs. Whelan.

"I could send along some potato salad," she offered.

"Thanks," Dave said, winking at me. "Your potato salad would make the evening complete. But only if you'll come too," he said.

"I never say no to a party," Mrs. Whelan said. "I'm a party animal."

As we laughed, Dave walked over to her and kissed her on the lips, bending her backward at the waist. She giggled when he finished.

Exit Dave, born for the theater.

I took the plate of toast Mrs. Whelan had just handed me and went to the phone in the parlor. Effie told me that Father Amos was just coming out of a counseling session if I could hold for a minute. I did, munching on toast as I waited.

"Sally?" His voice came over the line a few minutes later.

"Hi," I said, swallowing quickly.

"How goes the experiment?"

"I think I need a consultation. Do you have a few minutes this morning?"

I heard his voice, muffled, consulting with Effie. He came back on the line. "How about 11? I'll have half an hour."

"I'll be there." *Well*, I thought, *he's the one who got me into this; he can jolly well get me out.*

AT 10:30 MAC AND I SET OFF through the rain in the Buick with the Dave Brubeck Quartet playing Paul Desmond's "Take Five." We reached the church before 11. Mac left me outside Father Amos's office door. The woman Mac had called Effie, secretary extraordinaire, came down the hall after he walked away. She seated herself at a plain little wooden desk in the hall. A phone and a pad of paper were the only objects on the desk. She nodded at me.

"You're Sally?" she inquired.

"Yes, and you're Effie. I understand you run things here."

She shook her head. "No, I think it's the other way around."

I sat in an orange plastic chair several feet from her table.

"We're all thrilled that you're well again," she said. "It's such an encouragement to us to keep praying."

"Thank you. You're part of Annie Bosworth's prayer group?"

"Oh, yes. I surely am."

"I must thank all of you. I know your prayers made a difference in my recovery." I knew, in the seconds after I said it, that it wasn't just a gratuitous remark. It was true. I can't say how I knew. I just did.

"It's a privilege," she said. "To pray, I mean. We can take it for granted, but what greater privilege is there in life than getting to know who God really is, and then participating in His work? That's what prayer is, as Father Amos always says. We get involved in what God is doing. We change the world that way."

At that moment Father Amos's office door opened, and he came out with his arm around a young man's shoulder. Twenty years ago the boy would have been called a hippie. He had long, dirty-looking brown hair and a wispy beard. His eyes looked hollow and furtive. His clothes were filthy, and I could smell the sweat on them from ten feet away. Father Amos didn't seem to notice. The young man saw me and smiled. The smile transformed him into a sane person, right before my eyes. He hugged Father Amos, got a hug in return, and walked down the hall.

Effie handed Father Amos a stack of phone messages from her pad and said, "Remember now, half an hour—no more!"

He laughed happily. "Effie," he said, "you are a woman of faith!" She looked at him sternly. He stuck his arm out and grabbed mine, pulling me down the hall. "Come on, let's go for a walk!"

Outside, the rain had indeed stopped. Father Amos started toward the path that led up to the ridge. I took a deep breath and chugged along after him, my shoes squishing on the wet pebbles.

"Well, don't keep me in suspense!" he said as I caught up to him. His eyes were excited. "What's happened so far?"

"Oh, nothing much. Last night Mac tried to get me to marry him today."

"Aha! Straight to the heart of things, eh?"

"You might say that."

"Well, what did you say?"

"I didn't say no."

"Good, good." He was nodding vigorously, walking slower. I was grateful not to have to gasp for breath.

"But I didn't say yes."

He glanced at me. "Why?"

"I've been thinking about that. I tried very hard last night to look for options I hadn't considered before. Naturally, saying yes to Mac's proposal was one such option."

"Well?" His eyes were lit up like the Point Reyes lighthouse.

I sighed. "It isn't so easy." He was walking even slower, watching me. "Father, I can't say yes as if there were no tomorrow. I can't make decisions like that, leap of faith or no leap of faith. This is getting too complicated. There's so much I'll have to face tomorrow and the next day and the next. My whole life is elsewhere—not here. My work isn't even the most important thing—I could work here. It would just be a bit less convenient. But my *home* is Minneapolis, my son's home is there with me, my friends are there." I paused, thinking. "What am I saying? None of this is the real problem. There's more to it. Much more. And I don't fully understand what that's all about."

I walked along at a snail's pace, staring at the pebbles on the path. "I'm scared to death, Father Amos. I am absolutely terrified of walking away from the happy, very predictable life I had before Mac reappeared. And I'm afraid, more than I can tell you, of the pain he and I could cause each other. I can't ignore that. I guess that's actually why I didn't say yes."

"Well," he said. "That's fascinating." He watched me for a minute. "Perhaps God has a few things up his sleeve that He hasn't revealed yet. Perhaps the thing to do is just to wait."

"Wait for what?"

"Surprises. And perhaps for the fear to be displaced by courage. There's a Scripture that says, 'perfect love casts out fear.' God's love is always at work casting fear out of our lives."

I glanced at him. "My fears seem to be getting bigger, not smaller." That was something I hadn't thought about consciously, but it was true. I tried to remember a time when I hadn't been at

least a little afraid—of disapproval, of rejection, of disappoint-
ment, of intimacy and vulnerability most of all. It wasn't hard to
deal with faceless strangers; it was the person who *knew* me that
I feared above all others. That was the one who could mortally
wound me. And now, with Mac, I was feeling more fear, about
more things, than I could ever remember.

"I don't think we ever entirely stop being fearful," Father
Amos said. "Fear is a natural, sometimes even useful response to
the threats posed by the world around us. But God can enable
us to be courageous in the face of all we have to fear. As we get
to know and trust and believe in God's absolute love for us—a
love that actually forgives us for our sins—fear begins to lose its
grip. That makes it possible for us to forgive others for not loving us perfectly or painlessly—and it gives us the courage to
love and believe in spite of our fears, and in spite of the pain it
may bring us."

"Right now I'm so confused I don't know what I believe. I
don't even know what—or whom—I love, other than my son."

He stopped, turned, and looked me in the eye. "You only love
what you're willing to die for. We may *say* we love others or
believe in this or that cause or principle—and we may even 'feel,'
deep down, that we do. But unless we're willing to put our lives
on the line for them, it isn't true."

We started walking again, proceeding in silence for a few
minutes. I thought about the people and ideals I would be willing to die for, and I was surprised at the intensity of the love I
felt for my son in those moments. I thought of Angela and Saul,
of Biba, a few other old friends, of my family, my work, even my
country. Would I lay down my life for them? I would for my son,
yes. Without a second's hesitation. For my friends? I tried to picture myself in a life or death situation, and I wondered if I'd
throw myself in the path of a moving train to save them. It

seemed possible, but I wasn't sure. I felt ashamed, suddenly, of my hesitation.

"What are you thinking?" Father Amos said, startling me.

"I was trying to imagine throwing myself in front of a moving train to save the people I profess to love. I'm having trouble with that."

He smiled. "Try something a little more realistic. Think about what you're willing to sacrifice of yourself on a daily, practical basis. Love and faith are moment-to-moment acts— daily choices, commitments of our loyalty, our energy and resources, of our whole selves for the sake of another person. These acts reveal what we're really willing to die for. And also what we're willing to live for."

I sighed. "Father," I said, "I feel like I've been tossed into the middle of the Pacific Ocean without a life jacket. And I'm not a very good swimmer."

He smiled and put his arm around my shoulder in the sort of gesture Saul or Angela would have made. "It's okay," he said, smiling. "God is a great lifeguard. I'm pretty fair myself. We'll stick with you. You won't drown."

I looked at him. "I'd better learn to swim alone. You can't stay with me indefinitely," I said.

He was still smiling, still had his arm around me. "Oh, but I can," he said, "and I will. As long as I have breath. And of course, God will. You're perfectly safe, in spite of the way things look."

I stared into his eyes and knew—without knowing *how* I knew—that he was telling me the truth. How was it possible that this man who barely knew me could care so much, could be so willing to share himself with me? And how was it possible that a God I knew almost nothing about could go to such lengths to connect with me?

It occurred to me in that instant that I might have said no instead of yes when Mac had invited me to California the week before. I might not have come, might have decided not to risk it, might never have known Amos Whitcomb. And I might never have known this moment. Without thinking I grabbed the priest and hugged him. When I pulled away, I noticed tears in his eyes, which made me less self-conscious about my own.

After a few moments we began to walk again. As we came to a fork in the path I glanced at my watch and saw that we'd been gone twenty-five minutes. "We have to get you back to Effie," I said.

"Oh, yes, thank you for remembering!" he said. "There's a shortcut up ahead." Several yards up the path we came to an opening in the undergrowth that led down the hillside in a zig-zag pattern. We took it and made it back to the church in less than five minutes.

In the courtyard he turned and looked at me sympathetically. "Can I make a suggestion?"

"Sure."

"Don't try so hard. Let God do something surprising. It's His turn, remember?"

"Father," I said, "when I asked to talk with you about all this, it was because it's important to me that you understand my decision—whatever it turns out to be. If I end up saying no to Mac, it won't be a decision I'll have arrived at without a lot of soul-searching. And whatever I decide, I want to remain your friend."

He frowned thoughtfully. "Naturally, your decision won't affect our friendship. That is cemented by God. But just be a little patient about Mac, and don't decide too quickly. This is still the second day of seven you agreed to, remember? God didn't create the world in only two days."

"I'm a smaller project," I said.

"Not necessarily." We both smiled at that and then looked toward the front door of the church as it opened. Mac was there, waving us toward him.

"Come here," Mac said. "I want you to see something." We

followed him into the vestibule. There, standing on an easel, was a painting. It was acrylic, about 36 by 48 inches, an impressionistic rendering of a lamb being carried by a shepherd in a rocky, rural setting. It was absolutely stunning.

"It just arrived, along with two others. What do you think?" he said.

"What's it called?" I asked.

"*The Shepherd*," Mac said. "It represents the 23rd Psalm. I want everyone to see it on Sunday. It will help them envision what's going to happen when we begin construction on the cottages this coming week."

"It's wonderful," I said. "Don't you think so?" I looked at Father Amos.

"It is fabulous," he said. "Just fabulous." His eyes were glued to the canvas. "You were so right, Mac," he said.

I looked back at the painting. There was something vaguely familiar about it. Then I glanced down at the signature in the corner. "Marjorie Hennessy," it said.

Mac saw the look on my face. "I liked your painting, so I went to see her while I was in Minneapolis after your accident. She was very enthusiastic about our project. We ended up commissioning twenty paintings. The committee here was very excited. We knew these were going to be exactly what the cottages should have, and she gave us a good price, to say the least."

"If this is an example, they couldn't be more perfect," I said. "I can imagine how thrilled she is to be part of this."

"We're flying her out here when the cottages are finished, to hang each painting in its proper place," Mac said. He was tickled pink. So was I. I wished I could be there to see it.

THAT AFTERNOON MAC WENT OFF on newspaper business to someplace called Amity, several miles up the road, leaving me ensconced in the cottage with a pot of coffee and ten of his columns to read. I was almost afraid to begin. What if they were dull and pedestrian? What could I tell him? I hated reading the work of writers I knew. It was risky business.

By the time I got through the third, which was a funny, insightful, beautifully crafted piece about sibling rivalry, I knew that Dave had not been exaggerating when he said Mac's work was great. I also knew that Mac should be syndicating his columns, not just editing newspapers. His instincts were leading him in the right direction, and I planned to encourage those instincts. He had the "voice" to be memorable and unique; he was one of a kind. The discovery made my spirits soar.

After I finished all the columns—twice—I felt inspired to work on my own stuff. So I sat down at the computer and attacked chapter 7 of Saul's and my manuscript. Everything was humming along in high gear a couple of hours later when I heard a tap on my door.

It was Mrs. Whelan. "There's a phone call for you," she said.

"Is it Mac?" I asked as I followed her up the path.

"Your son," she said.

I had one of those moments every mother understands, when I tried not to think he was sick or injured or in trouble. It's instinct, pure and simple. *Please, God, let him be okay.*

"Hi, Mom," he said cheerfully when I got on the line. Sigh of relief. He could speak. A good sign.

"Hi, honey," I said, trying to sound unconcerned. "You sound happy."

"I am."

"What's happened? Did you ace an exam?"

"Much better than that."

"If you tell me Valerie is pregnant, I'll come right through this line and choke the life out of you."

"Mom, you've got to get your mind out of the gutter."

"Okay, so what is it?"

"I've been offered a job. Starting a week after I graduate."

"That's wonderful!" I knew he'd been worried about that, sending off resumés and samples of his work to a lot of different newspapers—both in Minneapolis and in larger communities. I'd forced myself not to ask him about responses, wanting to avoid putting extra pressure on him.

"There's just one small problem," he said.

"Oh. What's that?" Why was there always one small problem where my kid was concerned?

"Mom, I won't take this job if you tell me not to. I'll understand. I won't be mad. At least not permanently. So please tell me the truth."

"What are you talking about? Why wouldn't I want you to take it? Did *Kiddie Porn Journal* make you an offer?"

"It's more complicated than that."

"Come on, quit dragging it out."

"Well, the paper that wants to hire me is a small daily called *The Amity Courier.* It's a great job. Exactly what I wanted. Full-time reporting. Some investigative stuff. It's a progressive paper, and they have a great managing editor, George Michael. I applied there a couple of months ago after one of my instructors told me about the paper. It's a terrific opportunity."

"Yes? So what's the problem?"

"The thing is, *The Amity Courier* is owned by one Matthew MacDonald. By the way, I never knew until today that his first name is really Matthew. Isn't that interesting?"

"What?"

"Look, I didn't tell you about applying there because I didn't think I stood a chance. Believe me, I wasn't hired by Mac, Mom. I was hired by his managing editor. I didn't know Mac had anything to do with the paper until today. When Mac found out

about it this afternoon, he called me. He's very happy about it—
he thinks it's fate or something."

"My goodness," I said.

"Huh?" my son replied.

"Nothing," I said. "It's just very surprising. So what's involved
in this?"

"Well, Mac and I talked for quite a while. We just hung up
before I called you. He says the only thing that worries him is that
you could look on this as outside pressure on your relationship
with him. I gather you and he haven't really, uh, come to terms
yet. He doesn't want you to feel *coerced*, he said."

"Hmmm," I said.

"Mac says it's got to be up to you, and I agreed to that. Mom,
he invited me to live in the guest cottage at his house if this thing
works out. It would mean I wouldn't have any overhead. I could
save to get a place of my own. And, hey, it would be sort of like
having a chaperone, right? Mac would keep me out of trouble."

"You never get into trouble."

"If you believe that, why did you think Valerie was pregnant?"

I took a breath. "I'm thinking, I'm thinking . . . Don't press
me."

"Well, I don't have to give *The Courier* an answer until
Monday morning. You can take the weekend to think it over. This
is pretty weird, isn't it?"

"That's putting it mildly." Conspiracy theories were already
forming in my mind. My serious talk with Mac couldn't be put
off any longer.

"Can I call you Sunday?"

"That would be good. And, honey, congratulations. I'm very
proud of you."

"Thanks, Mom," Matt said. "I'm proud of you, too." He hung
up.

23

Mac got home just after dark, went right to the barn, and did some horsy chores before coming into the house. I was laying in wait for him in the parlor, ready to pounce.

"Hi," he said as he saw me. He tossed his jacket on the back of the sofa. "Have you eaten, I hope?"

"I told Mrs. Whelan to take the night off. I'll fix you something if you're hungry."

"Maybe later, thanks." He sat. His eyebrows went up. "Well?"

I was sitting in the armchair by the fireplace. I'd lit a fire, and it was just catching. The room was filling with the sweet smell of it.

"Well," I said.

"Look, Sal, I don't know what to say. I promise you, I didn't know Matt was applying at *The Courier*, and I didn't know until today that he'd been offered a job. He's by far the best candidate, believe me, and there were a lot of good applicants. My editor will be very disappointed if Matt doesn't come. He thinks he's the best he's seen in ten years. So do I, as a matter of fact. He's a chip off the old block. He's going to be a great reporter, a great writer." He looked at me sharply.

"I think so, too. But I'm prejudiced."

Mac sighed. "My editor's very upset with me about this, and I don't blame him. It isn't easy to find somebody as good as Matt."

He was fingering the arm of his chair, pulling on the fabric. "Well, it can't be helped," he said. "I realize I should have kept my mouth shut about his staying here at the cottage. I mean, I knew better than to toss that into the equation, but it just slipped out. I was excited, I guess. But it was stupid of me to say it, and I apologize. Anyway, I explained things to him. As I'm sure he's told you, he's willing to live with whatever you decide, and so am I." He sighed and shook his head. "My editor may be another matter."

Thinking hard, I watched him. The fire was blazing now. It felt good and warm.

"So what do you think?" he said.

"I think it's very surprising," I said.

"Yes?"

I looked at him. "You really didn't know Matt was being considered? And you really didn't influence things at all?"

His eyes widened, hurt. I felt bad for asking. After a few seconds he said, very deliberately, "I didn't know. But today when George told me he'd hired a U. of Missouri grad as a reporter, for some reason I immediately thought it had to be Matt. I don't know why. It couldn't have been anyone else, I guess. Could it?"

"I guess not," I said. I sat forward in the chair, thinking. "How about some buttered popcorn?" I said.

"And a bottle of Snapple," he answered, looking relieved that the inquisition seemed to be over. He started to get up.

"No," I said. "I'll do it." He sat back and watched me as I got up and started out to the kitchen. At the door I stopped. I came back and went over to stand by his chair. He looked up at me, eyebrows lifted.

"I'm going to tell Matt to go ahead and take the job."

He smiled. "Good."

"I can't deprive him of this."

"You could," he said. "He'd forgive you. So would I. He'll get plenty of other good offers."

"Well, I'm not going to. He deserves it. He earned it."

"True."

I smiled and turned, starting toward the kitchen again. Then I stopped, turned again to face him.

"I have an important question."

"Yes?" he said.

"If I decide to love you, will you break my heart?" I didn't say it lightly.

He pushed himself out of his chair and took two steps toward me.

"No doubt about it," he said.

"Somehow, that wasn't the answer I was hoping for."

"It's the truth. I'll break your heart, and you'll break mine. We'll do it more than once, most likely. Not on purpose, but it will happen."

"It gets better and better."

"I'll do everything in my power not to, I can promise you that. And I can promise I'll never stop loving you."

I looked at him, hard. "That isn't just a feeling," I said. "I mean, you're not just 'in love' with me. You've made a decision to love me and never stop, no matter what. Haven't you?" My awareness of this had grown to the point where it was no longer merely an abstract concept. It was true. This surprised me and moved me immensely. As I stood there, I was suddenly awed by the magnitude of this certainty.

Mac was watching me. He had reached up and was pushing my hair back from my face with his hand. "I'm glad you understand that," he said.

I turned my face into the palm of his hand and kissed it, closing my eyes. His arms went around me, and mine around him.

"I want to love you," I said. "I want to love you the same way. But I'm not sure I'm capable of it. I'm scared to death of it, Mac. I am absolutely terrified."

He pulled me even closer. It was, I thought, the best place in the world to be.

"You're very brave," he said, smiling a little, "to be so terrified, and to want to love me in spite of it." He pulled back and looked at me, his smile fading.

"Brave, or stupid," I said. "Or crazy."

He touched my hair again, pulling it behind my ear and then kissing me very tenderly. "Well," he said when he finished, "if it's any help, I'll love you even if it turns out you're stupid or crazy. But I admit, brave is better."

We stood there holding each other for a long time.

LATER, AS WE SIPPED kiwi-flavored Snapple and nibbled Orville Redenbacher's best, Mac said, ever so casually, "Did you have a chance to read the columns?"

"*Of course* I had a chance to read the columns. Twice."

I let him suffer in silence for a minute. "They're brilliant, Mac. Absolutely terrific. I'm so impressed, I hardly know where to begin."

"You don't have to say that."

"Oh, thanks. I thought I did."

More silence.

"Do you think they're good *enough*?"

I smiled. "Oh, yes. They're definitely good enough."

He was watching me for signs of insincerity. Writers. What can I say? We're all alike.

"Well," Mac said, pulling in a deep breath, "that's more than just an idle question. I got a *bona fide* offer for the papers today. Do you think I should take it?"

That left me speechless for a moment. Then I laughed. "Mac, that's incredible! All three papers?"

"All of them. If I accept the offer, Matt wouldn't be working for me by the time he comes here; he'd be working for the new owners. Same managing editor, however. They're insisting on a long-term contract with George Michael. It shows they've got good sense. They're fine people, very responsible and committed to the same kinds of things I am. I'd feel comfortable selling to them."

"Did they meet your price?"

He nodded. "If I become a failed columnist, I'll be able to pay for the psychiatrist and antidepressants. But I won't be independently wealthy."

"I think you should go for it, Mac."

He looked at me, eyes wide. "After all the years I've spent working for what I have, it isn't easy. This is one of those major life crises they always talk about in articles about stress."

"I know. But isn't it exciting, too?"

"Yes." He thought for a minute. "Is this how you felt when you moved to Minneapolis?"

"I think so. It was very scary. Like that moment when you're at the top of the roller coaster and your heart's in your throat, but you know it's too late to get out, so you have no choice but to just hang on and scream all the way to the end of the ride." I remembered that drive to Minneapolis, and that feeling, as if it had happened only yesterday. Maybe because I'd felt a little like that yesterday. And today.

"That's it," he said. He scrutinized my face for a minute. What was he looking for?

"Welcome to the world of free-lance writing," I said. "You'll get used to it. It's a lot like high-stakes poker at Monte Carlo, I suppose."

Mac poured a little more Snapple into our glasses, and I made a toast to his new career. He drank to it too and then said, seriously, "It's going to be okay."

"I know. You're a great writer. You're going to be famous and powerful."

"That's not what I meant," he said.

I thought about it. "I hope you're right."

"You'll see," he smiled. "Have a little faith."

I thought about that for a few seconds, too, and munched on the popcorn.

"That's all I have. Just a little."

He leaned forward and kissed me. "That's enough," he said.

After that we fooled around a little more, if you could call it that. It was the sort of fooling around Debbie Reynolds did with Carlton Carpenter while they sang "Abba Dabba Honeymoon" in that fifties movie. What was it? *Two Weeks With Love?* I thought how frustrating things were getting, and for a brief moment I couldn't recall why we'd decided on this kind of restraint. Then I remembered.

Half an hour later I went to bed feeling discombobulated, as I imagine Mac did, and wishing I was still as innocent as I was in the mid-fifties, when Debbie and Carlton's fooling around was the most libidinous behavior I could imagine. As I said in the beginning, everything was much easier then.

24

On Saturday we went riding in the late morning. The horses were ready to gallop, but I wasn't. I hung back while Mac ran his mare into the woods and back out again all along our route. They were full of vim and vigor, both Mac and his steed.

Mrs. Whelan didn't come until mid-afternoon because she'd had a funeral to attend. She got started on potato salad as soon as she arrived. I went into the kitchen to help, putting the eggs on to boil and chopping up some onions and celery.

After that it was a lazy day. I sat in the parlor and listened to an Anita O'Day album and then found, upon inspecting the record and tape shelf, six older Melissa Manchester albums, a Doris Day with Les Brown and His Band of Renown, and Linda Keene backed up by Henry Levine and his Strictly From Dixie Jazz Band. I listened to Linda first, then Doris and Les, and finally turned to M.M. Nobody could sing "Don't Cry Out Loud" but Melissa, and nobody should try. Once she sang almost any song, it was hers alone.

Mac did some bookkeeping chores at the dining room table, writing checks, paying bills, and working on some of the details for the sale of his newspapers. I tried to read but was constantly distracted by the music and my musings about Mac and me. Finally I just sat back and let the music carry me along. A little later I did manage to write some short notes to friends back in Minneapolis, including Angela, not mentioning when I'd be home.

At 5:30 I showered and put on my best celebrity barbecue togs, a pair of dark blue jeans, and an oversize purple turtleneck sweater that was softer than cashmere, and more expensive. I'd bought it six years before and expected it to last another fifty. At least.

Mac came to the cottage in tan cords and a heavy navy cable knit turtleneck. We were the nicely coordinated California country couple.

"You're looking extremely sexy," Mac said after appraising me.

"Well, what with Dave Higgins lusting after me and all, I feel an obligation to keep up appearances. You think it's easy to compete with Jamie Lee Curtis?" I wrapped a big flowered silk scarf around my shoulders and tied it, western-style.

"Dave is not the only one."

"The only one what?"

He grinned at me.

"I thought you were above all that," I said, fluffing my hair.

"Sure, I am," he said.

MRS. WHELAN TOOK HER OWN CAR. The potato salad went with her. Dave's house, it turned out, was about twenty minutes away, north on Highway One. It was a neat little white-picket-fenced oceanside English country cottage. It surprised me because I'd imagined him living in something more modern. Inside, the house was comfortable, designed for bachelor living. It was, however, extraordinarily neat. I commented on it to him.

"I'm obsessive-compulsive," he said. "I line up my shoes in the closet by color and function." He was dressed at that moment in a neatly pressed western outfit, complete with a silver and turquoise belt buckle. I wished I could look in his closet.

"You're going to make some woman very happy one of these days," I said.

"What do you mean?" he said, a lecherous look on his face. "I've been doing that for years."

We'd been among the first to arrive. Mac and Dave went out to the deck behind the house, where they set up six barbecue grills with mesquite briquettes and assorted implements for cooking. Fifteen minutes later a Chevy Caprice full of women arrived, about eight of them piling out like clowns from a funny car. They all carried Tupperware bowls and cartons full of food. One of them came up to me right away.

"Sally? I'm Annie Bosworth," she said, sticking out her hand.

"Annie, I'm so glad to have a face to connect with your name—at last," I said. She looked just the way I thought she would—the Helen Hayes type, gray-haired, compact, with the sort of pink-and-white, happily wrinkled face that smiled even in repose. She looked smart, funny, alert.

"This will be a celebration," she said, twinkling. "Of your recovery and of your visit."

"I have you to thank for my recovery," I said.

She laughed a girlish little laugh, grabbing my hand. "Oh no, you don't! I was only one of a whole group of middlemen. We all know Who to thank."

It wasn't a rebuke, just a happy comment. A very nice woman, indeed. I squeezed her hand.

"Now that you're here," she said, "I hope you'll get involved in our prayer group. Now that you've experienced such a miraculous recovery you could have a powerful ministry, you know."

"I'm not sure I understand," I said. "I'm presuming you mean 'ministry' in the generic sense."

She looked at me with the look Margaret Rutherford as Miss Marple gave to guilty felons in the old Agatha Christie movies— chin tucked in, one eye slightly closed. "I mean you could be interceding for others who need healing and comfort. Your experience gives you a unique ability to do that."

Hmm, I thought. This woman saw me as some sort of spiritual tower of strength, and I wasn't sure how to disabuse her of that notion without hurting her feelings or her faith. Then I thought how unlikely it was that I could faze her in either regard.

"Annie, I'm not in your league," I said. She pulled one corner of her mouth into a small smile. I patted her shoulder. "I wouldn't have the faith to do what you're suggesting."

"Nonsense," she said, looking up at me with both eyes squinted. "You have it. You just don't know it yet. You simply need practice!" Her smile was big now. She patted my arm.

"I think you're giving me too much credit."

She shook her head. "No, no. It's not you I'm giving credit to. God is in the business of turning unlikely people like us into his emissaries. The less qualified you feel, the better. I worry about anyone who thinks he's got what it takes to be a CEO in God's business. That's trouble. But you—well, my dear, perhaps you and I will even have a joint ministry of some sort. That strikes me as a distinct possibility."

I smiled. "I'll believe that when I see it," I said.

"That's fine," she said. "That's soon enough."

PEOPLE WERE MILLING AROUND, more than I imagined lived in the entire area. Dave and Annie and Mrs. Whelan kept pulling me around to introduce me. I couldn't remember most of their names. I was introduced as "Mac's friend, the mystery writer," which was nice. Nobody made sly remarks about our relationship. They were people I liked immensely, right from the start. They were attractive to me in a way I couldn't define. It puzzled me. What was it?

I watched them laughing, exchanging stories, hugging each other. Was there something in the water that made these people so huggy? I'd never seen anything like this type of interaction before. They seemed to respect and love each other in a remarkably open and intense way. It showed in the ways they encouraged and accepted each other, listened eagerly, argued and challenged without rancor, asked probing questions, sought to really *know* each other. They were a giant family, in the best sense of the word. I knew that if any of them had a need or problem, the others would be there immediately to help. And I knew that none of them would have any fear of admitting they had a need or problem to begin with.

Amos Whitcomb arrived late, bursting into the living room like Bishop Fulton J. Sheen making an entrance. All he needed was a black cape with a scarlet satin lining. The man was totally captivating. He drew people like dogs draw fleas. The best part was that he wasn't aware of it.

"Sally!" he cried as he spied me. You'd think he hadn't seen me in ten years. I got hugged and patted again.

"Isn't she wonderful?" he asked everyone standing around us. "I've been telling everyone how wonderful you are," he added. "I hope you don't mind, but I also told several people they should bring their copies of your books for autographs." My agent and publicist. I grinned and said it was my pleasure. As soon as I said this, about ten books appeared in the hands of the guests, almost like magic. Maybe they'd been waiting for Father Amos's signal. I signed them all and felt more like a celebrity than I had in years.

The barbecue smells were wafting in from the deck. I was kept busy helloing and signing a few more books, some of which were worn and tattered enough that I knew they'd been passed around among a good half dozen friends over the years. It pleased me that as many people gushed over Mac's columns as gushed over my books. Inequity in that regard would have made me uncomfortable. I knew Mac wouldn't have resented it, but it would have bothered me; so I was glad he was as much admired as I.

A couple of hours later, while Mac was off in a corner listening to an exceptionally attractive, dimpled blonde who seemed to be holding his attention without effort, Dave sidled up to me, plate in hand, and said, "Have you seen *Perfect?*"

"Pardon?"

"The movie. It was great."

"Jamie Lee Curtis?"

"You didn't see it."

"No," I said. "I don't know how I could have missed that one."

"How about *Trading Places* or *A Fish Called Wanda?*"

"Sorry. I don't get around much."

"I have them on video."

"I'll bet you do."

He grinned at me. I tightened my tummy muscles. Any woman of my generation would have done the same thing. Even so, I kicked myself.

Father Amos appeared at my elbow. "David," he said, "unless I miss my guess, you are in great jeopardy, spiritually speaking."

Dave put his arm around the priest's shoulder. "You are a man of extraordinary perceptiveness. But I'm afraid you're too late."

Father Amos gave him an arch look. "There is no such thing as *too* late," he said. "Not while you're still breathing. Until then, there is early, on the dot, or just in the nick of time. And so far, at least where you're concerned, I believe I am still early."

Father Amos looked at me protectively. I laughed, glancing

across the room at Mac. He was still talking with the blonde, head down slightly, all ears. He held a plate in his hand, as did she. She was wiggling her fanny as she talked. Dave caught my look and lifted his eyebrows.

"You'd better get over there," he said.

"I'm not worried," I said. "She's wearing a 100 percent polyester dress." The woman could make polyester double knit all the rage again. It gave me pause. I'd bestowed my last polyester double knits on the Salvation Army a year before.

Father Amos was enjoying it, eyes bright. He looked alert and excited, like a puppy about to scramble after a tennis ball.

Dave was still watching Mac and Dolly Parton over in the corner. Actually he was watching Dolly, not Mac. Without looking at us he said, "Excuse me for a minute, will you? I think Mac needs some help." He headed toward them, elbowing his way through the crowd. *Men are so fickle*, I thought. I wondered how Dolly did that little wiggle.

Father Amos was nodding and waving at people as they jostled past us. I pulled him over toward the side of the room, where I'd spotted a couple of vacant chairs.

"Guess what?" I said as we sat. "Something surprising has happened."

"Aha!" he said, mashing the baked beans on his plate. "Tell me!"

I told him about Matt and his job. His eyes widened and gleamed. "Well, that's very exciting, isn't it? Very exciting! Go on, tell me more."

I looked at my hands. On my right hand was the little ruby ring. Tonight was the first time I'd worn it since Mac had given it to me. "I'm going to tell Matt to go ahead and take the job. It feels right." I paused, glancing up at him. "But it's scary, too."

He nodded, taking a mouthful of Mrs. Whelan's potato salad. "Naturally," he said.

"But I'm not as scared as I was this morning," I said.

He smiled, crunching the celery in the salad. "Perhaps you're just as scared, but more courageous," he said. "That's even better."

I gave that some thought. "Maybe."

Annie Bosworth had come up to us, and she was pulling up a folding chair to join us.

"Am I interrupting something?" she said as she sat.

I smiled at her. "No, of course not," I said. I wished I could look just like Annie when I got to be her age.

"Father," she said, leaning toward us confidentially, "you'll be so pleased. David Higgins has just told me he wants to donate the cost of one cottage for the retreat center!"

Father Amos smiled. "Well, isn't that a surprise!" he said, glancing over toward Dave with a pleased look. Somehow I thought it wasn't really such a surprise.

"He's a dear man," Annie went on, reaching out to touch my arm. "He said he hoped we could accept a donation from an admirer who'd like to visit God from time to time at St. Stephen's." She laughed a musical little laugh, as if Dave had made the cleverest remark in the world.

I glanced over at Dave. *He's a complicated man*, I thought. "Of course he's going to want you to put a plaque on the door," I said, looking at both of them. "The David Higgins Memorial Cottage." *Or the Jamie Lee Curtis Memorial Cottage*, I thought.

Both Annie and Father Amos laughed. *Go ahead and laugh*, I thought. *Wait 'til the plaque appears.*

Then, curious, I said, "I understood you already had the cottages paid for. Was I wrong?"

Father Amos looked at me, his eyes widening slightly. "I'll bet Mac hasn't told you," he said, shifting his glance to Annie. "That would be like him. Well, it's no secret. Mac originally underwrote the cost of the the entire project—all twenty cottages, plus a large meeting center with a kitchen and dining room and facilities to handle every kind of retreat group we could envision. It was all his idea to begin with."

I was floored. The entire project? Perhaps as much as a million dollars for the entire plan? I had no idea he had that kind of money. His lifestyle wasn't exactly material for a Robin Leach special.

"Wow," I said. Understatement was my strong suit.

Father Amos was watching Mac across the room. He and Dolly and Dave had been joined by another man who looked like Central Casting's choice to play the lead in the life story of Harry Belafonte. He even wore a calypso shirt. The four of them were having a jolly good time.

"We made an agreement with Mac," Father Amos went on. "I knew the people of the parish—and people from all over, for that matter—would want to have a part in the project. So Mac agreed that others could donate as they were moved to, provided we didn't go out asking for help, and he would pay whatever wasn't covered by others. That way, the project is actually the outgrowth of the work God is doing in many different lives. And we aren't taking resources away from essential services of the church. It's worked splendidly," he said, a look of satisfaction on his face. He forked a last bite of baked beans into his mouth.

Annie was thrilled. I had the feeling she was thrilled twenty-four hours a day, maybe more. "We've had donations of every conceivable sort, from all over the world," she said. "Some money, but mostly furnishings, building materials, seats for the meeting hall. Even shrubs and flowers have been promised to complete the landscaping. There have been increases in costs, but the donations have kept us within the resources we have at our disposal," she said. "It's such fun to be involved in what God is doing. Never a dull moment!"

I had to admit that it looked that way.

Amos Whitcomb was still looking at Mac across the room.

"He is a most extraordinary man," he said. Then after a few moments he added, "No, that's not quite true. He's a completely *ordinary* man who is extraordinary because of God's presence in his life. Mac's a constant source of inspiration to me . . . And to many others." Annie was nodding vigorously in agreement.

I glanced at Mac and Dave and Dolly, who had slipped off her shoes, making her a good twelve inches shorter. Just looking at her made me feel like a lummox. Mac glanced our way and caught us watching him. He waved, and I waved back, trying to look unconcerned. He *was* awfully cute. Dolly wasn't the only one who thought so. And yes, *extraordinary*. I even bought Father Amos's explanation of why.

We good-byed our way to the car at about 10. Half the crowd had already dissipated, including the blonde. I didn't see Dave Higgins, either, for about twenty minutes before we left. I wondered if he'd taken leave of his own party to see Dolly home. I was relieved, sort of, when he found us as we started to get into Mac's Buick.

"Thank you," I told him as he hugged me. "It was wonderful. I can't remember when I've enjoyed a party this much." He was feeling my waist again. I deliberately didn't bother to suck it in.

"Thanks for being the guest of honor. I'm sorry I abandoned you there at the end," he apologized.

"Well, she was pretty hot stuff," I said. "I can understand that."

"She's isn't you, of course," Dave said, "but I can see the handwriting on the wall where you're concerned. I've got to pull myself together and get on with my life."

"I admire you for it."

"Thank you for your support. Her name is Candy, by the way." Naturally. What else?

"Congratulations," I said. He winked at me. I wasn't sure what it meant. I figured it was better not to know.

When we got home, Mac built a fire and suggested that we sit on the sofa and listen to Duke Ellington. It sounded like a good, if somewhat risky, idea.

As Duke was playing "On the Sunny Side of the Street" and Mac was nuzzling my ear I casually said, "Amos and Annie let the cat out of the bag tonight." He stopped nuzzling and looked at me.

"Which cat is that?"

Alistair Cooke, who had been sleeping in a fetal position in the armchair by the fire, raised his head. Cats understand every word we say, of course. They like to keep us guessing, so they pretend to ignore us most of the time. Strategy is everything to a cat.

"I'm referring to the cat who's paying for the retreat center," I said.

"Oh," Mac said, looking chagrined. Alistair, satisfied that this was not going to be an important exchange, stretched and circled down for another nap.

"Why didn't you mention it to me?" I said.

"I suppose it seemed immodest. I'm a modest, humble kind of guy."

"I find myself wondering if I'm involved with a man of means. When did you get so rich?"

"Would rich work in my favor?" His eyebrows went up.

"Quit being clever. Talk."

"My parents left me their estate, which consisted of their house, two cars, and some stocks they'd bought years before and left in a blind trust during the years my dad was in political life. There were also some pretty big debts. Several years ago, after all the debts and expenses were covered, the bulk of it finally came to me. I'd been thinking about the need for an expanded retreat center at St. Stephen's; so I turned the whole thing over to Amos. It wasn't a big deal. It seemed like the best possible use for the money, that's all."

"A million dollars wasn't a big deal?"

"A little more than that, actually, give or take a few dollars. The meeting center will be a big item, almost as much as all the cottages put together."

"My word."

"It's not that much."

"As Everett Dirksen said, 'A billion here, a billion there, and pretty soon it starts to run into real money.'"

He shrugged. "I didn't need it, and I felt God and Amos Whitcomb could do interesting things with it. But it wasn't really sacrificial. I'm not exactly deprived."

"True," I said. "But you could have done a lot of other things—even with part of it. You must have been tempted."

He seemed to be thinking about that for the first time. "I don't know. I don't think much of anything else occurred to me. What would you have done with it?"

I stared at the fire for a few minutes. *There are not many people,* I thought, *who can look on a million dollars as not a big deal, and even fewer who can think of nothing to do with it but to give it away.* I tried to imagine what I'd do if I had a million dollars. Help Matt? No. He'd inherit my estate, such as it was. I knew his father's will had recently been rewritten to leave him $500,000 in zero coupon bonds—a strange gesture from a man who had not laid eyes on his son for seventeen years. Matt was well provided for. Maybe too well.

I thought about other ways to spend the million—a Mercedes, maid service, a little cottage in the south of France. Hmm. If I really wanted those things, I could have them without inheriting a million bucks. I could have had them already, so I guessed I didn't really want them very badly. Retirement? Nah, I never wanted to retire. Even the thought bored me. Of course, there were plenty of people who did long for that, and they would probably have no trouble thinking how to spend a million dollars to fend off boredom.

It finally dawned on me, to my amazement, that I couldn't think of much I'd rather do with that kind of money than spend it on the retreat center. It could be—well, it's the only term I could think of—a blast.

"I have a feeling," I said, "that I'd have done exactly what you did with the money."

Mac looked at me thoughtfully. "It probably seems a lot more unselfish than it really was."

"How do you mean?"

"It's been more fun than anything I've ever done. I've watched my dreams take shape and have helped the people in the church bring theirs to life, too. And it won't end when the buildings are finished. It'll go on as long as I live, and well beyond that. What else could I have done with the money that would have been that much fun?"

He'd given away his fortune just for the fun of it. And it made all the sense in the world. I wondered idly if I could be closer than I imagined to selling my possessions and joining Mother Theresa. Would I look good in a nun's habit? Would I be allowed to wear eye makeup? My eyes disappeared without mascara.

"I would like to have some fun right now," Mac said, "if you get my drift." He pulled closer to me on the sofa. So much for my holy vows.

"You're just feeling frisky because you and Candy were flirting all night," I said, stoutly resisting temptation. "You can't fool me."

He grinned. "She was flirting with me. I wasn't flirting with her."

"Good for you. I guess I wasn't close enough to catch that."

"I was rather proud of myself, actually." He took my hand and played with the little ruby ring.

"You have admirable powers of self-control," I said. "By the way, who is she?"

"Candy?" He laughed, seemingly at some private joke. "Amos invited her. She's just moved to town, opened a pottery studio near Amity. I think she was looking for some publicity from me."

"I think she was looking for more than publicity."

He looked at me innocently. "Really?"

"Not that I blame her." His innocent look was sweet, if insincere. "She and Dave seem made for each other," I said. "So to speak."

"If she can get over me, perhaps," he said.

He kissed me softly, tentatively. I put my arms around his neck. I looked at him, my eyes narrowed. "She'll *never* get over you."

"Maybe you're right. I am pretty unforgettable."

"I'll never get over you, either."

"I hope not."

"I don't think I'm going to try."

He was watching me, his eyes searching my face. "Could you elaborate on that a little?"

I thought about it. "Let me put it this way," I said. I kissed him eloquently. He reciprocated.

25

Easter Sunday. The sun was out; the air was cool and moist. The breeze carried scents of burning firewood with a hint of ocean fish when I got up. It had a peculiarly invigorating effect on me. I found myself breathing more deeply here than I could remember doing anywhere else. I wore a black and white silk print dress with long sleeves and a high Mandarin collar and a big red silk flower at the neck.

Mac and I arrived at St. Stephen's half an hour before the start of the late service. The sanctuary and courtyard were wall-to-wall people. Children weaved in and out among a sea of legs in the vestibule, where Marjorie Hennessy's painting stood. I heard murmured comments of admiration about the painting. I wanted to call Marjorie and let her know what a success she was in California.

We found folding chairs in the back. The crowd had already squeezed itself into pews and onto wooden chairs around the edges of the sanctuary. A woman I recognized as Libby Rooney from last night's party was seated at the organ playing a medley of Easter cantata music. Excitement was in the air. The faces around me looked expectant. It was not something I'd seen or felt before in any church I'd attended. It could grow on you, I thought. A person could get even get upset about missing something like this.

I wondered briefly if I was on the brink of becoming a religious fanatic. The notion didn't scare me nearly as much as it should have, which scared me. Then I thought, *Hey, didn't I see some research just last year showing that religious women were far more sensuous than either atheist or agnostic women?* That was a comforting thought. If I went over the edge, I could at least test the theory.

There was no choir. At the stroke of 11 o'clock the organ went up to full throttle, and the congregation joined in singing Charles Wesley's "Christ the Lord Is Risen Today" as the back doors swung open. A procession of several robed priests, candle-lighters, and an acolyte carrying a cross—led by Father Amos in dazzling gold and white, hand-embroidered vestments—entered the sanctuary and slowly made its way down the center aisle to the altar. It occurred to me that Amos Whitcomb had been born for a moment such as this.

I looked at Mac, and he took my hand. *Maybe*, I thought, *I had been born for it, too.*

After five rousing verses of "O for a Thousand Tongues," another Wesley hymn, the service got under way. As the mass proceeded, I found that I was deeply touched by ritual that had always seemed—from a distance—cold and impersonal. It now felt warm and intimate. As we stood at one point, I glanced toward the end of our row and spotted Annie Bosworth smiling happily and wiggling her fingers at me.

Father Amos's ten-minute sermon was a masterpiece. He called Jesus "God's living Word to mankind—the Word made flesh, the Word that brings the dead to life again, the Word that is God's great, loving, eternally powerful 'yes' in each human heart." As he finished his message he paused and looked at the audience with a broad smile.

"My friends," he said, "let none of us leave this sanctuary

today without knowing that the resurrected Christ is alive in our hearts. Let's respond to God's gift to us. Let's say, 'yes, Lord Jesus,' 'yes, risen Savior and King,' 'yes, Prince of Peace,' 'yes, be the Ruler of my heart!'" Several people in the sanctuary said, "yes" and "amen" quietly. It seemed appropriate but still surprising in an Episcopal church.

"Do you remember the words of the angel in the empty tomb after the Resurrection?" Father Amos asked us. "And do you remember what Jesus said when He first appeared to the disciples after that? 'Don't be afraid!' He said. 'Don't be afraid!' And those are His words to us today. 'Don't be afraid to say yes to Me!'"

At our left, without warning, Annie Boswell said "Yes!" in a ringing, fearless tone. It echoed in the sanctuary. Father Amos laughed a hearty laugh and said, "That's it! Come on, let's all say it! One, two, three—YES!" He swung his arms like a choir director, leading us. I joined in the chorus of "yes!" Father Amos beamed at us. It was his moment as much as ours. He basked in it. I thought, *If anybody had told me about this a week ago, I'd have said they were making it up.*

As the yeses died down, Father Amos lifted his arms in the air and shouted, "Hallelujah!" and at least two dozen perfectly respectable and sane-looking people in the congregation, including a gray-haired woman in a mink coat and Gucci shoes standing next to me, joined him without embarrassment. The organ roared to life with the "Hallelujah Chorus" from Handel's *Messiah*, and the audience spontaneously joined hands and sang it with one voice. I figured the real Easter, 2,000 years before, could not have been much more electrifying than this.

At the end of the service we went out to the courtyard, where Father Amos was greeting parishioners enthusiastically.

"I'm so glad you came!" he said to us, barely able to contain himself. "Isn't this the greatest of all days?" Everyone was filled

with it, laughing, hugging, shaking hands. We lingered, not wanting to leave.

After a few minutes Mac said, "Let's walk up to the ridge. I
have a surprise for you." We started up the path that was now
familiar to me. Near the top we came to a wooden bench I hadn't
seen before, off the path in a sea of flowering shrubbery. Mac
pulled me to it, and we sat looking out on the ocean, the valley
below, the church, the people still milling around, the cars
pulling out of the parking lot. I took a deep breath and let it out,
feeling alive and tingly. Mac put his arm around me, letting his
hand hang relaxed over my right shoulder.

"So what's the surprise?" I asked, leaning into him.

"Patience, patience," he said.

I waited, but he didn't say anything more. I looked around us
and thought I could not recall ever feeling such a deep sense of
well-being as I felt at that moment. It was, all at once, joyful and
peaceful and serene and—surprisingly—terribly romantic. I
wondered if this was the sort of feeling drug-users were looking for but never found.

I glanced at Mac and thought, as I had thought two days
before when I'd been up here with Father Amos, *You might have
missed this, Sally. You might have said no; and if you had, you might have
lived your whole life without knowing it was possible to feel like this.* It was
an unbearable thought.

"Mac?" I said, still looking at him. He was watching the parking lot.

"Hmm?"

"I love you."

His head turned. He stared at me for several long seconds. I'd
finally done it. He was speechless.

"That's not only an expression of feelings," I said. "It's also a
commitment. I don't want to be without you."

He hadn't blinked, hadn't moved since he'd turned to look at me. I leaned against his shoulder again. "Your silence is making me anxious," I said.

He pulled away from me a bit so he could see my face clearly. He was smiling a little now. My anxiety level decreased.

"Do you suppose," I said when he still didn't speak, "that Father Amos might be available tomorrow?"

He finally spoke. "Tomorrow?"

"For a wedding. Maybe in the early afternoon," I said. "Two-ish. You did say there was no waiting period in California, didn't you?"

Mac was beaming now. His eyes were riveted to my face. I looked down at the trees, the church, the sun illuminating the flowers. I could smell the moss, the lavender, the roses, the mimosa. It was glorious, the best day of my life by a long shot. But tomorrow just might be even better.

"Right," he said. "Two would not be any too early," he said. Yes, tomorrow would definitely be an even better day.

"Angela is going to kill me," I said. "She's never been a brides-maid or matron of honor. This was her big chance. Maybe Annie would be my maid of honor. Or Mrs. Whelan. Or both." I thought for a minute. "Oh, dear. Matt is going to disown me. I can't do this without him. Can children disown their parents? I suppose not." It's amazing how lucid and unflappable I can be when I put my mind to it.

I looked up at Mac. He started to laugh, then put his arms around me, hugging me hard. "I love you," he said. "You have no idea. You have absolutely no idea." He pulled me to him and hugged me again, mightily. Finally I felt him draw back a little and saw that he was looking down the hill.

"What?" I said, watching his face. It was a very handsome face, I thought. The face of The Man of My Dreams. No kidding.

"I think your surprise finally arrived," he said. He pointed down the hill. "Better late than never."

There, pulling into the parking lot, was a late-model beige generic sedan. It maneuvered carefully into an empty space near the steps that led toward the church. A minute later I saw Saul's head pop out of the driver's side, followed by Angela's from the opposite door. And right after that, from the backseat, came Matt, carrying a big bouquet of flowers.

"Happy Easter," Mac said.

I ran all the way down to meet them.

26

At 2 o'clock the next afternoon we were married in the sanctuary of St. Stephens-by-the-Bay. We used the old ceremony from the earliest *Book of Common Prayer*, which made me feel ten times as married as any other exchange of vows I could imagine. Matt and Saul and Dave jointly acted as best men, and Angela, Annie, and Mrs. Whelan were maids and matron of honor. It was, no doubt, the largest small wedding any of us had ever attended.

The bride wore an elegant little teal wool suit hastily purchased from a tiny shop in Amity, with a floral silk blouse that had a bow at the throat and pearl buttons. The groom wore a dark blue suit, as did the best men. I felt we were as fine a looking bunch as ever walked down the aisle, with the possible exception of Princess Grace and Prince Ranier's wedding party. Everyone, including Matt and Amos Whitcomb, cried.

Angela and Saul were staying in a motel several miles down the coast. It turned out that their visit had been the start of a vacation—which Mac had convinced them to take early so they could be part of my Easter surprise. Monday evening, after a late-afternoon celebratory dinner at our house (I was finally able to think of it that way), they planned to begin an eight-day drive down the coast to San Diego, with a promise to return for two more days at the end of the trip.

Matt was in high spirits all day Monday, partly because of the wedding and partly—maybe largely—because Mac had flown him out not only as an Easter surprise but also to enable him to spend a week hanging around *The Courier* before spring break was over. The wedding was just an unexpected bonus for him.

He carted most of my things into the house and transferred his suitcases to the cottage right after the wedding, while the rest of us were milling around the house eating hors d'oeuvres, listening to Benny Goodman, and saying the things you have to say to blend one set of old friends with another. He seemed totally at ease, which shouldn't have surprised me because Matt was always an adaptable boy; but even so I'd expected him to have some reservations about the life Mac and I were asking him to share. After all, he'd never lived anywhere other than a metropolitan area. This was country, even if it was beautiful, civilized country. There were no concerts down the street, no Twins or Vikings or Gophers tickets, no health clubs with racquetball courts, no 90-degree swimming pools, and not many people his own age that I knew of.

He might be disillusioned later, I decided, but at least for a while he seemed to be having the time of his life. I even found him at one point just before dinner sitting cross-legged on the kitchen counter telling Polish jokes to Mrs. Whelan, who was in stitches. She was so charmed by him that she'd sunk to the level of regaling him in turn with Scottish jokes. Her brogue was pretty good. His attempt at a Polish dialect was terrible. Later, I decided, I'd counsel him to stick to Swedish and Norwegian jokes; after most of a lifetime in Minnesota, the accent came naturally.

I was pleased to watch the relationship Matt seemed to be

building with Mac. It wasn't exactly a friendship. I suppose I'd have to describe it as part hero-worship and part warm affection on Matt's part. Mac didn't really treat it as a father-son sort of thing, though I was seeing hints of that. I was glad that Mac didn't try too hard, as I'd often seen men do with stepsons. He appeared to be content simply to enjoy Matt for the person he was, treating him with great respect—more than most fathers I'd seen, and even more than many friends had for each other. That seemed to bring out the best in my son, and I suspected I was going to learn a lot about both of them by watching their relationship develop.

At dinner Monday night Matt was the first to toast the bride and groom, and I thought his toast nicely symbolized what was happening in our new little three-person family. He said, "To Mom and Mac, who should have been married for the past quarter century. May you have twice as long to make up for lost time." As an afterthought, he looked at me and said with a grin, "And, Mom, if you don't treat him right, you'll never hear the end of it from me." As everyone laughed and drank, I glanced at Saul, who was sitting to my right at the dining room table. He winked at me, leaning over to whisper in my ear, "That goes double for me." Angela was beaming at me.

The conversation at dinner was a little weird. Dave traded flirtatious comments with Angela, who handled him with admirable aplomb and seemed to enjoy hearing about the columns he was planning for the next month. Saul glanced at the two of them with mild interest as he chatted with Father Amos and Annie about hospice care. I overheard just enough of their conversation to get the sense that the three of them were hatching a plan to start an experimental care center for the terminally ill, probably near or at St. Stephen's. Perhaps, I thought, they were not such an odd trio as they seemed at first glance. As I observed them, a funny picture flashed through my mind—of

Saul looking for all the world like a trout about to bite a nice, fat worm that just happened to be wiggling on a hook dangling from a fishing pole held by Amos Whitcomb and Annie Bosworth.

Matt and Mrs. Whelan continued to tell jokes through the entire meal, and Mac and I spent a lot of time just watching all the conversation that was going on. I think neither of us could quite believe it. After the entire group left *en masse* at about 9 P.M. (Matt went off to the cottage, yawning elaborately), Mac and I went out on the porch to take in the evening air.

We were quiet for a while. The silence was nice after the excitement of the day. Finally Mac looked over at me.

"We did it," he said.

"We sure did." I smiled at him, reaching out to take his hand. He took my hand and kissed it. Boy, I loved that.

"Do you suppose it's legal? They don't let people have this much fun legally, do they?" he said.

"They'll probably find some technicality tomorrow or the next day that invalidates the whole thing."

"Well," he said, "by then it will be too late. We'll have had a lot more fun by then."

We smiled at each other, neither of us anxious to leave the porch, the quiet, or the feelings that were passing between us.

Alistair Cooke strolled toward us from the south side of the house looking fatter than ever. He was licking his chops. Mousie dessert, I surmised.

"I've been thinking about Minneapolis," I told Mac as Cookie hopped into my lap and curled himself for a nap. I stroked his chin, and he purred like an outboard motor.

"So have I," Mac said. "You first."

I was still stroking the cat, who had now turned tummy up to get a more complete massage. "I wouldn't have believed I could ever miss everyone here as much as I miss everyone in Minneapolis, but tonight I've had to face the fact that I would." I glanced over at him. "I think the thing to do is for me to move here. I don't think I'll end up hating you for it. I mean, I doubt I'll ever look on it as a supreme sacrifice. I'll be doing it for myself more than for you." He was watching and listening with that intense look of his.

"I'm not sure how this will work logistically," I said, "but I suppose I'd better go back to Minneapolis and put the condo up for sale, sell my furniture, ship some of my art and other stuff out here—it seems dumb, with your house completely furnished, but there are a few things I really love, and I'd like to work them in here. And I'd better deal with the business end of things, get my work set up so I can do it remotely, all that." I stopped and looked at him. "I suppose I don't have to decide all this right now, but I feel we should start making some plans. I'm still unclear about what I ought do first. I could use your advice."

He looked over at me in the semi-darkness. The moon was up, giving the shrubs around the porch and down the hill a ghostly, colorless quality. Mac's face looked paler and younger in that light. I hoped mine did, too—at least enough to make me look my age.

"I was thinking," he said, "that maybe, instead of living one place or the other, we could spend half of our time in Minneapolis and half of it here. We might want to adjust the amount of time we're there or here eventually, but flights are inexpensive, so we can really have the best of both worlds. Our computers can keep us connected regardless of where we are. Why don't we give that a try? It might be fun."

I thought for a minute. "It sounds impractical. A lot of travel, a lot of extra expense. We'd be paying for upkeep on two places, after all."

"So what? Matt would be here to look after things when we're in Minneapolis, and he can take care of the animals and the house in exchange for his room and board—that would be a fair deal. Mrs. Whelan would love to be housemother. And your condo would be easy to lock up and leave unattended. There wouldn't be much upkeep there. And both our places are paid for, after all."

I gave it more thought. Something in me relished the notion that I might not have to give up 100 percent of my midwestern life after all.

"I suppose we can afford it," I said. "It's just that it seems like a lot of hassle. I'm willing, but then, I'm the one who's having a hard time letting go. Are you sure you're not going to feel like you're sacrificing half your life for me?"

"I'll let you know if that happens," he said. "Just like you'll let me know. Right?"

I smiled at him. "You *would* tell me, wouldn't you?"

"Sure. But I think I'm going to have to keep an eye on you. You have certain tendencies."

"You're right," I said. "Feel free to call me on it."

"You can count on it," he said. He was slouched in the wicker chair, feet against the railing, looking out at the moon. He put his feet down and stretched them out through the spindles of the railing. "So—what do you think?"

"I think you're a brilliant and creative man, and I don't know how I've lived without you."

"You haven't," he said, squeezing my hand.

"True," I said. "It has been mere existence." We stood, and Alistair Cooke hopped to the floor, stretching elaborately. Then Mac was kissing me on the cheek, on the nose, finally on the mouth—that kiss of his that just barely grazed my lips.

"Promise me something," he said. There was a funny little hint of a smile on his face.

"What?"

"Promise me you'll keep your name."

"You don't want me to be Sally MacDonald?"

"It isn't that," he said. "I just want to be able to tell people that I decided to keep my maiden name."

I laughed. "I don't blame you. It's a great line."

"Actually," he said, "I'm serious about your name. It's part of your identity. Why change it?"

"That isn't very Republican of you," I said. "But I appreciate your modern attitude."

"The Republican Party has vigorously advanced the cause of women since the day it came into existence," he said. "There are far more Republican women in positions of political power than Democrats. I did a full-page feature on it, with thirty examples. So don't give me that."

"Whew. I should have known you'd find a way to get on a soapbox on the first night of our honeymoon."

He raised his eyebrows and looked at me. "This is a honeymoon?"

"Yes. How are you enjoying things up to now?"

He leaned forward to hug me. "So far, so good," he said.